EXPANDED UNIVERSE

VOLUME TWO

EXPANDED UNIVERSE

VOLUME TWO

ROBERT A. HEINLEIN

an imprint of

Rockville, Maryland

ISBN: 978-1-61242-240-4

www.PhoenixPick.com
Great Science Fiction & Fantasy

Published by Phoenix Pick
an imprint of Arc Manor
P. O. Box 10339
Rockville, MD 20849-0339
www.ArcManor.com

To William Targ

CONTENTS

FOREWORD

This story was written twenty-one years before Dr. Neil Armstrong took "one short step for a man, a giant leap for mankind"—but in all important essentials it has not (yet) become dated. True, we do not know that formations such as "morning glories" exist on Luna and we do not know that there are areas where footgear midway between skis and snowshoes would be useful. But the Lunar surface is about equal in area to Africa; a dozen men have explored an area smaller than Capetown for a total of a few days. We will still *be exploring Luna and finding new wonders there when the first interstellar explorers return from Proxima Centauri or Tau Ceti.*

This story is compatible with the so-called "Future History" stories. It is also part of my continuing post-War-II attempt to leave the SF-pulp field and spread out. I never left the genre *pulps entirely, as it turned out to be easy to write a book-length job, then break it into three or four cliffhangers and sell it as a pulp serial immediately before book publication. I did this with a dozen novels in the '40s and '50s. But I recall only one story ("Gulf") specifically written for pulp, "Gulf" being for* Astounding's *unique "prophesied" issue.*

Deus volent, I may someday collect my Boy Scout stories as one volume just as I would like to do with the Puddin' stories.

"If you pray hard enough, water will run uphill. How hard? Why, hard enough to make water run uphill, of course!"

—L. Long

NOTHING EVER HAPPENS ON THE MOON

"I never knew a boy from Earth who wasn't cocky."

Mr. Andrews frowned at his Senior Patrol Leader. "That's childish, Sam. And no answer. I arrive expecting to find the troop ready to hike. Instead I find you and our visitor about to fight. And both of you Eagle Scouts! What started it?"

Sam reluctantly produced a clipping. "This, I guess."

It was from the Colorado Scouting News and read: "Troop 48, Denver—LOCAL SCOUT SEEKS SKY-HIGH HONOR. Bruce Hollifield, Eagle Scout, is moving with his family to South Pole, Venus. Those who know Bruce—and who doesn't—expect him to qualify as Eagle (Venus) in jig time. Bruce will spend three weeks at Luna City, waiting for the Moon-Venus transport. Bruce has been boning up lately on lunar Scouting, and he has already qualified in space suit operation in the vacuum chamber at the Pike's Peak space port. Cornered, Bruce admitted that he hopes to pass the tests for Eagle Scout (Luna) while on the Moon.

"If he does—and we're betting on Bruce!—he's a dead cinch to become the first Triple Eagle in history.

"Go to it, Bruce! Denver is proud of you. Show those Moon Scouts what real Scouting is like."

Mr. Andrews looked up. "Where did this come from?"

"Uh, somebody sent it to Peewee."

"Yes?"

"Well, we all read it and when Bruce came in, the fellows ribbed him. He got sore."

"Why didn't you stop it?"

"Uh ... well, I was doing it myself."

"Humph! Sam, this item is no sillier than the stuff our own Scribe turns in for publication. Bruce didn't write it, and you yahoos had no business making his life miserable. Send him in. Meantime call the roll."

"Yes, sir. Uh, Mr. Andrews—"

"Yes?"

"What's *your* opinion? Can this kid possibly qualify for lunar Eagle in three weeks?"

"No—and I've told him so. But he's durn well going to have his chance. Which reminds me: you're his instructor."

"Me?" Sam looked stricken.

"You. You've let me down, Sam; this is your chance to correct it. Understand me?"

Sam swallowed. "I guess I do."

"Send Hollifield in."

Sam found the boy from Earth standing alone, pretending to study the bulletin board. Sam touched his arm. "The Skipper wants you."

Bruce whirled around, then stalked away. Sam shrugged and shouted, "Rocket Patrol—fall in!"

Speedy Owens echoed, "Crescent Patrol—fall in!" As muster ended Mr. Andrews came out of his office, followed by Bruce. The Earth Scout seemed considerably chastened.

"Mr. Andrews says I'm to report to you."

"That's right." They eyed each other cautiously. Sam said, "Look, Bruce—let's start from scratch."

"Suits me."

"Fine. Just tag along with me." At a sign from the Scoutmaster Sam shouted, "By twos! Follow me." Troop One jostled out the door, mounted a crosstown slidewalk and rode to East Air Lock.

Chubby Schneider, troop quartermaster, waited there with two assistants, near a rack of space suits. Duffel was spread around in enormous piles—packaged grub, tanks of water, huge air bottles, frames of heavy wire, a great steel drum, everything needed for pioneers on the airless crust of the Moon.

Sam introduced Bruce to the Quartermaster. "We've got to outfit him, Chubby."

"That new G.E. job might fit him."

Sam got the suit and spread it out. The suit was impregnated glass fabric, aluminum-sprayed to silvery whiteness. It closed from crotch to collar with a zippered gasket. It looked expensive; Bruce noticed a plate on the collar: DONATED BY THE LUNA CITY KIWANIS KLUB.

The helmet was a plastic bowl, silvered except where swept by the eyes of the wearer. There it was transparent, though heavily filtered.

Bruce's uniform was stowed in a locker; Chubby handed him a loose-knit coverall. Sam and Chubby stuffed him into the suit and Chubby produced the instrument belt.

Both edges of the belt zipped to the suit; there were several rows of grippers for the top edge; thus a pleat could be taken. They fastened it with maximum pleat. "How's that?" asked Sam.

"The collar cuts my shoulders."

"It won't under pressure. If we leave slack, your head will pull out of the helmet like a cork." Sam strapped the air, water, radio, and duffel-rack backpack to Bruce's shoulders. "Pressure check, Chubby."

"We'll dress first." While Chubby and Sam dressed, Bruce located his intake and exhaust valves, the spill valve inside his collar, and the water nipple beside it. He took a drink and inspected his belt.

Sam and Bruce donned helmets. Sam switched on Bruce's walkie-talkie, clipped a blood-oxygen indicator to Bruce's ear, and locked his helmet on. "Stand by for pressure," he said, his words echoing in Bruce's helmet. Chubby hooked a hose from a wall gauge to Bruce's air intake.

Bruce felt the collar lift. The air in the suit grew stuffy, the helmet fogged. At thirty pounds Chubby cut the intake, and watched the gauge. Mr. Andrews joined them, a Gargantuan helmeted figure, toting a pack six feet high. "Pressure steady, sir," Chubby reported.

Sam hooked up Bruce's air supply. "Open your intake and kick your chin valve before you smother," he ordered. Bruce complied. The stale air rushed out and the helmet cleared. Sam adjusted Bruce's valves. "Watch that needle," he ordered, pointing to the blood-oxygen dial on Bruce's belt. "Keep your mix so that reads steady in the white without using your chin valve."

"I know."

"So I'll say it again. Keep that needle out of the red, or you'll explain it to Saint Peter."

The Scoutmaster asked, "What load are you giving him?"

"Oh," replied Sam, "just enough to steady him—say three hundred pounds, total."

Bruce figured—at one-sixth gravity that meant fifty pounds weight including himself, his suit, and his pack. "I'll carry my full share," he objected.

"We'll decide what's best for you," the Scoutmaster snapped. "Hurry up; the troop is ready." He left.

Sam switched off his radio and touched helmets. "Forget it," he said quietly. "The Old Man is edgy at the start of a hike." They loaded Bruce rapidly—reserve air and water bottles, a carton of grub, short, wide skis and ski poles—then hung him with field gear, first-aid kit, prospector's hammer, two climbing ropes, a pouch of pitons and snap rings, flashlight, knife. The Moon Scouts loaded up; Sam called, "Come on!"

Mr. Andrews handed the lockmaster a list and stepped inside; the three Scouts followed. Bruce felt his suit expand as the air sucked back into the underground city. A light blinked green; Mr. Andrews opened the outer door and Bruce stared across the airless lunar plain.

It dazzled him. The plain was bright under a blazing Sun. The distant needle-sharp hills seemed painted in colors too flat and harsh. He looked at the sky to rest his eyes.

It made him dizzy. He had never seen a whole skyful of stars undimmed by air. The sky was blacker than black, crowded with hard, diamond lights.

"Route march!" the Scoutmaster's voice rang in his helmet. "Heel and toe. Jack Wills out as pathfinder." A boy left the group in long, floating strides, fifteen feet at a bound. He stopped a hundred yards ahead; the troop formed a single column fifty yards behind him. The Pathfinder raised his arm, swung it down, and the troop moved out.

Mr. Andrews and a Scout joined Sam and Bruce. "Speedy will help you," he told Sam, "until Bruce gets his legs. Move him along. We can't heel-and-toe and still make our mileage."

"We'll move him."

"Even if we have to carry him," added Speedy.

The Scoutmaster overtook the troop in long leaps. Bruce wanted to follow. It looked easy—like flying. He had not liked the crack about carrying him. But Sam grasped him by his left belt grip while Speedy seized the one on his right. "Here we go," Sam warned. "Feet on the ground and try to swing in with us."

Bruce started off confidently. He felt that three days of low gravity in the corridors of Luna City had given him his "legs"; being taught to walk, like a baby, was just hazing.

Nothing to it—he was light as a bird! True, it was hard to keep heel-and-toe; he wanted to float. He gained speed on a downgrade; suddenly the ground was not there when he reached for it. He threw up his hands.

He hung head down on his belt and could hear his guides laughing. "Wha' happened?" he demanded, as they righted him.

"Keep your feet on the ground."

"I know what you're up against," added Speedy, "I've been to Earth. Your mass and weight don't match and your muscles aren't used to it. You weigh what a baby weighs, Earth-side, but you've got the momentum of a fat man."

Bruce tried again. Some stops and turns showed him what Speedy meant. His pack felt like feathers, but unless he banked his turns, it would throw him, even at a walk. It *did* throw him, several times, before his legs learned.

Presently, Sam asked, "Think you're ready for a slow lope?"

"I guess so."

"Okay—but remember, if you want to turn, you've *got* to slow down first—or you'll roll like a hoop. Okay, Speedy. An eight-miler."

Bruce tried to match their swing. Long, floating strides, like flying. It *was* flying! Up! ... float ... brush the ground with your foot and up again. It was better than skating or skiing.

"Wups!" Sam steadied him. "Get your feet out in front."

As they swung past, Mr. Andrews gave orders for a matching lope.

—◈—

The unreal hills had moved closer; Bruce felt as if he had been flying all his life. "Sam," he said, "do you suppose I can get along by myself?"

"Shouldn't wonder. We let go a couple o' miles back."

"Huh?" It was true; Bruce began to feel like a Moon hand.

Somewhat later a boy's voice called "Heel and toe!" The troop dropped into a walk. The pathfinder stood on a rise ahead, holding his skis up. The troop halted and unlashed skis. Ahead was a wide basin filled with soft, powdery stuff.

Bruce turned to Sam, and for the first time looked back to the west. *"Jee … miny Crickets!"* he breathed.

Earth hung over the distant roof of Luna City, in half phase. It was round and green and beautiful, larger than the harvest Moon and unmeasurably more lovely in forest greens, desert browns and glare white of cloud.

Sam glanced at it. "Fifteen o'clock."

Bruce tried to read the time but was stumped by the fact that the sunrise line ran mostly across ocean. He questioned Sam. "Huh? See that bright dot on the dark side? That's Honolulu—figure from there."

Bruce mulled this over while binding his skis, then stood up and turned around, without tripping. "Hmmm—" said Sam, "you're used to skis."

"Got my badge."

"Well, this is different. Just shuffle along and try to keep your feet."

Bruce resolved to stay on his feet if it killed him. He let a handful of the soft stuff trickle through his glove. It was light and flaky, hardly packed at all. He wondered what had caused it.

Mr. Andrews sent Speedy out to blaze trail; Sam and Bruce joined the column. Bruce was hard put to keep up. The loose soil flew to left and right, settling so slowly in the weak gravity that it seemed to float in air—yet a ski pole, swung through such a cloud, cut a knife-sharp hole without swirling it.

The column swung wide to the left, then back again. Off to the right was a circular depression perhaps fifty yards across; Bruce could not see the bottom. He paused, intending to question Sam; the Scoutmaster's voice prodded him. "Bruce! Keep moving!"

Much later Speedy's voice called out, "Hard ground!" Shortly the column reached it and stopped to remove skis. Bruce switched off his radio and touched his helmet to Sam's.

"What was that back where the Skipper yelled at me?"

"That? That was a morning glory. They're poison!"

"A 'morning glory'?"

"Sort of a sink hole. If you get on the slope, you never get out. Crumbles out from under you and you wind up buried in the bottom. There you stay—until your air gives out. Lot of prospectors die that way. They go out alone and are likely to come back in the dark."

"How do you know what happens if they go out alone?"

"Suppose you saw tracks leading up to one and no tracks going away?"

"Oh!" Bruce felt silly.

The troop swung into a lope; slowly the hills drew closer and loomed high into the sky. Mr. Andrews called a halt. "Camp," he said. "Sam, spot the shelter west of that outcropping. Bruce, watch what Sam does."

The shelter was an airtight tent, framed by a half cylinder of woven heavy wire. The frame came in sections. The Scoutmaster's huge pack was the air bag.

The skeleton was erected over a ground frame, anchored at corners and over which was spread an asbestos pad. The curved roof and wall sections followed. Sam tested joints with a wrench, then ordered the air bag unrolled. The air lock, a steel drum, was locked into the frame and gasketed to the bag. Meanwhile, two Scouts were rigging a Sun shade.

Five boys crawled inside and stood up, arms stretched high. The others passed in all the duffel except skis and poles. Mr. Andrews was last in and closed the air lock. The metal frame blocked radio communication; Sam plugged a phone connection from the lock to his helmet. "Testing," he said.

Bruce could hear the answer, relayed through Sam's radio. "Ready to inflate."

"Okay." The bag surged up, filling the frame. Sam said, "You go on, Bruce. There's nothing left but to adjust the shade."

"I'd better watch."

"Okay." The shade was a flimsy Venetian blind, stretched over the shelter. Sam half-opened the slats. "It's cold inside," he commented, "from expanding gas. But it warms up fast." Presently, coached by phone, he closed them a bit. "Go inside," he urged Bruce. "It may be half an hour before I get the temperature steady."

"Maybe I should," admitted Bruce. "I feel dizzy."

Sam studied him. "Too hot?"

"Yeah, I guess so."

"You've held still in the Sun too long. Doesn't give the air a chance to circulate. Here." Sam opened Bruce's supply valve wider; "Go inside."

Gratefully, Bruce complied.

As he backed in, and straightened up, two boys grabbed him. They closed his valves, unlocked his helmet, and peeled off his suit. The suit traveled from hand to hand and was racked. Bruce looked around.

Daylamps were strung from the air lock to a curtain at the far end that shut off the sanitary unit. Near this curtain suits and helmets were racked. Scouts were lounging on both sides of the long room. Near the entrance a Scout was on watch at the air conditioner, a blood-oxygen indicator clipped to his ear. Nearby, Mr. Andrews phoned temperature changes to Sam. In the middle of the room Chubby had set up his commissary. He waved. "Hi, Bruce! Siddown—chow in two shakes."

Two Scouts made room for Bruce and he sat. One of them said, "Y'ever been at Yale?" Bruce had not. "That's where I'm going," the Scout confided. "My brother's there now." Bruce began to feel at home.

When Sam came in Chubby served chow, beef stew, steaming and fragrant, packaged rolls, and bricks of peach ice cream. Bruce decided that Moon Scouts had it soft. After supper, the Bugler got out his harmonica and played. Bruce leaned back, feeling pleasantly drowsy.

"Hollifield!" Bruce snapped awake. "Let's try you on first aid."

For thirty minutes Bruce demonstrated air tourniquets and emergency suit patches, artificial respiration for a man in a space suit, what to do for Sun stroke, for anoxia, for fractures. "That'll do," the Scoutmaster concluded. "One thing: What do you do if a man cracks his helmet?"

Bruce was puzzled. "Why," he blurted, "you bury him."

"Check," the Scoutmaster agreed. "So be careful. Okay, sports— six hours of sleep. Sam, set the watch."

Sam assigned six boys, including himself. Bruce asked, "Shouldn't I take a watch?"

Mr. Andrews intervened. "No. And take yourself off, Sam. You'll take Bruce on his two-man hike tomorrow; you'll need your sleep."

"Okay, Skipper." He added to Bruce, "There's nothing to it. I'll show you." The Scout on duty watched several instruments, but, as with suits, the important one was the blood-oxygen reading. Stale air was passed through a calcium oxide bath, which precipitated carbon dioxide as calcium carbonate. The purified air continued through dry sodium hydroxide, removing water vapor.

"The kid on watch makes sure the oxygen replacement is okay," Sam went on. "If anything went wrong, he'd wake us and we'd scramble into suits."

Mr. Andrews shooed them to bed. By the time Bruce had taken his turn at the sanitary unit and found a place to lie down, the harmonica was sobbing: *"Day is done.... Gone the Sun ..."*

It seemed odd to hear *Taps* when the Sun was still overhead. They couldn't wait a week for sundown, of course. These colonials kept funny hours ... bed at what amounted to early evening, up at one in the morning. He'd ask Sam. Sam wasn't a bad guy—a little bit know-it-all. Odd to sleep on a bare floor, too—not that it mattered with low gravity. He was still pondering it when his ears were assaulted by *Reveille*, played on the harmonica.

Breakfast was scrambled eggs, cooked on the spot. Camp was struck, and the troop was moving in less than an hour. They headed for Base Camp at a lope.

The way wound through passes, skirted craters. They had covered thirty miles and Bruce was getting hungry when the pathfinder called, "Heel and toe!" They converged on an air lock, set in a hillside.

Base Camp had not the slick finish of Luna City, being rough caverns sealed to airtightness, but each troop had its own well-equipped troop room. Air was renewed by hydroponic garden, like Luna City;

there was a Sun power plant and accumulators to last through the long, cold nights.

Bruce hurried through lunch; he was eager to start his two-man hike. They outfitted as before, except that reserve air and water replaced packaged grub. Sam fitted a spring-fed clip of hiking rations into the collar of Bruce's suit.

The Scoutmaster inspected them at the lock. "Where to, Sam?"

"We'll head southeast. I'll blaze it."

"Hmm—rough country. Well; back by midnight, and stay out of caves."

"Yes, sir."

Outside Sam sighed, "Whew! I thought he was going to say not to climb."

"We're going to?"

"Sure. You can, can't you?"

"Got my Alpine badge."

"I'll do the hard part, anyhow. Let's go."

Sam led out of the hills and across a baked plain. He hit an eight-mile gait, increased it to a twelve-miler. Bruce swung along, enjoying it. "Swell of you to do this, Sam."

"Nuts. If I weren't here, I'd be helping to seal the gymnasium."

"Just the same, I need this hike for my Mooncraft badge."

Sam let several strides pass. "Look, Bruce—you don't really expect to make Lunar Eagle?"

"Why not? I've got my optional badges. There are only four required ones that are terribly different: camping, Mooncraft, pathfinding, and pioneering. I've studied like the dickens and now I'm getting experience."

"I don't doubt you've studied. But the Review Board are tough eggs. You've got to be a real Moon hand to get by."

"They won't pass a Scout from Earth?"

"Put it this way. The badges you need add up to one thing, Mooncraft. The examiners are old Moon hands; you won't get by with book answers. They'll know how long you've been here and they'll *know* you don't know enough."

Bruce thought about it. "It's not fair!"

Sam snorted. "Mooncraft isn't a game; it's the real thing. 'Did you stay alive?' If you make a mistake, you flunk—and they bury you."

Bruce had no answer.

Presently they came to hills; Sam stopped and called Base Camp. "Parsons and Hollifield, Troop One—please take a bearing."

Shortly Base replied, "One one eight. What's your mark?"

"Cairn with a note."

"Roger."

Sam piled up stones, then wrote date, time, and their names on paper torn from a pad in his pouch, and laid it on top. "Now we start up."

The way was rough and unpredictable; this canyon had never been a watercourse. Several times Sam stretched a line before he would let Bruce follow. At intervals he blazed the rock with his hammer. They came to an impasse, five hundred feet of rock, the first hundred of which was vertical and smooth.

Bruce stared. "We're going up that?"

"Sure. Watch your Uncle Samuel." A pillar thrust up above the vertical pitch. Sam clipped two lines together and began casting the bight up toward it. Twice he missed and the line floated down. At last it went over.

Sam drove a piton into the wall, off to one side, clipped a snap ring to it, and snapped on the line. He had Bruce join him in a straight pull on the free end to test the piton. Bruce then anchored to the snap ring with a rope strap; Sam started to climb.

Thirty feet up, he made fast to the line with his legs and drove another piton; to this he fastened a safety line. Twice more he did this. He reached the pillar and called, "Off belay!"

Bruce unlinked the line; it snaked up the cliff. Presently Sam shouted, "On belay!"

Bruce answered, "Testing," and tried unsuccessfully to jerk down the line Sam had lowered.

"Climb," ordered Sam.

"Climbing." One-sixth gravity, Bruce decided, was a mountaineer's heaven. He paused on the way up only to unsnap the safety line.

Bruce wanted to "leapfrog" up the remaining pitches, but Sam insisted on leading. Bruce was soon glad of it; he found three mighty differences between climbing on Earth and climbing here; the first was low gravity, but the others were disadvantages: balance climbing was awkward in a suit, and chimney climbing, or any involving knees and shoulders, was clumsy and carried danger of tearing the suit.

They came out on raw, wild upland surrounded by pinnacles, bright against black sky. "Where to?" asked Bruce.

Sam studied the stars, then pointed southeast. "The photomaps show open country that way."

"Suits me." They trudged away; the country was too rugged to lope. They had been traveling a long time, it seemed to Bruce, when they came out on a higher place from which Earth could be seen. "What time is it?" he asked.

"Almost seventeen," Sam answered, glancing up.

"We're supposed to be back by midnight."

"Well," admitted Sam, "I expected to reach open country before now."

"We're lost?"

"Certainly not! I've blazed it. But I've never been here before. I doubt if anyone has."

"Suppose we keep on for half an hour, then turn back?"

"Fair enough." They continued for at least that; Sam conceded that it was time to turn.

"Let's try that next rise," urged Bruce.

"Okay." Sam reached the top first. "Hey, Bruce—we made it!"

Bruce joined him. "Golly!" Two thousand feet below stretched a dead lunar plain. Mountains rimmed it except to the south. Five miles away two small craters formed a figure eight.

"I know where we are," Sam announced. "That pair shows up on the photos. We slide down here, circle south about twenty miles, and back to Base. A cinch—how's your air?"

Bruce's bottle showed fair pressure; Sam's was down, he having done more work. They changed both bottles and got ready. Sam drove a piton, snapped on a ring, fastened a line to his belt and passed it through the ring. The end of the line he passed between his legs, around a thigh and across his chest, over his shoulder and to his other hand, forming a rappel seat. He began to "walk" down the cliff, feeding slack as needed.

He reached a shoulder below Bruce. "Off rappel!" he called, and recovered his line by pulling it through the ring.

Bruce rigged a rappel seat and joined him. The pitches became steeper; thereafter Sam sent Bruce down first, while anchoring him above. They came to a last high sheer drop. Bruce peered over. "Looks like here we roost."

"Maybe." Sam bent all four lines together and measured it. Ten feet of line reached the rubble at the base.

Bruce said, "It'll reach, but we have to leave the lines behind us."

Sam scowled. "Glass lines cost money; they're from Earth."

"Beats staying here."

Sam searched the cliff face, then drove a piton. "I'll lower you. When you're halfway, drive two pitons and hang the strap from one. That'll give me a changeover."

"I'm against it," protested Bruce.

"If we lost our lines," Sam argued, "we'll never hear the last of it. Go ahead."

"I still don't like it."

"Who's in charge?"

Bruce shrugged, snapped on the line and started down.

Sam stopped him presently. "Halfway. Pick me a nest."

Bruce walked the face to the right, but found only smooth wall. He worked back and located a crack. "Here's a crack," he reported, "but just one. I shouldn't drive two pitons in one crack."

"Spread 'em apart," Sam directed. "It's good rock."

Reluctantly, Bruce complied. The spikes went in easily but he wished he could hear the firm ring that meant a piton was biting properly. Finished, he hung the strap. "Lower away!"

In a couple of minutes he was down and unsnapped the line. "Off belay!" He hurried down the loose rock at the base. When he reached the edge of it he called, "Sam! This plain is soft stuff."

"Okay," Sam acknowledged. "Stand clear." Bruce moved along the cliff about fifty feet and stopped to bind on skis. Then he shuffled out onto the plain, kick-turned, and looked back. Sam had reached the pitons. He hung, one foot in the strap, the bight in his elbow, and recovered his line. He passed his line through the second piton ring, settled in rappel, and hooked the strap from piton to piton as an anchor. He started down.

Halfway down the remaining two hundred feet he stopped. "What's the matter?" called Bruce.

"It's reached a shackle," said Sam, "and the pesky thing won't feed through the ring. I'll free it." He raised himself a foot, then suddenly let what he had gained slip through the ring above.

To Bruce's amazement Sam leaned out at an impossible angle. He heard Sam cry "Rock!" before he understood what had happened—the piton had failed.

Sam fell about four feet, then the other piton, connected by the strap, stopped him. He caught himself, feet spread. But the warning cry had not been pointless; Bruce saw a rock settling straight for Sam's helmet. Bruce repeated the shout.

Sam looked up, then jumped straight out from the cliff. The rock passed between him and the wall; Bruce could not tell if it had struck him. Sam swung in, his feet caught the cliff—and again he leaned out crazily. The second piton had let go.

Sam again shouted, "*Rock!*" even as he kicked himself away from the cliff.

Bruce watched him, turning slowly over and over and gathering momentum. It seemed to take Sam forever to fall.

Then he struck.

Bruce fouled his skis and had to pick himself up. He forced himself to be careful and glided toward the spot.

Sam's frantic shove had saved him from crashing his helmet into rock. He lay buried in the loose debris, one leg sticking up ridiculously. Bruce felt an hysterical desire to laugh.

Sam did not stir when Bruce tugged at him. Bruce's skis got in his way; finally he stood astraddle, hauled Sam out. The boy's eyes were closed, his features slack, but the suit still had pressure. "Sam," shouted Bruce, "can you hear me?"

Sam's blood-oxygen reading was dangerously in the red; Bruce opened his intake valve wider—but the reading failed to improve. He wanted to turn Sam face down, but he had no way of straightening

Sam's helmeted head, nor would he then be able to watch the blood-oxygen indicator unless he took time to remove the belt. He decided to try artificial respiration with the patient face up. He kicked off skis and belt.

The pressure in the suit got in his way, nor could he fit his hands satisfactorily to Sam's ribs. But he kept at it—swing! and one, and two and up! and one, and two and swing!

The needle began to move. When it was well into the white Bruce paused.

It stayed in the white.

Sam's lips moved but no sound came. Bruce touched helmets. "What is it, Sam?"

Faintly he heard, "Look out! Rock!"

Bruce considered what to do next.

There was little he could do until he got Sam into a pressurized room. The idea, he decided, was to get help—fast!

Send up a smoke signal? Fire a gun three times? Snap out of it, Bruce! You're on the Moon now. He wished that someone would happen along in a desert car.

He would have to try radio. He wasn't hopeful, as they had heard nothing even from the cliff. Still, he must try—

He glanced at Sam's blood-oxygen reading, then climbed the rubble, extended his antenna and tried. "*M'aidez!*" he called. "Help! Does anybody hear me?" He tried again.

And again.

When he saw Sam move he hurried back. Sam was sitting up and feeling his left knee. Bruce touched helmets. "Sam, are you all right?"

"Huh? This leg won't work right."

"Is it broken?"

"How do I know? Turn on your radio."

"It *is* on. Yours is busted."

"Huh? How'd that happen?"

"When you fell."

"Fell?"

Bruce pointed. "Don't you remember?"

Sam stared at the cliff. "Uh, I don't know. Say, this thing hurts like mischief. Where's the rest of the troop?"

25

Bruce said slowly, "We're out by ourselves, Sam. Remember?"

Sam frowned. "I guess so. Bruce, we've got to get out of here! Help me get my skis on."

"Do you think you can ski with that knee?"

"I've got to." Bruce lifted him to his feet, then bound a ski to the injured leg while Sam balanced on the other. But when Sam tried shifting his weight he collapsed—and fainted.

Bruce gave him air and noted that the blood-oxygen reading was still okay. He untangled the ski, straightened out Sam's legs, and waited. When Sam's eyes fluttered he touched helmets. "Sam, can you understand me?"

"Yeah. Sure."

"You can't stay on your feet. I'll carry you."

"No."

"What do you mean, 'No'?"

"No good. Rig a toboggan." He closed his eyes.

Bruce laid Sam's skis side by side. Two steel rods were clipped to the tail of each ski; he saw how they were meant to be used. Slide a rod through four ring studs, two on each ski; snap a catch—*so!* Fit the other rods. Remove bindings—the skis made a passable narrow toboggan.

He removed Sam's pack, switched his bottles around in front and told him to hold them. "I'm going to move you. Easy, now!" The space-suited form hung over the edges, but there was no help for it. He found he could thread a rope under the rods and lash his patient down. Sam's pack he tied on top.

He made a hitch by tying a line to the holes in the tips of the skis; there was a long piece left over. He said to Sam, "I'll tie this to my arm. If you want anything, just jerk."

"Okay."

"Here we go." Bruce put on his skis, brought the hitch up to his armpits and ducked his head through, forming a harness. He grasped his ski poles and set out to the south, parallel to the cliff.

The toboggan drag steadied him; he settled down to covering miles. Earth was shut off by the cliff; the Sun gave him no estimate of hour. There was nothing but blackness, stars, the blazing Sun, a burning desert underfoot, and the towering cliff—nothing but silence and the urgency to get back to base.

Something jerked his arm. It scared him before he accounted for it. He went back to the toboggan. "What is it, Sam?"

"I can't stand it. It's too hot." The boy's face was white and sweat-covered.

Bruce gave him a shot of air, then thought about it. There was an emergency shelter in Sam's pack, just a rolled-up awning with a collapsible frame. Fifteen minutes later he was ready to move. One awning support was tied upright to the sole of one of Sam's boots; the other Bruce had bent and wedged under Sam's shoulders. The contraption looked ready to fall apart but it held. "There! Are you okay?"

"I'm fine. Look, Bruce, I think my knee is all right now. Let me try it."

Bruce felt out the knee through the suit. It was twice the size of its mate; he could feel Sam wince. He touched helmets. "You're full of hop, chum. Relax." Bruce got back into harness.

Hours later, Bruce came across tracks. They swung in from northeast, turned and paralleled the hills. He stopped and told Sam.

"Say, Sam, how can I tell how old they are?"

"You can't. A track fifty years old looks as fresh as a new one."

"No point in following these?"

"No harm in it, provided they go in our direction."

"Roger." Bruce went back to towing. He called hopefully over the radio every few minutes and then listened. The tracks cheered him even though he knew how slim the chance was that they meant anything. The tracks swung out from the hills presently or, rather, the hills swung in, forming a bay. He took the shorter route as his predecessor had.

He should have seen what was coming. He knew that he should keep his eyes ahead, but the need to watch his instruments, the fact that he was leaning into harness, and the circumstance that he was following tracks combined to keep his head down. He had just glanced back at Sam when he felt his skis slipping out from under him.

Automatically he bent his knees and threw his skis into a "snowplow." He might have been able to stop had not the toboggan been scooting along behind. It plowed into him; boy, skis, and toboggan went down, tangled like jackstraws.

He struggled for footing, felt the sand slip under him. He had time to see that he had been caught—in daylight!—by that lunar equivalent of quicksand, a morning glory. Then the sifting dust closed over his helmet.

He felt himself slip, slide, fall, slide again, and come softly to rest.

Bruce tried to get his bearings. Part of his mind was busy with horror, shock, and bitter self blame for having failed Sam; another part seemed able to drive ahead with the business at hand. He did not seem hurt—and he was still breathing. He supposed that he was buried in a morning glory; he suspected that any movement would bury him deeper.

Nevertheless he had to locate Sam. He felt his way up to his neck, pushing the soft flakes aside. The toboggan hitch was still on him. He got both hands on it and heaved. It was frustrating work, like swimming in mud. Gradually he dragged the sled to him—or himself to the sled. Presently he felt his way down the load and located Sam's helmet. "*Sam!* Can you hear me?"

The reply was muffled. "Yeah, Bruce!"

"Are you okay?"

"Okay? Don't be silly! We're in a *morning glory!*"

"Yes, I know. Sam, I'm terribly sorry!"

"Well, don't cry about it. It can't be helped."

"I didn't mean to—"

"Stow it, can't you!" Sam's voice concealed panic with anger. "It doesn't matter. We're goners—don't you realize that?"

"Huh? No, we're not! Sam, I'll get you out—I swear I will."

Sam waited before replying. "Don't kid yourself, Bruce. Nobody ever gets out of a morning glory."

"Don't talk like that. We aren't dead yet."

"No, but we're going to be. I'm trying to get used to the idea." He paused. "Do me a favor, Bruce—get me loose from these confounded skis. I don't want to die tied down."

"Right away!" In total darkness, his hands in gloves, with only memory to guide him, and with the soft, flaky dust everywhere, unlashing the load was nearly impossible. He shifted position, then suddenly noticed something—his left arm was free of the dust.

He shifted and got his helmet free as well. The darkness persisted; he fumbled at his belt, managed to locate his flashlight.

He was lying partly out and mostly in a sloping mass of soft stuff. Close overhead was a rocky roof; many feet below the pile spilled over a floor of rock. Sideways the darkness swallowed up the beam.

He still clutched the toboggan; he hauled at it, trying to drag Sam out. Failing, he burrowed back in. "Hey, Sam! We're in a cave!"

"Huh?"

"Hang on. I'll get you out." Bruce cautiously thrashed around in an attempt to get his entire body outside the dust. It kept caving down on him. Worse, his skis anchored his feet. He kicked one loose, snaked his arm in, and dragged it out. It slid to the base of the pile. He repeated the process, then rolled and scrambled to the floor, still clinging to the hitch.

He set the light on the rock floor, and put the skis aside, then heaved mightily. Sam, toboggan, and load came sliding down, starting a small avalanche. Bruce touched helmets. "Look! We're getting somewhere!"

Sam did not answer. Bruce persisted, "Sam, did you hear me?"

"I heard you. Thanks for pulling me out. Now untie me, will you?"

"Hold the light." Bruce got busy. Shortly he was saying, "There you are. Now I'll stir around and find the way out."

"What makes you think there is a way out?"

"Huh? Don't talk like that. Who ever heard of a cave with no exit?"

Sam answered slowly, "*He* didn't find one."

"'He'?"

"Look." Sam shined the light past Bruce. On the rock a few feet away was a figure in an old-fashioned space suit.

Bruce took the light and cautiously approached the figure. The man was surely dead; his suit was limp. He lay at ease, hands folded across his middle, as if taking a nap. Bruce pointed the torch at the glass face plate. The face inside was lean and dark, skin clung to the bones; Bruce turned the light away.

He came back shortly to Sam. "He didn't make out so well," Bruce said soberly. "I found these papers in his pouch. We'll take them with us so we can let his folks know."

"You *are* an incurable optimist, aren't you? Well, all right." Sam took them. There were two letters, an old-style flat photograph of a little girl and a dog, and some other papers. One was a driver's license for the Commonwealth of Massachusetts, dated June 1995 and signed *Abner Green.*

Bruce stared. "1995! Gee whiz!"

"I wouldn't count on notifying his folks."

Bruce changed the subject. "He had one thing we can use. This." It was a coil of manila rope. "I'll hitch all the lines together, one end to your belt and one to mine. That'll give me five or six hundred feet. If you want me, just pull."

"Okay. Watch your step."

"I'll be careful. You'll be all right?"

"Sure. I've got *him* for company."

"Well ... here goes."

One direction seemed as good as another. Bruce kept the line taut to keep from walking in a circle. The rock curved up presently and his flash showed that it curved back on itself, a dead end. He followed the wall to the left, picking his way, as the going was very rough. He found himself in a passage. It seemed to climb, but it narrowed. Three hundred feet and more out by the ropes, it narrowed so much that he was stopped.

Bruce switched off his light and waited for his eyes to adjust. He became aware of a curious sensation. It was panic.

He forced himself not to turn on the light until he was certain that no gleam lay ahead. Then thankfully he stumbled back into the main cavern.

Another series of chambers led steadily downward. He turned back at a black and bottomless hole.

The details varied but the answers did not: At the furthest reach of the lines, or at some impassable obstacle, he would wait in the dark—but no gleam of light ever showed. He went back to Sam after having covered, he estimated, about 180°.

Sam had crawled up to the heap of fallen dust. Bruce hurried to him. "Sam, are you all right?"

"Sure. I just moved to a feather bed. That rock is terribly cold. What did you find?"

"Well, nothing yet," he admitted. He sat down in the flaky pile and leaned toward Sam. "I'll start again in a moment."

"How's your air supply?" asked Sam.

"Uh, I'll have to crack my reserve bottle soon. How's yours?"

"Mine is throttled to the limit. You're doing all the work; I can save my reserve bottle for you—I think."

Bruce frowned. He wanted to protest, but the gesture wouldn't make sense. They would have to finish up all even; naturally he was using much more air than was Sam.

One thing was sure—time was running out. Finally he said, "Look, Sam—there's no end of those caves and passages. I couldn't search them all with all the air in Luna City."

"I was afraid so."

"But we *know* there's a way out right above us."

"You mean *in*."

"I mean *out*. See here—this morning glory thing is built like an hour glass; there's an open cone on top, and this pile of sand down below. The stuff trickled down through a hole in the roof and piled up until it choked the hole."

"Where does that get you?"

"Well, if we dug the stuff away we could clear the hole."

"It would keep sifting down."

"No, it wouldn't, it would reach a point where there wasn't enough dust close by to sift down any further—there would still be a hole."

Sam considered it. "Maybe. But when you tried to climb up it would collapse back on you. That's the bad part about a morning glory, Bruce; you can't get a foothold."

"The dickens I can't! If I can't climb a slope on skis without collapsing it, when I've got my wits about me and am really trying, why, you can have my reserve air bottle."

Sam chuckled. "Don't be hasty. I might hold you to it. Anyhow," he added, "I can't climb it."

"Once I get my feet on the level, I'll pull you out like a cork, even if you're buried. Time's a-wastin'." Bruce got busy.

Using a ski as a shovel he nibbled at the giant pile. Every so often it would collapse down on him. It did not discourage him; Bruce knew that many yards of the stuff would have to fall and be moved back before the hole would show.

Presently he moved Sam over to the freshly moved waste. From there Sam held the light; the work went faster. Bruce began to sweat. After a while he had to switch air bottles; he sucked on his water tube and ate a march ration before getting back to work.

He began to see the hole opening above him. A great pile collapsed on him; he backed out, looked up, then went to Sam. "Turn out the light!"

There was no doubt; a glimmer of light filtered down. Bruce found himself pounding Sam and shouting. He stopped and said, "Sam, old boy, did I ever say what patrol I'm from?"

"No. Why?"

"Badger Patrol. Watch me dig!" He tore into it. Shortly sunlight poured into the hole and reflected dimly around the cavern. Bruce shoveled until he could see a straight rise from the base of the pile clear to the edge of the morning glory high above them. He decided that the opening was wide enough to tackle.

He hitched himself to Sam with the full length of all the glass ropes and then made a bundle of Sam's pack save air and water bottles, tied a bowline on Sam's uninjured foot, using the manila line, and secured the bundle to the end of that line. He planned to drag Sam out first, then the equipment. Finished, he bound on skis.

Bruce touched helmets. "This is it, pal. Keep the line clear of the sand."

Sam grabbed his arm. "Wait a minute."

"What's the matter?"

"Bruce—if we don't make it, I just want to say that you're all right."

"Uh ... oh, forget it. We'll make it." He started up.

A herringbone step suited the convex approach to the hole. As Bruce neared the opening he shifted to side-step to fit the narrow passage and the concave shape of the morning glory above. He inched up, transferring his weight smoothly and gradually, and not remaining in one spot too long. At last his head, then his whole body, were in sunshine; he was starting up the morning glory itself.

He stopped, uncertain what to do. There was a ridge above him, where the flakes had broken loose when he had shoveled away their support. The break was much too steep to climb, obviously unstable. He paused only a moment as he could feel his skis sinking in; he went forward in half side-step, intending to traverse past the unstable formation.

The tow line defeated him. When Bruce moved sideways, the line had to turn a corner at the neck of the hole. It brushed and then cut into the soft stuff. Bruce felt his skis slipping backwards; with cautious haste he started to climb, tried to ride the slipping mass and keep above it. He struggled as the flakes poured over his skis. Then he was fouled, he went down, it engulfed him.

Again he came to rest in soft, feathery, darkness. He lay quiet, nursing his defeat, before trying to get out. He hardly knew which way was up, much less which way was out. He was struggling experimentally when he felt a tug on his belt. Sam was trying to help him.

A few minutes later, with Sam's pull to guide him, Bruce was again on the floor of the cave. The only light came from the torch in Sam's hand; it was enough to show that the pile choking the hole was bigger than ever.

Sam motioned him over. "Too bad, Bruce," was all he said.

Bruce controlled his choking voice to say, "I'll get busy as soon as I catch my breath."

"Where's your left ski?"

"Huh? Oh! Must have pulled off. It'll show up when I start digging."

"Hmmm … how much air have you?"

"Uh?" Bruce looked at his belt. "About a third of a bottle."

"I'm breathing my socks. I've got to change."

"Right away!" Bruce started to make the switch; Sam pulled him down again.

"You take the fresh bottle, and give me your bottle."

"But—"

"No 'buts' about it," Sam cut him off. "You have to do all the work; you've *got* to take the full tank."

33

Silently Bruce obeyed. His mind was busy with arithmetic. The answer always came out the same; he knew with certainty that there was not enough air left to permit him again to perform the Herculean task of moving that mountain of dust.

He began to believe that they would never get out. The knowledge wearied him; he wanted to lie down beside the still form of Abner Green and, like him, not struggle at the end.

However he could not. He knew that, for Sam's sake, he would have to shovel away at that endless sea of sand, until he dropped from lack of oxygen. Listlessly he took off his remaining ski and walked toward his task.

Sam jerked on the rope.

Bruce went back. "What's got into you, kid?" Sam demanded.

"Nothing. Why?"

"It's got you whipped."

"I didn't say so."

"But you think so. I could see it. Now you listen! You convinced me that you could get us out—and, by Jiminy! you're going to! You're just cocky enough to be the first guy to whip a morning glory and you can do it. Get your chin up!"

Bruce hesitated. "Look, Sam, I won't quit on you, but you might as well know the truth: there isn't air enough to do it again."

"Figured that out when I saw the stuff start to crumble."

"You knew? Then if you know any prayers, better say them."

Sam shook his arm. "It's not time to pray; it's time to get busy."

"Okay." Bruce started to straighten up.

"That's not what I meant."

"Huh?"

"There's no point in digging. Once was worth trying; twice is wasting oxygen."

"Well, what do you want me to do?"

"You didn't try *all* the ways out, did you?"

"No." Bruce thought about it. "I'll try again, Sam. But there isn't air enough to try them all."

"You can search longer than you can shovel. But don't search haphazardly; search back toward the hills. Anywhere else will be just another morning glory; we need to come out *at the hills*; away from the sand."

"Uh … look, Sam, where *are* the hills? Down here you can't tell north from next week."

"Over that way," Sam pointed.

"Huh? How do you know?"

"You showed me. When you broke through I could tell where the Sun was from the angle of the light."

"But the Sun is overhead."

"Was when we started. Now it's fifteen, twenty degrees to the west. Now listen: these caves must have been big blow holes once, gas pockets. You search off in that direction and find us a blow hole that's not choked with sand."

"I'll do my darndest!"

"How far away were the hills when we got caught?"

Bruce tried to remember. "Half a mile, maybe."

"Check. You won't find what we want tied to me with five or six hundred feet of line. Take that pad of paper in my pouch. Blaze your way—and be darn sure you blaze enough!"

"I will!"

"Attaboy! Good luck."

Bruce stood up.

It was the same tedious, depressing business as before! Bruce stretched the line, then set out at the end of it, dropping bits of paper and counting his steps. Several times he was sure that he was under the hills, only to come to an impasse. Twice he skirted the heaps that marked other morning glorys. Each time he retraced his steps he gathered up his blazes, both to save paper and to keep from confusing himself.

Once, he saw a glimmer of light and his heart pounded—but it filtered down from a hole too difficult even for himself and utterly impossible for Sam.

His air got low; he paid no attention, other than to adjust his mix to keep it barely in the white. He went on searching.

A passage led to the left, then down; he began to doubt the wisdom of going further and stopped to check the darkness. At first his eyes saw nothing, then it seemed as if there might be a suggestion of light ahead. Eye fatigue? Possibly. He went another hundred feet and tried again. It was light!

Minutes later he shoved his shoulders up through a twisted hole and gazed out over the burning plain.

"Hi!" Sam greeted him. "I thought you had fallen down a hole."

"Darn near did. Sam, I found it!"

"Knew you would. Let's get going."

"Right. I'll dig out my other ski."

"Nope."

"Why not?"

"Look at your air gauge. We aren't going anywhere on skis."

"Huh? Yeah, I guess not." They abandoned their loads, except for air and water bottles. The dark trek was made piggy-back, where the ceiling permitted. Some places Bruce half dragged his partner. Other places they threaded on hands and knees with Sam pulling his bad leg painfully behind him.

Bruce climbed out first, having slung Sam in a bowline before he did so. Sam gave little help in getting out; once they were above ground Bruce picked him up and set him against a rock. He then touched helmets. "There, fellow! We made it!"

Sam did not answer.

Bruce peered in; Sam's features were slack, eyes half closed. A check of his belt told why; the blood-oxygen indicator showed red.

Sam's intake valve was already wide open; Bruce moved fast, giving himself a quick shot of air, then transferring his bottle to Sam. He opened it wide.

He could see Sam's pointer crawl up even as his own dropped toward the red. Bruce had air in his suit for three or four minutes if he held still.

He did not hold still. He hooked his intake hose to the manifold of the single bottle now attached to Sam's suit and opened his valve. His own indicator stopped dropping toward the red. They were

Siamese twins now, linked by one partly-exhausted bottle of utterly necessary gas. Bruce put an arm around Sam, settled Sam's head on his shoulder, helmet to helmet, and throttled down both valves until each was barely in the white. He gave Sam more margin than himself, then settled down to wait. The rock under them was in shadow, though the Sun still baked the plain. Bruce looked out, searching for anyone or anything, then extended his aerial. "*M'aidez!*" he called. "Help us! We're lost."

He could hear Sam muttering. "May day!" Sam echoed into his dead radio. "May day! We're lost."

Bruce cradled the delirious boy in his arm and repeated again, "*M'aidez!* Get a bearing on us." He paused, then echoed, "May day! May day!"

After a while he readjusted the valves, then went back to repeating endlessly, "May day! Get a bearing on us."

He did not feel it when a hand clasped his shoulder. He was still muttering "May day!" when they dumped him into the air lock of the desert car.

Mr. Andrews visited him in the infirmary at Base Camp. "How are you, Bruce?"

"Me? I'm all right, sir. I wish they'd let me get up."

"My instructions. So I'll know where you are." The Scoutmaster smiled; Bruce blushed.

"How's Sam?" he asked.

"He'll get by. Cold burns and a knee that will bother him a while. That's all."

"Gee, I'm glad."

"The troop is leaving. I'm turning you over to Troop Three, Mr. Harkness. Sam will go back with the grub car."

"Uh, I think I could travel with the Troop, sir."

"Perhaps so, but I want you to stay with Troop Three. You need field experience."

"Uh—" Bruce hesitated, wondering how to say it. "Mr. Andrews?"

"Yes?"

"I might as well go back. I've learned something. You were right. A fellow can't get to be an old Moon hand in three weeks. Uh ... I guess I was just conceited."

"Is that all?"

"Well—yes, sir."

"Very well, listen to me. I've talked with Sam and with Mr. Harkness. Mr. Harkness will put you through a course of sprouts; Sam and I will take over when you get back. You plan on being ready for the Court of Honor two weeks from Wednesday." The Scoutmaster added, "Well?"

Bruce gulped and found his voice. "Yes, sir!"

Once opened, the box could never be closed. But after the myriad swarming Troubles came Hope.

Science fiction is not prophecy. It often reads as if it were prophecy; indeed the practitioners of this odd genre (pun intentional—I won't do it again) of fiction usually strive hard to make their stories sound as if they were true pictures of the future. Prophecies.

Prophesying is what the weatherman does, the race track tipster, the stock market adviser, the fortuneteller who reads palms or gazes into a crystal. Each one is predicting the future—sometimes exactly, sometimes in vague, veiled, or ambiguous language, sometimes simply with a claim of statistical probability, but always with a claim seriously made of disclosing some piece of the future.

This is not at all what a science fiction author does. Science fiction is almost always laid in the future—or at least in a fictional possible-future—and is almost invariably deeply concerned with the shape of that future. But the method is not prediction; it is usually extrapolation and/or speculation. Indeed the author is not required to (and usually does not) regard the fictional "future" he has chosen to write about as being the events most likely to come to pass; his purpose may have nothing to do with the *probability* that these storied events may happen.

"Extrapolation" means much the same in fiction writing as it does in mathematics: exploring a trend. It means continuing a curve, a path, a trend into the future, by extending its present direction and continuing the *shape* it has displayed in its past performance—i.e., if it is a sine curve in the past, you extrapolate it as a sine curve in the future, not as an hyperbola, nor a Witch of Agnesi, and *most certainly not* as a tangent straight line.

"Speculation" has far more elbowroom than extrapolation; it starts with a "What if?"—and the new factor thrown in by the what-if may be both wildly improbable and so revolutionary in effect as to throw a sine-curve trend (or a yeast-growth trend, or any trend) into something unrecognizably different. What if little green men land on the White House lawn and invite us to join a Galactic union?—or big green men land and enslave us and eat us? What if we solve the problem of immortality? What if New York City really does go dry? And not just the present fiddlin' shortage tackled by fiddlin' quarter-measures—can you imagine a man being lynched for wasting an ice cube? Living, as I do, in a state (Colorado—1965) which has just two sorts of water, too little and too much—we just finished seven years of drought with seven inches of rain in two hours, and one was about as disastrous as the other—I find a horrid fascination in Frank Herbert's *Dune World*, in Charles Einstein's *The Day New York Went Dry*, and in stories about Bible-type floods such as S. Fowler Wright's *Deluge*.

Most science fiction stories use both extrapolation and speculation. Consider "Blowups Happen," in volume one. It was written in 1939, updated very slightly for book publication just after World War II by inserting some words such as "Manhattan Project" and "Hiroshima," but not rewritten, and is one of a group of stories published under the pretentious collective title of *The History of the Future* (!) (an editor's title, *not* mine!)—which certainly sounds like prophecy.

I disclaim any intention of prophesying; I wrote that story for the sole purpose of making money to pay off a mortgage and with the single intention of entertaining the reader. As prophecy the story falls flat on its silly face—any tenderfoot Scout can pick it to pieces—but I think it is still entertaining as a *story*, else it would not be here; I have a business reputation to protect and wish to continue making money. Nor am I ashamed of this motivation. Very little of the great literature of our heritage arose solely from a wish to "create art"; most writing, both great and not-so-great, has as its proximate cause a need for money combined with an aversion to, or an inability to perform, hard "honest labor." Fiction writing offers a legal and reasonably honest way out of this dilemma.

A science fiction author may have, and often does have, other motivations *in addition to* pursuit of profit. He may wish to create "art for art's sake," he may want to warn the world against a course he feels to be disastrous (Orwell's *1984*, Huxley's *Brave New World*—but please note that each is intensely entertaining, and that each made stacks of money), he may wish to urge the human race toward a course which he considers desirable (Bellamy's *Looking Backward*, Wells' *Men Like Gods*), he may wish to instruct, or uplift, or even to dazzle. But the science fiction writer—*any* fiction writer—must keep entertainment consciously in mind as his prime purpose ... or he may find himself back dragging that old cotton sack.

If he succeeds in this purpose, his story is likely to remain gripping entertainment long years after it has turned out to be false "prophecy." H. G. Wells is perhaps the greatest science fiction author of all time—and his greatest science fiction stories were written around sixty years ago (i.e., about 1895) ... under the whip. Bedfast with consumption, unable to hold a job, flat broke, paying alimony—he *had* to make money somehow, and writing was the heaviest work he could manage. He was clearly aware (see his autobiography) that to stay alive he must be entertaining. The result was a flood of some of the most brilliant speculative stories about the future ever written. As prophecy they are all hopelessly dated ... which matters not at all; they are as spellbinding now as they were in the Gay 'Nineties and the Mauve Decade.

Try to lay hands on his *The Sleeper Awakes*. The gadgetry in it is ingenious—and all wrong. The projected future in it is brilliant—and did not happen. All of which does not sully the story; it is a great story of love and sacrifice and blood-chilling adventure set in a matrix of mind-stretching speculation about the nature of Man and his Destiny. I read it first in 1923, and at least a dozen times since ... and still reread it whenever I get to feeling uncertain about just how one does go about the unlikely process of writing fiction for entertainment of strangers—and again finding myself caught up in the sheer excitement of Wells' story.

"Solution Unsatisfactory" (volume one) is a consciously Wellsian story. No, no, I'm not claiming that it is of H. G. Wells' quality—its quality is for you to judge, not me. But it was written by the method which Wells spelled out for the speculative story: Take one, just one, basic new assumption, then examine all its consequences—but express those consequences in terms of human beings. The assumption I chose was the "Absolute Weapon"; the speculation concerns what changes this forces on mankind. But the "history" the story describes simply did not happen.

However the problems discussed in this story are as fresh today, the issues just as poignant, for the grim reason that we have not reached even an "unsatisfactory" solution to the problem of the Absolute Weapon; we have reached *no* solution.

In the years that have passed since I wrote that story (in 1940) the world situation has grown much worse. Instead of one Absolute Weapon there are now at least five distinct types—an "Absolute Weapon" being defined as one against which there is no effective defense and which kills indiscriminately over a very wide area. The earliest of the five types, the A-bomb, is now known to be possessed by at least five nations; at least twenty-five other nations have the potential to build them in the next few years.

But there is a possible sixth type. Earlier this year (1965—R.A.H.) I attended a seminar at one of the nation's new think-factories. One of the questions discussed was whether or not a "Doomsday Bomb" could be built—a single weapon which would destroy all life of all sorts on this planet; *one* weapon, not an all-out nuclear holocaust involving hundreds of thousands of ICBMs. No, this was to be a world-wrecker of the sort Dr. E. E. Smith used to use in his interstellar sagas back in the days when SF magazines had bug-eyed monsters on the cover and were considered lowbrow, childish, fantastic.

The conclusions reached were: Could the Doomsday Machine be built?—yes, no question about it. What would it cost?—quite cheap.

A seventh type hardly seems necessary.

And that makes the grimness of "Solution Unsatisfactory" seem more like an Oz book in which the most harrowing adventures always turn out happily.

"Searchlight" is almost pure extrapolation, almost no speculation. The gadgets in it are either hardware on the shelf, or hardware which will soon be on the shelf because nothing is involved but straightforward engineering development. "Life-Line" (my first story) is its opposite, a story which is sheer speculation and either impossible or very highly improbable, as the What-If postulate will never be solved—I think. I hope. But the two stories are much alike in that neither depends on when it was written nor when it is read. Both are independent of any particular shape to history; they are timeless.

"Free Men" is another timeless story. As told, it looks like another "after the blowup"—but it is not. Although the place is nominally the United States and the time (as shown by the gadgetry) is set in the not-distant future, simply by changing names of persons and places and by inserting other weapons and other gadgets this story could be any country and any time in the past or future—or could even be on another planet and concern a non-human race. But the story does also apply here-and-now, so I told it that way.

"Pandora's Box" was the original title of an article researched and written in 1949 for publication in 1950, the end of the half-century. Inscrutable are the ways of editors: it appeared with the title "Where To?" and purported to be a nonfiction prophecy concerning the year 2000 A.D. as seen from 1950. (I agree that a science fiction writer should avoid marijuana, prophecy, and time payments—but I was tempted by a soft rustle.)

Our present editor (1965) decided to use this article, but suggested that it should be updated. Authors who wish to stay in the business listen most carefully to editors' suggestions, even when they think an editor has been out in the sun without a hat; I agreed.

And reread "Where To?" and discovered that our editor was undeniably correct; it needed updating. At least.

But at last I decided not to try to conceal my bloopers. Below is reproduced, unchanged, my predictions of fifteen years back. But here and there through the article I have inserted signs for footnotes—like this: (z)—and these will be found at the end of the 1950 article ... calling attention to bloopers and then forthrightly excusing myself by rationalizing how anyone, even Nostradamus, would have made the same mistake ... hedging my bets in other cases, or chucking in

43

brand-new predictions and carefully laying them farther in the future than I am likely to live … and, in some cases, crowing loudly about successful predictions. (Addendum 1979: I have interpolated the later comments, and marked each item 1950, or 1965, or 1980.) So—

—— WHERE TO? ———————————————————

A bloomin', foolish sparrow
Built his nest in a spout,
And along—

—came a building inspector, looked over the site, and the plans, and okayed them, after requiring the sparrow to buy eleven different licenses totalling 18% of the sparrow's building budget, plus something called special service, and along—

—the bleedin' rains came,
And washed the sparrow out.

Again the foolish sparrow,
Built his nest in the spout,
And again—

—came that building inspector, bawled out the sparrow for failing to get special licenses and permits covering typhoons, sun spots, and ice ages, required him to buy seventeen permits and/or licenses and appear before boards controlling zoning, economic impact, ecological protection, energy conservation, and community esthetics, plus something called "very special service"—and a second mortgage, and along—

—the bleedin' rains came,
And washed the sparrow out. (Around again ... and again ... and—)

1950 Where To?

Most science fiction consists of big-muscled stories about adventures in space, atomic wars, invasions by extra-terrestrials, and such. All very well—but now we will take time out for a look at ordinary home life half a century hence.

Except for tea leaves and other magical means, the only way to guess at the *future* is by examining the *present* in the light of the *past*. Let's go back half a century and visit your grandmother before we attempt to visit your grandchildren.

1900: Mr. McKinley is President and the airplane has not yet been invented. Let's knock on the door of that house with the gingerbread, the stained glass, and the cupola.

The lady of the house answers. You recognize her—your own grandmother, Mrs. Middleclass. She is almost as plump as you remember her, for she "put on some good, healthy flesh" after she married.

She welcomes you and offers coffee cake, fresh from her modern kitchen (running water from a hand pump; the best coal range Pittsburgh ever produced). Everything about her house is modern—hand-painted china, souvenirs from the Columbian Exposition, beaded portières, shining baseburner stoves, gas lights, a telephone on the wall.

There is no bathroom, but she and Mr. Middleclass are thinking of putting one in. Mr. Middleclass's mother calls this nonsense, but your grandmother keeps up with the times. She is an advocate of clothing reform, wears only one petticoat, bathes twice a week, and her corsets are guaranteed rust proof. She has been known to defend female suffrage—but not in the presence of Mr. Middleclass.

Nevertheless, you find difficulty in talking with her. Let's jump back to the present and try again.

The automatic elevator takes us to the ninth floor, and we pick out a door by its number, that being the only way to distinguish it.

"Don't bother to ring," you say? What? It's *your* door and you know exactly what lies beyond it—

Very well, let's move a half century into the future and try another middle class home.

It's a suburban home not two hundred miles from the city. You pick out your destination from the air while the cab is landing you—a cluster of hemispheres that makes you think of the houses Dorothy found in Oz.

You set the cab to return to its hangar and go into the entrance hall. You neither knock nor ring. The screen has warned them before you touched down on the landing flat and the autobutler's transparency is shining with: PLEASE RECORD A MESSAGE.

Before you can address the microphone a voice calls out, "Oh, it's you! Come in, come in." There is a short wait, as your hostess is not at the door. The autobutler flashed your face to the patio—where she was reading and sunning herself—and has relayed her voice back to you.

She pauses at the door, looks at you through one-way glass, and frowns slightly; she knows your old-fashioned disapproval of casual nakedness. Her kindness causes her to disobey the family psychiatrist; she grabs a robe and covers herself before signaling the door to open.

The psychiatrist was right; you have thus been classed with strangers, tradespeople, and others who are not family intimates. But you must swallow your annoyance; you cannot object to her wearing clothes when you have sniffed at her for not doing so.

There is no reason why she should wear clothes at home. The house is clean—not somewhat clean, but *clean*—and comfortable. The floor is warm to bare feet; there are no unpleasant drafts, no cold walls. All dust is precipitated from the air entering this house. All textures, of floor, of couch, of chair, are comfortable to bare skin. Sterilizing ultra-violet light floods each room whenever it is unoccupied, and, several times a day, a "whirlwind" blows house-created dust from all surfaces and whisks it out. These auto services are unobtrusive because automatic cut-off switches prevent them from occurring whenever a mass in a room is radiating at blood temperature.

Such a house can become untidy, but not dirty. Five minutes of straightening, a few swipes at children's fingermarks, and her day's housekeeping is done. Oftener than sheets were changed in Mr. McKinley's day, this housewife rolls out a fresh layer of sheeting on each sitting surface and stuffs the discard down the oubliette. This is easy; there is a year's supply on a roll concealed in each chair or couch. The tissue sticks by pressure until pulled loose and does not obscure the pattern and color.

You go into the family room, sit down, and remark on the lovely day. "Isn't it?" she answers. "Come sunbathe with me."

The sunny patio gives excuse for bare skin by anyone's standards; thankfully she throws off the robe and stretches out on a couch. You hesitate a moment. After all, she is your own grandchild, so why not? You undress quickly, since you left your outer wrap and shoes at the door (only barbarians wear street shoes in a house) and what remains is easily discarded. Your grandparents had to get used to a mid-century beach. It was no easier for them.

On the other hand, their bodies were wrinkled and old, whereas yours is not. The triumphs of endocrinology, of cosmetics, of plastic surgery, of figure control in every way are such that a woman need not change markedly from maturity until old age. A woman can keep her body as firm and slender as she wishes—and most of them so wish. This has produced a paradox: the United States has the highest percentage of old people in all its two and a quarter centuries, yet it seems to have a larger proportion of handsome young women than ever before.

(Don't whistle, son! That's your grandmother—)

This garden is half sunbathing patio, complete with shrubs and flowers, lawn and couches, and half swimming pool. The day, though sunny, is quite cold—but not in the garden, and the pool is not chilly. The garden appears to be outdoors, but is not; it is covered by a bubble of transparent plastic, blown and cured on the spot. You are inside the bubble; the sun is outside; you cannot see the plastic.

She invites you to lunch; you protest. "Nonsense!" she answers, "I like to cook." Into the house she goes. You think of following, but it is deliriously warm in the March sunshine and you are feeling relaxed to be away from the city. You locate a switch on the side of the couch, set it for gentle massage, and let the couch knead your troubles away. The couch notes your heart rate and breathing; as they slow, so does it. As you fall asleep it stops.

Meanwhile your hostess has been "slaving away over a hot stove." To be precise, she has allowed a menu selector to pick out an 800-calorie, 4-ration-point luncheon. It is a random-choice gadget, somewhat like a slot machine, which has in it the running inventory of her larder and which will keep hunting until it turns up a balanced meal. Some housewives claim that it takes the art out of cookery, but our hostess is one of many who have accepted it thankfully as an endless source of new menus. Its choice is limited today as it has been three months since she has done grocery shopping. She rejects several menus; the selector continues patiently to turn up combinations until she finally accepts one based around fish disguised as lamb chops.

Your hostess takes the selected items from shelves or the freezer. All are prepared; some are pre-cooked. Those still to be cooked she puts into her—well, her "processing equipment," though she calls it a "stove." Part of it traces its ancestry to diathermy equipment; another feature is derived from metal enameling processes. She sets up cycles, punches buttons, and must wait two or three minutes for the meal to cook. She spends the time checking her ration accounts.

Despite her complicated kitchen, she doesn't eat as well as her great grandmother did—too many people and too few acres.

Never mind; the tray she carries out to the patio is well laden and beautiful. You are both willing to nap again when it is empty. You wake to find that she has burned the dishes and is recovering from her "exertion" in her refresher. Feeling hot and sweaty from your nap you decide to use it when she comes out. There is a wide choice offered by the 'fresher, but you limit yourself to a warm shower growing gradually cooler, followed by warm air drying, a short massage, spraying with scent, and dusting with powder. Such a simple routine is an insult to a talented machine.

Your host arrives home as you come out; he has taken a holiday from his engineering job and has had the two boys down at the beach. He kisses his wife, shouts, "Hi, Duchess!" at you, and turns to the video, setting it to hunt and sample the newscasts it has stored that day. His wife sends the boys in to 'fresh themselves then says, "Have a nice day, dear?"

He answers, "The traffic was terrible. Had to make the last hundred miles on automatic. Anything on the phone for me?"

"Weren't you on relay?"

"Didn't set it. Didn't want to be bothered." He steps to the house phone, plays back his calls, finds nothing he cares to bother with—but the machine goes ahead and prints one message; he pulls it out and tears it off.

"What is it?" his wife asks.

"Telestat from Luna City—from Aunt Jane."

"What does she say?"

"Nothing much. According to her, the Moon is a great place and she wants us to come visit her."

"Not likely!" his wife answers. "Imagine being shut up in an air-conditioned cave."

"When you are Aunt Jane's age, my honey lamb, and as frail as she is, with a bad heart thrown in, you'll go to the Moon and like it. Low gravity is not to be sneezed at—Auntie will probably live to be a hundred and twenty, heart trouble and all."

"Would *you* go to the Moon?" she asks.

"If I needed to and could afford it." He turns to you. "Right?"

You consider your answer. Life still looks good to you—and stairways are beginning to be difficult. Low gravity is attractive even though it means living out your days at the Geriatrics Foundation on the Moon. "It might be fun to visit," you answer. "One wouldn't have to stay."

Hospitals for old people on the Moon? Let's not be silly—

Or is it silly? Might it not be a logical and necessary outcome of our world today?

Space travel we will have, not fifty years from now, but much sooner. It's breathing down our necks. As for geriatrics on the Moon, for most of us no price is too high and no amount of trouble is too great to extend the years of our lives. It is possible that low gravity (one sixth, on the Moon) may not lengthen lives; nevertheless it *may*—we don't know yet—and it will most certainly add greatly to comfort on reaching that inevitable age when the burden of dragging around one's body is almost too much, or when we would otherwise resort to an oxygen tent to lessen the work of a worn-out heart.

By the rules of prophecy, such a prediction is *probable*, rather than impossible.

But the items and gadgets suggested above are examples of *timid* prophecy.

What are the rules of prophecy, if any?

Look at the graph shown here. The solid curve is what has been going on this past century. It represents many things—use of power, speed of transport, numbers of scientific and technical workers, advances in communication, average miles traveled per person per year, advances in mathematics, the rising curve of knowledge. Call it the curve of human achievement.

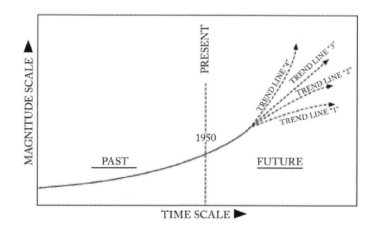

What is the correct way to project this curve into the future? Despite everything, there is a stubborn "common sense" tendency to project it along dotted line number one—like the patent office official of a hundred years back who quit his job "because everything had already been invented." Even those who don't expect a slowing up at once tend to expect us to reach a point of diminishing returns (dotted line number two).

Very daring minds are willing to predict that we will continue our present rate of progress (dotted line number three—a tangent).

But the proper way to project the curve is dotted line number four—for there is no reason, mathematical, scientific, or historical, to expect that curve to flatten out, or to reach a point of diminishing returns, or simply to go on as a tangent. The correct projection, by all facts known today, is for the curve to go on up indefinitely with *increasing* steepness.

The timid little predictions earlier in this article actually belong to curve one, or, at most, to curve two. You can count on the changes in the next fifty years at least *eight times* as great as the changes of the past fifty years.

The Age of Science *has not yet opened.*

AXIOM: A "nine-days' wonder" is taken as a matter of course on the tenth day.

AXIOM: A "common sense" prediction is sure to err on the side of timidity.

AXIOM: The more extravagant a prediction sounds the more likely it is to come true.

So let's have a few free-swinging predictions about the future.

Some will be wrong—but cautious predictions are *sure* to be wrong.

1. 1950 Interplanetary travel is waiting at your front door— C.O.D. It's yours when you pay for it.

1965 And now we are paying for it and the cost is high. But, for reasons understandable only to bureaucrats, we have almost halted development of a nuclear-powered spacecraft when success was in sight. Never mind; if we don't another country will. By the end of this century space travel will be cheap.

1980 And now the Apollo-Saturn Man-on-the-Moon program has come and gone, and all we have now in the U.S.A. as a new man-in-space program is the Space Shuttle—underfinanced and two years behind schedule. See my article "Spinoff" on page 211 (Volume II), especially the last two pages.

Is space travel dead? *No, because the United States is not the only nation on this planet.* Today both Japan and Germany seem to be good bets—countries aware that endless wealth is out there for the taking. USSR seems to be concentrating on the military aspects rather than on space travel, and the People's Republic of China does not as yet appear to have the means to spare—but don't count out either nation; the potential is there, in both cases.

And don't count out the United States! Today most of our citizens regard the space program as a boondoggle (totally unaware that it is one of the very few Federal programs that paid for themselves, manyfold). But we are talking about twenty years from now, 2000 A.D. Let's see it in perspective. Exactly thirty years ago George Pal and Irving Pichel and I—and ca. 200 others—were making the motion picture *Destination Moon*. I remember sharply that most of the people working on that film started out thinking that it was a silly fantasy, an impossibility. I had my nose rubbed in it again and again, especially if the speaker was unaware that I had written it. (Correction: written the first version of it. By the time it was filmed, even the banker's wife was writing dialog.)

As for the general public—A trip to the *Moon*? Nonsense!

That was thirty years ago, late 1949.

Nineteen years and ten months later Apollo 11 landed on the Moon.

Look again at the curves on page 51 (Volume II). With respect to space travel (and industry, power, and colonization) we have dropped to that feeble curve #1—but we could shift back to curve #4 overnight if our President and/or Congress got it through their heads that not one but all of our crisis problems can be solved by exploiting space. Employment, inflation, pollution, population, energy, running out of nonrenewable resources—there is pie in the sky for the U.S.A. and for the entire planet including the impoverished "Third World."

I won't try to prove it here. See *The Third Industrial Revolution* by G. Harry Stine, 1979, Ace Books, 51 Madison Avenue, New York, NY 10010, and see *A Step Farther Out* by Dr. Jerry Pournelle, also Ace Books 1979—and accept my assurance that I have known both authors well for twenty-odd years, know that each has years of experience in aerospace, and that each has both the formal education and the continuing study—and the horse sense!—to be a true expert in this matter.

From almost total disbelief about space travel (99.9+%) to a landing on the Moon in twenty years ... from President Kennedy's announcement of intention to that Lunar landing in only *seven* years ... and still twenty years to go until the year 2000—we can still shift to curve #4 (and get rich) almost overnight. By 2000 A.D. we could have O'Neill colonies, self-supporting and exporting power to Earth, at both Lagrange-4 and Lagrange-5, transfer stations in orbit about Earth and around Luna, a permanent base on Luna equipped with an electric catapult—and a geriatrics retirement home.

However, I am not commissioned to predict what we *could* do but to predict (guess) what is *most likely* to happen by 2000 A.D.

Our national loss of nerve, our escalating anti-intellectualism, our almost total disinterest in anything that does not *directly* and *immediately* profit us, the shambles of public education throughout most of our nation (especially in New York and California) cause me to predict that *our space program will continue to dwindle*. It would not surprise me (but would distress me mightily!) to see the Space Shuttle canceled.

In the meantime some other nation or group will start exploiting space—industry, power, perhaps Lagrange-point colonies—and suddenly we will wake up to the fact that we have been left at the post.

That happened to us in '57; we came up from behind and passed the competition. Possibly we will do it again. Possibly—

But I am making no cash bets.

2. 1950 Contraception and control of disease is revising relations between the sexes to an extent that will change our entire social and economic structure.

1965 This trend is so much more evident now than it was fifteen years ago that I am tempted to call it a fulfilled prophecy. Vast changes in sex relations are evident all around us—with the oldsters calling it "moral decay" and the youngsters ignoring them and taking it for granted. Surface signs: books such as *Sex and the Single Girl* are smash hits; the formerly-taboo four-letter words are now seen both in novels and popular magazines; the neologism "swinger" has come into the language; courts are conceding that nudity and semi-nudity are now parts of the cultural *mores*. But the end is not yet; this revolution will go much farther and is now barely started.

The most difficult speculation for a science fiction writer to undertake is to imagine correctly the *secondary* implications of a new factor. Many people correctly anticipated the coming of the horseless carriage; some were bold enough to predict that everyone would use them and the horse would virtually disappear. But I know of no writer, fiction or nonfiction, who saw ahead of time the vast change in the courting and mating habits of Americans which would result primarily from the automobile—a change which the diaphragm and the oral contraceptive merely confirmed. So far as I know, no one even dreamed of the change in sex habits the automobile would set off.

There is some new gadget in existence today which will prove to be equally revolutionary in some other way equally unexpected. You and I both know of this gadget, by name and by function—but we don't know which one it is nor what its unexpected effect will be. This is why science fiction is *not* prophecy—and why fictional speculation can be so much fun both to read and to write.

1980 (No, I still don't know what that revolutionary gadget is—unless it is the computer chip.) The sexual revolution: it continues apace—FemLib, GayLib, single women with progeny and never a lifted eyebrow, staid old universities and colleges that permit unmarried couples to room together on campus, group marriages, "open" marriages, miles and miles of "liberated" beaches. Most of this can be covered by one sentence: What used to be concealed is now done openly. But sexual attitudes are in flux; the new ones not yet cultural *mores*.

But I think I see a trend, one that might jell by 2000 A.D. The racial biological function of "family" is the protection of children and pregnant women. To accomplish that, family organization must be rewarding to men as well ... and I do *not* mean copulation. There is a cynical old adage covering that: "Why keep a cow when milk is so cheap?" A marriage must offer its members emotional, spiritual, and physical comforts superior to those to be found in living alone if that prime function is to be accomplished.

(Stipulated: there are individuals, both sexes, who prefer to live alone. This is racially self-correcting.)

The American core family (father, mother, two or three children) has ceased to be emotionally satisfying—if it ever was. It is a creation of our times: mobility, birth control, easy divorce. Early in this century the core family was mother, father, four to eight children ... and was itself a unit in an extended family of grandparents, aunts, uncles, and cousins living near enough (if not in the same house) to be mutually supportive. If a child was ill, Aunt Cora came over to help while Aunt Abby took the other kids into her home. See Mauve Decade fiction.

With increased mobility and fewer children this undefined extended-family pattern disappeared almost without its disappearance being noticed. To the extent to which it was noticed there was often glee at being free of the nuisance of in-laws and kinfolk. It took considerably longer to realize that the advantages had also disappeared.

We will not get a return of the extended family of the sort that characterized the 19th century and the early 20th ... but the current flux of swingers' clubs, group marriages, spouse swapping, etc., is, in my opinion, fumbling and almost unconscious attempts to regain the pleasure, emotional comfort, and mutual security once found in the extended family of two or more generations back.

Prediction: by 2000 A.D. or soon thereafter extended families of several sorts will be more common than core families. The common characteristic of the various types will be increased security for children under legally enforceable contracts.

3. 1950 The most important military fact of this century is that there is no way to repel an attack from outer space.

1965 I flatly stand by this one. True, we are now working on Nike-Zeus and Nike-X and related systems and plan to spend billions on such systems—and we know that others are doing the same thing. True, it is possible to hit an object in orbit or trajectory. Nevertheless this prediction is as safe as predicting tomorrow's sunrise. Anti-aircraft fire never stopped air attacks; it simply made them expensive. The disadvantage in being at the bottom of a deep "gravity well" is very great; gravity gauge will be as crucial in the coming years as wind gauge was in the days when sailing ships controlled empires. The nation that controls the Moon will control the Earth—but no one seems willing these days to speak that nasty fact out loud.

1980 I have just heard a convincing report that the USSR has developed lasers far better than ours that can blind our eyes-in-the-sky satellites and, presumably, destroy our ICBMs in flight. Stipulate that this rumor is true: It does not change my 1950 assertion one iota. Missiles tossed from the Moon to the Earth need not be H-bombs or any sort of bomb—or even missile-shaped. All they need be is massive ... because they arrive at approximately *seven miles per second*. A laser capable of blinding a satellite and of disabling an ICBM to the point where it can't explode would need to be orders of magnitude more powerful in order to volatilize a house-size chunk of Luna. For further details see my *The Moon Is a Harsh Mistress*.

4. 1950 It is utterly impossible that the United States will start a "preventive war." We will fight when attacked, either directly or in a territory we have guaranteed to defend.

1965 Since 1950 we have done so in several theaters and are doing so in Viet Nam as this is written. "Preventive" or "pre-emptive" war seems as unlikely as ever, no matter who is in the White House.

Here is a new prediction: World War III (as a major, all-out war) will not take place at least until 1980 and could easily hold off until 2000. This is a very happy prediction compared with the situation in 1950, as those years of grace may turn up basic factors which (I hope!) may postpone disaster still longer. We were *much* closer to ultimate disaster around 1955 than we are today—much closer indeed than we were at the time of the Cuban confrontation in 1962. But the public never knew it. All in all, things look pretty good for survival, for the time being—and that is as good a break as our ancestors ever had. It was far more dangerous to live in London in 1664-5 than it is to live in a city threatened by H-bombs today.

1980 I am forced to revise the 1950 prediction to this extent: It is no longer certain that we will fight to repel attack on territory we have guaranteed to defend; our behavior both with respect to Viet Nam and to Taiwan is a clear warning to our NATO allies. The question is not whether we should ever have been in Viet Nam or whether we should ever have allied ourselves to the Nationalist Chinese. I do not know of *any* professional military man who favored ever getting into combat on the continent of Asia; such war for us is a logistic and strategic disaster.

But to break a commitment to an ally *once it has been made* is to destroy our credibility.

5. 1950 In fifteen years the housing shortage will be solved by a "breakthrough" into new technology which will make every house now standing as obsolete as privies.

1965 Here I fell flat on my face. There has been no breakthrough in housing, nor is any now in prospect—instead the ancient, wasteful methods of building are now being confirmed by public subsidies. The degree of our backwardness in the field is hard to grasp; we have never seen a modern house. Think what an automobile would be if each one were custom-built from materials fetched to your home—what would it look like, what would it do, and how much would it cost. But don't set the cost lower than $100,000 or the speed higher than 10 m/h, if you want to be realistic about the centuries of difference between the housing industry and the automotive industry.

I underestimated (through wishful thinking) the power of human stupidity—a fault fatal to prophecy.

1980 I'm still flat on my face with my nose rubbed in the mud; the situation is worse than ever. See "A Bathroom of Her Own" in volume one. And that figure of $100,000 just above was with gold at $35 per troy ounce—so change it to one million dollars—or call it 2700 troy ounces of gold. Or forget it. The point is that it would be very nearly impossible to build even a clunker automobile at- any price if we built them the way we build houses.

We have the technology to build cheap, beautiful, efficient, flexible (modular method) houses, extremely comfortable and with the durability of a Rolls Royce. But I cannot guess when (if ever) the powers that be (local bureaucrats, unions, building materials suppliers, county and state officials) will permit us poor serfs to have modern housing.

6. 1950 We'll all be getting a little hungry by and by.

1965 No new comment.

1980 Not necessarily. In 1950 I was too pessimistic concerning population. Now I suspect that the controlling parameter is oil. In modern agriculture oil is the prime factor—as power for farm machinery (obviously) but also for insecticides and for fertilizers. Since our oil policies in Washington are about as boneheaded—counterproductive—as they can be, I have no way to guess how much food we can raise in 2000 A.D. But no one in the United States should be hungry in 2000 A.D.—unless we are conquered and occupied.

7. 1950 The cult of the phony in art will disappear. So-called "modern art" will be discussed only by psychiatrists.

1965 No new comment.

1980 One may hope. But art reflects culture and the world is even nuttier now than it was in 1950; these are the Crazy Years. But, while "fine" art continues to look like the work of retarded monkeys, commercial art grows steadily better.

8. 1950 Freud will be classed as a pre-scientific, intuitive pioneer and psychoanalysis will be replaced by a growing, changing "operational psychology" based on measurement and prediction.

1965 No new comment.

1980 This prediction is beginning to come true. Freud is no longer taken seriously by informed people. More and more professional psychologists are skilled in appropriate mathematics; most of the younger ones understand inductive methodology and the nature of scientific confirmation and are trying hard to put rigor into their extremely difficult, still inchoate subject. For some of the current progress see Dr. Pournelle's book, cited on page 54 (Volume II).

By 2000 A.D. we will know a great deal about how the brain functions ... whereas in 1900 what little we knew was wrong.

I do *not* predict that the basic mystery of psychology—how mass arranged in certain complex patterns becomes aware of itself—will be solved by 2000 A.D. I hope so but do not expect it.

9. 1950 Cancer, the common cold, and tooth decay will all be conquered; the revolutionary new problem in medical research will be to accomplish "regeneration," i.e., to enable a man to grow a new leg, rather than fit him with an artificial limb.

1965 In the meantime spectacular progress has been made in organ transplants—and the problem of regeneration is related to this one. Biochemistry and genetics have made a spectacular breakthrough in "cracking the genetic code." It is a tiny crack, however, with a long way to go before we will have the human chromosomes charted and still longer before we will be able to "tailor" human beings by gene manipulation. The possibility is there—but not by year 2000. This is probably just as well. If we aren't bright enough to build decent houses, are we bright enough to play God with the architecture of human beings?

1980 I see no reason to change this prediction if you will let me elaborate (weasel) a little. "The common cold" is a portmanteau expression for upper respiratory infections which appear to be caused by a very large number of different viruses. Viruses are pesky things. It is possible to immunize against them, e.g., vaccination against smallpox, a virus disease. But there are almost no chemotherapies, medicines, against viruses. That is why "the common cold" is treated much the same way today as in 1900, i.e., support the patient with bed rest, liquids, aspirin to make him more comfortable, keep him warm. This was standard in 1900 and it is still standard in 1980.

It is probable that your body makes antibodies against the virus of any cold you catch. But this gives you no protection against that virus's hundreds of close relatives found in any airport, theater, supermarket, or gust of dust off the street. In the meantime, while his kinfolk take turns making you miserable, virus #1 has mutated and you have no antibodies against the mutation.

Good news: Oncology (cancer), immunology, hematology, and "the common cold" turn out to be strongly interrelated subjects; research in all these is moving fast—and a real breakthrough in any one might mean a breakthrough in all.

10. 1950 By the end of this century mankind will have explored this solar system, and the first ship intended to reach the nearest star will be a building.

1965 Our editor suggested that I had been too optimistic on this one—but I still stand by it. It is still thirty-five years to the end of the century. For perspective, look back thirty-five years to 1930—the American Rocket Society had not yet been founded. Another curve, similar to the one herewith in shape but derived entirely from speed of transportation, extrapolates to show faster-than-light travel by year 2000. I guess I'm chicken, for I am not predicting FTL ships by then, if ever. But the prediction still stands without hedging.

1980 My money is still on the table at twenty years and counting. Senator Proxmire can't live forever. In the last 10½ years men have been to the Moon several times; much of the Solar system has been most thoroughly explored within the limits of "black box" technology and more will be visited before this year is out.

Ah, but not explored by *men*—and the distances are so great. Surely they are ... by free-fall orbits, which is all that we have been using. But there are numerous proposals (and not all ours!) for constant-boost ships, proposals that require R&D on present art only—no breakthroughs.

Reach for your pocket calculator and figure how long it would take to make a trip to Mars and back if your ship could boost at one-tenth gee. We will omit some trivia by making it from parking orbit to parking orbit, use straight-line trajectories, and ignore the Sun's field—we'll be going uphill to Mars, downhill to Earth; what we lose on the roundabouts we win on the shys.

These casual assumptions would cause Dan Alderson, ballistician at Jet Propulsion Laboratory, to faint. But after he comes out of his faint he would agree that our answers would be of correct close order of magnitude—and all I'm trying to prove is that even a slight constant boost makes an enormous difference in touring the Solar System. (Late in the 21st century we'll offer the Economy Tour: Ten Planets in Ten Days.)

There are an unlimited number of distances between rather wide parameters for an Earth-Mars-Earth trip but we will select one that is nearly minimum (it's cheating to wait in orbit at Mars for about a year in order to take the shortest trip each way ... and unthinkable to wait years for the closest approach). We'll do this Space Patrol style: There's Mars, here we are at L-5; let's scoot over, swing around Mars, and come straight home. Just for drill.

Conditions: Earth-surface gravity (one "gee") is an acceleration of 32.2 feet per second squared, or 980.7 centimeters per second squared. Mars is in or near opposition (Mars is rising as Sun is setting). We will assume that the round trip is 120,000,000 miles. If we were willing to wait for closest approach we could trim that to less than 70,000,000 miles ... but we might have to wait as long as 17 years. So we'll take a common or garden variety opposition—one every 26 months—for which the distance to Mars is about 50- to 60,000,000 miles and never over 64 million.

(With Mars in conjunction on the far side of the Sun, we could take the scenic route of over 500 million miles—how much over depends on how easily you sunburn. I suggest a minimum of 700 million miles.)

You now have all necessary data to figure the time it takes to travel Earth-Mars-Earth in a constant-boost ship—*any* constant-boost ship—when Mars is at opposition. (If you insist on the scenic route, you can't treat the trajectory approximations as straight lines and you can't treat space as flat but a bit uphill. You'll need Alderson or his equal and a *big* computer, not a pocket calculator; the equations are very hairy and sometimes shoot back.)

But us two space cadets are doing this by eyeballing it, using Tennessee windage, an aerospace almanac, a Mickey Mouse watch, and an SR-50 Pop discarded years ago.

We need just one equation: Velocity equals acceleration times elapsed time: $v = at$

This tells us that our average speed is $\frac{1}{2}at$—and from that we know that the distance achieved is the average speed times the elapsed time: $d = \frac{1}{2}at^2$

If you don't believe me, check any physics text, encyclopedia, or nineteen other sorts of reference books—and I did that derivation without cracking a book but now I'm going to stop and find out whether I've goofed—I've had years of practice in goofing. (Later—seems okay.)

Just two things to remember: 1) This is a 4-piece trip—boost to midpoint, flip over and boost to brake; then do the same thing coming home. Treat all four legs as being equal or 30,000,000 miles, so figure one of them and multiply by four. (Dan, stop frowning; this is an *approximation* ... done with a Mickey Mouse watch.)

2) You must keep your units straight. If you start with centimeters, you are stuck with centimeters; if you start with feet, you are stuck with feet. So we have $\frac{1}{4}$ of the trip equals $5280 \times 30,000,000 = 1.584 \times 10^{11}$ feet, or 4.827×10^{12} centimeters.

One last bit: Since it is elapsed time we are after, we will rearrange that equation ($d = \frac{1}{2}at^2$) so that you can get the answer in one operation on your trusty-but-outdated pocket calculator ... or even on a slide rule, as those four-significant-figures data are mere swank; I've used so many approximations and ignored so many minor variables that I'll be happy to get answers correct to two significant figures.

$$\frac{d}{\frac{1}{2}a} = t^2 \qquad \text{This gives us: } t = \sqrt{d/\tfrac{1}{2}a}$$

*d is 30,000,000 miles expressed in feet, or 158,400,000,000. Set that into your pocket calculator. Divide it by one half of one tenth of gee, or 1.61. Push the square root button. Multiply by 4. You now have the elapsed time of the round trip expressed in seconds so divide by 3600 and you have it in hours, and divide that by 24 and you have it in days.

At this point you are supposed to be astonished and to start looking for the mistake. While you are looking, I'm going to slide out to the refrigerator.

There is no mistake. Work it again, this time in metric. Find a reference book and check the equation. You will find the answer elsewhere in this book but don't look for it yet; we'll try some other trips you may take by 2000 A.D. if you speak Japanese or German—or even English if Proxmire and his ilk fail of reelection.

Same trip, worked the same way, but at only one percent of gee. At that boost I would weigh less than my shoes weigh here in my study.

Hmmph! Looks as if one answer or the other must be wrong.

Bear with me. This time we'll work it at a full gee, the acceleration you experience lying in bed, asleep. (See Einstein's 1905 paper.)

(Preposterous. All three answers must be wrong.)

Please stick with me a little longer. Let's run all three problems for a round trip to Pluto—in 2006 A.D., give or take a year. Why 2006? Because today Pluto has ducked inside the orbit of Neptune and won't reach perihelion until 1989—and I want it to be a bit farther away; I've got a rabbit stashed in the hat.

Pluto ducks outside again in 2003 and by 2006 it will be (give or take a few million miles) 31.6 A.U. from the Sun, figuring an A.U. at 92,900,000 miles or 14,950,000,000,000 centimeters as we'll work this both ways, MKS and English units. (All right, all right—1.495 x 10^{13} centimeters; it gets dull here at this typewriter.)

Now work it all three ways, a round trip of 63.2 A.U. at a constant boost of one gravity, one tenth gravity, and one hundredth of a gee—and we'll dedicate this to Clyde Tombaugh, the only living man to discover a new planet—through months of tedious and painstaking examination of many thousands of films.

Some think that Pluto was once a satellite and its small size makes this possible. But it is *not* a satellite today. It is both far too big and hundreds of millions of miles out of position to be an asteroid. It can't be a comet. So it's a planet—or something so exotic as to be still more of a prize.

Its size made it hard to find and thus still more of an achievement. But Tombaugh continued the search for seventeen weary years and many millions more films. If there is an Earth-size planet out there, it is at least three times as distant as Pluto, and a gas giant would have to be six times as far. Negative data win no prizes but they are the bedrock of science.

Until James W. Christy on 22 June 1978 discovered Pluto's satellite, Charon, it was possible for us romantics to entertain the happy thought that Pluto was loaded with valuable heavy metals; the best estimate of its density made this plausible. But the mass of a planet with a satellite can be calculated quite easily and accurately, and from that, its density.

The new figure was much too low, only half again as heavy as water. Methane snow? Perhaps.

So once again a lovely theory is demolished by an awkward fact.

Nevertheless Pluto remains a most mysterious and most intriguing heavenly body. A planet the size and mass of Mars might not be too much use to us out there ... but think of it as a fuel dump. Many stories and many nonfictional projections speak of using the gas giants and/or the rings of Saturn as sources of fuel. But if Pluto is methane ice or water ice or frozen hydrogen or all three, as a source of fuel—conventional, or fusion, or even reaction mass—Pluto has one supremely important advantage over the gas giants: Pluto is *not* at the bottom of a horridly deep gravity well.

Finished calculating? Good. Please turn to page 94 (Volume II) and see why I wanted our trip to Pluto to be a distance of 31.6 A.U.—plus other goodies, perhaps.

11. 1950 Your personal telephone will be small enough to carry in your handbag. Your house telephone will record messages, answer simple inquiries, and transmit vision.

1965 No new comment.

1980 This prediction is trivial and timid. Most of it has already come true and the telephone system will hand you the rest on a custom basis if you'll pay for it. In the year 2000, with modern telephones tied into home computers (as common then as flush toilets are today) you'll be able to have 3-dimensional holovision along with stereo speech. Arthur C. Clarke says that this will do away with most personal contact in business. I agree with all of Mr. Clarke's arguments and disagree with his conclusion; with us monkey folk there is no substitute for personal contact; we enjoy it and it fills a spiritual need.

Besides that, the business conference is often an excuse to loaf on the boss's time and the business convention often supplies some of the benefits of the Roman Saturnalia.

Nevertheless I look forward to holovideostereophones *without* giving up personal contacts.

12. 1950 Intelligent life will be found on Mars.

1965 Predicting intelligent life on Mars looks pretty silly after those dismal photographs. But I shan't withdraw it until Mars has been *thoroughly* explored. As yet we really have no idea—and no data—as to just how ubiquitous and varied life may be in this galaxy; it is conceivable that life as we *don't* know it can evolve on *any* sort of a planet ... and nothing in our present knowledge of chemistry rules this out. All the talk has been about life-as-we-know-it—which means terrestrial conditions.

But if you feel that this shows in me a childish reluctance to give up thoats and zitidars and beautiful Martian princesses until forced to, I won't argue with you—I'll just wait.

1980 The photographs made by the Martian landers of 1976 and their orbiting companions make the prediction of intelligent Martian life look even sillier. But the new pictures and the new data make Mars even more mysterious. I'm a diehard because I suspect that life is ubiquitous—call that a religious opinion if you wish. But remember two things: Almost all discussion has been about Life-as-we-know-it ... but what about Life-as-we-*don't*-know-it? If there were Martians around the time that those amazing gullies and canyons were formed, perhaps they went underground as their atmosphere thinned. At present, despite wonderful pictures, our data are very sparse; those two fixed landers are analogous to two such landing here: one on Canadian tundra, the other in Antarctica—hardly sufficient to solve the question: Is there intelligent life on Sol III?

(Is there intelligent life in Washington, D.C.?)

Whistling in the dark—I think I goofed on this one. But if in fact Mars is uninhabited, shortly there will be a land rush that will make the Oklahoma land stampede look gentle. Since E = mc² came into our lives, *all* real estate is potentially valuable; it can be terraformed to suit humans. There has been so much fiction and serious, able nonfiction published on how to terraform Mars that I shan't add to it, save to note one thing:

Power is no problem. Sunshine at that distance has dropped off to about 43% of the maximum here—but Mars gets *all* of it and gets it all day long save for infrequent dust storms ... whereas the *most* that Philadelphia (and like places) ever gets is 35%—and overcast days are common. Mars won't need solar power from orbit; it will be easier to do it on the ground.

But don't be surprised if the Japanese charge you a very high fee for stamping their visa into your passport plus requiring deposit of a prepaid return ticket or, if you ask for immigrant's visa, charge you a much, much higher fee plus proof of a needed colonial skill.

For there *is* intelligent life in Tokyo.

13. 1950 A thousand miles an hour at a cent a mile will be commonplace; short hauls will be made in evacuated subways at extreme speed.

1965 I must hedge number thirteen; the "cent" I meant was scaled by the 1950 dollar. But our currency has been going through a long steady inflation, and no nation in history has ever gone as far as we have along this route without reaching the explosive phase of inflation. Ten-dollar hamburgers? Brother, we are headed for the hundred-dollar hamburger—for the barter-only hamburger.

But this is only an inconvenience rather than a disaster as long as there is plenty of hamburger.

1980 I must scale that "cent" again. In 1950 gold was $35/troy ounce; this morning the London fix was $374/troy ounce. Just last week my wife and I flew San Francisco to Baltimore and return. We took neither the luxury class nor any of the special discounted fares; we simply flew what we could get.

Applying the inflation factor—35/374—our tickets cost a hair less than one cent a mile in *1950* dollars. From here on I had better give prices in troy ounces of gold, or in Swiss francs; not even the Man in the White House knows where this inflation is going. About those subways: possible, even probable, by 2000 A.D. But I see little chance that they will be financed until the dollar is stabilized—a most painful process our government hates to tackle.

14. 1950 A major objective of applied physics will be to control gravity.

1965 This prediction stands. But today physics is in a tremendous state of flux with new data piling up faster than it can be digested; it is anybody's guess as to where we are headed, but the wilder you guess, the more likely you are to hit it lucky. With "elementary particles" of nuclear physics now totaling about half the number we used to use to list the "immutable" chemical elements, a spectator needs a program just to keep track of the players. At the other end of the scale, "quasars"—quasi-stellar bodies—have come along; radio astronomy is now bigger than telescopic astronomy used to be; and we have redrawn our picture of the universe several times, each time enlarging it and making it more complex—I haven't seen this week's theory yet, which is well, as it would be out of date before this gets into print. Plasma physics was barely started in 1950; the same for solid-state physics. This is the Golden Age of physics—and it's an anarchy.

1980 I stick by the basic prediction. There is so much work going on both by mathematical physicists and experimental physicists as to the nature of gravity that it seems inevitable that twenty years from now applied physicists will be trying to control it. But note that I said "trying"—succeeding may take a long time. If and when they do succeed, a spinoff is likely to be a spaceship that is in no way a rocket ship—and the Galaxy is ours! (Unless we meet that smarter, meaner, tougher race that kills us or enslaves us or eats us—or all three.)

Particle physics: the situation is even more confusing than in 1965. Physicists now speak of more than 200 kinds of hadrons, "elementary" heavy particles. To reduce this confusion a mathematical construct called the "quark" was invented. Like Jell-O quarks come in many colors and flavors ... plus spin, charm, truth, and beauty (or top and bottom in place of truth and beauty—or perhaps "truth" doesn't belong in the list, and no jokes, please, as the physicists aren't joking and neither am I). Put quarks together in their many attributes and you can account for (maybe) all those 200-odd hadrons (and have a system paralleling the leptons or light particles as a bonus).

All very nice ... except that no one has ever been able to pin down even one quark. Quarks, if they exist, come packaged in clumps as hadrons—not at random but by rules to account for each of that mob of hadrons.

Now comes Kenneth A. Johnson, Ph.D. (Harvard '55), Professor of Physics at the Massachusetts Institute of Technology (which certainly places him in the worldwide top group of physicists) with an article (*Scientific American*, July 1979, p. 112, "The Bag Model of Quark Confinement"), an article which appears to state that quarks will never be pinned down because they are in sort of an eternal purdah, never to be seen even as bubble tracks.

Somehow it reminds me of the dilemma when the snark is a boojum.

I'm not poking fun at Dr. Johnson; he is very learned and trying hard to explain his difficult subject to the unlearned such as I.

But, in the meantime I suggest reading *The Hunting of the Snark* while waiting patiently for 2000 A.D. We have a plethora of data; perhaps in twenty more years the picture will be simplified. Perhaps—

15. 1950 We will not achieve a "World State" in the predictable future. Nevertheless, Communism will vanish from this planet.

1965 I stand flatly behind prediction number fifteen.

1980 I still stand flatly behind the first sentence of that two-part prediction above. The second part I could weasel out of by pointing out that on this planet *no* state that calls itself Marxist or Socialist or Communist has ever established a system approximating that called for by the works of Karl Marx and Friedrich Engels. And never will; Marx's Utopia does not fit human beings. The state will not "wither away."

But I shan't weasel as I am utterly dismayed by the political events of the past 15-20 years. At least two thirds of the globe now calls itself Marxist. Another large number of countries are military dictatorships. Another large group (including the United States) are constitutional democratic republics but so heavily tinged with socialism ("welfare state") that all of them are tottering on the brink of bankruptcy and collapse.

So far as I can see today the only thing that could cause the soi-disant Marxist countries to collapse in as little time as twenty years would be for the United States to be conquered and occupied by the USSR—and twenty years ago I thought that this was a strong possibility. (I'm more optimistic now, under the present three-cornered standoff.)

If we were to be conquered and occupied, the Communist world might collapse rather quickly. We have been propping them up whenever they were in real trouble (frequently!) for about half a century.

16. 1950 Increasing mobility will disenfranchise a majority of the population. About 1990 a constitutional amendment will do away with state lines while retaining the semblance.

1965 No further comment.

1980 I goofed. I will be much surprised if either half of this double prediction comes to pass by 2000—at least in the form described and for the reasons I had in mind. The franchise now extends to any warm body over eighteen years of age and that franchise can be transferred to another state in less time than it takes the citizen to find housing in his/her new state.

Thus no constitutional amendment is needed. But the state lines are fading year by year anyhow as power continues to move from the states to the Federal government and especially into the hands of non-elected bureaucrats.

17. 1950 All aircraft will be controlled by a giant radar net run on a continent-wide basis by a multiple electronic "brain."

1965 No further comment.

1980 This prediction still stands—although it may be my wishful thinking. Such a system was designed over thirty years ago; Congress wouldn't buy it. It would be more expensive today ... and is far more urgently needed. Anyone who has ever been in the tower of a busy field or has ever ridden in the "office" of a commercial plane during a takeoff or landing at a busy field knows what I mean. All our fields are overloaded but anyone who goes in or out of San Diego or of O'Hare-Chicago or—but why go on? Our airplanes are pretty durn wonderful ... but our method of handling air traffic at fields is comparable to Manhattan without traffic lights.

I shall continue to fly regularly for two reasons: 1) Mrs. Heinlein and I hope to go out in a common disaster. 2) Consider the alternatives: AMTRAK (ugh!), buses (two ughs!), and driving oneself. The latter is fine for short distances (OPEC and Washington permitting) but, while in my younger days I drove across this continent so many times that I've lost count, today I am no longer physically up to such a trip even with a chauffeur.

But that totally-automated traffic control system *ought* to be built. Expensive, yes—but what price do we place on a hundred dead passengers, a flight crew, and a modern airliner? In the present state of the art in computers and in radar neither the pilot nor the controller should be in the loop at landing or takeoff; they should simply be alert, ready to override, because even the most perfect machinery is subject to Murphy's Law. But all routine (99.9+%) takeoffs and landings should be made by computer.

If this pushes small private planes onto separate and smaller fields, so be it. Bicycles do not belong on freeways. I hate to say that, as there is nothing more fun than a light sports plane.

(Nothing that is not alive, I mean. Vive la difference!)

71

(On air traffic control I speak with a modicum of authority. I returned to the aircraft industry for a short time in 1948 to research this subject, then wrote an article aimed at the slicks: "The Billion-Dollar Eye." I missed; it is still unpublished.)

18. 1950 Fish and yeast will become our principal sources of proteins. Beef will be a luxury; lamb and mutton will disappear.

1965 I'll hedge number eighteen a little. Hunger is not now a problem in the USA and need not be in the year 2000—but hunger *is* a world problem and would at once become an acute problem for us if we were conquered ... a distinct possibility by 2000. Between our present status and that of subjugation lies a whole spectrum of political and economic possible shapes to the future under which we would share the worldwide hunger to a greater or lesser extent. And the problem grows. We can expect to have to feed around half a billion Americans circa year 2000—our present huge surpluses would then represent acute shortages even if we never shipped a ton of wheat to India.

1980 It would now appear that the USA population in 2000 A.D. will be about 270,000,000 instead of 500,000,000. I have been collecting clippings on demography for forty years; all that the projections have in common is that all of them are wrong. Even that figure of 270,000,000 may be too high; today the only reason our population continues to increase is that we oldsters are living longer; our current birthrate is not sufficient even to replace the parent generation.

19. 1950 Mankind will *not* destroy itself, nor will "Civilization" be destroyed.

1965 I stand by prediction number nineteen.

1980 I still stand by prediction number nineteen. There will be wars and we will be in some of them—and some may involve atomic weapons. But there will *not* be that all-destroying nuclear holocaust that forms the background of so many SF stories. There are three reasons for this: The United States, the Soviet Union, and the People's Republic of China.

Why? Because the three strongest countries in the world (while mutually detesting each the other two) have nothing to gain and everything to lose in an all-out swapping of H-bombs. Because Kremlin bosses are not idiots and neither are those in Beijing (Peiping) (Peking).

If another country—say Israel, India, or the South African Republic—gets desperate and tosses an A- or H-bomb, that country is likely to receive three phone calls simultaneously, one from each of the Big Three: "You have exactly three minutes to back down. Then we destroy you."

After World War II I never expected that our safety would ever depend on a massive split in Communist International—but that is exactly what has happened.

1950 Here are things we *won't* get soon, if ever:

Travel through time.

Travel faster than the speed of light.

"Radio" transmission of matter.

Manlike robots with manlike reactions.

Laboratory creation of life.

Real understanding of what "thought" is and how it is related to matter.

Scientific proof of personal survival after death.

Nor a permanent end to war. (I don't like that prediction any better than you do.)

1950 Prediction of gadgets is a parlor trick anyone can learn; but only a fool would attempt to predict details of future history (except as fiction, so labeled); there are too many unknowns and no techniques for integrating them even if they were known.

Even to make predictions about overall trends in technology is now most difficult. In fields where before World War II there was one man working in public, there are now ten, or a hundred, working in secret. There may be six men in the country who have a clear picture of what is going on in science today. *There may not be even one.*

This is in itself a trend. Many leading scientists consider it a factor as disabling to us as the nonsense of Lysenkoism is to Russian technology. Nevertheless there are clear-cut trends which are certain to make this coming era enormously more productive and interesting than the frantic one we have just passed through. Among them are:

Cybernetics: The study of communication and control of mechanisms and organisms. This includes the wonderful field of mechanical and electronic "brains"—but is not limited to it. (These "brains" are a factor in themselves that will speed up technical progress the way a war does.)

Semantics: A field which seems concerned only with definitions of words. It is not; it is a frontal attack on epistemology—that is to say, *how* we know *what* we know, a subject formerly belonging to long-haired philosophers.

New tools of mathematics and logic, such as calculus of statement, Boolean logic, morphological analysis, generalized symbology, newly invented mathematics of every sort—there is not space even to name these enormous fields, but they offer us hope in every field—medicine, social relations, biology, economics, anything.

Biochemistry: Research into the nature of protoplasm, into enzyme chemistry, viruses, etc., gives hope not only that we may conquer disease, but that we may someday understand the mechanisms of life itself. Through this, and with the aid of cybernetic machines and radioactive isotopes, we may eventually acquire a rigor of chemistry. Chemistry is not a discipline today; it is a jungle. We know that chemical behavior depends on the number of orbital electrons in an atom and that physical and chemical properties follow the pattern called the Periodic Table. We don't know much else, save by cut-and-try, despite the great size and importance of the chemical industry. When chemistry becomes a discipline, mathematical chemists will design new materials, predict their properties, and tell engineers how to make them—without ever entering a laboratory. We've got a *long* way to go on that one!

Nucleonics: We have yet to find out what makes the atom tick. Atomic power?—yes, we'll have it, in convenient packages—when we understand the nucleus. The field of radioisotopes alone is larger than was the entire known body of science in 1900. Before we are through with these problems, we may find out how the universe is shaped and *why.* Not to mention enormous unknown vistas best represented by ?????

Some physicists are now using two time scales, the T-scale, and the *tau*-scale. Three billion years on one scale can equal an incredibly split second on the other scale—and yet both apply to you and your kitchen stove. Of such anarchy is our present state in physics.

For such reasons we must insist that *the Age of Science has not yet opened.*

(**Still 1950**) The greatest crisis facing us is not Russia, not the Atom Bomb, not corruption in government, not encroaching hunger, not the morals of young. It is a crisis in the *organization* and *accessibility* of human knowledge. We own an enormous "encyclopedia"—which isn't even arranged alphabetically. Our "file cards" are spilled on the floor, nor were they ever in order. The answers we want may be buried somewhere in the heap, but it might take a lifetime to locate two already known facts, place them side by side and derive a third fact, the one we urgently need.

Call it the Crisis of the Librarian.

We need a new "specialist" who is not a specialist, but a synthesist. We need a new science to be the perfect secretary to all other sciences.

But we are not likely to get either one in a hurry and we have a powerful lot of grief before us in the meantime.

Fortunetellers can always be sure of repeat customers by predicting what the customer wants to hear … it matters not whether the prediction comes true. Contrariwise, the weatherman is often blamed for bad weather.

Brace yourself.

In 1900 the cloud on the horizon was no bigger than a man's hand—but what lay ahead was the Panic of 1907, World War I, the panic following it, the Depression, Fascism, World War II, the Atom Bomb, and Red Russia.

Today the clouds obscure the sky, and the wind that overturns the world is sighing in the distance.

The period immediately ahead will be the roughest, crudest one in the long, hard history of mankind. It will probably include the worst World War of them all. It might even end with a war with Mars, God save the Mark! Even if we are spared that fantastic possibility, it is certain that there will be no security anywhere, save that which you dig out of your own inner spirit.

But what of that picture we drew of domestic luxury and tranquility for Mrs. Middleclass, style 2000 A.D.?

She lived through it. She survived.

Our prospects need not dismay you, not if you or your kin were at Bloody Nose Ridge, at Gettysburg—or trudged across the Plains. You and I are here because we carry the genes of uncountable ancestors who fought—and won—against death in all its forms. We're tough. We'll survive. Most of us.

We've lasted through the preliminary bouts; the main event is coming up.

But it's not for sissies.

The last thing to come fluttering out of Pandora's Box was Hope—without which men die.

The gathering wind will not destroy everything, nor will the Age of Science change everything. Long after the first star ship leaves for parts unknown, there will still be outhouses in upstate New York, there will still be steers in Texas, and—no doubt—the English will still stop for tea.

Afterthoughts, fifteen years later—(1965)

I see no reason to change any of the negative predictions which follow the numbered affirmative ones. They are all conceivably possible; they are all wildly unlikely by year 2000. Some of them are debatable if the terms are defined to suit the affirmative side—definitions of "life" and "manlike," for example. Let it stand that I am not talking about an amino acid in one case, or a machine that plays chess in the other.

Today the forerunners of synthesists are already at work in many places. Their titles may be anything; their degrees may be in anything—or they may have no degrees. Today they are called "operations researchers," or sometimes "systems development engineers," or other interim tags. But they are all interdisciplinary people, generalists, not specialists—the new Renaissance Man. The very explosion of data which forced most scholars to specialize very narrowly created the necessity which evoked this new non-specialist. So far, this "un-specialty" is in its infancy; its methodology is inchoate, the results are sometimes trivial, and no one knows how to train to become such a man. But the results are often spectacularly brilliant, too—this new man may yet save all of us.

I'm an optimist. I have great confidence in Homo sapiens.

We have rough times ahead—but when didn't we? Things have always been "tough all over." H-bombs, Communism, race riots, water shortage—all nasty problems. But not basic problems, merely current ones.

We have three basic and continuing problems: The problem of population explosion; the problem of data explosion; and the problem of government.

Population problems have a horrid way of solving themselves when they are not solved rationally; the Four Horsemen of the Apocalypse are always saddled up and ready to ride. The data explosion is now being solved, mostly by cybernetics and electronics men rather than by librarians—and if the solutions are less than perfect, at least they are better than what Grandpa had to work with. The problem of government has not been solved either by the "Western Democracies" or the "People's Democracies," as of now. (Anyone who thinks the people of the United States have solved the problem of government is using too short a time scale.) The peoples of the world are now engaged in a long, long struggle with no end in sight, testing whether one concept works better than another; in that conflict millions have already died and it is possible that hundreds of millions will die in it before year 2000. But not all.

I hold both opinions and preferences as to the outcome. But my personal preference for a maximum of looseness is irrelevant; what we are experiencing is an evolutionary process in which personal preference matters, at most, only statistically. Biologists, ecologists in particular, are working around to the idea that natural selection and survival of the fittest is a notion that applies more to groups and how they are structured than it does to individuals. The present problem will solve itself in the cold terms of evolutionary survival, and in the course of it both sides will make changes in group structure. The system that survives might be called "Communism" or it might be called "Democracy" (the latter is my guess)—but one thing we can be certain of: it will not resemble very closely what either Marx or Jefferson had in mind. Or it might be called by some equally inappropriate neologism; political tags are rarely logical.

For Man is rarely logical. But I have great confidence in Man, based on his past record. He is mean, ornery, cantankerous, illogical, emotional—and amazingly hard to kill. Religious leaders have faith in the spiritual redemption of Man; humanist leaders subscribe to a belief in the perfectibility of Man through his own efforts; but I am not discussing either of these two viewpoints. My confidence in our species lies in its past history and is founded quite as much on Man's so-called vices as on his so-called virtues. When the chips are down, quarrelsomeness and selfishness can be as useful to the survival of the human race as is altruism, and pig-headedness can be a trait superior to sweet reasonableness. If this were not true, these "vices" would have died out through the early deaths of their hosts, at least a half million years back.

I have a deep and abiding confidence in Man as he is, imperfect and often unlovable—plus still greater confidence in his potential.

No matter how tough things are, Man copes. He comes up with adequate answers from illogical reasons. But the answers work.

Last to come out of Pandora's Box was a gleaming, beautiful thing—eternal Hope.

(**1980**—I see no point in saying more. R.A.H.)

If It's Sinful, It's More Fun.

FOREWORD

The editor who disliked science fiction (and me) but liked my sales grum-
bled to me, on my delivering my annual boys' novel, that she did wish that
someone would write girls' stories. I answered, "Very well, I'll write a story
for girls. When do you want it?"

She was simultaneously astonished, offended, and amused at the ri-
diculous and arrogant notion that a mere man could write stories for girls.
So that's how Puddin' was born: I started writing first-person-female-
adolescent stories—but not for that old harridan.

Since this is not the first of the Puddin' stories, let me introduce her:
her name is Maureen, her nickname derives from her weight problem. She
is eternally an undergraduate on a small campus in Somewhere, U.S.A.,
where her father teaches anthropology, smokes his pipe, and reads—where-
as her mother is a Renaissance Man who does everything. *Maureen has*
an unbearable younger brother (all younger brothers are unbearable; I
should know, I was one).

I grew so fond of Maureen that I helped her to get rid of that excess
weight, changed her name to "Podkayne," and moved her to Mars (along
with her unbearable kid brother). And now and again she turns up under
other names in other science fiction stories.

Nevertheless Maureen still attends classes on this campus in Never-
Neverland. I had intended to do a full book of Puddin' short stories under
the title Men Are Exasperating. *I have enough stories for a fat volume*
but as yet I have not written all of them down. One in particular ("Mother
and the Animal Kingdom") keeps niggling at me to write it—a character
in it, a little gray donkey named Mr. Jenkins, keeps looking at me with

mournful eyes. I can write that one anytime I get a full day absolutely free of other pressures—say about 1997.

Three others are almost as ready to write, and I would have enough for a book.

And yet ... and yet—Is Puddin' totally obsolete? This campus never has riots. The girls are not "on the Pill." (Or if they are, the subject is not mentioned.) There is no drug problem. In short, I have described college life of a bygone day.

But don't misunderstand me. My teens were the Torrid Twenties and exactly the same things went on then as now ... but were kept under cover. When I was a freshman in college, the nearest connection for marijuana was a drugstore a hundred yards off campus; for H or C it was necessary to walk another block. But bootleg liquor (tax-free) would be delivered on or off campus at any hour.

Did I avail myself of any of these amenities? None of your business, Buster!

As for sex, each generation thinks it invented sex; each generation is totally mistaken. Anything along that line today was commonplace both in Pompeii and in Victorian England; the differences lie only in the degree of coverup—if any.

I may never publish the book Men Are Exasperating; *I'm not sure it has a market and, at my age, there are more stories that I want to write (and are certain of publication) than I can possibly write before the black camel kneels at my door.*

I hope you like Puddin'.

81

CLIFF AND THE CALORIES

According to Daddy I'll eat anything standing still or even moving slowly. But Mother said nonsense, I simply have a high metabolic rate.

Daddy answered, "You haven't had it checked, so how do you know? Puddin', stand sideways and let me look at you."

Junior said, "She hasn't got a 'sideways,'" and let loose a perfectly horrible laugh that is supposed to sound like Woody Woodpecker and does, only worse. Of what use is the male of the species between the ages of two and sixteen? Later on, they are bearable, even indispensable—at least I would find it difficult to dispense with Cliff, although Junior may never be an asset.

That's how I went on a diet.

It started with Cliff—most things do. I am going to marry Cliff, only I haven't told him yet. I have never had any cause to doubt the sincerity of Cliff's devotion, but I have sometimes wondered what it was he found most attractive about me: my character, disposition, and true worth, or my so-to-speak physical attributes.

The bathroom scales were beginning to make me think it was the former. Perhaps that should have made me happy, but I have yet to find the girl who would swap a twenty-one-inch waist and a good silhouette for sterling merit. Not that I could hope to be a raving beauty, but a few wolf whistles never did any harm and are good for the morale.

I had just had a chance to test Cliff's point of view. A girl showed up at school who was exactly my size; we compared measurements. The point is, on Clarice it looked good—cursive and bountiful but good. Maureen, I told myself, here is a chance to get an honest opinion out of Cliff.

I saw to it that he got a good look at her at tennis practice. As we left I said craftily, "That new girl, Clarice—she has a lovely figure."

Cliff looked over his shoulder and replied. "Oh, sure—from her ankles down."

I had my answer and I didn't like it. Cliff didn't care for my type of figure; divorced from my personality it did not appeal to him. I should have felt a warm glow, knowing it for true love. I didn't; I felt terrible.

It was when I refused a second helping of potatoes that evening that the subject of my metabolism came up.

I went to the library next day and looked into this matter of diet. I hadn't known there were so many books about it. Finally I found one that made sense: *Eat and Grow Slender*. That struck me as an excellent idea.

I took it home to study. I got a few crackers and some cheese and ate them absent-mindedly while I thumbed through the book. There was a plan for losing ten pounds in ten days; the menus looked pretty skimpy. There was another for losing ten pounds in a month. That's for me, I said; no need to be fanatic.

There was a chapter about calories. They make it so simple: one ice-cream cone, one hundred and fifty calories; three dates, eighty-four calories.

My eye lit on "soda crackers"; I knew they wouldn't count much and they didn't—only twenty-one calories apiece. Then I looked up "cheese."

Arithmetic stirred in my brain and I had a chilly feeling. I went into Daddy's study and used his postal scale to weigh the cheese that had not already become Maureen.

I did the arithmetic three times. Including two little bits of fudge I had eaten six hundred and seventy calories, *more than half of a day's allowance as given in the reducing diet!* And I had only meant to stay the pangs until dinnertime.

Maureen, I said, this time you've got to be a fanatic; its the ten-day die-trying diet for you.

I planned to keep my affairs to myself, selecting the diet from what was placed before me, but such a course is impossible in a family that combines the worst aspects of a Senate investigation with the less brutal methods of a third degree. I got away with passing up the cream-of-tomato soup by being a little bit late, but when I refused the gravy, there was nothing to do but show them the book.

Mother said a growing girl needed her food. I pointed out that I had quit growing vertically and it was time I quit horizontally. Junior opened his mouth and I stuffed a roll into it. That gave Daddy a chance to say, "Let's put it up to Doc Andrews. If he gives her the green light, she can starve herself gaunt. She's a free agent."

So Daddy and I went to Doctor Andrews' office next day. Daddy had an appointment anyhow—he has terrible colds every spring. Doctor Andrews sent Daddy across the hall to Doctor Grieb who specializes in allergies and things, then he saw me.

I've known Doctor Andrews since my first squawk, so I told him everything, even about Cliff, and showed him the book. He thumbed through it, then he weighed me and listened to my heart and took my blood pressure. "Go ahead," he told me, "but make it the thirty-day diet. I don't want you fainting in the classroom."

I guess I had counted on him to save me from my will power. "How about exercise?" I said hopefully. "I'm pretty active. Won't I need to eat more to offset it?"

He roared. "Honey child," he said, "do you know how far you would have to hike to burn up one chocolate malt? *Eight miles!* It will help, but not much."

"How long do I keep this up?"—I asked faintly.

"Until you reach the weight you want—or until your character plays out."

I marched out with my jaw set. If a girl doesn't have a figure or character either, what has she got left?

Mother was home when we got there. Daddy picked her up and kissed her and said, "Now you've got two of us on diets!"

"Two?" said Mother.

"Look." Daddy peeled off his shirt. His arms were covered with little red pin pricks, some redder than others, arranged in neat rows. "I'm allergic," he announced proudly. "Those aren't real colds. I'm allergic to practically everything. That one"—he pointed to a red welt—"is bananas. That one is corn. That one is cow's milk protein. And there is pollen in honey. Wait." He hauled out a list: "Rhubarb, tapioca, asparagus, lima beans, coconut, mustard, cow's milk, apricot, beets, carrots, lamb, cottonseed oil, lettuce, oysters, chocolate—here, you read it; it's your problem."

"It's a good thing that I went to the campus today and signed up for an evening class in domestic dietetics. From now on this family is going to be fed scientifically," Mother said.

That should have been the worst of it, but it wasn't. Junior announced that he was training for hockey and he had to have a training-table diet—which to him meant beef, dripping with blood, whole-wheat toast, and practically nothing else. Last season he had discovered that, even with lead weights in his pockets, he didn't have what it took for a body check. Next season he planned to be something between Paul Bunyan and Gorgeous George. Hence the diet.

By now, Mother was on a diet, too, a scientific one, based on what she had learned during the two weeks she had actually attended classes. Mother pored over charts and we each had separate trays like a hospital, the time I broke my ankle playing second base for the West Side Junior Dodgers. Mother says a girl with my figure should not be a tomboy, but I said that a tomboy should not have my figure. Anyhow, I am no longer a tomboy since Cliff came into my life.

Somehow, Mother found things that weren't on Daddy's verboten list—stewed yak and pickled palm fronds and curried octopus and such. I asked if Daddy had been checked for those too? He said, "Tend to your knitting, Puddin'," and helped himself to more venison pasty. I tried not to watch.

Mother's own diet was as esoteric, but less attractive. She tried to tempt Junior and me with her seaweed soup or cracked wheat or raw rhubarb, but we stuck to our own diets. Eating is fun, but only if it's food.

Breakfast was easiest; Daddy breakfasted later than I did—he had no lectures earlier than ten o'clock that semester.

I would lie abed while our budding athlete wolfed down his Breakfast of Champions, then slide out at the last minute, slurp my glass of tomato juice (twenty-eight calories), and be halfway to school before I woke up. By then it would be too late to be tempted.

I carried my pitiful little lunch. Cliff started packing his lunch, too, and we picnicked together. He never noticed what I ate or how much.

I didn't want Cliff to notice, not yet. I planned to make him faint with the way I would look in my new formal at graduation prom.

It did not work out. Cliff took two final exams early and left for California for the summer and I spent the night of the prom in my room, nibbling celery (four calories per stalk) and thinking about life.

We got ready for our summer trip immediately thereafter. Daddy voted for New Orleans.

Mother shook her head. "Impossibly hot. Besides, I don't want you tempted by those Creole restaurants."

"Just what I had in mind," Daddy answered. "Finest gourmet restaurants in the country. You can't keep us on diets while traveling; it isn't practical. Antoine's, here I come!"

"No," said Mother.

"Yes," said Daddy.

So we went to California. I was ready to throw my weight (which was still too much) in with Daddy, when California was mentioned. I hadn't expected to see Cliff until fall. I put thoughts of *bouillabaisse* and Shrimp Norfolk out of mind; Cliff won, but it was nearer than I like to think.

The trip was hardly a case of merrie-merrie-be. Junior sulked because he wasn't allowed to take along his lifting weights, and Mother was loaded with charts and reference books and menus. Each time we stopped she would enter into long negotiations, involving a personal interview with the chef, while we got hungrier, and hungrier.

We were coming to Kingman, Arizona, when Mother announced that she didn't think we could find a restaurant to take care of our needs. "Why not?" demanded Daddy. "The people there must eat."

Mother shuffled her lists and suggested that we go on through to Las Vegas. Daddy said that if he had known this trip was going to be another Donner party, he would have studied up on how to cook human flesh.

While they discussed it we slid through Kingman and turned north toward Boulder Dam. Mother looked worriedly at the rugged hills and said, "Perhaps you had better turn back, Charles. It will be hours before we reach Las Vegas and there isn't a thing on the map."

Daddy gripped the wheel and looked grim. Daddy will not backtrack for less than a landslide, as Mother should have known.

I was beyond caring. I expected to leave my bones whitening by the road with a notice: *She tried and she died.*

We had dropped out of those hills and into the bleakest desert imaginable when Mother said, "You'll have to turn back, Charles. Look at your gasoline gauge."

Daddy set his jaw and speeded up. "Charles!" said Mother.

"Quiet!" Daddy answered. "I see a gas station ahead."

The sign read Santa Claus, Arizona. I blinked at it, thinking I was at last seeing a mirage. There was a gas station, all right, but that wasn't all.

You know what most desert gas stations look like—put together out of odds and ends. Here was a beautiful fairytale cottage with wavy candy stripes in the shingles. It had a broad brick chimney—*and Santa Claus was about to climb down the chimney!*

Maureen, I said, you've overdone this starvation business; now you are out of your head.

Between the station and the cottage were two incredible little dolls' houses. One was marked *Cinderella's House* and Mistress Mary Quite Contrary was making the garden grow. The other one needed no sign; the Three Little Pigs, and Big Bad Wolf was stuck in its chimney.

"Kid stuff!" says Junior, and added, "Hey, Pop, do we eat here? Huh?"

"We just gas up," answered Daddy. "Find a pebble to chew on. Your mother has declared a hunger strike."

Mother did not answer and headed toward the cottage. We went inside, a bell bonged, and a sweet contralto voice boomed, "Come in! Dinner is ready!"

The inside was twice as big as the outside and was the prettiest dining room imaginable, fresh, new, and clean. Heavenly odors drifted out of the kitchen. The owner of the voice came out and smiled at us.

We knew who she was because her kitchen apron had "Mrs. Santa Claus" embroidered across it. She made me feel slender, but for her it was perfectly right. Can you imagine Mrs. Santa Claus being *skinny*?

"How many are there?" she asked.

"Four," said Mother, "but—" Mrs. Santa Claus disappeared into the kitchen.

Mother sat down at a table and picked up a menu. I did likewise and started to drool—here is why:

Minted Fruit Cup Rouge
Pot-au-feu à la Creole
Chicken Velvet Soup
Roast Veal with Fine Herbs
Ham Soufflé
Yankee Pot Roast
Lamb Hawaii
Potatoes Lyonnaise
Riced Potatoes
Sweet Potatoes Maryland
Glazed Onions
Asparagus Tips with Green Peas
Chicory Salad with
Roquefort Dressing
Artichoke Hearts with Avocado
Beets in Aspic
Cheese Straws
Miniature Cinnamon Rolls
Hot Biscuits
Sherry Almond Ice Cream
Rum Pie
Pêches Flambées Royales
Peppermint Cloud Cake
Devil's Food Cake

Angel Berry Pie
Coffee   Tea   Milk

*(Our water is trucked fifteen miles;
please help us save it.)*
Thank you. Mrs. Santa Claus

It made me dizzy, so I looked out the window. We were still spang in the middle of the grimmest desert in the world.

I started counting the calories in that subversive document. I got up to three thousand and lost track, because fruit cups were placed in front of us. I barely tasted mine—and my stomach jumped and started nibbling at my windpipe.

Daddy came in, said, "Well!" and sat down, too. Junior followed.

Mother said, "Charles, there is hardly anything here you can touch. I think I had better—" She headed for the kitchen.

Daddy had started reading the menu. He said, "Wait, Martha! Sit down." Mother sat.

Presently he said, "Do I have plenty of clean handkerchiefs?"

Mother said, "Yes, of course. Why—"

"Good. I feel an attack coming on. I'll start with the *pot-au-feu* and—"

Mother said, "Charles!"

"Peace, woman! The human race has survived upwards of five million years eating anything that could be chewed and swallowed." Mrs. Santa Claus came back in and Daddy ordered lavishly, every word stabbing my heart. "Now," he finished, "if you will have that carried in by eight Nubian slaves—"

"We'll use a jeep," Mrs. Santa Claus promised and turned to Mother.

Mother was about to say something about chopped grass and vitamin soup but Daddy cut in with, "That was for both of us. The kids will order for themselves." Mother swallowed and said nothing.

Junior never bothers with menus. "I'll have a double cannibal sandwich," he announced.

Mrs. Santa Claus flinched. "What," she asked ominously, "is a cannibal sandwich?"

Junior explained. Mrs. Santa Claus looked at him as if she hoped he would crawl back into the woodwork. At last she said, "Mrs. Santa Claus always gives people what they want. But you'll have to eat it in the kitchen; other people will be coming in for dinner."

"Oke," agreed Junior.

"Now what would you like, honey?" she said to me.

"I'd like everything," I answered miserably, "but I'm on a reducing diet."

She clucked sympathetically. "Anything special you mustn't eat?"

"Nothing in particular—just food. I mustn't eat food."

She said, "You will have a hard time choosing a low-caloric meal here. I've never been able to work up interest in such cooking. I'll serve you the same as your parents; you can eat what you wish and as little as you wish."

"All right," I said weakly.

Honestly, I tried. I counted up to ten between bites, then I found I was counting faster so as to finish each course before the next one arrived.

Presently I knew I was a ruined woman and I didn't care. I was surrounded by a warm fog of calories. Once my conscience peeked over the edge of my plate and I promised to make up for it tomorrow. It went back to sleep.

Junior came out of the kitchen with his face covered by a wedge of pinkstriped cake. "Is that a cannibal sandwich?" I asked.

"Huh?" he answered. "You should see what she's got out there. She ought to run a training table."

A long time later Daddy said, "Let's hit the road. I hate to."

Mrs. Santa Claus said, "Stay here if you like. We can accommodate you."

So we stayed and it was lovely.

I woke up resolved to skip even my twenty-eight calories of tomato juice, but I hadn't reckoned with Mrs. Santa Claus. There were no menus; tiny cups of coffee appeared as you sat down, then other things, deceptively, one at a time. Like this: grapefruit, milk, oatmeal and cream, sausage and eggs and toast and butter and jam, bananas and cream—then when you were sure that they had played themselves out, in came the fluffiest waffle in the world, more butter and strawberry jam and syrup, and then more coffee.

I ate all of it, my personality split hopelessly between despair and ecstasy. We rolled out of there feeling wonderful. "Breakfast," said Daddy, "should be compulsory, like education. I hypothesize that correlation could be found between the modern tendency to skimp breakfast and the increase in juvenile delinquency."

I said nothing. Men are my weakness; food my ruin—but I didn't care.

We lunched at Barstow, only I stayed in the car and tried to nap.

Cliff met us at our hotel and we excused ourselves because Cliff wanted to drive me out to see the university. When we reached the parking lot he said, "What has happened? You look as if you had lost your last friend—and you are positively emaciated."

"Oh, Cliff!" I said, and blubbered on his shoulder.

Presently he wiped my nose and started the car. As we drove I told him about it. He didn't say anything, but after a bit he made a left turn. "Is this the way to the campus?" I asked.

"Never you mind."

"Cliff, are you disgusted with me?"

Instead of answering me, he pulled up near a big public building and led me inside; it turned out to be the art museum. Still refusing to talk, he steered me into an exhibition of old masters. Cliff pointed at one of them. "That," he said, "is my notion of a beautiful woman."

I looked. It was *The Judgment of Paris* by Rubens. "And that—and that—" added Cliff. Every picture he pointed to was by Rubens, and I'll swear his models had never heard of dieting.

"What this country needs," said Cliff, "is more plump girls—and more guys like me who appreciate them."

I didn't say anything until we got outside; I was too busy rearranging my ideas. Something worried me, so I reminded him of the time I had asked his opinion of Clarice, the girl who is just my size and measurements. He managed to remember. "Oh, yes! Very beautiful girl, a knockout!"

"But, Cliff, you said—"

He grabbed my shoulders. "Listen, featherbrain, think I've got rocks in my head? Would I say anything that might make you jealous?"

"But I'm never jealous!"

"So *you* say! Now where shall we eat? Romanoffs? The Beach-comber? I'm loaded with dough."

Warm waves of happiness flowed over me. "Cliff?"

"Yeah, honey?"

"I've heard of a sundae called Moron's Delight. They take a great big glass and start with two bananas and six kinds of ice cream and—"

"That's passé. Have you ever had a Mount Everest?"

"Huh?"

"They start with a big platter and build up the peak with twenty-one flavors of ice cream, using four bananas, butterscotch syrup, and nuts to bind it. Then they cover it with chocolate syrup, sprinkle malted-milk powder and more nuts for rock, pour marshmallow syrup and whipped cream down from the top for snow, stick parsley around the lower slopes for trees, and set a little plastic skier on one of the snow banks. You get to keep him as a souvenir of the experience."

"Oh, my!" I said.

"Only one to a customer and I don't have to pay if you finish it."

I squared my shoulders. "Lead me to it!"

"I'm betting on you, Puddin'."

Cliff is such a wonderful man.

AFTERWORD

Santa Claus, Arizona, is still there; just drive from Kingman toward Boulder Dam on 93; you'll find it. But Mrs. Santa Claus (Mrs. Douglas) is no longer there, and her gourmet restaurant is now a fast-food joint. If she is alive, she is at least in her eighties. I don't want to find out. In her own field she was an artist equal to Rembrandt, Michelangelo, and Shakespeare. I prefer to think of her in that perfect place where all perfect things go, sitting in her kitchen surrounded by her gnomes, preparing her hearty ambrosia for Mark Twain and Homer and Praxiteles and others of her equals.

THE ANSWERS

(to Problems on pages 61-69, Volume II)

N.B.: All trips are Earth parking orbit to Earth parking orbit without stopping at the target planet (Mars or Pluto). I assume that Hot Pilot Tom Corbett will handle his gravity-well maneuvers at Mars and at Pluto so as not to waste mass-energy—but that's his problem. Now about that assumption of "flat space" only slightly uphill: The Sun bas a fantastically deep gravity well; its "surface" gravity is 28 times as great as ours and its escape speed is 55+ times as great—but at the distance of Earth's orbit that grasp has attenuated to about one thousandth of a gee, and at Pluto at 31.6 A.U. it has dropped off to a gnat's whisker, one *millionth* of gee.

(No wonder it takes 2½ centuries to swing around the Sun. By the way, some astronomers seem positively gleeful that *today* Pluto is not the planet farthest from the Sun. The facts: Pluto spends nine-tenths of its time outside Neptune's orbit, and it averages being 875,000,000 miles farther out than Neptune—and at maximum is nearly 2 billion miles beyond Neptune's orbit (1.79×10^9 miles)—friends, that's more than the distance from here to Uranus, nearly four times as far as from here to Jupiter. When Pluto is out there—1865 or 2114 A.D.—it takes light 6 hours and 50 minutes to reach it. Pluto—the Winnuh and still Champeen! Sour grapes is just as common among astronomers as it is in school yards.)

ROUNDTRIP BOOST
COMPARISON OF ELAPSED TIME

Earth–Mars–Earth		Earth–Pluto–Earth
	@1 gee	
4.59 days	vs.	4.59 weeks
	@$\frac{1}{10}$ gee	
14.5 days	vs.	14.5 weeks
	@$\frac{1}{100}$ gee	
45.9 days	vs.	45.9 weeks
	@$\frac{1}{1000}$ gee	
145 days	vs.	145 weeks

—and the rabbit is out of the hat. You will have noticed that the elapsed-time figures are exactly the same in both columns, but in days for Mars, weeks for Pluto—i.e., with constant-boost ships of any sort Pluto is *only 7 times* as far away for these conditions as is Mars *even though in miles Pluto is about 50 times as far away.*

If you placed Pluto at its aphelion (stay alive another century and a quarter—quite possible), at one gee the Pluto round trip would take 5.72 weeks, at $\frac{1}{10}$ gee 18.1 weeks, at $\frac{1}{100}$ gee 57.2 weeks—and at $\frac{1}{1000}$ gee 181 weeks, or 3 yrs & 25 wks.

I have added on the two illustrations at $\frac{1}{1000}$ of one gravity boost because today (late 1979 as I write) we do not as yet know how to build constant-boost ships for long trips at 1 gee, $\frac{1}{10}$ gee, or even $\frac{1}{100}$

gee; Newton's Third Law of Motion (from which may be derived all the laws of rocketry) has us (temporarily) stumped. But only temporarily. There is $E = mc^2$, too, and there are several possible ways of "living off the country" like a foraging army for necessary reaction mass. Be patient; this is all very new. Most of you who read this will live to see constant-boost ships of $1/10$ gee or better—and will be able to afford vacations in space—soon, soon! I probably won't live to see it, but *you* will. (No complaints, Sergeant—I was born in the horse & buggy age; I have lived to see men walk on the Moon and to see live pictures from the soil of Mars. I've had my share!)

But if you are willing to settle today for a constant-boost on the close order of magnitude of $1/1000$ gee, we can start the project later this afternoon, as there are several known ways of building constant-boost jobs with that tiny acceleration—even light-sail ships.

I prefer to talk about light-sail ships (or, rather, ships that sail in the "Solar wind") because those last illustrations I added ($1/1000$ gee) show that we have the entire Solar System available to us *right now*; it is not necessary to wait for the year 2000 and new breakthroughs.

Ten weeks to Mars ... a round trip to Pluto at 31.6 A.U. in 2 years and 9 months ... or a round trip to Pluto's aphelion, the most remote spot we know of in the Solar System (other than the winter home of the comets).

Ten weeks—it took the Pilgrims in the *Mayflower* nine weeks and three days to cross the Atlantic.

Two years and nine months—that was a normal commercial voyage for a China clipper sailing out of Boston in the last century ... and the canny Yankee merchants got rich on it.

Three years and twenty-five weeks is excessive for the China trade in the 19th century ... but no one will ever take that long trip to Pluto *because Pluto does not reach aphelion until 2113* and by *then* we'll have ships that can get out there (constant boost with turnover near midpoint) *in three weeks.*

Please note that England, Holland, Spain, and Portugal all created worldwide empires with ships that took as long to get anywhere and back as would a $1/1000$-gee spaceship. On the high seas or in space it is not distance that counts but *time.* The magnificent accomplishments of our astronauts up to now were made in free fall and are therefore analogous to floating down the Mississippi on a raft. But even the tiniest constant boost turns sailing the Solar System into a money-making commercial venture.

Now return to page 69.

FOREWORD

One of the very few advantages of growing old is that one can reach an age at which he can do as he damn well pleases within the limits of his purse.

A younger writer, still striving, has to put up with a lot of nonsense—interviews, radio appearances, TV dates, public speaking here and there, writing he does not want to do—and all of this almost invariably unpaid.

In 1952 I was not a young writer (45) but I was certainly still striving. Here is an unpaid job I did for a librarians' bulletin because librarians can make you or break you. But today, thank Allah, if I don't want to do it, I simply say, "No." If I get an argument, I change that to: "Hell, No!"

—— RAY GUNS AND ROCKET SHIPS ——————

"When I make a word do a lot of work like that," said Humpty Dumpty, "I always pay it extra."

"Science Fiction" is a portmanteau term, and many and varied are the things that have been stuffed into it. Just as the term "historical fiction" includes in its broad scope *Quo Vadis*, nickel thrillers about the James Boys or Buffalo Bill, and *Forever Amber*, so does the tag "science fiction" apply both to Alley Oop and to Aldous Huxley's *After Many a Summer Dies the Swan*. It would be more nearly correctly descriptive to call the whole field "speculative fiction" and to limit the name "science fiction" to a sub-class—in which case some of the other sub-classes would be: undisguised fantasy (Thorne Smith, the Oz books), pseudo-scientific fantasy (C. S. Lewis's fine novel *Out of the Silent Planet*, Buck Rogers, Bradbury's delightful Martian stories), sociological speculation (More's *Utopia*, Michael Arlen's *Man's Mortality*, H. G. Wells' *The World Set Free*, Plato's *Republic*), adventure stories with exotic and non-existent locales (Flash Gordon, Burroughs' Martian stories, the *Odyssey*, *Tom Sawyer Abroad*). Many other classes will occur to you, since the term "speculative fiction" may be defined negatively as being fiction about things that have not happened.

One can see that the name "science fiction" is too Procrustean a bed, too tight a corset, to fit the whole field comfortably. Nevertheless, since language is how we talk, not how we might talk, it seems likely that the term "science fiction" will continue to be applied to the whole field; we are stuck with it, as the American aborigines are stuck with the preposterous name "Indian."

But what, under rational definition, is *science* fiction? There is an easy touchstone; science fiction is speculative fiction in which the author takes as his first postulate the real world as we know it, including all established facts and natural laws. The result can be extremely fantastic in content, but it is not fantasy; it is legitimate—and often very tightly reasoned—speculation about the possibilities of the real world. This category excludes rocket ships that make U-turns, serpent men of Neptune that lust after human maidens, and stories by authors who flunked their Boy Scout merit badge tests in descriptive astronomy.

But the category includes such mindstretchers as Olaf Stapledon's *Last and First Men,* William Sloane's *To Walk the Night,* Dr. Asimov's *The Stars, Like Dust,* even though these stories are stranger than most outright fantasies.

But how is one to distinguish between legitimate science fiction and ridiculous junk? Place of original publication is no guide; some of the best have appeared in half-cent-a-word pulp magazines, with bug-eyed monsters on their covers; some of the silliest have appeared in high-pay slicks or in the "prestige" quality group.

"The Pretzel Men of Pthark"—that one we can skip over; the contents are probably like the title. Almost as easy to spot is the Graustark school of space opera. This is the one in which the dashing Nordic hero comes to the aid of the rightful Martian princess and kicks out the villainous usurper through superscience and sheer grit. It is not being written very often these days, although it still achieves book publication occasionally, sometimes with old and respectable trade book houses. But it does not take a Ph.D. in physics to recognize it for what it is.

But do not be too quick to apply as a test to science fiction what are merely the conventions of better known fields of literature. I once heard a librarian say that she could not stand the unpronounceable names given by science-fiction writers to extraterrestrials. Have a heart, friend! These strings of consonants are honest attempts to give unearthly names to unearthly creatures. As Shaw pointed out, the customs of our tribe are not laws of nature. You would not expect a Martian to be named "Smith." (Say—how about a story about a Martian named "Smith"? Ought to make a good short. Hmmmm—)

But are there reliable criteria by which science fiction can be judged by one who is not well acquainted with the field? In my opinion, there are. Simply the criteria which apply to all fields of fiction, no more, no less.

First of all, an item of science fiction should be a story, i.e., its entertainment value should be as high as that which you expect from other types of stories. It should be entertaining to almost anyone, whether he habitually reads the stuff or not. Second, the degree of literacy should be as high as that expected in other fields. I will not labor this point, since we are simply applying an old rule to a new field, but there is no more excuse here than elsewhere for split infinitives, dangling participles, and similar untidiness, or for obscurity and doubletalk.

The same may be said for plotting, characterization, motivation, and the rest. If a science-fiction writer can't *write*, let him go back to being a fry cook or whatever he was doing before he gave up honest work.

I want to make separate mention of the author's evaluations. Granted that not all stories need be morally edifying, nevertheless I would demand of science-fiction writers as much exercise of moral sense as I would of other writers. I have in mind one immensely popular series which does not hold my own interest very well because the protagonist seems to be guided only by expediency. Neither the writer nor his puppet seems to be aware of good and evil. For my taste this is a defect in any story, nor is the defect mitigated by the wonderful and gaudy trappings of science fiction. In my opinion, such abstractions as honor, loyalty, fortitude, self-sacrifice, bravery, honesty, and integrity will be as important in the far reaches of the Galaxy as they are in Iowa or Korea. I believe that you are entitled to apply your own evaluating standards to science fiction quite as rigorously as you apply them in other fiction.

The criteria outlined above take care of every aspect of science fiction but one—the *science* part. But even here no new criterion is needed. Suppose you were called on to purchase or to refuse to purchase a novel about a Mexican boy growing up on a Mexican cattle ranch; suppose that you knew no Spanish, had never been to Mexico and were unacquainted with its history and customs, and were unsure of the competence of the author. What would you do?

I suspect that you would farm out the decision to someone who was competent to judge the authenticity of the work. It might be a high school Spanish teacher, it might be a friend or neighbor who was well acquainted with our neighboring culture, it might be the local Mexican consul. If the expert told you that the background material of the book was nonsense, you would not give the book shelf room.

The same procedure applies to science fiction. No one can be expected to be expert in everything. If you do not happen to know what makes a rocket go when there is no air to push against, you need not necessarily read Willy Ley's *Rockets, Missiles, and Space Travel*—although it is a fine book, a "must" for every library, desirable for any home. You may instead consult anyone of your acquaintance who *does* know about rocket ships—say an Air Force or Artillery officer, a physics teacher, or almost any fourteen-year-old boy, especially boys who are active in high school science clubs. If the novel being judged concerns cybernetics, nuclear physics, genetics, chemistry, relativity, it is necessary only to enlist the appropriate helper.

You would do the same, would you not, with a novel based on the life of Simón Bolívar?

Of course, there is the alternate, equivalent method of testing the authenticity of any book by checking on the author. If the Simón Bolívar novel was written by a distinguished scholar of South American history, you need concern yourself only with the literary merit of the book. If a book about space travel is written by a world-famous astronomer (as in the case of the one who writes under the pen name of "Philip Latham"), you can put your mind at rest about the correctness of the science therein. In many cases science-fiction writers have more than adequate professional background in the sciences they use as background material and their publishers are careful to let you know this through catalog and dustjacket blurb. I happen to be personally aware of and can vouch for the scientific training of Sprague de Camp, George O. Smith, "John Taine," John W.

Campbell, Jr., "Philip Latham," Will Jenkins, Jack Williamson, Isaac Asimov, Arthur C. Clarke, E. E. Smith, Philip Wylie, Olaf Stapledon, H. G. Wells, Damon Knight, Harry Stine, and "J. J. Coupling." This listing refers to qualifications in science only and is necessarily incomplete, nor do I mean to slight the many fine writers without formal scientific training who are well read in science and most careful in their research.

But some means of checking on a writer of alleged science fiction is desirable. Most writers of historical fiction appear to go to quite a lot of trouble to get the facts of their historical scenes correct, but some people seem to feel that all that is necessary to write science fiction is an unashamed imagination and a sprinkling of words like "ray gun," "rocket tube," "mutant," and "space warp." In some cases the offense is as blatant as it would be in the case of an author of alleged historical fiction who founded a book on the premise that Simón Bolívar was a Chinese monk! It follows that, in order to spot these literary fakers it is necessary to know that Bolívar was not a Chinese monk—know something of the sciences yourself or enlist competent advisers.

AFTERWORD

Writers talking about writing are about as bad as parents boasting about their children. I have not done much of it; the few times that I have been guilty, I did not instigate the project, and in almost all cases (all, I think) my arm was twisted.

I promise to avoid it in the future.

The item above, however, I consider worthy of publication (even though my arm was twisted) because there really are many librarians who earnestly wish to buy good science fiction ... but don't know how to do it. In this short article I tried very hard to define clearly and simply how to avoid the perils of Sturgeon's Law in buying science fiction.

Part way through you will notice the origin of the last name of the Stranger in a Strange Land.

FOREWORD

Superficially this looks like the same sort of article as "Pandora's Box"; it is not, it is fiction—*written by request to celebrate the 30th anniversary of* Amazing Stories. *In "Pandora's Box" I was trying hard to extrapolate rationally to most probable answers 50 years in the future (and in November 1979 I gave myself a score of 66%—anybody want to buy a used crystal ball with a crack in it?).*

But in this short-short I wrote as if I were alive in 2001 and writing a retrospective of the 20th century. Of course everyone knows what happened in 2001; they found a big black monolith on Luna—but in 1956 I didn't know that. So I wrote as far out as I thought I could get away with (to be entertaining) while trying to make the items sound plausible and possible if not likely.

Figures in parentheses refer to notes at the end.

THE THIRD MILLENNIUM OPENS

Now, at the beginning of the year 2001, it is time to see where we
have been and guess at where we are going. A thousand years ago
Otto III ruled the Holy Roman Empire, William the Conqueror was
not yet born, and the Discovery of America was almost five hundred
years in the future. The condition of mankind had not changed in
most important respects since the dawn of history. Aside from language and local custom a peasant of 1000 B.C. would have been right
at home in a village of 1001 A.D.

He would not be so today!

The major changes took place in the last two centuries, but the
most significant change of all occurred in the last fifty years, during
the lifetimes of many of us. In 1950 six out of ten persons could neither read nor write; today an illiterate person is a freak.(1)

*More people have learned to read and write in the past fifty years than
in all the thousands of years preceding 1950.*

This one change is more worldshaking than the establishment
this last year of the laboratory outpost on Pluto. We think of this
century just closed as the one in which mankind conquered space; it
would be more appropriate to think of it as the century in which the
human race finally learned to read and write.

(Let's give the Devil his due; the contagious insanities of the past
century—communism, xenophobia, aggressive nationalism, the explosions of the formerly colonial peoples—have done more to spread
literacy than the efforts of all the do-gooders in history. The Three

R's suddenly became indispensable weapons in mankind's bloodiest struggles—learn to read, or die. Out of bad has come good; a man who can read and write is nine-tenths free even in chains.)

But something else has happened as important as the ABC's. The big-muscled accomplishments of the past fifty years—like sea-farming, the fantastic multiplication of horsepower, and spaceships, pantographic factories, the Sahara Sea, reflexive automation, tapping the Sun—overshadow the most radical advance, i.e., the first fumbling steps in founding a science of the human mind.

Fifty years ago hypnotism was a parlor trick, clairvoyance was superstition, telepathy was almost unknown, and parapsychology was on a par with phrenology and not as respectable as the most popular nonsense called astrology.

Do we have a "science of the mind" today? Far from it. But we do have—

A Certainty of Survival after Death, proved with scientific rigor more complete than that which we apply to heat engines. It is hard to believe that it was only in 1952 that Morey Bernstein, using hypnotic regression, established the personal survival of Bridget Murphy—and thereby turned the western world to a research that Asia and Africa had always taken for granted. (2)

Telepathy and Clairvoyance for Military Purposes. The obvious effect was the changing of war from a "closed" game to an "open" game in the mathematical sense, with the consequence that assassination is now more important than mass weapons. It may well be that no fusion bomb or plague weapon will ever again be used—it would take a foolhardy dictator even to consider such when he knows that his thoughts are being monitored ... and that assassination is so much harder to stop than a rocket bomb. He is bound to remember that Tchaka the Ruthless was killed by one of his own bodyguard.

But the less obvious effect has been to take "secrecy" wraps off scientific research. It is hard to recall that there was once a time when scientific facts could not be freely published, just as it is hard to believe that our grandfathers used to wear things called "swimming suits"— secrecy in science and swimming with clothes on are almost equally preposterous to the modern mind. Yet clothing never hampered a swimmer as much as "classification" hampered science. Most happily, controlled telepathy made secrecy first futile, then obsolete. (3)

But possibly the most important discovery we have made about ourselves is that *Man is a Wild Animal*. He cannot be tamed and remain Man; his genius is bound up in the very qualities which make him wild. With this self-knowledge, bleak, stern, and proud, goes the last hope of permanent peace on Earth; it makes world government unlikely and certainly unstable. Despite the fact that we are (as always) in a condition of marginal starvation, this fact makes all measures of population control futile—other than the ancient, grisly Four Horsemen, and even they are not effective; we finished World War III with a hundred million more people than when we started.

Not even the H-bomb could change our inner nature. We have learned most bloodily that the H-bomb does nothing that the stone axe did not do—and neither weapon could tame us. Man can be chained but he cannot be domesticated, and eventually he always breaks his chains.

Nor can we be "improved" by genetic breeding; it is not in our nature to accept it. Someday we may be conquered by superbeings from elsewhere, then bred according to their notions—and become dogs, rather than wolves. (I'm betting that we will put up a fight!) But, left to our own resources, improvements in our breed must come the hard way, through survival ... and we will still remain wild animals.(4)

But we have barely begun to study ourselves. Now that mankind has finally learned to read and write what can we expect him to accomplish?

We have no idea today of how self-awareness is linked to protoplasm. Now that we know that the ego survives the body we should make progress on this mystery.

Personal survival necessitates *Cosmic Purpose* as a "least hypothesis" for the universe. Scientists are tending to take teleology away from theologians and philosophers and give it a shaking. But concrete results this century seem unlikely. As of now, we still don't know why we are here or what we are supposed to do—but for the first time in history it is scientifically probable that the final answers are not null answers. It will be interesting indeed if one of the religious faiths turns out to be correct to nine decimals.

Since ESP talents seem to be independent of space-time it is theoretically possible that we may achieve a mental form of time travel. This is allowable under the mathematics being developed to describe mind phenomena. If so, we may eventually establish history, and even prophecy, as exact sciences.

On the physical side we can be certain that the speed-of-light barrier will be cracked this century. This makes it statistically likely that we will soon encounter races equal or superior to ourselves. This should be the most significant happening to mankind since the discovery of fire. It may degrade or destroy us, it may improve us; it cannot leave us unchanged.

On the mundane side we can expect a population of five billion by the middle of this century. Emigration to other planets will not affect the total here.

Scientific facts will continue to be discovered much faster than they can be classified and cross-referenced, but we cannot expect any accompanying increase in human intelligence. No doubt the few remaining illiterates will continue to be employed in the subscription departments of periodicals; the same bigmouths who now complain about rocket service to Luna (but who can't thread a needle themselves) will in 2050 be complaining about service to the stars (and they still won't be able to thread a needle).

Unquestionably the Twentieth Century will be referred to as the "Good Old Days," we will continue to view with alarm the antics of the younger generation, and we probably will still be after a cure for the common cold.

Notes: 1980

1. He's still a freak but he's all too common. There is a special circle in Hell for the "Educators" who decided that the Three R's really weren't all that important. Concerning our public schools today: Never have so many been paid so much for so little. I thank whatever gods there be that I went to school so many years ago that I had no choice but to be tightly disciplined in classes in which the teachers did not hesitate to fail and to punish.

My first-grade class had 63 kids in it, one teacher, no assistant. Before the end of the second semester all 63 could read.

2. Many people seem to feel that the "Bridey Murphy" case has been invalidated. Maybe so, maybe not—the investigative reporter who went to Ireland had no special qualifications and the "disproof" came from Time *magazine.* Time *magazine probably publishes many facts ... but since its founding in the early 1920's I have been on the spot eight or nine times when something that wound up as a news story in* Time *happened. Not once—not once—did the* Time *magazine story match what I saw and heard.*

I have the "Bridey Murphy" recording and Bernstein's book about it. I am not an expert witness ... but I found the recording highly interesting. To me it sounded like what it purported to be: regression under hypnosis to memory of a former existence. Some years later I learned from an ethical hypnotherapist (i.e., he accepted patients only by referrals from M.D.'s, his own doctorate being in psychology) that regression to what seemed to be former lives was a commonplace among patients of hypnotherapists— they discussed it among themselves but never published because they were bound by much the same rule as physicians and priests taking confession.

I have no data to offer of my own. I decided many years back that I was too busy with this *life to fret about what happens afterwards. Long before 2001 I will know ... or I will know nothing whatever because my universe has ceased to exist.*

3. Anyone today who simply brushes off ESP phenomena as being ridiculous is either pigheaded or ignorant. But I do not expect controlled telepathy by 2001; that is sheer fiction, intended to permit me to get in that bit about Tchaka, et al.

4. I lifted this "Man is a wild animal" thesis bodily from Charles Gallon Darwin (grandson of the author of The Origin of Species) *in his book* The Next Million Years, *Doubleday, 1953. I am simply giving credit; I shan't elaborate here. But* The Next Million Years *is a follow-on to* The Origin of Species *and is, in my opinion, one of the most important works of this century. It has not been a popular book—but I seem to recall that his grandfather's seminal work wasn't too popular, either.*

FOREWORD

This polemic was first published on Saturday 12 April 1958. Thereafter it was printed many other places and reprints of it were widely circulated inside and outside the science fiction community, inside and outside this country.

It brought down on me the strongest and most emotional adverse criticism I have ever experienced—not to my surprise.

After more than twenty years my "misdeed" seems to have been largely forgotten, or perhaps forgiven. But I do not ask to be forgiven and I do not want it to be forgotten. So I now republish it in permanent form. I have not consulted my editor or my publisher; each is free to denounce my opinions here expressed—but is not free to refuse this item while accepting the rest of this book.

A few specific details below are outdated by new technology—e.g., earthquakes can now be distinguished with certainty (we hope) from nuclear explosions, while other aspects of detection and inspection grow more complex. Technical details change; basic principles do not.

"Supreme excellence in war is to subdue the enemy without fighting."

—*Sun Tzu, ca. 350 B.C.*

The Soviet Union is highly skilled at this—and so are the Chinese leaders. During the last twenty-odd years we have been outmaneuvered endlessly. Today it's the Backfire bomber (a B-1 with a Russian accent); tomorrow it is an international (U.N.) treaty to socialize all aspects of space and thereby kill such enterprise as the L-5 Society, Sabre, Otrag (already

111

killed), Robert Truax's Do-It-Yourself projects. The treaty will permit a KGB agent ("A rose by any other name—") to inspect in detail anything of ours, private or public, on the ground or in the sky, if it is **in any way** *connected with space—or the KGB man claims to suspect that it might be.*

(But if you think that gives us a free ticket into every building, every room, at the Byakonur space complex, you don't know how the USSR does business.)

The President has already announced that he will sign it. 10 to 1 he will, 7 to 2 the Senate will pass it—and 100 to 1 we will regret it.

This declaration is more timely than ever; I am proud to reprint it— and deeply sorry that it was ever needed.

Any rational person may well disagree with me on details of this broadside. But on the moral principles expressed here, a free man says: "Give me liberty, or give me death!" No quibbling, no stopping to "think it over." He means it.

Fools and poltroons do not.

STAND UP AND BE COUNTED!

"Is life so dear, or peace so sweet, as to be purchased at the price of chains and slavery? Forbid it, Almighty God! I know not what course others may take, but as for me, give me liberty, or give me death!!"

—Patrick Henry

Last Saturday in this city appeared a full-page ad intended to scare us into demanding that the President stop our testing of nuclear weapons. This manifesto was a curious mixture of truth, half-truth, distortion, exaggeration, untruth, and Communist-line goals concealed in idealistic-sounding nonsense.

The instigators were seventy-odd local people and sixty-odd national names styling themselves "The National Committee for a Sane Nuclear Policy." It may well be that none of the persons whose names are used as the "National" committee are Communists and we have no reason to suppose that any of the local people are Communists—possibly all of them are loyal and merely misguided. But this manifesto is the rankest sort of Communist propaganda.

A tree is known by its fruit. The purpose of their manifesto is to entice or frighten you into signing a letter to President Eisenhower, one which demands that he take three actions. The first demand is the old, old Communist-line gimmick that nuclear weapons and their vehicles should be "considered apart" in disarmament talks. It has had a slight restyling for the post-Sputnik era and now reads: "That nuclear test explosions, missiles, and outer-space satellites be considered apart from other disarmament problems."

This proposal sounds reasonable but is booby-trapped with outright surrender of the free world to the Communist dictators. Mr. Truman knew it, Mr. Eisenhower knows it; both have refused it repeatedly. The gimmick is this: if nuclear weapons and their vehicles are outlawed while conventional weapons (tanks and planes and bayonets and rifles) are not, then—but you figure it out. 170,000,000 of us against 900,000,000 of them. Who wins?

Even if you count our allies (on the assumption that every last one of them will stick by us no matter how bone-headed our behavior), the ratio is still two-to-one against us when it comes to slugging it out with infantry divisions, Yalu River style.

Oh yes! Khrushchev would like very much to have nuclear weapons "considered apart" from infantry divisions. And he is delighted when soft-headed Americans agree with him.

"The Mice Voted to Bell the Cat"

—Aesop

Their second proposal has been part of the Communist line for twelve long years. It reads: "That all nuclear test explosions be stopped immediately and that the U.N. then proceed with the mechanics necessary for monitoring this cessation." This is the straight Communist gospel direct from the Kremlin. This was and is today their phony counter-proposal to the Baruch Proposals of 1946—banning first, policing the ban if, when, and maybe … and subject to the veto of the U.S.S.R. It would leave us at the "mercy" of the butchers of Budapest, our lives staked on the "honor" of men to whom honesty is a bourgeois weakness, our freedom resting on the promises of a gangster government that has broken every promise it ever made.

The Committee's manifesto claims: "—the problems in monitoring such tests are relatively uncomplicated." This is either an outright lie or ignorant wishful thinking; the problems are so complicated that

WHO ARE THE HEIRS OF PATRICK HENRY?

nothing short of on-the-spot inspection will work—an underground test cannot be told from an earthquake shock by any known method of monitoring.

Before you trust your lives and freedom to the promises of the Kremlin, remember Budapest—

—remember Poland in 1945
—remember Prague
—remember Estonia, Latvia, Lithuania
—remember Korea
—remember brave little Finland
—and keep your powder dry!

The third proposal is largely pious window-dressing but it has the same sort of booby-trap buried in it. It reads: "That missiles and outer-space satellites be brought under United Nations-monitored control, and that there be a pooling of world science for space exploration under the United Nations." The harmless part could be done if the U.S.S.R. were willing; the booby-trap is the word "missiles."

We Americans live in a goldfish bowl; we could not conceal rocket tests even if we tried. But in the vast spaces of Russia, Siberia, and China missiles of every sort—even the long-range ICBMs—can be tested in secret, manufactured and stockpiled and installed ready to go, despite all "monitoring." Anything less than on-the-spot inspection of the entire vast spaces of the Communist axis would leave us at the mercy of the bland promises of the Butchers of Budapest.

The last paragraph of this letter that they want you to send to the President is not a proposal; it is simply another attempt to strike terror into the hearts of free men by reminding us of the horrors of nuclear war.

"'Will you walk into my parlor?' said the Spider to the Fly."

It is no accident that this manifesto follows the Communist line, no coincidence that it "happens" to appear all over the United States the very week that Khrushchev has announced smugly that the U.S.S.R. has ended their tests—and demands that we give up our coming, long-scheduled, and publicly announced tests of a weapon with minimum fall-out.

This follows the pattern of a much-used and highly-refined Communist tactic: plan ahead to soften up the free world on some major point, package the propaganda to appeal to Americans with warm hearts and soft heads, time the release carefully, then let the suckers carry the ball while the known Communists stay under cover.

They used this method to gut our army after the Japanese surrender with the slogan of "Bring the Boys Home." They used it to make us feel guilty about the A-bomb—while their spies were stealing it. They dreamed up the pious theme of "Don't Play Politics with Hunger"—then used our charity to play their politics. They used it to put over the infamous "Oxford Oath" and the phony "Peace Strikes" of the thirties. They have used this tactic many times to soften up the free world and will use it whenever they can find dupes.

They are using it now. Today both sides, Freedom and Red Tyranny, are armed with nuclear weapons ... and the Communists are again using our own people to try to shame or scare us into throwing our weapons away.

These proposals are not a road to world peace, they are abject surrender to tyranny. If we fall for them, then in weeks or months or a few years at most, Old Glory will be hauled down for the last time and the whole planet will be ruled by the Butchers of Budapest.

For more than a hundred years, ever since the original Communist Manifesto, it has been the unswerving aim of the Communist Party to take over all of this planet. The only thing blocking their conquest is the fact that the tragically-shrunken free world still possesses nuclear weapons. They can destroy us ... but they know that we can destroy them.

So they want us to throw away the equalizer.

If we do, we can expect the same "mercy" that Budapest received. They will say to us: "Surrender—or be destroyed!"

"God grants liberty only to those who love it and are always ready to guard and defend it."

—Daniel Webster

We the undersigned are not a committee but simply two free citizens of these United States. We love life and we want peace ... but not "peace at any price"—not the price of liberty!

Poltroons and pacifists will think otherwise.

Those who signed that manifesto have made their choice; consciously or unconsciously they prefer enslavement to death. Such is their right and we do not argue with them—we speak to you who are still free in your souls.

In a free country, political action can start anywhere. We read that insane manifesto of the so-called "Committee for a 'Sane' Nuclear Policy" and we despised it. So we are answering it ourselves—by our own free choice and spending only our own money.

We say to the commissars: "You will never enslave us. The worst you can do is kill us. But we are resolved to die free!"

> **"They that can give up essential liberty to obtain a little temporary safety deserve neither liberty nor safety."**
> **—Benjamin Franklin**

No scare talk of leukemia, mutation, or atomic holocaust will sway us. Is "fall-out" dangerous? Of course it is! The risk to life and posterity has been willfully distorted by these Communist-line propagandists—but if it were a hundred times as great we still would choose it to the dead certainty of Communist enslavement. If atomic war comes, will it kill off the entire human race? Possibly—almost certainly so if the Masters of the Kremlin choose to use cobalt bombs on us. Their command of science in these matters seems equal to ours, they appear to be some years ahead of us in the art of rocketry; they almost certainly have the power to destroy the human race.

If it comes to atomic war, the best we can hope for is tens of millions of American dead—perhaps more than half our population wiped out in the first few minutes.

Colorado Springs is at least a secondary target; all of us here may be killed.

These are the risks. The alternative is surrender. We accept the risks.

"The liberties of our country, the freedom of our civil Constitution, are worth defending at all hazards."

—Samuel Adams

We have no easy solution to offer. The risks cannot be avoided other than by surrender; they can be reduced only by making the free world so strong that the evil pragmatists of Communism cannot afford to murder us. The price to us will be year after weary year of higher taxes, harder work, grim devotion ... and perhaps, despite all this—death. But we shall die free!

To this we pledge our lives, our fortunes, and our sacred honor.

We the undersigned believe that almost all Americans agree with us. Whoever you are, wherever you are, you sons of Patrick Henry— let us know your name! Sign the letter herewith and mail it to us—we will see that it gets to Congressman Chenoweth, to both our Senators, and to the President.

1958 address— Robert and Virginia Heinlein
1776 Mesa Avenue
Colorado Springs, Colorado

1980 address— (Care Spectrum Literary Agency
60 East 42nd Street
New York City, New York 10017)

"WHAT CAN I DO?"

This much has been done by two people acting alone. Let's call ourselves "The Patrick Henry League" and prove to our government that the Spirit of '76 is still alive. We are two, you and your spouse make four, your neighbor and his wife make six—we can snowball this until it sweeps the country.

We can advertise in other counties, in other states.

If you who are reading this are not in Colorado Springs, stand up, speak up, and start your own chapter of "The Patrick Henry League" now. You are a free citizen, you need no permission, nor any charter from us. Run an ad—quote or copy this one if you like. Dig down in the sock to pay for it, or pass the hat, or both—but sound the call in your own home town, mail copies of your ad out of town, and get some more letters started toward Washington.

And let us hear from you!

Let us all stand up and shout aloud again and forever:

"Give Me Liberty or Give Me Death!"

President Eisenhower,
The White House
Washington, D.C.

Dear Mr. President:

We know that you are being pressured to stop our nuclear weapons tests, turn our missile and space program over to the U.N., and in other ways to weaken our defenses.

We urge you to stand steadfast.

We want America made supremely strong and we are resolved to accept all burdens necessary to that end. We ask for total effort—nuclear testing, research, and development, highest priorities for rocketry, sterner education, anything that is needed. We are ready to pay higher taxes, forego luxuries, work harder.

To this we pledge our lives, our fortunes, and our sacred honor.

Respectfully yours,

. . . .
(names)

. . . .
(address)

AFTERWORD

When the soi-disant "SANE" committee published its page ad in Colorado Springs (and many other cities) on 5 April 1958, I was working on The Heretic *(later to be published as* Stranger in a Strange Land*). I stopped at once and for several weeks Mrs. Heinlein and I did nothing but work on this "Patrick Henry" drive. We published our ad in three newspapers, encouraged its publication elsewhere, mailed thousands of reprints, spoke before countless meetings, collected and mailed to the White House thousands of copies of the letter above—always by registered mail—no acknowledgement of any sort was ever received, not even in response to "Return Receipt Requested."*

Then the rug was jerked out from under us; by executive order Mr. Eisenhower canceled all testing without requiring mutual inspection. (The outcome of that is now history; when it suited him, Khrushchev resumed testing with no warning and with the dirtiest bombs ever set off in the atmosphere.)

I was stunned by the President's action. I should not have been as I knew that he was a political general long before he entered politics—stupid, all front, and dependent on his staff. But that gets me *the stupid hat, too; I had learned, years earlier that many politicians (not all!) will do* anything *to get elected ... and Adlai Stevenson had him panting.*

Presently I resumed writing—not Stranger *but* Starship Troopers.

The "Patrick Henry" ad shocked 'em; Starship Troopers *outraged 'em. I still can't see how that book got a Hugo. It continues to get lots of nasty "fan" mail and not much favorable fan mail ... but it sells and sells and sells and sells, in eleven languages. It doesn't slow down—four new contracts just this year. And yet I almost never hear of it save when someone wants to chew me out over it. I don't understand it.*

The criticisms are usually based on a failure to understand simple indicative English sentences, couched in simple words—especially when the critics are professors of English, as they often are. (A shining counterexample, a professor who can read and understand English, is one at Colorado College—a professor of history.)

We have also some professors of English who write science fiction but I do not know of one who formally reviewed or criticized Starship Troopers. *However, I have gathered a strong impression over the years that professors of English who write and sell science fiction average being much more grammatical and much more literate than their colleagues who do not (cannot?) write saleable fiction.*

Their failures to understand English are usually these:

1. "Veteran" does not mean in English dictionaries or in this novel solely a person who has served in military forces. I concede that in commonest usage today it means a war veteran ... but no one hesitates to speak of a veteran fireman or veteran school teacher. In Starship Troopers *it is stated flatly and more than once that nineteen out of twenty veterans are not military veterans. Instead, 95% of voters are what we call today "former members of federal civil service."*

Addendum: The volunteer is not given a choice. He/she can't win a franchise by volunteering for what we call civil service. He volunteers ... then for two years plus-or-minus he goes where he is sent and does what he is told to do. If he is young, male, and healthy, he may wind up as cannon fodder. But there are long chances against it.

2. He/she can resign at any time other than during combat—i.e., 100% of the time for 19 out of 20; 99+% of the time for those in the military branches of federal service.

3. There is no conscription. (I am opposed to conscription for any reason at any time, war or peace, and have said so repeatedly in fiction, in nonfiction, from platforms, and in angry sessions in think tanks. I was sworn in first in 1923, and have not been off the hook since that time. My principal pride in my family is that I know of not one in over two centuries who was drafted; they all volunteered. But the draft is involuntary servitude, immoral, and unconstitutional no matter what the Supreme Court says.)

4. Criticism: "The government in Starship Troopers *is militaristic."* "Militaristic" *is the adjective for the noun "militarism," a word of several definitions but not one of them can be correctly applied to the government described in this novel. No military or civil servant can vote or hold office until after he is discharged and is again a civilian. The military tend to be despised by most civilians and this is made explicit. A career military man is most unlikely ever to vote or hold office; he is more likely to be dead—and if he does live through it, he'll vote for the first time at 40 or older.*

"That book glorifies the military!" Now we are getting somewhere. It does indeed. Specifically the P.B.I., the Poor Bloody Infantry, the mudfoot who places his frail body between his loved home and the war's desolation—but is rarely appreciated. "It's Tommy this and Tommy that and chuck him out, the brute!—but it's 'thin red line of heroes' when the guns begin to shoot."

My own service usually doesn't have too bad a time of it. Save for very special situations such as the rivers in Nam, a Navy man can get killed but he is unlikely to be wounded ... and if he is killed, it is with hot food in his belly, clean clothes on his body, a recent hot bath, and sack time in a comfortable bunk not more than 24 hours earlier. The Air Force leads a comparable life. But think of Korea, of Guadalcanal, of Belleau Wood, of Viet Nam. The H-bomb did not abolish the infantryman; it made him essential ... and he has the toughest job of all and should be honored.

Glorify the military? Would I have picked it for my profession and stayed on the rolls the past 56 years were I not proud of it?

I think I know what offends most of my critics the most about Starship Troopers*: It is the dismaying idea that a voice in governing the state should be earned instead of being handed to anyone who is 18 years old and has a body temperature near 37°C.*

But there ain't no such thing as a free lunch.

Democracies usually collapse not too long after the plebs discover that they can vote themselves bread and circuses ... for a while. Either read history or watch the daily papers; it is now happening here. Let's stipulate for discussion that some stabilizing qualification is needed (in addition to the body being warm) for a voter to vote responsibly with proper consideration for the future of his children and grandchildren—and yours. The Founding

Fathers never intended to extend the franchise to everyone; their debates and the early laws show it. A man had to be a stable figure in the community through owning land or employing others or engaged in a journeyman trade or something.

But few pay any attention to the Founding Fathers today—those ignorant, uneducated men—they didn't even have television (have you looked at Monticello lately?)—so let's try some other "poll taxes" to insure a responsible electorate:

a) Mark Twain's "The Curious Republic of Gondour"—if you have not read it, do so.

b) A state where anyone can buy for cash (or lay-away installment plan) one or more franchises, and this is the government's sole source of income other than services sold competitively and non-monopolistically. This would produce a new type of government with several rabbits tucked away in the hat. Rich people would take over the government? Would they, now? Is a wealthy man going to impoverish himself for the privilege of casting a couple of hundred votes? Buying an election today, under the warm-body (and tombstone) system is much cheaper than buying a controlling number of franchises would be. The arithmetic on this one becomes unsolvable ... but I suspect that paying a stiff price (call it 20,000 Swiss francs) for a franchise would be even less popular than serving two years.

c) A state that required a bare minimum of intelligence and education—e.g., step into the polling booth and find that the computer has generated a new quadratic equation just for you. Solve it, the computer unlocks the voting machine, you vote. But get a wrong answer and the voting machine fails to unlock, a loud bell sounds, a red light goes on over that booth—and you slink out, face red, you having just proved yourself too stupid and/or ignorant to take part in the decisions of the grownups. Better luck next election! No lower age limit in this system—smart 12-yr-old girls vote every election while some of their mothers—and fathers—decline to be humiliated twice.

There are endless variations on this one. Here are two: Improving the Breed—*No red light, no bell ... but the booth opens automatically—empty.* Revenue—*You don't risk your life, just some gelt. It costs you a ¼ oz troy of gold in local currency to enter the booth. Solve your quadratic and vote, and you get your money back. Flunk—and the state keeps it. With this one*

I guarantee that no one would vote who was not interested and would be most unlikely to vote if unsure of his ability to get that hundred bucks back.

I concede that I set the standards on both I.Q. and schooling too low in calling only for the solution of a quadratic since (if the programming limits the machine to integer roots) a person who deals with figures at all can solve that one with both hands behind him (her) and her-his eyes closed. But I just recently discovered that a person can graduate from high school in Santa Cruz with a straight-A record, be about to enter the University of California on a scholarship ... but be totally unable to do simple arithmetic. Let's not make things too difficult at the transition.

d) I don't insist on any particular method of achieving a responsible electorate; I just think that we need to tighten up the present warm-body criterion before it destroys us. How about this? For almost a century and a half women were not allowed to vote. For the past sixty years they have voted ... but we have not seen the enormous improvement in government that the suffragettes promised us.

Perhaps we did not go far enough. Perhaps men are still corrupting government ... so let's try the next century and a half with males disenfranchised. (Fair is fair. My mother was past forty before she was permitted to vote.) But let's not stop there; at present men outnumber women in elective offices, on the bench, and in the legal profession by a proportion that is scandalous.

Make males ineligible to hold elective office, or to serve in the judiciary, elective or appointed, and also reserve the profession of law for women.

Impossible? That was exactly *the situation the year I was born, but male instead of female, even in the few states that had female suffrage before the XIXth Amendment, with so few exceptions as to be unnoticed. As for rooting male lawyers out of their cozy niches, this would give us a pool of unskilled manual laborers—and laborers are very hard to hire these days; I've been trying to hire one at any wages he wants for the past three months, with no success.*

The really good ones could stay on as law clerks to our present female lawyers, who will be overworked for a while. But not for long. Can you imagine female judges (with no male judges to reverse them) permitting attorneys to take six weeks to pick a jury? Or allowing a trial to ramble along for months?

Women are more practical than men. Biology forces it on them.

Speaking of that, let's go whole hog. Until a female bears a child her socio-economic function is male no matter how orthodox her sexual prefer-ence. But a woman who is mother to a child knows *she has a stake in the future. So let's limit the franchise and eligibility for office and the practice of law to mothers.*

The phasing over should be made gentle. Let males serve out their terms but not succeed themselves. Male lawyers might be given as long as four years to retire or find other jobs while not admitting any more males into law schools. I don't have a candidate for President but the events of the last fifty years prove that anybody *can sit in the Oval Office; it's just that some are more impressive in appearance than others.*

Brethren and Sistern, have you ever stopped to think that there has not been one rational decision out of the Oval Office for fifty years?

An all-female government could not possibly be worse than what we have been enduring. Let's try it!

FOREWORD

After I got Starship Troopers *out of the way, I indulged in some stone masonry (my favorite recreation and reconditioning after writing when I was younger), installed a fountain in our lower irrigation pool and landscaped it—then got back to work on* The Heretic *aka* Stranger in a Strange Land, *and finally finished it more than ten years after I had plotted it. I had been in no hurry to finish it, as that story could not be published commercially until the public* mores *changed. I could see them changing and it turned out that I had timed it right.*

Many people have said that it is clear that Stranger *was written in two parts; the division point showed. But no two people have ever picked the same putative division point ... and this is the first time I have ever admitted that it was not written in two chunks but in four.*

No one ever will spot the actual starts and stops because Stranger *is one of the very few stories in which I plotted every detail before writing it, and then stuck precisely to that plot. What readers pick as places where I "must have" broken the writing are in fact division points planned for dramatic reasons.*

Then I had to cut the damned thing; sticking to that complex and ponderous plot resulted in a MS more than twice as long as it should have been, either commercially or dramatically. Cutting it took more working time than writing it.

In the meantime my wife signed up for University of Colorado Extension classes in Russian. She has always believed that anything worth doing at all is worth overdoing; for two solid years she lived and breathed Russian.

She never missed a class, was always thoroughly prepared, hired a private conversation tutor to supplement her classroom work, bought every brand of Russian language instruction records available then, kept them stacked on the record changer and played them all day long while she did other things— our home had a speaker in every room, and a large speaker for the garden.

(This did not bother my work; since I knew no Russian then, it was random noise to me.)

Two years of this and she could read Russian, write Russian, speak Russian, understand Russian—and think in Russian.

Then we went to the USSR.

Other countries, too, of course—Poland and Czechoslovakia won my undying sympathy, as well as the captive Baltic states. I should include the Turkestan countries, too, but they don't seem quite as oppressed—much farther from Moskva and off the beaten track. All in all we traveled about 10,000 miles inside USSR and saw about twenty cities. Ginny's hard work paid off; we saw and heard far, far more than we could have learned had we been dependent on a politically-cleared guide—we often ducked out without our guide. I picked up some pidgin Russian but never learned to speak it—I could give directions, ask directions, order a meal, pay a bill—and swear in Russian (essential!).

The article below I wrote in Hotel Torni, Helsinki, immediately after "escaping" (that's how it felt) from the Soviet Union. The lighter article following "Pravda" I wrote a couple of weeks later in Stockholm. By then my nerves had relaxed in the free air of Scandinavia and I could see humor in things that had not seemed at all funny at the time.

Being intelligent is not a felony.
But most societies evaluate it as at
least a misdemeanor."

—L. Long

"PRAVDA" Means "TRUTH"

"**P**ravda" means "truth."

That's what it says, right here in my English-Russian dictionary: Pravda—Truth. Surely one may depend on the dictionary.

In Al Smith's bleak, skeptical words: "Let's take a look at the record."

On May Day, 1960, a United States U-2 reconnaissance plane made some type of unplanned landing in the Soviet Union. This much is both "truth" and "pravda." Beyond this bare fact, "truth" and "pravda" diverge widely.

TRUTH: On May 1 this U-2 plane grounded near Sverdlovsk in the heartland of the Soviet Union about 1,500 miles from the border it crossed. The plane was wrecked but the pilot was not killed. Much of the equipment in the plane, such as radio gear, was undamaged. The pilot's survival and the condition of the wreckage, plus the undamaged equipment, suggest a forced landing in rough country, such as would result from engine failure.

The U-2 is extremely fast and it cruises at very high altitude, 60-70,000 feet. The kinetic energy stored in a moving object varies as the square of its velocity ($E = \frac{1}{2}MV^2$). A staggering amount of kinetic energy is stored in a U-2. If such a plane is hit by anti-aircraft rocket fire what happens in the next split second would make a head-on collision between two hot-rodders seem like a mother's loving pat. The anti-aircraft damage merely triggers the disaster; the major violence comes from the plane's great speed—it explodes! Suddenly the sky is filled with junk.

The chance of the pilot's surviving is small. He may escape if the plane's ejection capsule is not damaged when the plane is hit. But there is only the tiniest chance that radios and other relatively fragile pieces of equipment would reach the ground undamaged. Nevertheless, such items were "recovered" from the "shot-down" U-2. A crate of eggs, uncracked, would be equally convincing.

We may never know the exact truth of what happened to that U-2. Only Soviet officials talked to unlucky pilot Powers before his trial.

But the nervous nellies among us should stop beating their breasts over the shame of it all. Photo reconnaissance is not the same thing as a bombing run. An overflight by an unarmed plane is not in the same league with what Khrushchev did to Budapest. What we are dealing with here is the security of the United States and—very possibly—the survival, and certainly the freedom, of the entire human race.

Espionage is not illegal under International Law. Neither is it immoral. The penalty for getting caught at it is very high. It usually means the spy's neck. It is not illegal under U.S. laws for us to attempt to spy on the USSR, nor is it illegal under Soviet law for them to attempt to spy on us. Nor, in either case, is it an act of war. Throughout history every country has striven to learn the military secrets of any potential enemy, and to protect its own. Spying is wise and necessary insurance against utter military disaster.

That we have been conducting photo reconnaissance over the Soviet Union so successfully and for four vital years is the most encouraging news in the past decade. Among other things it means we have accurate maps by which to strike back. The Soviet Union does not have to send spy planes over us to obtain similar information. Excellent large-scale maps with our military installations and industrial complexes clearly marked may be obtained free from Standard Oil or Conoco. Still better maps may be ordered by the Soviet Embassy from our Coast and Geodetic Survey at very low prices. Soviet agents move freely among us and many of them enjoy the immunity and complete freedom of travel afforded by U.N. passports. If a Red spy wants aerial color photographs at low altitude of our Air Defense installation just south of Kansas City—in America's heartland—until recently he could hire a pilot and a plane at the Kansas City airport for about $25 an hour and snap pictures to his heart's content without taking any of the risks of being hanged or shot down that Francis Powers took for us. If Mr. Eisenhower had failed to obtain by any possible means the military intelligence that the USSR gets so easily and cheaply about us, he would have been derelict in his duty.

So, if you hear anyone whining about how "shameful" the U-2 flights were, take his lollipop away and spank him with it.

PRAVDA: It took the fat boy with the bad manners five days to decide just what sort of "pravda" to feed his people. The situation must have been acutely embarrassing for him, much more so than it was to us, because for four years he had been totally unable to stop the flights, despite his boasts and missile brandishing, despite the fact that every flight was certainly observed in Soviet radar screens.

K. could keep quiet, in which case there was little chance that the Free World news services would ever learn about it, and no chance that the Russian people would ever find out. Our Central Intelligence Agency would know that a reconnaissance plane was missing, but it would not have advertised a top secret.

K. could refurbish the incident, give it a new paint job and peddle it as propaganda.

Or K. could tell the simple truth. This alternative is mentioned simply to keep the record technically complete, as the simple truth is a tactic not contemplated under Marxism-Leninism doctrines. Here we have the essential distinction between truth and pravda.

Truth, to the West, consists of all the facts without distortion.

Pravda is that which serves the World Communist Revolution. Pravda can be a mixture of fact and falsehood, or a flat-footed, brass-bound, outright lie. In rare cases and by sheer coincidence, pravda may happen to match the facts. I do not actually know of such a case but it seems statistically likely that such matching must have taken place a few times in the past 43 years.

This comparison is not mere cynicism. I appeal to the authority of V. I. Lenin himself, in his tactics of revolution. By the doctrines of dialectical materialism, simple truth as we know it is abolished as a concept. It can have no existence of its own separate from the needs and purposes of the Communist Party and the World Revolution. Our ingrained habit of believing that the other fellow must be telling the truth at least most of the time is perhaps our greatest weakness in dealing with the Kremlin.

Apparently K. and his cohorts encountered much trouble in deciding just what the pravda should be about the U-2. They spent almost a week making up their minds. I was in Moscow at the time and there was no indication of any sort that anything unusual had happened on May 1; Russians continued to treat us American visitors with their customary almost saccharine politeness and the daily paper (I hesitate to call it a newspaper) known as *Pravda* hinted not of U-2's. This situation continued for several days thereafter. I was not dependent on an Intourist guide-interpreter in reaching this impression as my wife reads, writes, understands and fluently speaks Russian. She's not of Russian descent. She learned it at a University of Colorado Extension night school, plus a private tutor and a lot of hard work.

After May Day, we went on out to Alma Ata in Kazakhstan, north of India and a very short distance from the Red China border, about 2,000 miles beyond Moscow. Be-Kind-To-Americans Week continued. Three Americans, the only travelers in that remote part of Asia, received the undivided attention of the Alma Ata Director of Intourist, two school teachers (pulled off their teaching jobs to act as guides), two chauffeurs, and most of the attention of the hotel staff. We had but to express a wish and it was granted.

As of Thursday morning, May 5, the pravda was still that nothing had happened.

Thursday afternoon the climate abruptly changed. K's cohorts had at last decided on a pravda; to wit: an American military plane had attempted to cross the border of the Soviet Union. Soviet rocket fire had shot it down from an altitude of 60,000 feet as soon as it had crossed the border. The Soviet peoples were very much distressed that America would even attempt such an act of bald aggression. The Soviet peoples wanted peace. Such aggression would not be tolerated. Any other such planes would not only be shot down but the bases from which the attacks were made would be destroyed. Such was K's new pravda at the end of a five-hour speech.

The only connection between pravda and fact lay in the existence of an American plane down on Soviet soil. The locale of the incident shifted 1,500 miles. The plane is "shot down" at an extremely high altitude (if true then those exhibits in Gorky Park were as phony as K's promises of safety to Nagy and Pal Maleter). No mention at all is made of four long years of humiliating defeat. Pravda suppresses the truth and turns the incident into a triumph of Soviet arms. The Soviet newspapers and radio stations, all state-owned, spout the same line. All during this period the Voice of America was jammed. K. made certain his serfs heard nothing but the pravda.

We learned it by being ordered—not requested—to report to the Alma Ata office of the Director of Intourist. There we were given a long, very stern, but fatherly, lecture on the aggressive misbehavior of our government, a lecture that included a careful recital of the U-2 pravda.

Once I understood, I did something no American should ever do in the Soviet Union. I lost my temper completely. I out-shouted the director on the subject of American grievances against the Soviet Union. My red-headed wife most ably supported me by scorching him about Soviet slave labor camps, naming each one by name, pointing out their location to him on the big map of the Soviet Union which hung back of his desk, and telling him how many people had died in them—including Americans.

We stomped out of his office, went to our room and gave way to the shakes. I had lost my temper and with it my judgment and thereby endangered not merely myself but my wife. I had forgotten that I was not protected by our Bill of Rights, that I was not free to bawl out a public official with impunity—that I was more than 2,000 miles from any possible help.

Communism has no concern for the individual. The Soviets have liquidated some 20 to 30 millions of their own in "building socialism." They kept after Trotsky until they got him. They murdered a schoolmate of mine between stations on a train in Western Europe and dumped his body. Terror and death are as fixed a part of their tactics as is distortion of the truth. Their present gang boss is the "liberator" of Budapest, the "pacifier" of the Ukraine—a comic butcher personally responsible for the deaths of millions of innocent people.

All this I knew. I knew, too, that our own policies had softened beyond recognition since the day when Teddy Roosevelt demanded the return of an American citizen alive—or the man who gabbed him, dead—and made his threat stick. In these present sorry days no American citizen abroad can count on protection from our State Department. We have even voluntarily surrendered our own soldiers' Constitutional rights, drafted and sent willy-nilly to foreign lands. We still permit the Red Chinese to hold prisoner hundreds of our boys captured nearly ten years ago in Korea. We do nothing about it. I did have the cold comfort of knowing that I had behaved as a free man, an American. I cherished the thought. But I could not honestly pat myself on the back. My anger had been a reflex, not courage. Pride would not be much to chew on if it had got my wife and myself into a Soviet slave labor camp.

I began to listen for that knock on the door, the one you read about in *Darkness at Noon*, the knock that means your next address may be Vorkuta or Karaganda. The address doesn't matter. You are never, never going to receive mail.

My fears were not groundless. I'd read Philip Wylie's *The Innocent Ambassadors* and I knew what had happened to his brother. I vividly recalled Kravchenko's *I Chose Freedom*.

The knock never came because the political climate engendered by the new pravda was "more-in-sorrow-than-in-anger." The next morning, May 6, we were again ordered to report to the Director's office. We had decided to brazen it out. We refused to go. Presently, we were allowed to catch a plane for Tashkent.

Pravda lasted 12 days, until K. shattered the Summit and revealed a new pravda.

We arrived in Leningrad just as the news reached there that the Summit had failed and that President Eisenhower had cancelled his proposed trip to the USSR and that Khrushchev was returning to Moscow via East Berlin.

The climate suddenly turned very chilly.

A month earlier, in Moscow, we had been picked up by two Russians the very first time we went out on the street. One was a technical translator; the other, a lady, was a museum curator. They were very friendly and stayed with us almost three hours, asking questions about the U.S. and inviting questions about the Soviet Union. This happened to us daily thereafter; we were always making casual acquaintance with Soviet citizens, on the street, in parks, in restaurants, during intermissions at the theatre, everywhere. They were always curious about America, very friendly and extremely polite. This attitude on the part of individual Soviet citizens toward individual Americans continued throughout the first pravda, ending May 6. It lessened slightly during the "more-in-sorrow" second pravda.

K's Paris news conference set up a new pravda. From the time we reached Leningrad until we left for Helsinki, Finland, not one Soviet citizen other than Intourist employees—who had to deal with us professionally—spoke to us under any circumstances. Not one.

In dealing with Intourist it is always difficult to tell whether one's frustrations arise from horrendous red tape or from intentional obstructionism. In Leningrad it at once became clear that Intourist now just did not want to give service. Even the porter who took up our bags made trouble.

Our first afternoon we were scheduled to visit the Hermitage, one of the world's great art museums. The tour had been set with Intourist for that particular afternoon before we left the States.

At the appointed time our guide (you have to have one) had not arranged for a car. After awhile it whisked up and the guide said, "Now we will visit the stadium."

We said that we wanted to visit the Hermitage, as scheduled. The guide told us that the Hermitage was closed. We asked to be taken to another museum (Leningrad has many). We explained that we were not interested in seeing another stadium.

We visited the stadium.

That is all Intourist permitted us to see that afternoon.

When we got back to the hotel we found someone in our room, as always in Leningrad. Since maid service in Intourist hotels varies from non-existent to very ubiquitous we did not at once conclude that we were being intentionally inconvenienced. But one afternoon we found six men in our room, busy tearing out all the pipes and the question of intent became academic. A hotel room with its plumbing torn up and its floor littered with pipes and bits of wood and plaster is only slightly better than no hotel room at all.

We went to the ballet once in Leningrad. Intermissions are very long in Soviet theatres, about half an hour, and on earlier occasions these had been our most fruitful opportunity for meeting Russians.

Not now, not after K's Paris pravda. No one spoke to us. No Russian would even meet our eyes as we strolled past. The only personal attention we received that evening at the ballet was an unmistakably intentional elbow jab in the ribs from a Russian major in uniform. Be-Kind-To-Americans Week had adjourned, sine die.

How can the attitudes of 200 million people be switched on and off like a light bulb? How can one set of facts be made to produce three widely differing pravdas? By complete control of all communications from the cradle to the grave.

Almost all Soviet women work. Their babies are placed in kindergartens at an average age of 57 days, so we were told, and what we saw supported the allegation. We visited several kindergartens, on collective farms and in factories. By the posted schedules, these babies spend 13½ hours each day in kindergarten—they are with their mothers for perhaps an hour before bedtime.

At the Forty-Years-of-October Collective Farm outside Alma Ata some of the older children in one of the kindergartens put on a little show for us. One little girl recited a poem. A little boy gave a prose recitation. The entire group sang. The children were clean and neat, healthy and happy. Our guide translated nothing so, superficially, it was the sort of beguiling performance one sees any day in any American kindergarten.

However, my wife understands Russian:

The poem recounted the life of Lenin.

The prose recitation concerned the Seven-Year Plan.

The group singing was about how "we must protect our Revolution."

These tots were no older than six.

That is how it is done. Starting at the cradle, never let them hear anything but the official version. Thus "pravda" becomes "truth" to the Russian children.

What does this sort of training mean to a person when he is old enough, presumably, to think for himself? We were waiting in the Kiev airport, May 14. The weather was foul, planes were late and some 30 foreigners were in the Intourist waiting room. One of them asked where we were going and my wife answered that we were flying to Vilno.

Vilno? Where is that? My wife answered that it was the capital of Lithuania, one of the formerly independent Baltic republics which the USSR took over 20 years ago—a simple historic truth, as indisputable as the fact of the Invasion of Normandy or the bombing of Pearl Harbor.

But the truth is not pravda.

A young Intourist guide present understood English, and she immediately interrupted my wife, flatly contradicted her and asserted that Lithuania had *always* been part of the Soviet Union.

The only result was noise and anger. There was no possibility of changing this young woman's belief. She was telling the pravda the way she had been taught it in school and that was that. She had probably been about three when this international rape occurred. She had no personal memory of the period. She had never been to Vilno, although it is less than 400 miles from Kiev. (Soviet people do not travel much. With few exceptions the roads are terrible and the railroads are scarce. Russians are required to use internal passports, secure internal visas for each city they visit and travel by Intourist, just like a foreigner. Thus, traveling for pleasure, other than to designated vacation spots on the Black Sea, is almost unheard of.)

In disputing the official pravda we were simply malicious liars and she made it clear that she so considered us.

About noon on Sunday, May 15, we were walking downhill through the park surrounding the castle that dominates Vilno. We encountered a group of six or eight Red Army cadets. Foreigners are a great curiosity in Vilno. Almost no tourists go there. So they stopped and we chatted, myself through our guide and my wife directly, in Russian.

Shortly one of the cadets asked us what we thought of their new manned rocket. We answered that we had had no news lately—what was it and when did it happen?. He told us, with the other cadets listening and agreeing, that the rocket had gone up that very day, and at that very moment a Russian astronaut was in orbit around the earth—and what did we think of that?

I congratulated them on this wondrous achievement but, privately, felt a dull sickness. The Soviet Union had beaten us to the punch again. But later that day our guide looked us up and carefully corrected the story: The cadet had been mistaken, the rocket was not manned.

That evening we tried to purchase *Pravda*. No copies were available in Vilno. Later we heard from other Americans that *Pravda* was not available in other cities in the USSR that evening—this part is hearsay, of course. We tried also to listen to the Voice of America. It was jammed. We listened to some Soviet stations but heard no mention of the rocket.

This is the rocket the Soviets tried to recover and later admitted that they had had some trouble with the retrojets; they had fired while the rocket was in the wrong attitude.

So what is the answer? Did that rocket contain only a dummy, as the pravda now claims? Or is there a dead Russian revolving in space?—an Orwellian "unperson," once it was realized that he could not be recovered.

I am sure of this: At noon on May 15 a group of Red Army cadets were unanimously positive that the rocket was manned. That pravda did not change until later that afternoon.

Concerning unpersons—

Rasputin is a fairly well known name in America. I was unable to find anyone in Russia who would admit to having heard of him. He's an unperson.

John Paul Jones is known to every school child in America. After the American Revolution Catherine the Great called him to Russia where he served as an Admiral and helped found the Russian Navy, negligible up to that time. I tried many, many times to find a picture of him in Russian historical museums and I asked dozens of educated Russians about him—with no results. In Russian history John Paul Jones has become an unperson.

Trotsky and Kerensky are not unpersons yet. Too many persons are still alive who recall their leading roles in recent Russian history. But they will someday be unpersons, even though Dr. Kerensky is living today in California. In the USSR it is always tacitly assumed that the Communists overthrew the Tsar. This leaves no room for

Dr. Kerensky. If pinned down, a Soviet guide may admit that there was such a person as Kerensky, then change the subject. The same applies to Trotsky; his role, for good or bad, is being erased from the records. We saw literally thousands of pictures of Lenin, including several hundred group pictures which supposedly portrayed all the Communist VIP's at the time of the Revolution. Not one of these pictures shows Trotsky even though many of them were alleged to be news photos taken at the time when Lenin and Trotsky were still partners and buddies.

This is how unpersons are made. This is how pravda is created.

The theme of the May Day celebration this year was "Miru Mir": "Peace to the World." A sweet sentiment. But it isn't safe to assume that the dictionary definition of peace has any connection with the official Communist meaning, since even yesterday's pravda may be reversed tomorrow.

"Has it ever occurred to you that God might be a *committee*?"

—Jubal Harshaw

FOREWORD

"Don't Go To Russia If You Expect Tidy Toilets" is the heading on an article by H. Marlin Landwehr (Newspaper Enterprise Association) in the Santa Cruz Sentinel, *Sunday, December 2, 1979. "Russian toilets," writes Mr. Landwehr, "are uniformly filthy, with no toilet seats, coarse (if any) toilet paper, and extremely low pressure."*

From this and from many recent (1979) personal reports I know that my 1960 article "Inside Intourist" is still timely despite minor changes. Intourist still has three classes of travel: Bad—Worse—Horrible. These are now called: "Deluxe Suite, Deluxe, and First Class"—i.e., "First Class" is in fact third class—an Orwellian pravda.

Dirty toilets and bad food explain themselves; relative prices are harder to make clear, as the 1960 prices I cite as being outrageously high seem like bargain prices in 1979. So I must adjust for inflation, not too easy when dealing with four sorts of currency: 1) the 1960 dollar fully convertible to gold in the world market at $35 = 1 troy ounce of fine gold; 2) the 1979 floating dollar having today, 3 December 1979, a price per troy ounce of fine gold on the world market of $432 and some odd cents; 3) the 1960 western-tourist ruble, a currency not traded (= "blocked") in the world market, not convertible, not spendable outside its own country, and having its official rate set by decree and in direct consequence a very different black market (= free market) rate; and 4) the 3-Dec-79 western-tourist ruble, a blocked currency not equivalent to the 1960 western-tourist ruble.

To define the relationships between a fully-convertible gold currency, a floating currency, and two different blocked currencies is a task that causes headaches. The arithmetic is simple, the semantic problem is not, and it is further complicated by both conscious and subconscious personal attitudes. You may not "believe in" a gold standard, for example (and I readily concede the truth of the old saw that one cannot eat gold), but it does not matter what I believe or you believe, our floating dollar is now worth in gold whatever the rest of the world tells us it is worth, i.e., the price at which they will buy dollars or sell gold. The only yardstick I can apply to all four currencies is the troy ounce of fine gold (= 480 grains in both troy and avoirdupois, or 31.1035 grams in metric).

Since the ruble is not traded in the gold market, I must equate rubles first in dollars, then translate into gold. (This fiscal discussion is not my idea; our editor complained—correctly—that a much shorter discussion was unclear.) In 1960 the Kremlin-decreed rate was 4 rubles = $1.00 USA. Today Monday 3 December 1979 the Kremlin-decreed rate to U.S. tourists is 1 ruble = $1.52 USA.

Now to work—

In 1960 $1.00 USA equalled
$\frac{1}{35}$ tr. oz. Au = 13.715 grains =
0.888671+ grams gold,
and one ruble equalled $0.25, or
$\frac{1}{140}$ tr. oz. Au = 3.429 grains =
0.222167+ grams gold.

While on Dec. 3, 1979, $1.00 USA equalled
$\frac{1}{432}$ tr. oz. Au = 1.1111 ... grains =
0.071998+ grams gold,
and one ruble equalled $1.52 USA, or
0.003518+ tr. oz. Au = 1.7 grains =
0.109438+ grams gold.

—which doesn't tell us much, especially as the dollar floats and changes every day, and the ratio between the dollar and the U.S.-tourist ruble is by decree and subject to change without notice. In the following article I show all prices three ways: 1) 1960 prices; 2) 3-Dec-79 equivalent by world free-market conversion; and 3) 3-Dec-79 equivalent by Kremlin-decreed dollar/ruble ratio.

The conversion factor for the world free market is 432/35 = 12.343; the Kremlin-decreed conversion factor is 1520/250 = 6.08. You are free to believe either one or neither.

But the above still doesn't tell you very much as the floating dollar changes daily and the ruble/dollar ratio changes whenever the Kremlin changes it ... and you will not be reading this on December 3, 1979. But all is not lost; you can obtain and apply the conversion factors for the day you read this in the same fashion in which I did it:

For the world free-market conversion factor first get that day's gold fix from newspaper or radio, then divide by 35. For the Kremlin factor telephone a Soviet consulate or Intourist New York, get the current price of a ruble in dollars and cents, divide by 250. Then reach for your pocket calculator.

It would have been simpler to state that travel in USSR in 1960 was extremely, outrageously expensive—a planned swindle.

The Early Worm
Deserves the Bird

INSIDE INTOURIST

How to Break Even

(or Almost)

in the Soviet Union

To enjoy a thing requires that it be approached in the proper mood. A woman who has been promised a luxury suite at Miami Beach won't cheer at the thought of roughing it in the north woods, especially if her husband pulls this switch after the vacation has started.

But, with proper pre-conditioning, it is possible to enjoy anything—some people are addicted to parachute jumping. To experience the Soviet Union without first getting in the mood for it is too much like parachute jumping when the chute fails to open. The proper mood for the Soviet Union is that of the man who hit himself on the head with a hammer because it felt so good when he stopped.

This article assumes that you have already, for good and sufficient reasons, decided to visit the USSR, one good and sufficient reason being a wish to see for yourself this Communist paradise that Khrushchev has promised our grandchildren. But to set out for Russia in the holiday spirit in which you head for the Riviera, Las Vegas, or Rio is like going to a funeral for the ride.

You can avoid the worst shocks to your nervous system by knowing in advance that you are not going to get what you have paid for;

then you can soothe the residual nerve jangling with your favorite pacifier. I used small quantities of vodka—"small" by Russian standards, as Russians also use it to insulate themselves from the slings and arrows of outrageous fortune but they dose to unconsciousness. Drunks, passed out in public places, are more truly symbolic of the USSR than is the Hammer & Sickle.

My wife found methyl meprobamate (Equanil, Miltown) more useful. For you it might be yoga, or silent prayer, but, whatever it is, don't neglect it. Travel in the Soviet Union is not like travel anywhere else in the world. My wife and I have visited more than sixty countries on six continents, by freight ship, helicopter, dog sled, safari, jet plane, mule back, canal boat, etc.; as "seasoned travelers" these are our credentials. To visit the USSR we prepared by extensive reading and my wife learned the Russian language. Nevertheless, again and again we ran into surprises, difficulties, and maddening frustrations.

You can travel all through the Soviet Union without knowing a word of Russian—which will suit Khrushchev just fine because you will thereby be a prisoner of "Intourist," the state-owned travel bureau, seeing only what they want you to see, hearing only what they want you to hear.

But the Russian language is difficult; it took my wife two years of hard work to master it. The alphabet is weirdly strange, the pronunciation is hard for us, and the language is heavily inflected—a proper noun, such as "Smith" or "Khrushchev," has eighteen different forms.

Obviously most tourists can't take two years off to master Russian. What then? Depend entirely on Intourist guides?

No, no, no! Better to save your money and stay home. With no Russian at all you'll be as helpless as a bed patient. Instead you should prepare by learning a smattering of Russian. Forget about grammar; grammatical Russian is found only in formal literary compositions. Khrushchev has never learned to speak Russian well and Mikoyan speaks it with an accent thick enough to slice—so why should you worry?

First learn the alphabet, capitals and lower case, printed and written. This alone is half the battle. You can now find the men's room (or the ladies' room). The men's room is marked with "M" (for "muzhcheen," but think of "M" for "men") and the ladies' room is marked with a letter which looks like two capital K's, back to back: Ж. You are now past the greatest crisis confronting a traveler: finding the plumbing.

You now know many of the most useful Russian words just from knowing the alphabet. Hungry? Watch for a sign reading: "PEC-TOPAH." Sound it in your head as "restauran"—and it is!—the same word as in English save that the final "t" has been dropped.

There are hundreds of words which turn out to be the same as the English, or near enough. If you know French or German, your immediate vocabulary is further enriched, as, despite their boasts, Russian culture is very backward and most of their vocabulary for anything more complex than weeding a turnip patch has been borrowed from French, English, or German by converting the foreign word phonetically.

But don't stop with the alphabet; get a set of phonograph records for teaching Russian. Play them while following the lessons in the book—and play them without the book while bathing, shaving, cooking, gardening, etc. A few hours of this will pay off to the point where you will no longer be dependent on an Intourist guide; it will triple what you get out of a trip behind the Iron Curtain. For a few dollars in records and a little work you change it from a losing game into one in which your investment will be well repaid in education if not in pleasure.

But to get fun out of it, too, you must understand the Intourist game, play it, and win. Winning consists in outwitting the system so that you get more than they intend you to get; it does *not* mean fair value in the fashion (for example) that a traveler invariably gets his money's worth in any Scandinavian country. It is not possible to get fair value in the USSR; the game is rigged against the American tourist. But there are ways to minimize the expense and maximize the return while having quite a lot of fun.

All travel in the USSR is controlled at every point by Intourist; you must buy from it all travel, all automobile and guide service, all hotel rooms, all meals—or if you buy a meal not from Intourist you simply waste a meal already paid for.

You buy from Intourist at four rubles to the dollar—and you are licked from scratch as the value of the ruble is closer to forty to the dollar (which is the rate the Soviet government gives to favored visitors such as Asians they are trying to woo into the Communist camp).

You can cut costs by ordering cheap accommodations. Three grades are offered: Luxe, Tourist A, and Tourist B. A single man might risk Tourist B if he did not mind public toilets and baths of uncertain cleanliness, plus sharing sleeping space, dormitory style; a couple might risk Tourist A, which is supposed to be (but is not) equal to first-class travel elsewhere. But I cannot honestly urge anything short of "Luxe" class because even the best in Russia is often shockingly bad by our standards—bathrooms without baths, even hotels with no baths, tubs with no hot water, plumbing that is "quaint" or worse, poor cooking, dirty utensils, maddening waits. The lodging for Luxe class is often a huge and fantastically furnished suite, but a first-class double room & bath in any other country is more comfortable.

Luxe class costs $30 per day per person (3 Dec 79—Kremlin rate $182.40—World free-market rate $370.29) and includes lodging, meal coupons, and three hours of guide and automobile service per person (thus six hours for a couple)—if you get it. It does not include *any* train, plane, or bus fares. Add these in, plus round trip aircoach fares from New York, and a month in the Soviet Union will cost an American couple at least $4,500 (3 Dec 79—Kremlin rate $27,360.00—World rate $55,543.50), plus spending money and extras.

You will get at least twice as much for your money in any other part of Europe, but the real problem always is to get what you have paid for and Intourist has contracted to furnish you.

Start by realizing that Intourist is not really a travel service in the sense in which Thos. Cook or American Express is. It is a bureau of the Communist government and its function is to get those Yankee dollars in advance, channel you through a fixed route, then spill you out at the far end almost as ignorant of their country as when you started. P. T. Barnum's famous sign "*This Way to the Egress*" anticipated the basic Intourist principle: Get the sucker's money first, then get rid of him with the least trouble to the management.

So treat it as a game and don't fret when you lose. Try to get a good night's sleep—the bed may be awful but it will be quiet because there is almost no traffic—and try again the next day.

For example: the guide is not there to guide you, the guide is there to make sure that you see the stadium—so try not to see a stadium anywhere in the Soviet Union. Surely they have stadiums; any people so devoted to "Togetherness" have stadiums—how else could they display ten thousand people all doing physical jerks at once? (A "Spartakiad") But remember that your fixed cost is about $20 just to look at a stadium (with no football game thrown in) and that, in diverting you to the stadium, Intourist has kept you from seeing something of real interest, a factory, a slum area, or a school.

Stadiums haven't changed much since the Romans built the Colosseum; if you have seen Yankee Stadium, Soldiers' Field, or the Rose Bowl—or even the football stands of Podunk High—you've seen enough empty stadiums to last a lifetime. So refuse!

But the guide has orders that you *must* see the stadium; no other theory will account for the persistence with which all Intourist guides *insist* that you see the local stadium. If you manage to get in and out of the Soviet Union without visiting a stadium, award yourself the Order of Hero of Soviet Travel, First Class.

(We saw a lot of them—nobody had warned us.)

Each Intourist hotel has a place called the "Service Bureau." "Service" in this usage is an example of Communist semantics comparable to "co-existence," "peace-loving," "democratic," etc. Here most of your battles with Intourist will take place. Second only to the passed-out drunk, the most typical sight in the Soviet Union is an American tourist seated in a service bureau, his expression getting tighter as the weary, expensive minutes trickle away.

Intourist rarely uses the blunt refusal on this unhappy creature; instead the standard tactics are please-sit-down-and-wait-for-just-a-moment (which usually turns out to be at least an hour), I'm-sorry-but-the-Director-is-out (and won't return as long as *you* keep hanging around) come-back-later, (when the desk will be closed), and go-to-that-desk-at-the-far-end-of-the-room (where, after more delay and much consultation, you will be sent back to the desk from which you started).

When facing this, to get part of what you have paid for (and anything over 70% is a triumph, with 50% par for the course) you must stick to pre-planned defensive tactics and never, never, never lose your temper, or you will wind up a fit candidate for wet packs and sedation.

Their first weapon is politeness. You *must* resist this soporific politeness or you will not get anything.

First-Stage Defense: Be just as polite as they are—but utterly stubborn. Above all, *don't sit down when invited to.* If you do, this retires you from the game for an indefinite penalty period. Hold your ground, standing firmly against the desk and taking up as much space as possible—lean on it with hands spread wide to double your combat frontage. Say firmly and politely: "No, thank you, I'll wait right here"—then monopolize that desk and clerk, making it impossible for business to be transacted until Intourist has honored your contract on the point you have raised.

Keep talking. It does not matter what you say nor whether the clerk understands English—*keep talking!* Your purpose is to take that unit of Intourist out of the game until your request has been met, not with promises but with immediate action—whereas *their* purpose is to get *you* out of the game by persuading you to sit down away from the desk.

So hold your ground and be softly, politely stubborn. Usually someone with authority will arrive in a few minutes and satisfy your request.

Defense in Depth: Be prepared to simulate anger at any instant. It is much better to *pretend* to lose your temper *before* things have grown so unbearable that you actually do blow your top; it saves wear and tear on your ulcers and enables you to conduct your tactics more efficiently.

(And I must say a word on behalf of Intourist employees. About three quarters of them are young women, girls really. They are nice people, polite, harassed, overworked, and underpaid. They are prisoners of a system which automatically frustrates the traveler, and they are more imprisoned by it than you are, for you will escape (we hope) on the date set forth on your exit visa. They can't. These poor kids did not invent the silly red tape and mountains of useless paperwork and those in the lower ranks have no authority to vary from it. So don't be too harsh and try not to lose your temper in fact.)

But be prepared to simulate anger whenever the log jam does not break under the pianissimo tactics of the first-stage defense. When you refuse to sit down and wait, the clerk will sometimes turn away and ignore you.

It is then time to throw a fit.

You must (1) hold your blocking position, (2) make lots of noise, and (3) show that you are bitterly and righteously angry and cannot possibly be shut up short of complete satisfaction.

Keep shouting. It helps to cuss a bit and one all-purpose word will do: "*Borjemoi!*" This is a phonetic approximation of two words meaning "My God!"—which is merely an expression of disgust in this atheistic society. Another good phrase is "Yah Haw*chew*!" which is the abrupt way of saying "I want it!" (The polite idiom is "Mnyeh *Khaw*chettsuh.")

You can shout, "I want to see the Director!"—or, in Russian, "Yah *Khaw*chew veedyets Direktora!" She may possibly answer, "The Director's office (or desk) is over there," but she is more likely to give you what you want rather than let you complain to the boss.

But if she does, *don't move.* Hold your ground, keep on being unreasonable, and let the boss come to you. If you let them chivvy you into his office, away from spectators, and you yourself sitting down and being polite, you've lost that round. The Director will be polite, apologetic, and regretful about "shortages"—but firmly unhelpful. The place to win is in public.

For most of us it is not easy to be intentionally rude. I think one should never be impolite unnecessarily—but we can do much to uphold our national dignity and to improve our relations with the Soviet Union by never keeping quiet when we are cheated, by answering the great stubbornness of Russians by being twice as stubborn, and by being intentionally and loudly rude whenever Intourist refuses to keep its contract despite polite protest. Intourist is an integral part of a government with a forty-three year record (now 63 years—R.A.H.) of not honoring its most solemn commitments; one must assume that its blatant cheating is planned from the top and that every employee of Intourist is schooled in his role, right down to the sweet little girl who insists that you must see the stadium.

You may prefer to think that this horrendous swindle is merely an unintentional by-product of a fantastic, all embracing, and incredibly inefficient bureaucracy bogged down in its own red tape to the point where it can't give service. Either way, a contract with Intourist works exactly like that long list of broken treaties. You start by making a contract with the Soviet government; you are required to pay in advance and in full. Then you attempt to collect what you have paid for—and discover that a Communist contract is worth what it usually is. "Room with bath" turns out to be without, "jet planes" become prop planes, guide and auto service is less than half the time you have paid for, dining rooms are locked at meal hours, and your extremely expensive time is wasted sitting, sitting, sitting in "service" bureaus.

Unless you raise hell about it, right at the time. No use complaining later, you won't get your money back.

If neither polite stubbornness nor noisy rudeness will work, use the insult direct. Shake your finger in the face of the most senior official present, simulate extreme rage, and shout, "Nyeh Kuhl-*toor*nee!" ("Uncultured!") Hit that middle syllable and roll the r's.

Subordinates will turn a sickly green and pretend to be elsewhere. The official will come close to apoplexy—but will probably make an extreme effort to satisfy your demand in order to shut you up. This is the worst insult you can hand a Russian, one that hits him in cracks of his armor. *Use it only as a last resort.*

I do not think you will be in personal danger as the officials you will meet will probably not be high enough in the hierarchy to punish you for insulting them. But if anything goes wrong and you wind up in Siberia, *please understand that you use it at your own risk.*

If "nyeh kuhltoornee" does not work, I have nothing more to suggest but a hot bath and a sedative.

But the above campaign usually wins in the first or second stage and rarely fails in the third as it is based on Russian temperament and Communist social organization. Even the most arrogant Soviet citizen suffers from an inferiority complex when faced with free citizens of the western world, especially Americans. The questions they ask most frequently are: How much money do you make? How big is your house? Do you own an automobile? Each one is a dead give-away.

So if you make it clear that Intourist service is contemptible by free-world standards, a Russian may want to take a poke at you but he is much more likely to attempt to restore face by meeting those standards. The rest of the picture has to do with socialist "equality," another example of Communist semantics, because in the egalitarian paradise there is *no* equality, nowhere anything like the easy-going equality between an American taxi driver and his fare. In the USSR you are either on top or underneath—never even.

An American does not fit. Some Soviet citizens react by subordinating themselves to the tourist; grandmothers sweeping the streets will scurry out of your way, taxi drivers will rush to open doors, porters and waitresses and such are servile in a fashion we are not used to. But an employee of Intourist is in an indeterminate position vis-à-vis a tourist. Dominant? Or subordinate? It must be one or the other. Often there is a quick test of wills, then an immediate assumption of one role or the other depending on how the tourist responds. For example, we were met in Kiev by a guide who gave his name as "Sasha." I asked his surname; he told me quite arrogantly that there was no need for me to know it.

We had been in the USSR several weeks and I had had my fill of arrogance; I told him bluntly that I was not interested in his name, that I had asked out of politeness as practiced in all *civilized* countries—but that if good manners were not customary in his country, forget it!

An American or other free man might have given me a rough answer or icy silence; he did neither, he groveled. When he left us at the hotel he thanked us effusively for having been so kind as to talk with him. His manner was cringingly servile.

I don't like servility any more than the next American—but if there is going to be any groveling done it won't be by me. Nor, I hope, by you. In dealing with Intourist people you will often run into situations where one of you must knuckle under—and many are much tougher cases than this man. It will be a clash of will and all too often polite stubbornness won't be enough to get them to honor your contract—then you need to model your behavior after the worst temper tantrums you have seen Khrushchev pull on television; this they understand. In the USSR only a boss ever behaves that way; therefore you *must* be entitled to Red Carpet service. The Intourist functionary *knows* you are just an American tourist, to be frustrated and cheated, but his conditioned reflex bypasses his brain; a lifetime of conditioning tells him to kowtow to any member of the master class ... which you *must* be, even though his brain tells him you are not.

It usually works. In a bully-boy society often nothing but bullying will work.

The "Coupon Game": When you arrive you will be handed a lot of documents in exchange for your tour voucher; one will be a book of meal tickets, four coupons for each day. For Luxe class their values are twelve rubles for a breakfast coupon, twenty for a lunch, three for tea, thirty for dinner. If you and your spouse have contracted to spend a month in the USSR, your meal tickets have cost you one thousand dollars (3 Dec 79—Kremlin rate $6,080.00—World free-market $12,343.00) (28½ oz. of gold). The gouging starts here, because Diamond Jim Brady and his twin could not eat a thousand dollars of Intourist food in a month. Intourist eateries range from passable to very bad. Hotel Berlin in Moscow is perhaps the best but even it would have trouble making the Duncan Hines list. There are three or four good restaurants in the Soviet Union but their prices are *very* high and they won't accept coupons.

You can minimize your losses in ways that Intourist does not tell you. You can combine coupons as you wish—a "lunch" and a "breakfast" to pay for dinner, for example. The possible combinations in rubles are 3, 6, 9, 12, 15, 18, 20, 21, 23, 24, 26, 27, 29, 30, 32, 33, 35, 36, 38, and all higher numbers—but the hitch is that too many of them take more than one "tea" coupon. So figure out the best way to work each combination and write it on the back of your coupon book; this will help you to decide whether to overpay for food already horribly overpriced, or to pay the difference in cash. Skill in the coupon game can save you many, many dollars.

There is nothing fair in the coupon system but it isn't meant to be; it is the prime fashion in which the Soviet government squeezes more dollars out of American tourists than they want or need to spend.

There are other ways to reduce your losses. You can swap coupons for liquor, candy, canned caviar, cigarettes, and bottled water. Tap water in Moscow and Leningrad is said to be safe but elsewhere it is wise to buy mineral water—get enough bottles at a time to come out even in coupons. Their cigarettes are corrosive but a brand called "Trud" is smokable. Candy is extremely expensive but a welcome change in a tedious diet (I lost twelve pounds); caviar is cheap and is the best buy to use up leftover coupons on your last day. Don't expect to find whiskey nor any imported liquor, but local "kawnyahk" and "chahm-*pahn*skoyeh" are good. The vodka like ours is "*vawt*-kah stel*leech*na-yuh"—the other sorts are very highly spiced. Their wines are good.

My favorite relief from a hard day with Intourist was a Bloody Mary—"Staw grahm vawt-kee, p'jalst, ee taw*maht*nee sawk." This is "nyeh kuhltoornee" as the proper way to drink vodka is with beer (*pee*vaw), or with black bread, sweet butter, and caviar.

In Moscow and Leningrad very few Russian waiters speak English and almost none elsewhere, but you will usually be handed a huge four-language menu on which you can pick out what you want in English and point to it in Russian. But only the few items with prices written in are offered and maybe half of those will be available—when the waiter says "Nyeh-taw" he means it's all gone. Allow at least two hours for dinner; I've never heard of any way to speed up the service. But, once you are served, the waiter may try to rush you out, claiming that the table is reserved ten minutes hence for a delegation or such. He may simply want to sell food to someone else—he gets a commission. Ignore him—you've waited a long time, paid a high price in advance, and are entitled to eat in peace.

Pick a table as far from the orchestra as possible. Some orchestras are good but most are very loud and sound like a fully automated boiler factory.

Tipping is never necessary but waiters, chambermaids, and porters are paid very little. Tips can be coupons or cash.

The dining room is often locked—for a political delegation from Asia or Africa, for a traveling theatrical troupe, or anything. Any service may be chopped off without warning in any Intourist hotel. Complain ... but be prepared to fall back on the buffet (pronounced "*boof*-yet"). There are usually three or four on the upper floors of large hotels, open from seven a.m. to eleven at night and serving omelets, snacks, beer, wine, juice, coffee, tea, cakes, etc. The guides and clerks in Intourist often do not know about them because *they have never been upstairs*, so **watch for the sign (БУФЕТ)** or wander the corridors saying inquiringly to maids and floor clerks: "*Boof*-yet?"

Buffets are cozy, friendly, little places run by cheerful, helpful, dreadfully overworked women. They won't know English and the menu will be in Russian—here a memorandum in English & Russian of your favorite foods is most useful. But even the buffet doesn't serve breakfast before seven and Russian transportation often leaves at such an hour that you must leave the hotel before then. Russian hotels have room service but not at such hours. If you have your *own* thermos bottle, room service can fetch you hot coffee and a cold breakfast the night before. (They've heard of thermos bottles—the word is the same—but the hotel won't have one.)

Keep iron rations in your room and carry food and drink on long flights and train trips. Both trains and planes often stop for meals but you can't count on it and usually can't find out in advance.

Minor Ways to Improve Your Score: Go for walks without your guide; you will usually be picked up by someone who knows English—but you will never be picked up while a guide is with you. This is your chance to get acquainted and to get answers which are not the official answers. Don't talk politics—but these venturesome souls may ask you political questions and you can learn almost as much by the questions they ask as by raising such issues yourself.

Your guide may not be a hardshell Communist; he, or she, may open up once he thinks he can trust you. If so, be careful not to mention anything even faintly political when others are in earshot, *especially the driver.* The driver may be a political chaperone who knows English but pretends not to. More than one guide has told me this and *all* guides talk more freely when no one can overhear.

In this country children are brought to Moscow and decorated for having informed on their parents. *Never forget this.*

When you are shown a party headquarters, a palace of culture, a stadium, an auditorium, or such, ask when it was built. We discovered that, in the areas not occupied by Nazis, many of the biggest and fanciest were built right at the time Americans were dying to keep the Murmansk lend-lease route open.

There is new brick construction all over the Soviet Union. We asked repeatedly to be shown a brick yard, were never quite refused, but the request was never granted. We have since heard a rumor that this is prison labor and that is why a tourist can't see something as unsecret as a brick yard. So try it yourself—you may merely prove to yourself that Intourist exists to keep tourists from seeing what they want to see, rather than vice versa.

Offer your passport to casual acquaintances; they will usually offer theirs in return—*internal* passports. Intourist people have been coached to deny that such a thing exists but everybody in the USSR carries one and the owner must get a visa to go from one Russian city to another. It is a brown book with "**ПАСПОРТ**" (passport) on the cover. Try it when your guide is not around.

The USSR is the only country in which we were never able to get into a private home. Other tourists report the same but one couple from Los Angeles almost cracked this; they said to their guide, "*Why* can't we see the inside of one of those apartment houses? Are you people *ashamed* of them?" The next day they were shown through a not-yet-occupied one.

This could be varied endlessly, as it works on that Russian basic, their inferiority complex. The key word is "ashamed"—simply asking "Why?" gets you nowhere. I think it could be used to get into farms, schools, courts, factories, anything not a military secret. It tops my list of things I wish I had thought of first.

In meeting anyone, including guides, try to use "democracies" as an antonym for "Communist countries" as soon as possible—drag it in by the heels, i.e., "I think all of us from the democracies earnestly hope for peace with the Communist countries," etc. The much abused word "democratic" means "Communist" in Russia and it always introduces a propaganda pitch. If you deny him his definition by preempting the word, you leave him with his mouth hanging open, unable to proceed.

We got tripped on this several times before we caught on.

The official list of things you must not photograph is short but the unofficial list is long and ranges from old, broken-down buildings to old, broken-down women sweeping the streets. You can photograph such by having them appear "accidentally" in a background but if you are suspected of this, they have a silent counter to it. At some later time you will find that your film has been exposed to light, then re-spooled. You could keep all your film with you at all times and hope to get it across the border … but such behavior might cause you to be arrested on suspicion of espionage, as one American tourist was this summer. At best, sneaking a picture of one passed-out drunk risks losing *all* your pictures—too high a price even if you aren't accused of being a spy.

The most-used plane, the Ilyushin-14, flies very low; you can see a lot and compare it with elsewhere. Are railroads single or double track? How much traffic on the roads? On the rivers? How about factory smokestacks and other signs of industry? How busy are the airfields? Or a dozen other things. I think you will conclude that no Russian claim should be accepted as true until fully verified. A "great industrial center" often turns out to be a jerkwater town.

But don't make written notes about such things! *Don't!!!*

Will your mail be opened? You must assume so. Will your rooms be bugged? If seems impossible to monitor every room of every In-tourist hotel—but if the police get interested in *you* it takes just three minutes in these days of miniaturization to bug a room. I do know, from several incidents, that Soviet citizens *believe* that all hotel rooms are bugged.

I wish that a million of us would visit the USSR; the dollars the Kremlin would reap would be more than offset by the profit to us in having so many free men see with their own eyes what Communism is.

But go there with your eyes open—Intourist is as fully an agency of the Kremlin as is Gromyko or Mikoyan. Its functions are (1) to get your money in advance, (2) to deliver as little as possible by down-grading accommodations, by forced overcharges on food, and by clip-ping you on auto and guide service, (3) to waste your time so that you will see as little as possible, and (4) to see that what little time you have left is spent only on those things the Kremlin does not mind your seeing—"new construction" (from the outside), parks of "rest & culture" (filled with loudspeakers blaring propaganda), ballets, muse-ums, stadiums, and the outsides of public buildings.

The first point you must accept; the game is crooked but it is the only game in town. Points two and three you can struggle against—I hope the tactics suggested in here will help. Point four is the toughest. After trimming you down to about three hours a day of useful time, Intourist can and will use up what is left in "stadium sightseeing" unless you fight it constantly. Even then, Intourist is adept in parrying with: "It's closed today—too bad you're not staying another day," and "That must be arranged in advance through the Ministry of Culture, etc." and "You should have requested that in Moscow."

The essence of Intourist tactics is: "Jam yesterday and jam tomorrow, but never jam today." The way to answer it is: "No! I will *not* look at the stadium, I do *not* want to see another subway station, I will *not* visit a museum to see another five hundred pictures of Lenin. I want to see thus-and-so and I want to see it *now*. Stop the car, get on the phone, and arrange it—or tell the Director that, as far as I am concerned, you're fired! I am keeping the car and the driver and will go on without you—I've got hours more of car service due me today and I *won't* be cheated out of it."

You will find whether your guide is truly a guide ... or a guard placed with you to make sure you see only the facade of this regime. Whether or not you see "thus-and-so" you are sure to learn a surprising amount about how a police state is run ... and thereby get your full money's worth in education.

AFTERWORD

After twenty years it would seem logical for me to return to the USSR to see what improvements, if any, they have made in handling tourism. I could plead age and health but I shan't—one trip to the USSR is educational; twice is masochism.

If you have been to the USSR recently and if you know enough Russian that you could and did slip the leash occasionally and poke around and get acquainted without permission of Intourist, please write to me and tell me about it—what you saw with your own eyes, what you touched, what you counted, how you were treated. I am not interested in second-hand reports, not even from other Americans you trust, and I most emphatically am not interested in anything *your guides told you.*

If you know no Russian and took one of the standard Intourist trips—around the Black Sea, or the Leningrad-Moskva-Sochi trip—don't waste your time writing. I hope you had fun.

If you took the long railway trip, Vladivostok to Leningrad or Moskva—or vice versa—do please *write to me. If you knew no Russian at first, I'm betting high odds that you spoke fluent (if ungrammatical) Russian long before you completed the trip. You will know many things I don't know as I have never been across Siberia. Alma Ata, KSSR, north of the Himalayas and just short of Sinkiang, is as far as I got.*

Concerning believing what you see and ignoring reports: *In thirty-odd years of habitual travel, Mrs. Heinlein and I have not been simply sightseeing; we have been studying other people's ways. Sometimes trivia—e.g., in Peru they make* far *better apple pie than Mom ever baked (treason!), Chile has us beat all hollow when it comes to ice-cream sodas,* *and the Finnish ice-cream cone is a work of art that makes what we call an ice-cream cone look sad.*

But usually we are dead serious. Lately I've been making a global survey of blood services—but that is another story. Two things we have done consistently throughout the world: 1) See the slums; 2) evaluate the diet.

The fancy hotels and the museums and the parks are much the same the world over—but the slums are honest criteria even though a traveller can't assign a numerical value. The street people of Bombay and of Calcutta tell far more about India than does the glorious Taj Mahal.

Two other questions give direct, numerical comparisons: Q: How many long tonnes of protein (meat, fish, cheese) does this country consume in one year? (Then, privately, divide by the population.) Q: How many minutes must a journeyman carpenter work to earn enough to buy one kilogram of the local standard bread?

The first question tells the quality of the average diet; the second tells you how rich (or poor) that country averages. If you have also managed to see the slums, you have some idea of the range of wealth. You can't tell by looking at the extremely wealthy; all over the world they are careful to dress like upper middle class, no higher. But slums are honest and the most extreme wealth range is to be found in India.

The range of personal wealth in Russia, in 1960, was high, possibly greater than the range in the U.S.A. But the range showed in "perks," not in money—privately-assigned automobiles and chauffeurs, summer houses, assigned living quarters. The Latvian Secretary (a Russian, not a Lett) of the Writers Union had as his offices a marble palace, extremely ornate inside and outside and loaded with sculpture and paintings (built—I was told—by the late Tsar for his favorite mistress. True? I don't know but I've never been in a more lavish palace and I have been in many). After meeting his colleagues—and living through a Russian drinking duel better left undescribed—we were taken by him out to the Baltic and shown his dacha ... thereby showing us that he had a private car, a chauffeur, and a summer home, as well as offices literally fit for a king. No mention of money, no need to—I was convinced that he was not going home to a meal of black bread, potatoes, and boiled cabbage.

Yet he was merely writer boss in Latvia, a small captive country—not General Secretary of the Writers Union in Moskva. I was in the Writers Union general headquarters in Moskva, a large office building; I did not meet the General Secretary. I assume that he lived at least as well as his stooge in Latvia.

How many levels are there between this minor boss in Riga and the members of the Praesidium? How well does Khrushchev—excuse me; Brezhnev—live? I shan't guess.

In the USSR it was not politic (risky) to ask the two key questions that I always asked in other countries, and seeing slums was forbidden. Twice we saw slums by accident, were hurried on past—primitive log cabins just outside Moskva, 1st century mud huts in Alma Ata that were concealed by screening but from one elevation we could see over the screening ... until we were seen and cautioned not to stop there and not to take pictures.

Since we couldn't ask our standard comparison questions, Mrs. Heinlein devised some "innocent" ones, and I concentrated on certain signs; both of us were sizing up population. At that time the USSR claimed a population of 225,000,000 and claimed a population for Moskva of 5,000,000+. (Today, twenty years later, they claim almost 300,000,000 and over 7,000,000.)

For many days we prowled Moskva—by car, by taxi when we did not want Intourist with us, by subway, by bus, and on foot. In the meantime Mrs. Heinlein, in her fluent Russian, got acquainted with many people— Intourist guides, drivers, people who picked us up on the streets, chambermaids, anyone. The Russians are delightful people, always happy to talk with visitors, in English if they know it (and many do), in Russian if they do not.

Let me add that, if it suited her, Ginny could charm pictures off a wall.

She was able to ask personal questions (but ones people anywhere usually are pleased to answer) by freely answering questions about us and showing warm interest in that person—not faked; she is a warm person.

But, buried in chitchat, she always learned these things:

How old are you?

Are you married?

How many children do you have?

How many brothers and sisters do you have? What ages?

How many nieces and nephews do you have?

Put baldly, that sounds as offensive as a quiz by a Kinsey reporter. But it was not put baldly—e.g., "Oh, how lucky you are! Gospodin Heinlein and I didn't even meet until the Great Patriotic War ... and we have no children although we wanted them. But we have lots of nieces and neph-ews." Etc., etc. She often told more than she got but she accumulated, pain-lessly, the data she wanted, often without asking questions.

One day we were seated on a park bench, back of the Kremlin and facing the Moskva river, with no one near us—a good spot to talk; a direc-tional mike would have to be clear across the river as long as we kept our backs to the Kremlin.

I said, "How big does that guide book say this city is?"

"Over five million."

"Hmmph! Look at that river. Look at the traffic on it." (One lonely scow—) "Remember the Rhine?" We had taken a steamer up the Rhine three years earlier; the traffic was so dense the river had traffic lights on it, just like the Panama Canal. "Ginny, this dump isn't anything like five million. More the size of Copenhagen, if that. Pittsburgh. New Orleans. San Francisco, possibly." (These are all cities I know well, on foot and by every form of transportation. In 1960 all of them were in the 600,000-800,000 range.) "Yet they are trying to tell us that this dump is bigger than Philadelphia, bigger than Los Angeles, bigger than Chicago. Nonsense."

(I have lived in all three cities. A big city feels big, be it Yokohama or New York.) "Three quarters of a million, not five million."

"I know," she agreed.

"Huh?"

(I think I must mention that Mrs. Heinlein is a close student of Rus-sian history, history of the Russian Revolution, history of the Third Inter-national or Comintern, and so skilled in Marxist dialectical materialism that she can argue theory with a Russian party member and get him so mixed up that he's biting his own tail.)

She answered, "They claim to have finished the War with about two hundred million and Moscow at four million. Now they are claiming twenty-five million more in the Union, and over a million increase in Moscow." She thought a bit. "It's a lie. Unless they are breeding like flies everywhere outside Moscow, they have lost population since the War—not gained. I haven't found even one family with more than three children. The average is less than two. And they marry late. Robert, they aren't even replacing themselves."

She looked at that empty river. "Not quite as big as Copenhagen is my guess."

161

We stopped in many other cities—Alma Ata, Tashkent, Samarkand, Minsk, Vilno, Kiev, Riga, Leningrad, etc.—and she continued her gentle questioning but never found reason to change her opinion. Even out in the Muslim countries of Turkestan the birthrate was low, or the answers seemed to show it. She did not write down her figures (Well, I don't think she did; I warned her not to) but she has a memory that is effectively perfect as long as necessary ... then she can wash out useless details, which I can't do.

How was it possible for the Russians to claim that Moscow was seven times as big as it actually was? How could I be right and the whole world wrong? The World Almanac gave the same figures the Russians did, all news services seemed to accept Russian population figures—how could a Big Lie that big not be noticed—and denounced?

About a year later I had a chance to discuss it with an old shipmate, an admiral now retired but then holding a major command. I asked him how many people there were in Moscow.

He answered, "I don't know. Why don't you look it up?" (When a high brass answers, "I don't know," he may mean, "Don't be nosy and let's change the subject." But I persisted.)

"Make a guess. You must have some idea."

"Okay." He closed his eyes and kept quiet for several minutes. "Seven hundred and fifty thousand, not over that."

(Jackpot!)

I said, "Mister Ought Ought Seven, have you made a special study of Russia? Or shouldn't I ask?"

"Not at all. [His command] gives me all the trouble I need without worrying about Russia. I simply worked it as a logistics problem, War College style. But I had to stop and visualize the map first. Roads, rivers, railroads, size of marshalling yards, and so forth. You know." (I did, vaguely. But I wasn't a War College graduate. He is.) "That city just doesn't have the transportation facilities to be any bigger than that. Get much over three quarters of a million and they'd starve. Until they double their tracks and increase their yards they can't risk a bigger population. You don't do that over night. They can pick up some slack with the river—but it doesn't go where they need it most."

And there it stands. Either all three of us are crazy despite the fact that all three of us got the same answer to a numerical question using three en-

tirely different but logical methods … or for many, many years the Krem-lin lie factory has peddled their biggest and fanciest "Pravda" without ever being questioned.

Look—both the Pentagon and the State Department know exactly how big Moscow is, and the Kremlin knows that they know. We were high-flying 'em with the U-2 for four years; you can bet Moscow was care-fully photographed many times. Our present Eye-in-the-Sky satellites are so sharp-eyed that they can come close to reading the license plate on your car; our top officials know precisely what the logistics situation is for Mos-cow—and every economist knows that one of the parameters that controls strictly the upper limit to the size of a city is how many tons of food it can ship in, week in and week out, never failing. Most big cities are only a day or two away from hunger, only a week or so away from beginning starva-tion and panic.

Moscow isn't even a seaport; she's a riverport and not a good one. Most food must come overland by train or lorry.

Maybe she's built enough more facilities since 1960 … but in 1960 she just didn't have what it takes. Since I can't believe the 5,000,000+ figure for 1960, I don't believe the 7,000,000+ figure for this year.

I have one very wild theory. Our State Department may see no ad-vantage in calling them liars on this point. Through several administra-tions we have been extremely careful not to hurt their feelings. I think this is a mistake … but I am neither president nor secretary of state; my opinion is not important and may be wrong.

("'But the Emperor is not wearing any clothes,' said the child.")

The three biggest lies in the USA
today:
1) The check is in the mail.
2) I gave at the office.
3) [Big, cheery smile] "Hello!
I'm from Washington.
I'm here to help you!"

—Anon.

FOREWORD

In April 1962 I received a letter from the advertising agents of Hoff-
man Electronics: They had a wonderful idea—SF stories about electronics,
written by well-known SF writers, just long enough to fill one column of
Scientific American *or* Technology Review *or such, with the other two*
thirds of the page an ad for Hoffman Electronics tied into the gimmick of
the story. For this they offered a gee-whiz word rate—compared with SF
magazines.

A well-wrought short story is twice as hard to write as a novel; a
short-short is at least eight times as hard—but one that short ... there are
much easier ways of making a living. I dropped them a postcard saying,
*"Thanks but I'm busy on a novel." (True—*Glory Road*)*

They upped the ante. This time I answered, "Thanks and I feel flat-
tered—but I don't know anything about electronics." (Almost true.)

They wrote back offering expert advice from Hoffman's engineers on
the gimmick—and a word rate six times as high as The Saturday Evening Post *had paid me.*

I had finished Glory Road; *I sat down and drafted this one—then*
sweated endlessly to get it under 1200 words as required by contract.
Whereas I had written Glory Road *in 23 days and enjoyed every minute*
of it. This is why lazy writers prefer novels.

* * *

ON THIS SITE
THE AFTERNOON OF JUNE 5TH, 1834
NOTHING OF ANY IMPORTANCE HAPPENED

SEARCHLIGHT

"**W**ill she hear you?"

"If she's on this face of the Moon. If she was able to get out of the ship. If her suit radio wasn't damaged. If she has it turned on. If she is alive. Since the ship is silent and no radar beacon has been spotted, it is unlikely that she or the pilot lived through it."

"She's got to be found! Stand by, Space Station. Tycho Base, acknowledge."

Reply lagged about three seconds, Washington to Moon and back. "Lunar Base, Commanding General."

"General, put every man on the Moon out searching for Betsy!"

Speed-of-light lag made the answer sound grudging. "Sir, do you know how big the Moon is?"

"No matter! Betsy Barnes is there somewhere—so every man is to search until she is found. If she's dead, your precious pilot would be better off dead, too!"

"Sir, the Moon is almost fifteen million square miles. If I used every man I have, each would have over a thousand square miles to search. I gave Betsy my best pilot. I won't listen to threats against him when he can't answer back. Not from anyone, sir! I'm sick of being told what to do by people who don't know Lunar conditions. My advice—my official advice, sir—is to let Meridian Station try. Maybe they can work a miracle."

The answer rapped back, "Very well, General! I'll speak to you later. Meridian Station! Report your plans."

—◈—

166

Elizabeth Barnes, "Blind Betsy," child genius of the piano, had been making a USO tour of the Moon. She "wowed 'em" at Tycho Base, then lifted by jeep rocket for Farside Hardbase, to entertain our lonely missile-men behind the Moon. She should have been there in an hour. Her pilot was a safety pilot; such ships shuttled unpiloted between Tycho and Farside daily.

After lift-off her ship departed from its programming, was lost by Tycho's radars. It was ... somewhere.

Not in space, else it would be radioing for help and its radar beacon would be seen by other ships, space stations, surface bases. It had crashed—or made emergency landing—somewhere on the vastness of Luna.

"Meridian Space Station, Director speaking—" Lag was unnoticeable; radio bounce between Washington and the station only 22,300 miles up was only a quarter second. "We've patched Earthside stations to blanket the Moon with our call. Another broadcast blankets the far side from Station Newton at the three-body stable position. Ships from Tycho are orbiting the Moon's rim—that band around the edge which is in radio shadow from us and from the Newton. If we hear—"

"Yes; yes! How about radar search?"

"Sir, a rocket on the surface looks to radar like a million other features the same size. Our one chance is to get them to answer ... if they can. Ultrahigh-resolution radar might spot them in months— but suits worn in those little rockets carry only six hours' air. We are praying they will hear and answer."

"When they answer, you'll slap a radio direction finder on them. Eh?"

"No, sir."

"In God's name, why *not*?"

"Sir, a direction finder is useless for this job. It would tell us only that the signal came from the Moon—which doesn't help."

"Doctor, you're saying that you might *hear* Betsy—and not know where she is?"

"We're as blind as she is. We hope that she will be able to lead us to her ... if she hears us."

"How?"

"With a laser. An intense, very tight beam of light. She'll hear it—"

"*Hear* a beam of light?"

"Yes, sir. We are jury-rigging to scan like radar—that won't show anything. But we are modulating it to give a carrier wave in radio frequency, then modulating that into audio frequency—and controlling that by a piano. If she hears us, we'll tell her to listen while we scan the Moon and run the scale on the piano—"

"All this while a little girl is *dying*?"

"Mister President—*shut up!*"

"*Who was THAT?*"

"I'm Betsy's father. They've patched me from Omaha. *Please*, Mr. President, keep quiet and let them work. I want my daughter back."

The President answered tightly, "Yes, Mr. Barnes. Go ahead, Director. Order anything you need."

In Station Meridian the Director wiped his face. "Getting anything?"

"No. Boss, can't something be done about that Rio Station? It's sitting right on the frequency!"

"We'll drop a brick on them. Or a bomb. Joe, tell the President."

"I heard, Director. They'll be silenced!"

"*Sh!* Quiet! Betsy—do you hear me?" The operator looked intent, made an adjustment.

From a speaker came a girl's light, sweet voice: "—to hear somebody! Gee, I'm glad! Better come quick—the Major is hurt."

The Director jumped to the microphone. "Yes, Betsy, we'll hurry. You've got to help us. Do you know where you are?"

"Somewhere on the Moon, I guess. We bumped hard and I was going to kid him about it when the ship fell over. I got unstrapped and found Major Peters and he isn't moving. Not dead—I don't think so; his suit puffs out like mine and I hear something when I push my helmet against him. I just now managed to get the door open." She added, "This can't be Farside; it's supposed to be night there. I'm in sunshine, I'm sure. This suit is pretty hot."

"Betsy, you must stay outside. You've got to be where you can see us."

She chuckled. "That's a good one. I see with my ears."

"Yes. You'll see us, with your ears. Listen, Betsy. We're going to scan the Moon with a beam of light. You'll hear it as a piano note. We've got the Moon split into the eighty-eight piano notes. When you hear one, yell, '*Now!*' Then tell us what note you heard. Can you do that?"

"Of course," she said confidently, "if the piano is in tune."

"It is. All right, we're starting—"

—◆—

"*Now!*"

"What note, Betsy?"

"E flat the first octave above middle C."

"This note, Betsy?"

"That's what I said."

The Director called out, "Where's that on the grid? In Mare Nubium? Tell the General!" He said to the microphone, "We're finding you, Betsy honey! Now we scan just that part you're on. We change setup. Want to talk to your Daddy meanwhile?"

"Gosh! Could I?"

"Yes indeed!"

Twenty minutes later the Director cut in and heard: "—of course not, Daddy. Oh, a teensy bit scared when the ship fell. But people take care of me, always have."

"Betsy?"

"Yes, sir?"

"Be ready to tell us again."

—◆—

"*Now!*" She added, "That's a bullfrog G, three octaves down."

169

"This note?"

"That's right."

"Get that on the grid and tell the General to get his ships up! That cuts it to a square ten miles on a side! Now, Betsy—we know *almost* where you are. We are going to focus still closer. Want to go inside and cool off?"

"I'm not too hot. Just sweaty."

Forty minutes later the General's voice rang out: "They've spotted the ship! *They see her waving!*"

AFTERWORD

In 1931 I was serving in Lexington *(CV-2). In March the Fleet held a war game off the coast of Peru and Ecuador; for this exercise I was assigned as radio compass officer. My principal duty was to keep in touch with the plane guards, amphibians (OL8-A), guarding squadrons we had in the air—i.e., the squadrons were carrier-based land planes; if one was forced to ditch, an amphibian was to land on the water and rescue the pilot.*

No radar in those days and primitive radio—the pilots of the plane guards were the only ones I could talk to via the radio compass. The fighters had dot-dash gear; the radio compass did not. To get a feeling for the limitations of those days, only 28 years after the Wright brothers' first flight, see my "The Man Who Was Too Lazy to Fail" in Time Enough For Love, *Putnam/Berkley/NEL.*

A radio compass depends on the directional qualities of a loop antenna. To talk you rotate the antenna for maximum signal; turn it 90° and you get a minimum signal that marks the direction of the other radio—or 180° from it but you are assumed to know whether your beacon is ahead or behind you—and you do in almost every case where it matters, such as going up a channel in a fog. That minimum will tell you direction within a degree or two if the other radio is close enough, loud enough.

If it's too far away, the signal can fade to zero before you reach the bearing you need to read, and stay zero until well past it. No use turning it back 90° to try to locate it by the maximum signal; that curve is much too flat.

Late afternoon the second day of the exercise we were in trouble; the other squadrons were landing but VF-2 squadron was lost—all too easy with one-man fighter planes before the days of radar. The captain of the squadron, a lieutenant commander, held one opinion; the pilot of the amphib held another—but his opinion did not count; he was a j.g. and not part of the squadron. The juniors in the squadron hardly had opinions; they were young, green, and depending on their skipper—and probably had fouled up their dead reckoning early in the flight.

The squadron captain vectored for rendezvous with the carrier, by his reckoning. No carrier. Just lots and lots of ocean. (I was in the air once, off Hawaii, when this happened. It's a lonely feeling.)

No sign of the U.S. Fleet. No Saratoga *(CV-3), no battleships, no cruisers. Not even a destroyer scouting a flank. Just water.*

At this point I found myself in exactly the situation described in "Searchlight"; I could talk to the plane guard pilot quite easily—but swing the loop 90° and zero signal was spread through such a wide arc that it meant nothing ... and, worse, the foulup in navigation was such that there was no rational choice between the two lobes 180° apart.

And I had a personal interest not as strong as that of Betsy Barnes' father but strong. First, it was my duty and my responsibility to give that squadron a homing vector—and I couldn't do it; the equipment wasn't up to it. Had I kept track of vectors on that squadron all day—but that was impossible; not only had I had four squadrons in the air all day and only one loop but also (and damning) there was war-game radio silence until the squadron commander in trouble was forced to break it.

But, second, the pilot of the plane guard was my closest friend in that ship—from my home town, at the Academy with me, shipmates before then in USS Utah, *shore-leave drinking companion, only other officer in the ship who believed in rocketry and space flight and read "those crazy magazines." My number-one pal—*

And I was forced to tell him: "Bud, you're either somewhere northeast of us, give or take twenty or thirty degrees, or somewhere southwest, same wide range of error, and signal strength shows that you must be at least fifty miles over the horizon, probably more; I've got no way to scale the reception."

Bud chuckled. "That's a lot of ocean."

"How much gas do you have?"

"Maybe forty minutes. Most of the fighters don't have as much. Hold the phone; the skipper's calling me."

So I tried again for a minimum—no luck—swung back. "Lex loop to Victor Fox Two guard."

"Gotcha, boy. Skipper says we all ditch before the sun goes down. First I land, then they ditch as close to me as possible. I'll have hitchhikers clinging to the float all night long—be lucky if they don't swamp me."

"What sea?"

"Beaufort three, crowding four."

"Cripes. No white water here at all. Just long swells."

"She'll take it, she's tough. But I'm glad not to have to dead-stick a galloping goose. Gotta sign off; skipper wants me, it's time. Been nice knowing you."

So at last I knew—too late—which lobe they were in, as it was already dark with the suddenness of the tropics where I was, whereas the sun was still to set where they were. That eliminated perhaps five hundred square miles. But it placed them still farther away ... which added at least a thousand square miles.

Suddenly out of the darkness endless searchlights shot straight up; the Fleet C-in-C had canceled war-condition darken-ship rather than let Victor Fox Two ditch—which was pretty nice of him because all those battleship admirals were veterans of World War One, not one of them had wings, and (with no exceptions worth noting) they hated airplanes, did not believe that planes were good for anything but scouting (if that), and despised pilots, especially those who had not attended the Academy (i.e., most of them).

I was still listening on Bud's frequency and heard some most prayerful profanity. At once Bud had a bearing on the battle line; our navigator had our bearing and distance to the battle line; my talker to the bridge gave me the course and distance VF-2 needed to home on, and I passed it to Bud. End of crisis—

—but not quite the end of tension. The squadron just barely had enough gas to get home, and more than half of those pilots had never checked out on night carrier landings ... with no margin of fuel to let the landing officer wave a man off for poor approach if there was any possible chance that his tail hook could catch a wire. I am happy to report that every pilot got down safely although one did sort of bend his prop around the crash barrier.

Bud did almost have to make a dead-stick landing with a galloping goose. As he was the only one who could land on water if necessary, he had

173

to come in last ... and his engine coughed and died just as his tail hook caught the wire.

In one of Jack Williamson's stories a character goes back in time and makes a very slight change in order to effect a major change in later history.

Bud is Albert Buddy Scoles, then a lieutenant (junior grade), now a retired rear admiral, and is the officer who in 1942 gathered me, Isaac Asimov, and L. Sprague de Camp into his R&D labs at Mustin Field, Philadelphia, later solicited help from all technically trained SF writers and, still later, just after World War Two, set up the Navy's first guided missile range at Point Mugu.

I do not assume that history would have changed appreciably had VF-2 been forced to ditch.

But let's assume a change in Buddy Scoles' career just sufficient that he would not have been in charge of those labs on 7 December 1941. It would not have to be his death—although he was in far greater danger than his cheerful attitude admitted. An amphibian of that era did not necessarily make a safe landing on the high seas, and the galloping goose was an awkward beast at best—hard to see out of it in landing. Assume a minor injury in landing, or several days' exposure to tropical sun—that's a big ocean; they would not necessarily have been picked up the next day or even that week.

Assume any one change that would have affected the pattern of Buddy Scoles' career enough to place him elsewhere than at Mustin Field December 1941:

Now let's take it in small, not in terms of history:

I would not have been at Mustin Field. I can't venture to guess where I would have been; the Navy Bureau of Medicine was being stuffy over my past medical history. I would not have met my wife; therefore I would have died at least ten years ago ... and I would not be writing this book. (All high probabilities. Among the low probabilities is winning the Irish Sweepstakes and moving to Monaco.)

Sprague de Camp would not have been at Mustin Field. He was already headed for a Naval commission but at my suggestion Scoles grabbed him. Perhaps he would have died gloriously in battle ... or he might have sat out the war in a swivel chair in the Navy Department.

But now I reach the important one. I practically kidnapped Isaac Asimov from Columbia University, where he was a graduate student bucking for his doctorate.

You can write endless scenarios from there. The Manhattan District is recruiting exceptionally bright graduate students in chemistry and physics; Isaac is grabbed and the A-bomb is thereby finished a year sooner. Or he stays on at Columbia, finishes his doctorate, and his draft board never does pick him up because he is already signed as an assistant professor at N.Y.U. the day he is invested. Etc., etc.

Here comes the rabbit—The first two books of the Foundation series (Foundation, Bridle and Saddle, The Big and the Little, The Wedge, Dead Hand, The Mule) *were written while Isaac was a chemist in the labs at Mustin Field.*

What would the Good Doctor have written during those years had I not fiddled with his karma? Exactly the same stories? Very similar stories? Entirely different stories? (Any scenario is plausible except one in which Dr. Asimov does no writing at all.)

All I feel sure of is that there is an extremely high probability that an almost–too–late decision by a battleship admiral in 1931 not only saved the lives of some fighter pilots whose names I do not know ... but also almost certainly changed the lives of Admiral Scoles, myself, L. Sprague de Camp, Dr. Asimov and, by direct concatenation, the lives of wives, sweethearts, and offspring—and quite a major chunk of modern science fiction. (Had Scoles not called me back to Philadelphia I think I would have wound up in a Southern California aircraft factory, and possibly stayed with it instead of going back to writing ... and helped build Apollo-Saturn. Maybe.)

If you think "Searchlight" derives from an incident off Ecuador, you may be right. Possibly I dredged it out of my subconscious and did not spot it until later.

FOREWORD

On 5 April 1973 I delivered the James Forrestal Memorial Lecture to the Brigade of Midshipmen at my alma mater the United States Naval Academy. As the first half of the lecture, at the request of the midshipmen, I discussed freelance writing. This is the second half:

"'Cooperate with the inevitable'
means 'Roll with the punch'—
it does not mean stooling
for the guards."

—L. Long

THE PRAGMATICS OF PATRIOTISM

In this complex world, science, the scientific method, and the consequences of the scientific method are central to everything the human race is doing and to wherever we are going. If we blow ourselves up we will do it by misapplication of science; if we manage to keep from blowing ourselves up, it will be through intelligent application of science. Science fiction is the only form of fiction which takes into account this central force in our lives and futures. Other sorts of fiction, if they notice science at all, simply deplore it—an attitude very chichi in the anti-intellectual atmosphere of today. But we will never get out of the mess we are in by wringing our hands.

Let me make one flat-footed prediction of the science-fiction type. Like all scenarios this one has assumptions—variables treated as constants. The primary assumption is that World War Three will hold off long enough—ten, twenty, thirty years—for this prediction to work out … plus a secondary assumption that the human race will not find some other way to blunder into ultimate disaster.

Prediction: In the immediate future—by that I mean in the course of the naval careers of the class of '73—there will be nuclear-powered, constant-boost spaceships—ships capable of going to Mars and back in a couple of weeks—and these ships will be armed with Buck-Rogersish death rays. Despite all treaties now existing or still to be signed concerning the peaceful use of space, these spaceships will be used in warfare. Space navies will change beyond recognition our present methods of warfare and will control the political shape of the

177

world for the foreseeable future. Furthermore—and still more important—these new spaceships will open the Solar System to colonization and will eventually open the rest of this Galaxy.

I did *not* say that the United States will have these ships. The present sorry state of our country does not permit me to make such a prediction. In the words of one of our most distinguished graduates in his *The Influence of Sea Power on History*: "Popular governments are not generally favorable to military expenditures, however necessary—"

Every military officer has had his nose rubbed in the wry truth of Admiral Mahan's observation. I first found myself dismayed by it some forty years ago when I learned that I was expected to maintain the ship's battery of USS *Roper* in a state of combat readiness on an allowance of less than a dollar a day—with World War Two staring down our throats.

The United States is capable of developing such spaceships. But the mood today does not favor it. So I am unable to predict that *we* will be the nation to spend the necessary R&D money to build such ships.

(Addressed to a plebe midshipman:)

Mister, how long is it to graduation?

Sixty-two days? Let's make it closer than that. I have ... 7.59, just short of eight bells. Assuming graduation for ten in the morning that gives ... 5,320,860 seconds to graduation ... and I have less than 960 seconds in which to say what I want to say.

(To the Brigade at large:)

Why are you here?

(To a second plebe:)

Mister, why are *you* here?

Never mind, son; that's a rhetorical question. You are here to become a naval officer. That's why this Academy was founded. That is why all of you are here: to become naval officers. If that is *not* why *you* are here, you've made a bad mistake. But I speak to the overwhelming majority who understood the oath they took on becoming midshipmen and look forward to the day when they will renew that oath as commissioned officers.

But why would anyone want to become a naval officer?

In the present dismal state of our culture there is little prestige attached to serving your country; recent public opinion polls place military service far down the list.

It can't be the pay. No one gets rich on Navy pay. Even a 4-star admiral is paid much less than top executives in other lines. As for lower ranks the typical naval officer finds himself throughout his career just catching up from the unexpected expenses connected with the last change of duty when another change of duty causes a new financial crisis. Then, when he is about fifty, he is passed over and retires ... but he can't really retire because he has two kids in college and one still to go. So he has to find a job ... and discovers that jobs for men his age are scarce and usually don't pay well.

Working conditions? You'll spend half your life away from your family. Your working hours? "Six days shalt thou work and do all thou art able; the seventh the same, and pound on the cable." A forty-hour week is standard for civilians—but not for naval officers. You'll work that forty-hour week but that's just a starter. You'll stand a night watch as well, and duty weekends. Then with every increase in grade your hours get longer—until at last you get a ship of your own and no longer stand watches. Instead you are on duty twenty-four hours a day ... and you'll sign your night order book with: "In case of doubt, do not hesitate to call me."

I don't know the average week's work for a naval officer but it is closer to sixty than to forty. I'm speaking of peacetime, of course. Under war conditions it is whatever hours are necessary—and sleep you grab when you can.

Why would anyone elect a career which is unappreciated, over-worked, and underpaid? It can't be just to wear a pretty uniform. There has to be a better reason.

As one drives through the bushveldt of East Africa it is easy to spot herds of baboons grazing on the ground. But not by looking at the ground. Instead you look up and spot the lookout, an adult male posted on a limb of a tree where he has a clear view all around him—which is why you can spot him; he has to be where he can see a leopard in time to give the alarm. On the ground a leopard can catch a baboon ... but if a baboon is warned in time to reach the trees, he can out-climb a leopard.

The lookout is a young male assigned to that duty and there he will stay, until the bull of the herd sends up another male to relieve him.

Keep your eye on that baboon; we'll be back to him.

Today, in the United States, it is popular among self-styled "intellectuals" to sneer at patriotism. They seem to think that it is axiomatic that any civilized man is a pacifist, and they treat the military profession with contempt. "Warmongers"—"Imperialists"—"Hired killers in uniform"—you have all heard such sneers and you will hear them again. One of their favorite quotations is: "Patriotism is the last refuge of a scoundrel."

What they never mention is that the man who made that sneering wisecrack was a fat, gluttonous slob who was pursued all his life by a pathological fear of death.

I propose to prove that that baboon on watch is morally superior to that fat poltroon who made that wisecrack.

Patriotism is the most practical of all human characteristics.

But in the present decadent atmosphere patriots are often too shy to talk about it—as if it were something shameful or an irrational weakness.

But patriotism is *not* sentimental nonsense. Nor something dreamed up by demagogues. Patriotism is as necessary a part of man's evolutionary equipment as are his eyes, as useful to the race as eyes are to the individual.

A man who is *not* patriotic is an evolutionary dead end. This is not sentiment but the hardest sort of logic.

To prove that patriotism is a necessity we must go back to fundamentals. Take any breed of animal—for example, tyrannosaurus rex. What is the most basic thing about him? The answer is that tyrannosaurus rex is dead, gone, extinct.

Now take homo sapiens. The first fact about him is that he is not extinct, he is alive.

Which brings us to the second fundamental question: Will homo sapiens stay alive? Will he survive?

We can answer part of that at once: Individually h. sapiens will *not* survive. It is unlikely that anyone here tonight will be alive eighty years from now; it approaches mathematical certainty that we will all be dead a hundred years from now as even the youngest plebe here would be 118 years old then—if still alive.

Some men do live that long but the percentage is so microscopic as not to matter. Recent advances in biology suggest that human life may be extended to a century and a quarter, even a century and a half—but this will create more problems than it solves. When a man reaches my age or thereabouts, the last great service he can perform is to die and get out of the way of younger people.

Very well, as individuals we all die. This brings us to the second half of the question: Does homo sapiens *as a breed* have to die? The answer is: No, it is *not* unavoidable.

We have two situations, mutually exclusive: Mankind surviving, and mankind extinct. With respect to morality, the second situation is a null class. An extinct breed has *no* behavior, moral or otherwise.

Since survival is the sine qua non, I now define "moral behavior" as "behavior that tends toward survival." I won't argue with philosophers or theologians who choose to use the word "moral" to mean something else, but I do not think anyone can define "behavior that tends toward extinction" as being "moral" without stretching the word "moral" all out of shape.

We are now ready to observe the hierarchy of moral behavior from its lowest level to its highest.

The simplest form of moral behavior occurs when a man or other animal fights for his own survival. Do not belittle such behavior as being merely selfish. Of course it is selfish ... but selfishness is the bedrock on which all moral behavior starts and it can be immoral only when it conflicts with a higher moral imperative. An animal so poor in spirit that he won't even fight on his own behalf is already an evolutionary dead end; the best he can do for his breed is to crawl off and die, and not pass on his defective genes.

The next higher level is to work, fight, and sometimes die for your own immediate family. This is the level at which six pounds of mother cat can be so fierce that she'll drive off a police dog. It is the level at which a father takes a moonlighting job to keep his kids in college—

and the level at which a mother or father dives into a flood to save a drowning child ... and it is still moral behavior even when it fails.

The next higher level is to work, fight, and sometimes die for a group larger than the unit family—an extended family, a herd, a tribe—and take another look at that baboon on watch; he's at that moral level. I don't think baboon language is complex enough to permit them to discuss such abstract notions as "morality" or "duty" or "loyalty"—but it is evident that baboons *do* operate morally and *do* exhibit the traits of duty and loyalty; we see them in action. Call it "instinct" if you like—but remember that assigning a name to a phenomenon does not explain it.

But that baboon behavior can be explained in evolutionary terms. Evolution is a process that never stops. Baboons who fail to exhibit moral behavior do not survive; they wind up as meat for leopards. Every baboon generation has to pass this examination in moral behavior; those who bilge it don't have progeny. Perhaps the old bull of the tribe gives lessons ... but the leopard decides who graduates—and there is no appeal from his decision. We don't have to understand the details to observe the outcome: Baboons behave morally—for baboons.

The next level in moral behavior higher than that exhibited by the baboon is that in which duty and loyalty are shown toward a group of your own kind too large for an individual to know all of them. We have a name for that. It is called "patriotism."

Behaving on a still higher moral level were the astronauts who went to the Moon, for their actions tend toward the survival of the entire race of mankind. The door they opened leads to the hope that h. sapiens will survive indefinitely long, even longer than this solid planet on which we stand tonight. As a direct result of what they did, it is now possible that the human race will *never* die.

Many short-sighted fools think that going to the Moon was just a stunt. But the astronauts knew the meaning of what they were doing, as is shown by Neil Armstrong's first words in stepping down onto the soil of Luna: "One small step for a man, one giant leap for mankind."

Let us note proudly that eleven of the Astronaut Corps are graduates of this our school.

And let me add that James Forrestal was the *first* high-ranking Federal official to come out flatly for space travel.

I must pause to brush off those parlor pacifists I mentioned earlier ... for they contend that *their* actions are on this highest moral level. They want to put a stop to war; they say so. Their purpose is to save the human race from killing itself off; they say that too. Anyone who disagrees with them must be a bloodthirsty scoundrel—and they'll tell you that to your face.

I won't waste time trying to judge their motives; my criticism is of their mental processes: Their heads aren't screwed on tight. They live in a world of fantasy.

Let me stipulate that, if the human race managed its affairs sensibly, we could do without war.

Yes—and if pigs had wings, they could fly.

I don't know what planet those pious pacifists are talking about but it can't be the third one out from the Sun. Anyone who has seen the Far East—or Africa—or the Middle East—knows or certainly should know that there is *no* chance of abolishing war in the foreseeable future. In the past few years I have been around the world three times, traveled in most of the communist countries, visited many of the so-called emerging countries, plus many trips to Europe and to South America; I saw nothing that cheered me as to the prospects for peace. The seeds of war are everywhere; the conflicts of interest are real and deep, and will not be abolished by pious platitudes.

The best we can hope for is a precarious balance of power among the nations capable of waging total war—while endless lesser wars break out here and there.

I won't belabor this. Our campuses are loaded with custard-headed pacifists but the yard of the Naval Academy is one place where I will not encounter them. We are in agreement that the United States still needs a navy, that the Republic will always have need for heroes—else you would not be here tonight and in uniform.

Patriotism— Moral behavior at the national level. Non sibi sed Patria. Nathan Hale's last words: "I regret that I have but one life to give for my country." Torpedo Squadron Eight making its suicidal attack. Four chaplains standing fast while the water rises around them. Thomas Jefferson saying, "The Tree of Liberty must be refreshed from time to time with the blood of patriots—" A submarine skipper giving the order "Take her *down!*" while he himself is still topside. Jonas Ingram standing on the steps of Bancroft Hall and shouting, "The Navy has no place for good losers! The Navy needs tough sons of bitches who can go out there and *win!*"

Patriotism— An abstract word used to describe a type of behavior as harshly practical as good brakes and good tires. It means that you place the welfare of your nation ahead of your own even if it costs you your life.

Men who go down to the sea in ships have long had another way of expressing the same moral behavior tagged by the abstract expression "patriotism." Spelled out in simple Anglo-Saxon words "Patriotism" reads "Women and children first!"

And that is the moral result of realizing a self-evident biological fact: Men are expendable; women and children are not. A tribe or a nation can lose a high percentage of its men and still pick up the pieces and go on ... as long as the women and children are saved. But if you fail to save the women and children, you've had it, you're done, you're *through!* You join tyrannosaurus rex; one more breed that bilged its final test.

I must amplify that. I know that women can fight and often have. I have known many a tough old grandmother I would rather have at my side in a tight spot than any number of pseudo-males who disdain military service. My wife put in three years and a butt active duty in World War Two, plus ten years reserve, and I am proud—very proud!—of her naval service. I am proud of every one of our women in uniform; they are a shining example to us men.

Nevertheless, as a mathematical proposition in the facts of biology, children, and women of child-bearing age, are the ultimate treasure that we must save. Every human culture is based on "Women and children first"—and any attempt to do it any other way leads quickly to extinction.

Possibly extinction is the way we are headed. Great nations have died in the past; it can happen to us.

Nor am I certain how good our chances are. To me it seems self-evident that any nation that loses its patriotic fervor is on the skids. Without that indispensable survival factor the end is only a matter of time. I don't know how deeply the rot has penetrated—but it seems to me that there has been a change for the worse in the last fifty years. Possibly I am misled by the offensive behavior of a noisy but unimportant minority. But it does seem to me that patriotism has lost its grip on a large percentage of our people.

I hope I am wrong ... because if my fears are well grounded, I would not bet two cents on this nation's chance of lasting even to the end of this century.

But there is no way to force patriotism on anyone. Passing a law will not create it, nor can we buy it by appropriating so many billions of dollars.

You gentlemen of the Brigade are most fortunate. You are going to a school where this basic moral virtue is daily reinforced by precept and example. It is not enough to know what Charlie Noble does for a living, or what makes the wildcat wild, or which BatDiv failed to splice the main brace and why—nor to learn matrix algebra and navigation and ballistics and aerodynamics and nuclear engineering. These things are merely the working tools of your profession and could be learned elsewhere; they do not require "four years together by the Bay where Severn joins the tide."

What you do have here is a tradition of service. Your most important classroom is Memorial Hall. Your most important lesson is the way you feel inside when you walk up those steps and see that shot-torn flag framed in the arch of the door: "Don't Give Up the Ship."

If you feel nothing, you don't belong here. But if it gives you goose flesh just to see that old battle flag, then you are going to find that feeling increasing every time you return here over the years ... until it reaches a crescendo the day you return and read the list of your own honored dead—classmates, shipmates, friends—read them with grief and pride while you try to keep your tears silent.

The time has come for me to stop. I said that "Patriotism" is a way of saying "Women and children first." And that no one can force a man to feel this way. Instead he must embrace it freely. I want to tell about one such man. He wore no uniform and no one knows his name, or where he came from; all we know is what he did.

In my home town sixty years ago when I was a child, my mother and father used to take me and my brothers and sisters out to Swope Park on Sunday afternoons. It was a wonderful place for lads, with picnic grounds and lakes and a zoo. But a railroad line cut straight through it.

One Sunday afternoon a young married couple were crossing these tracks. She apparently did not watch her step, for she managed to catch her foot in the frog of a switch to a siding and could not pull it free. Her husband stopped to help her.

But try as they might they could not get her foot loose. While they were working at it, a tramp showed up, walking the ties. He joined the husband in trying to pull the young woman's foot loose. No luck—

Out of sight around the curve a train whistled. Perhaps there would have been time to run and flag it down, perhaps not. In any case both men went right ahead trying to pull her free ... and the train hit them.

The wife was killed, the husband was mortally injured and died later, the tramp was killed—and testimony showed that neither man made the slightest effort to save himself.

The husband's behavior was heroic ... but what we expect of a husband toward his wife: his right, and his proud privilege, to die for his woman. But what of this nameless stranger? Up to the very last second he could have jumped clear. He did not. He was still trying to save this woman he had never seen before in his life, right up to the very instant the train killed him. And that's all we'll ever know about him.

This is how a man dies.
This is how a *man* ... lives!

> "They shall not grow old
>   as we that are left grow old,
>   age shall not wither them
>   nor the years condemn;

At the going down of the sun
   and in the morning,
   we shall remember them ..."

— Tomb of the Scottish
Unknown Soldier
Edinburgh

Paul A. M. Dirac

A Riddle

What have these in common?

1. 1926: A graduate student, Cambridge University
2. Billions of years ago: Quasars exploding
3. 1908: A Siberian forest devastated
4. 10 million years ago: A galaxy exploding
5. 1932: A cloud-chamber track, Pasadena, Calif.

Answer: All may, and 1 and 5 *do* involve antimatter.

(*ANTI*matter?)

Yes—like ordinary matter with electrical properties of particles reversed. Each atom of matter is one or more nucleons surrounded by one or more electrons; charges add up to zero. A hydrogen atom has a proton with positive charge as nucleus, surrounded by an electron with negative charge. A proton is 1836.11 times as massive as an electron, but their charges are equal and opposite: +1-1 = 0. Uranium-235 (or $_{92}U^{235}$, meaning "an isotope of element 92, uranium, nuclear weight 235") has 235 nucleons: 143 neutrons of zero charge and 92 protons of positive charge (143 + 92 = 235; hence its name); these 235 are surrounded by 92 electrons (negative), so total charge is zero: 0 + 92 - 92 = 0. (Nuclear weight is never zero, being the mass of all the nucleons.)

Make electrons positive, protons negative: charges still balance; nuclear weight is unchanged—but it is *not* an atom of matter; it is an antiatom of antimatter.

"Touch Me Not!"

In an antimatter world, antimatter behaves like matter. Bread dough rises, weapons kill, kisses still taste sweet. You would be antimatter and not notice it.

WARNING! Since your body is matter (else you could not be reading this), *don't* kiss an antimatter girl. You both would explode with violence unbelievable.

But you'll never meet one, nor will your grandchildren. (I'm not sure about *their* grandchildren.)

$E = mc^2$

Antimatter is no science-fiction nightmare; it's as real as Texas. That Cambridge graduate student was Paul A. M. Dirac inventing new mathematics to merge Albert Einstein's special theory of relativity with Max Planck's quantum theory. Both theories worked—but conflicted. Dirac sought to merge them without conflict.

He succeeded.

His equations were published in 1928, and from them, in 1930, he made an incredible prediction: each sort of particle had antiparticles of opposite charge: "antimatter."

Scientists have their human foibles; a scientist can grow as fond of his world concept as a cat of its "own" chair. By 1930 the cozy 19th-century "world" of physics had been repeatedly outraged. This ridiculous new assault insulted all common sense.

But in 1932 at the California Institute of Technology, Carl D. Anderson photographed proof of the electron's antiparticle (named "positron" for its positive charge but otherwise twin to the electron). Radical theory has seldom been confirmed so quickly or rewarded so promptly: Dirac received the Nobel prize in 1933, Anderson in 1936— each barely 31 years of age when awarded it.

Carl D. Anderson

Since 1932 so many sorts of antiparticles have been detected that no doubt remains: antimatter matches matter in every sort of particle. Matching is not always as simple as electron (e–) and positron (e+). Photons are their own antiparticles. Neutrons and neutrinos (zero charges) are matched by antineutrons and anti-neutrinos, also of zero charge—this sounds like meaningless redundancy because English is not appropriate language; abstract mathematics is the language required for precise statements in physical theory. (Try writing the score of a symphony solely in words *with no musical symbols whatever*.)

A photograph taken in 1932 by Carl D. Anderson through the glass wall of a Wilson cloud chamber at the California Institute of Technology provided the first proof of the existence of an antiparticle.

But a hint lies in noting that there are reaction series in which protons and electrons yield neutrons—one example: the *soi-disant* "Solar Phoenix" (solar power theory, Hans Bethe); if we ignore details, the Solar Phoenix can be summarized as changing four hydrogen atoms (four of $_1H^1$) into one helium atom ($_2He^4$). We start with four protons and four electrons; we end up six stages later with two neutrons, two protons, and two electrons—and that is neither precise nor adequate and is not an equation and ignores other isotopes involved, creation of positrons, release of energy through mutual annihilations of positrons and free electrons, and several other features, plus the fact that this transformation can occur by a variety of routes.

(But such are the booby traps of English or *any* verbal language where abstract mathematics is the *only* correct language.)

A wide variety of other transformations permits antiprotons and positrons to yield antineutrons. The twin types of varieties of transformations mentioned above are simply samples; there are many other types being both predicted mathematically and detected in the laboratories almost daily—and many or most transformation series involve antiparticles of antimatter.

Nevertheless, antimatter is scarce in our corner of the universe—lucky for us because, when matter encounters antimatter, *both* explode in total annihilation. E = mc² is known to everyone since its awful truth was demonstrated at Hiroshima, Japan. It states that energy is equivalent to mass, mass to energy, in this relation: energy equals mass times the square of the velocity of light in empty space.

That velocity is almost inconceivable. In blasting for the moon our astronauts reached nearly 7 miles/second; light travels almost 27,000 times that speed—186,282.4 (±0.1) miles or 299,792.5 (±0.15) kilometers each second. Round off that last figure as 300,000; then use the compatible units of science (grams, centimeters, ergs) and write in centimeters 3×10^{10}, then square it: 9×10^{20}, or 900,000,000,000,000,000,000. (!!!)

This fantastic figure shouts that a tiny mass can become a monstrous blast of energy—grim proof: Hiroshima.

But maximum possible efficiency of U^{235} fission is about ¹⁄₁₀ of 1%; the Hiroshima bomb's actual efficiency was much lower, and H-bomb fusion has still lower maximum (H-bombs can be more powerful through having no limit on size; all fission bombs have sharp limits). But fission or fusion, almost all the reacting mass splits or combines into other elements; only a trifle becomes energy.

In matter-antimatter reaction, however, *all* of *both* become energy. An engineer might say "200% efficient" as antimatter undergoing annihilation converts into raw energy an equal mass of matter.

Mathematical Physicists

An experimental physicist uses expensive giant accelerators to shoot particles at 99.9+% of the speed of light, or sometimes gadgets built on his own time with scrounged materials. Large or small, cheap or costly, he works with *things*.

A mathematical physicist uses pencil, paper, and brain. Not my brain or yours—unless you are of the rare few with "mathematical intuition."

Nicolaus Copernicus
1473—1543

Johannes Kepler
1571—1630

Sir Isaac Newton
1643—1727

James Clerk Maxwell
1831—1879

Max Plank
1858—1947

Albert Einstein
1879—1955

Paul A. M. Dirac
1902—1984

SOME OF THE WORLD'S GREATEST PHYSICISTS

EXPANDED UNIVERSE: VOLUME TWO

That's a tag for an unexplainable. It is a gift, not a skill, and cannot be learned or taught. Even advanced mathematics ("advanced" to laymen) such as higher calculus, Fourier analysis, n-dimensional and non-Euclidean geometries are skills requiring only patience and normal intelligence ... *after* they have been invented by persons having mathematical intuition.

The oft-heard plaint "I can't cope with math!" may mean subnormal intelligence (unlikely), laziness (more likely), or poor teaching (extremely likely). But that plaint usually refers to common arithmetic—a trivial skill in the eyes of a mathematician. (*Creating* it was not trivial. Zero, positional notation, decimal-or-base point all took genius; imagine doing a Form 1040 in Roman numerals.)

Of billions living and dead perhaps a few thousand have been gifted with mathematical intuition; a few hundred have lived in circumstances permitting use of it; a smaller fraction have been mathematical physicists. Of these a few dozen have left permanent marks on physics.

But without these few we would not have science. Mathematical physics is basic to *all* sciences. No exceptions. *None.*

Mathematical physicists sometimes hint that experimentalists are frustrated pipefitters; experimentalists mutter that theoreticians are so lost in fog they need guardians. But they are indispensable to each other. Piling up facts is not science—science is facts-*and*-theories. Facts alone have limited use and lack meaning; a valid theory organizes them into far greater usefulness. To be valid a theory must be confirmed by *all* relevant facts. A "natural law" is theory repeatedly confirmed and drops back to "approximation" when *one* fact contradicts it. Then search resumes for better theory to embrace old facts plus this stubborn new one.

No "natural law" of 500 years ago is "law" today; all our present laws are probably approximations, useful but not perfect. Some scientists, notably Paul Dirac, suspect that perfection is unattainable.

A powerful theory not only embraces old facts and new but also discloses unsuspected facts. These are landmarks of science: Nicolaus Copernicus' heliocentric theory, Johannes Kepler's refining it into conic-sections ballistics, Isaac Newton's laws of motion and theory of universal gravitation, James C. Maxwell's equations linking electricity with magnetism, Planck's quantum theory, Einstein's relativity, Dirac's synthesis of quantum theory and special relativity—a few more, not many.

Mathematical physicists strive to create a mathematical structure interrelating all space-time events, past and future, from infinitesimally small to inconceivably huge and remote in space and time, a "unified field theory" embracing 10 or 20 billion years and light-years, more likely 80 billion or so—or possibly eternity in an infinity of multiple universes.

Some order!

They try. Newton made great strides. So did Einstein. Nearly 50 years ago Dirac brought it closer, has steadily added to it, is working on it today.

Paul Dirac may be and probably is the greatest living theoretical scientist. Dirac, Newton, and Einstein are equals.

Paul A. M. Dirac

The experimentalists' slur about theoretical physicists holds a grain of truth. Newton apparently never noticed the lovely sex in all his years. Einstein ignored such trivialities as socks. One mathematical physicist who swayed World War II could not be trusted with a screwdriver.

Dirac is *not* that sort of man.

Other than genius, his only unusual trait is strong dislike for idle talk. (His Cambridge students coined a unit the _dirac_—one word per light-year.) But he lectures and writes with admirable clarity. Taciturn, he is not unsocial; in 1937 he married a most charming Hungarian lady. They have two daughters and a son.

He can be trusted with tools; he sometimes builds instruments, and performs his own experiments. He graduated in engineering before he became a mathematical physicist; this influenced his life. Engineers find working solutions from incomplete data; approximations are close enough if they do the job—too fussy wastes man-hours. But when a job needs it, a true engineer gives his utmost to achieve as near perfection as possible.

Dirac brought this attitude to theoretical physics; his successes justify his approach.

He was born in Bristol, England, Aug. 8, 1902, and named Paul Adrien Maurice Dirac. His precocity in mathematics showed early; his father supplied books and encouraged him to study on his own. Solitary walks and study were the boy's notion of fun—and are of the man today. Dirac works (and plays) hardest by doing and saying *nothing* ... while his mind roams the universe.

When barely 16 years old, he entered the University of Bristol. At 18 he graduated, bachelor of science in electrical engineering. In 1923 a grant enabled him to return to school at the foremost institution for mathematics, Cambridge University. In three years of study for a doctorate Dirac published 12 papers in mathematical physics, 5 in *The Proceedings of the Royal Society*. A cub with only an engineering degree from a minor university has trouble getting published in *any* journal of science; to appear at the age of 22 in the most highly respected of them all is amazing.

Dirac received his doctorate in May 1926, his dissertation being "Quantum Mechanics"—the stickiest subject in physical science. He tackled it his first year at Cambridge and has continued to unravel its paradoxes throughout his career; out of 123 publications over the last 50 years the word *quantum* can be found 45 times in his titles.

Dirac remained at Cambridge—taught, thought, published. In 1932, the year before his Nobel prize, he received an honor rarer than that prize, one formerly held by Newton: Lucasian professor of mathematics. Dirac kept it 37 years, until he resigned from Cambridge. He accepted other posts during his Cantabrigian years: member of the Institute for Advanced Study at Princeton, N.J., professor of the Dublin Institute for Advanced Studies, visiting professorships here and there.

Intuitive mathematicians often burn out young. Not Dirac!—he is a Michelangelo who started very young, never stopped, is still going strong. Antimatter is not necessarily his contribution most esteemed by colleagues, but his other major ones are so abstruse as to defy putting them into common words:

A mathematical attribute of particles dubbed "spin"; coinvention of the Fermi-Dirac statistics; an abstract mathematical replacement for the "pellucid aether" of classical mechanics. For centuries, ether was used and its "physical reality" generally accepted either as "axiomatic" or "proved" through various negative proofs. Both "axiom" and "negative proof" are treacherous; the 1887 Michelson-Morley experiment showed no physical reality behind the concept of ether, and many variations of that experiment over many years gave the same null results.

So Einstein omitted ether from his treatments of relativity—while less brilliant men ignored the observed facts and clung to classical ether for at least 40 years.

Dirac's ether (circa 1950) is solely abstract mathematics, more useful thereby than classical ether as it avoids the paradoxes of the earlier concepts. Dirac has consistently warned against treating mathematical equations as if they were pictures of something that could be visualized in the way one may visualize the Taj Mahal or a loaf of bread; his equations are *rules* concerning space-time events—*not* pictures. (This may be the key to his extraordinary successes.)

One more example must represent a long list: Dirac's work on Georges Lemaître's "primeval egg"—later popularized as the "big bang."

Honors also are too many to list in full: fellow of the Royal Society, its Royal Medal, its Copley Medal, honorary degrees (always refused), foreign associate of the American Academy of Sciences, Oppenheimer Memorial Prize, and (most valued by Dirac) Great Britain's Order of Merit.

Dirac "retired" by accepting a research professorship at Florida State University, where he is now working on gravitation theory. In 1937 he had theorized that Newton's "constant of gravitation" was in fact a decreasing variable ... but the amount of decrease he predicted was so small that it could not be verified in 1937.

Today the decrease can be measured. In July 1974 Thomas C. Van Flandern of the U.S. Naval Observatory reported measurements showing a decrease in gravitation of about a ten-billionth each year (1 per 10^{10} per annum). This amount seems trivial, but it is *very* large in astronomical and geological time. If these findings are confirmed and if they continue to support Dirac's mathematical theory, he will have upset physical science even more than he did in 1928 and 1930.

Here is an incomplete list of the sciences that would undergo radical revision: physics from micro- through astro-, astronomy, geology, paleontology, meteorology, chemistry, cosmology, cosmogony, geogony, ballistics. It is too early to speculate about effects on the life sciences, but we exist inside this physical world and gravitation is the most pervasive feature of our world.

Theory of biological evolution would certainly be affected. It is possible that understanding gravitation could result in changes in engineering technology too sweeping easily to be imagined.

Antimatter and You

Of cosmologies there is no end; astrophysicists enjoy "playing God." It's safe fun, too, as the questions are so sweeping, the data so confusing, that any cosmology is hard to prove or disprove. But since 1932 antimatter has been a necessary datum. Many cosmologists feel that the universe (universes?) has as much antimatter as matter—but they disagree over how to balance the two.

Some think that, on the average, every other star in our Milky Way galaxy is antimatter. Others find that setup dangerously crowded—make it every second galaxy. Still others prefer universe-and-antiuniverse with antimatter in ours only on rare occasions when energetic particles collide so violently that some of the energy forms antiparticles. And some like higher numbers of universes—even an unlimited number.

One advantage of light's finite speed is that we can see several eons of the universe in action, rather than just one frame of a *very* long moving picture. Today's instruments reach not only far out into space but also far back into time; this permits us to test in some degree a proposed cosmology. The LST (Large Space Telescope), to be placed in orbit by the Space Shuttle in 1983, will have 20 times the resolving power of the best ground-based and atmosphere-distorted conventional telescope—therefore 20 times the reach, or more than enough to see clear back to the "beginning" by one cosmology, the "big bang."

(Q: What happened *before* the beginning? A: *You* tell *me*.)

When we double that reach—someday we will—what will we see? Empty space? Or the backs of our necks?

(Q: What's this to *me*? A: Patience one moment....)

The star nearest ours is a triplet system; one of the three resembles our sun and may have an Earthlike planet—an inviting target for our first attempt to cross interstellar space. Suppose that system is anti-matter—*BANG!* Scratch one starship.

(Hooray for Zero Population Growth! To hell with space-travel boondoggles!)

Then consider this: June 30, 1908, a meteor struck Siberia, so blindingly bright in broad daylight that people 1,000 miles away saw it. Its roar was "deafening" at 500 miles. Its ground quake brought a train to emergency stop 400 miles from impact. North of Vanavara its air blast killed a herd of 1,500 reindeer.

Trouble and war and revolution—investigation waited 19 years. But still devastated were many hundreds of square miles. How giant trees lay pinpointed impact.

A meteor from inside our Galaxy can strike Earth at 50 miles/second.

But could one hit us from *outside* our Galaxy?

Yes! The only unlikely (but not impossible) routes are those plowing edgewise or nearly so through the Milky Way; most of the sky is an open road—step outside tonight and *look.* An antimeteor from an antigalaxy could sneak in through hard vacuum—losing an antiatom whenever it encountered a random atom but nevertheless could strike us massing, say, one pound.

One pound of antimatter at any speed or none would raise as much hell as *28,000 tons* of matter striking at 50 miles/second.

Today no one knows how to amass even a gram of antimatter or how to handle and control it either for power or for weaponry. Experts assert that all three are impossible.

However ...

Two relevant examples of "expert" predictions:

Robert A. Millikan, Nobel laureate in physics and distinguished second to none by a half-century of research into charges and properties of atomic particles, in quantum mechanics, and in several other areas, predicted that all the power that could ever be extracted from atoms would no more than blow the whistle on a peanut vendor's cart. (In fairness I must add that most of his colleagues agreed—and the same is true of the next example.)

Forest Ray Moulton, for many years top astronomer of the University of Chicago and foremost authority in ballistics, stated in print (1935) that there was "not the slightest possibility of such a journey" as the one the whole world watched 34 years later: Apollo 11 to the moon.

In 1938, when there was not a pinch of pure uranium-235 anywhere on Earth and no technology to amass or control it, Lise Meitner devised mathematics that pointed straight to atom bombs. Less than seven years after she did this, the first one blazed "like a thousand suns."

No *possible* way to amass antimatter?

Or *ever* to handle it?

Being smugly certain of *that* (but mistaken) could mean to *you* ... and me and everyone ...

The END

"It is far, far better to have a bastard
In the family than an
unemployed son-in-law."

—Jubal Harshaw

AFTERWORD

I am precluded from revising this article because Encyclopaedia Britannica owns the copyright; I wrote it under contract. But in truth it needs no revision but can use some late news flashes.

*1) Jonathan V. Post reports (*Omni, *May '79) that scientists in Geneva have announced containment of a beam of antiprotons in a circular storage ring for* 85 *hours. Further deponent sayeth not as today (Nov. '79) I have not yet traced down details. The total mass could not have been large (Geneva is still on the map) as the storage method used is not suited to large masses—or, as in this case, a massive sum total of very small masses.*

But I am astonished at any containment even though with dead seriousness I predicted it in the section just above. I did not expect it in the near future but now I learn it happened at least 10 months ago, only 4 years after I wrote the above article.

Too frighteningly soon! A very small (anti) mass to be sure—but when Dr. Lise Meitner wrote the equations that implicitly predicted the A-bomb, there was not enough purified U-235 *anywhere to cause a gnat's eye to water.*

How soon will we face a LARGE mass—say about an ounce—planted in Manhattan by someone who doesn't like us very well? If he releases the magnetic container by an alarm-clock timer or nine other simple make-it-in-your-own-kitchen devices, he can be in Singapore when it goes off. Or in Trenton if he enjoys watching his own little practical jokes—he won't worry about witnesses; they will be dead.

Too big? Too cumbersome? Too expensive? I don't know—and neither does anyone else today. I am not proposing sneaking a CERN particle ac-

celerator past Hoboken customs ... but note that the first reacting atomic pile (University of Chicago) was massive—but it was not flown to Hiroshima. The bomb that did go was called "Little Boy" for good reason. Now we can fire them from 8-inch guns. As for the "suitcase" bomb—change that to a large briefcase; all the other essentials can be bought off the shelf for cash in any medium-large city, no questions asked as they are commonplace items.

Antimatter, containment and all, might turn out to be even smaller, lighter, simpler.

2) That variable constant: Dr. Van Flandern is still plugging away at Dr. Dirac's 1937 prediction about the "Constant" of Gravitation. The latest figures I have seen show (by his measurements) that the "Constant" is decreasing by 3.6 ± 1.8 parts in 10^{11} years, a figure surprisingly close to Dirac's 1937 prediction (5.6) in view of the extreme difficulty of making the measurements and of excluding extraneous variables. But all this is based on a universe 18–20 billion years old since the "big bang"—an assumption on current best data but still an assumption. If the universe is actually materially older than that (there are reasons to think so, and all the revisions since Abbé Lemaître first formulated the theory have all been upward, never downward), then Dirac's prediction may turn out to be right on the nose of observed data to their limit of accuracy.

The data above are from an article by Dr. Herbert Friedman of Naval Research Laboratory. Our Baker Street Irregulars have just established a pipeline to Dr. Van Flandern; if major new data become available before this book is closed for press, I will add a line to this.

3) In "Where To" see prediction number fourteen, page 68 (Volume II): At the Naval Academy I slept my way through the course in physics; nothing had changed since I had covered the same ground in high school. "Little did I dream" that a young man at Cambridge, less than five years older than I, was at that very moment turning the world upside down. This quiet, polite, soft-spoken gentleman was going to turn out to be the enfant terrible of physics. This has been the stormiest century in natural philosophy of all history and the storms are not over. We would not today have over 200 "elementary" particles (an open scandal) if Paul Dirac had not simplified the relation of spin and magnetism in an electron into one equation over fifty years ago, then shown that the equation implied antimatter.

202

Many thousands of man-hours, many millions of dollars have been spent since then exploring the byways opened up by this one equation. And the end is not yet. The four forces (strong, weak, gravitic, electromagnetic) are still to be combined into one system. Einstein died with the work unfinished, Hawking (although young) is tragically ill, Dirac himself has reached the age when he really should not climb stepladders (as I know too well; I'm not that much younger).

$E = mc^2$ everybody knows; it's short and simple. But the Dirac equation, at least *as important, is known only to professionals—not surprising; it's hairy and uses symbols a layman never sees.*

I include it here just for record; I won't try to explain it. For explanations, get a late text on quantum mechanics and be prepared to learn some not-easy mathematics. Lotsa luck!

$$\iiint \left[|\Psi_1|^2 + |\Psi_2|^2 + |\Psi_3|^2 + |\Psi_4|^2 \right] \, dxdydz = 1$$

LATE BULLETIN:

Newton's "Constant" of Gravitation is *a decreasing variable.*

Just as I was about to dispatch this book MS to New York, through the good offices of Dr. Yoji Kondo (astrophysicist NASA Goddard) I received from Dr. Thomas C. Van Flandern a preprint of his latest results. They tend to confirm Dr. Dirac's 1937 prediction even more closely AND ARE BACKED UP BY TWO OTHER APPROACHES; all three show Gravitation as a variable decreasing with time.

I have just telephoned Dr. Van Flandern. With caution proper to a scientist he does not say that he has "proved" Dr. Dirac's prediction ... but that data to date support it; no data that he knows of contradict it—and adds that some of his colleagues disagree with him.

I don't have to be cautious; this man has established the fact beyond any reasonable doubt. Twenty-odd years of endless Lunar data, done by atomic (cesium) clock, electrically-automatically timed occultations of stars, backed by both triangulation and radar ranging, counterchecked by similar work done on the inner planets by other astronomers at other observatories— Certainly he could be wrong ... and I could be elected President!

T. C. Van Flandern turns out to be the sort of Renaissance Man Dirac is, but a generation younger (38 years). B.S. mathematics, Xavier, Cincin-

nati; Ph.D. astronomy, Yale—he has three other disciplines: biochemistry, nutrition, psychiatry. (When does he sleep?)

Reread that list of sciences affected (page 198, Volume II), then batten down the hatches! Dirac has done it again, and the World will never be the same.

——— LARGER THAN LIFE ———

A Memoir in Tribute to Dr. Edward E. Smith

August 1940—a back road near Jackson, Michigan—a 1939 Chevrolet sedan:

"Doc" Smith is at the wheel; I am in the righthand seat and trying hard to appear cool, calm, fearless—a credit to the Patrol. Doc has the accelerator floor-boarded ... but has his head tilted over at ninety degrees so that he can rest his skull against the frame of the open left window—in order to listen by bone conduction for body squeaks.

Were you to attempt this position yourself—car parked and brakes set, by all means; I am not suggesting that you *drive*—you would find that your view of the road ahead is between negligible and zero.

I must note that Doc was *not* wearing his Lens.

This leaves (by Occam's Razor) his sense of perception, his almost superhuman reflexes, and his ability to integrate instantly all available data and act therefrom decisively and correctly.

Sounds a lot like the Gray Lensman, does it not?

It should, as no one more nearly resembled (in character and in ability—not necessarily in appearance) the Gray Lensman than did the good gray doctor who created him.

Doc could do almost anything and do it quickly and well. In this case he was selecting and road-testing for me a secondhand car. After rejecting numberless other cars, he approved this one; I bought it. Note the date: August 1940. We entered World War Two the fol-

205

lowing year and quit making automobiles. I drove that car for twelve years. When I finally did replace it, the mechanic who took care of it asked to be permitted to buy it rather than have it be turned in on a trade ... because, after more than thirteen years and hundreds of thousands of miles, it was *still* a good car. Doc Smith had not missed *anything*.

Its name? *Skylark Five*, of course.

So far as I know, Doc Smith could not play a dulcimer (but it would not surprise me to learn that he had been expert at it). Here are some of the skills I know he possessed:

Chemist & chemical engineer—and anyone who thinks these two professions are one and the same is neither a chemist nor an engineer. (My wife is a chemist and is also an aeronautical engineer—but she is not a chemical engineer. All clear? No? See me after class.)

Metallurgist—an arcane art at the Trojan Point of Black Magic and science.

Photographer—all metallurgists are expert photographers; the converse is not necessarily true.

Lumberjack

Cereal chemist

Cook

Explosives chemist—research, test, & development—product control

Blacksmith

Machinist (tool & diemaker grade)

Carpenter

Hardrock miner—see chapter 14 of *First Lensman*, titled "Mining and Disaster." That chapter was written by a man who had *been* there. And it is a refutation of the silly notion that science fiction does not require knowledge of science. Did I hear someone say that there is no *science* in that chapter? Just a trick vocabulary—trade argot—plus description of some commonplace mechanical work—

So? The science (several sciences!) lies just below the surface of the paper ... and permeates every word. In some fields I could be fooled, but not in this one. I've been in mining, off and on, for more than forty years.

Or see *Spacehounds of IPC*, chapters 3 & 4, pp. 40-80 ... and especially p. 52 of the Fantasy Press hardcover edition. Page 52 is almost purely autobiographical in that it tells *why* the male lead, "Steve" Stevens, knows how to fabricate from the wreckage at hand everything necessary to rescue Nadia and himself. I once discussed with Doc these two chapters, in detail; he convinced me that his hero character could do these things by convincing me that he, Edward E. Smith, could do all of them ... and, being myself an experienced mechanical engineer, it was not possible for him to give me a "snow job." (I think he lacked the circuitry to give a "snow job" in any case; incorruptible honesty was Dr. Smith's prime attribute—with courage to match it.)

What else could he do? He could call square dances. Surely, almost anyone can square-dance ... but to become a caller takes longer and is much more difficult. When and how he found time for this I do not know—but, since he did everything about three times as fast as ordinary people, there is probably no mystery.

Both Doc and his beautiful Jeannie were endlessly hospitable. I stayed with them once when they had *nine* houseguests. They seemed to enjoy it.

But, above all, Doc Smith was the perfect, gallant knight, sans peur et sans reproche.

And all of the above are reflected in his stories.

It is customary today among self-styled "literary critics" to sneer at Doc's space epics—plot, characterization, dialog, motivations, values, moral attitudes, etc. "Hopelessly old-fashioned" is one of the milder disparagements.

As Al Smith used to say: "Let's take a look at the record."

Edward Elmer Smith was born in 1890, some forty years before the American language started to fall to pieces—long, long before the idiot notion of "restricted vocabulary" infected our schools, a half century before our language was corrupted by the fallacy that popular usage defines grammatical correctness.

In consequence Dr. Smith made full use of his huge vocabulary, preferring always the exact word over a more common but inexact word. He did not hesitate to use complex sentences. His syntactical constructions show that he understood and used with precision the conditional and the subjunctive modes as well as the indicative. He did not split infinitives. The difference between "like" and "as" was not a mystery to him. He limited barbarisms to quoted dialog used in characterization.

("Oh, but that dialog!") In each story Doc's male lead character is a very intelligent, highly educated, cheerful, emotional, enthusiastic, and genuinely modest man who talks exactly like Doc Smith, who was a very intelligent, highly educated, cheerful, emotional, enthusiastic, and genuinely modest man.

In casual conversation Doc used a number of clichés … and his male lead characters used the same or similar ones. This is a literary fault? I think not. In casual speech most people tend to repeat each his own idiosyncratic pattern of clichés. Doc's repertory of clichés was quite colorful, especially so when compared with patterns heard today that draw heavily on "The Seven Words That Must Never Be Used in Television." A 7-word vocabulary offers little variety.

("But those embarrassing love scenes!") E. E. Smith's adolescence was during the Mauve Decade; we may assume tentatively that his attitudes toward women were formed mainly in those years. In 1914, a few weeks before the war in Europe started, he met his Jeannie—and I can testify of my own knowledge that, 47 years later (i.e., the last time I saw him before his death) he was still dazzled by the wonderful fact that this glorious creature had consented to spend her life with him.

Do you remember the cultural attitudes toward romantic love during the years before the European War? Too early for you? Never mind, you'll find them throughout Doc Smith's novels. Now we come to the important question. The Lensman novels are laid in the far future. Can you think of any reason why the attitudes between sexes today (ca. 1979) are more likely to prevail in the far future than are attitudes prevailing before 1914?

(I stipulate that there are many other possible patterns. But we are now comparing just these two.)

I suggest that the current pattern is contrasurvival, is necessarily most temporary, and is merely one symptom of the kaleidoscopic and possibly catastrophic rapid change our culture is passing through (or dying from?).

Contrariwise, the pre-1914 values, whatever faults they may have, are firmly anchored in the concept that a male's first duty is to protect women and children. *Pro*survival!

"Ah, but those hackneyed plots!" Yes, indeed!—and for excellent reason: The ideas, the cosmic concepts, the complex and sweeping plots, all were brand new when Doc invented them. But in the past half century dozens of other writers have taken his plots, his concepts, and rung the changes on them. The ink was barely dry on *Skylark of Space* when the imitators started in. They have never stopped—pygmies, standing on the shoulders of a giant.

But all the complaints about "Skylark" Smith's alleged literary faults are as nothing to the (usually unvoiced) major grievance:

Doc Smith did not go along with *any* of the hogwash that passes for a system of social values today.

He believed in Good and Evil. He had no truck with the moral relativism of the neo- (cocktail-party) Freudians.

He refused to concede that "mediocre" is better than "superior."

He had no patience with self-pity.

He did not think that men and women are equal—he would as lief have equated oranges with apples. His stories assumed that men and women are *different*, with different functions, different responsibilities, different duties. Not equal but complementary. Neither complete without the other.

Worse yet, in his greatest and longest story, the 6-volume Lensman novel, he assumes that all humans are unequal (and, by implication, that the cult of the common man is pernicious nonsense), and bases his grand epic on the idea that a planned genetic breeding program thousands of years long can (and *must*) produce a new race superior to *h. sapiens* … supermen who will become the guardians of civilization.

209

The Lensman novel was left unfinished; there was to have been at least a seventh volume. As always, Doc had worked it out in great detail but never (so far as I know) wrote it down … because it was un-publishable—then. But he told me the ending, orally and in private.

I shan't repeat it; it is not my story. Possibly somewhere there is a manuscript—I *hope* so! All I will say is that the ending develops by inescapable logic from clues in *Children of the Lens*.

So work it out for yourself. The original Gray Lensman left us quite suddenly—urgent business a long way off, no time to spare to tell us more stories.

On 2 July 1979 I received a letter calling me to testify July 19th before a joint session of the House Select Committee on Aging (Honorable Claude Pepper, M.C., Chairman) and the House Committee on Science and Technology (Honorable Don Fuqua, M.C., Chairman)—subject: Applications of Space Technology for the Elderly and the Handicapped.

I stared at that letter with all the enthusiasm of a bridegroom handed a summons for jury duty. Space technology? Yeah, sure, I was gung-ho for space technology, space travel, spaceships, space exploration, space colonies—anything about space, always have been.

But "applications of space technology for the elderly and the handicapped"? Why not bee culture? Or Estonian folk dancing? Or the three-toed salamander? Tantric Yoga?

I faced up to the problem the way any married man does: "Honey? How do I get out of this?"

"Come clean," she advised me. "Tell them bluntly that you know nothing about the subject. Shall I write a letter for you to sign?"

"It's not that simple."

"Certainly it is. We don't want to go to Washington. In *July?* Let's not be silly."

"You don't have to go."

"You don't think I'd let you go alone, do you? After the time and trouble I've spent keeping you alive? Then let you drop dead on a Washington sidewalk? *Hmmph!* You go—*I* go."

Some hours later I said, "Let's sum it up. We both know that any Congressional committee hearing, no matter how the call reads, has as its real subject 'Money'—who gets it and how much. And we know that the space program is in bad trouble. This joint session may not help—it looks as if it would take a miracle to save the space program—but it *might* help. Some, maybe. The only trouble is that I don't know anything about the subject I'm supposed to discuss."

"So you've said, about twenty times."

"I don't know anything about it *today*. But on July 19th I'm going to be a fully-qualified Expert Witness."

"So I told you, two hours ago."

Ginny and I have our own Baker Street Irregulars. Whether the subject be Chaucer or chalk, pulsars or poisons, we either know the man who knows the most about it, or we know a man who knows the man who knows the most. Within twenty-four hours we had a couple of dozen ~~spaceflight fanatics~~ public-spirited citizens helping us. Seventy-two hours, and information started to trickle in—within a week it was a flood and I was starting to draft my written testimony.

I completed my draft and immediately discarded it; galley proofs had arrived of *Technologies for the Handicapped and the Aged* by Trudy E. Bell, NASA July 1979. This brochure was to be submitted by Dr. Frosch, Administrator of NASA, as his testimony at the same hearing. Trudy Bell had done a beautiful job—one that made 95% of what I had written totally unnecessary.

So I started over.

What follows is condensed and abridged from both my written presentation and my oral testimony:

"Honorable Chairman, ladies, and gentlemen—

"Happy New Year!

"Indeed a happy New Year beginning the 11th year in the Age of Space, greatest era of our race—the *greatest!*—despite gasoline shortages, pollution, overpopulation, inflation, wars and threats of war. 'These too shall pass'—but the stars abide.

"Our race will spread out through space—unlimited room, unlimited energy, unlimited wealth. This is certain.

"But I am not certain that the working language will be English. The people of the United States seem to have suffered a loss of nerve. However, I am limited by the call to a discussion of 'spinoffs' from our space program useful to the aged and the handicapped.

"In all scientific research, the researcher may or may not find what he is looking for—indeed, his hypothesis may be demolished—but he is *certain* to learn something new ... which may be and often is more important than what he had hoped to learn.

"This is the Principle of Serendipity. It is so invariant that it can be considered an empirically established natural law.

"In space research we always try to do more with less, because today the payload is tightly limited in size and in weight. This means endless research and development to make everything smaller, lighter, foolproof, and fail-proof. It works out that almost everything developed for space can be used in therapy ... and thereby benefits both the elderly and the handicapped, the two groups requiring the most therapy of all sorts.

"When you reach old age—say 70 and up—it approaches certainty that you will be in some way handicapped. Not necessarily a wheelchair or crutches or a white cane—most handicaps do not show. So all of us are customers for space spinoffs—if not today, then soon."

Witness holds up NASA brochure. "There is no need for me to discuss applications that NASA has already described. But this I must say: NASA's presentation is *extremely* modest; it cites only 46 applications—whereas there are hundreds. Often one bit of research results in 2nd, 3rd, and 4th generations; each generation usually has multiple applications—spinoffs have spinoffs, branching out like a tree. To get a feeling for this, think of the endless applications of Lee DeForest's vacuum tube, Dr. Shockley's transistor.

"Here is a way to spot space-research spinoffs: If it involves microminiaturization of *any* sort, minicomputers, miniaturized long-life power sources, highly reliable microswitches, remotely-controlled manipulators, image enhancers, small and sophisticated robotics or cybernetics, then, *no matter where you find the item*, at a critical point in its development it was part of our space program.

213

"Examples:

"*Image enhancer*: This magic gadget runs an x-ray or fluoroscope picture through a special computer, does things to it, then puts it back onto the screen. Or stores it for replay. Or both. It can sharpen the contrast, take out 'noise,' remove part of the picture that gets in the way of what you need to see, and do other Wizard-of-Oz stunts.

"This is the wonder toy that took extremely weak digital code signals and turned them into those beautiful, sharp, true-color photographs from the surface of Mars in the Viking program and also brought us the Voyager photographs of Jupiter and its moons.

"I first saw one in 1977 at the Medical School of the University of Arizona—saw them put a long catheter up through a dog's body in order to inject an x-ray-opaque dye into its brain. This does not hurt the dog. More about this later—

"I did not know what an image enhancer was until I saw one demonstrated and did not learn until this year that it came from our space program. Possibly the doctor did not know. M.D.'s can use instruments with no notion that they derive from space research.... and a patient usually knows as little about it as did that dog.

"The most ironical thing about our space program is that there are thousands of people alive today who would be dead were it not for some item derived from space research—but are blissfully unaware of the fact—and complain about 'wasting all that money on stupid, useless space stunts when we have so many really important problems to solve right here on Earth.'

"'—all that money—'!

"That sort of thinking would have kept Columbus at home.

"NASA's annual budget wouldn't carry H.E.W. ten days. The entire 10 years of the Moon program works out to slightly *less than five cents per citizen per day*.

"Would you like to be a wheelchair case caught by a hurricane such as that one that failed to swing east and instead hit the Texas and Louisiana coast? That storm was tracked by weather satellite; there was ample warning for anyone who would heed it—plenty of time to evacuate not only wheelchair cases but bed patients.

"A similar storm hit Bangladesh a while back; it too was tracked by satellite. But Bangladesh lacks means to warn its people; many thousands were killed. Here in the United States it would take real effort to *miss* a hurricane warning; even houses with no plumbing have television.

"*Weather satellites* are not spinoff; they *are* space program. But they must be listed because bad weather of any sort is much rougher on the aged and the handicapped than it is on the young and able-bodied.

"*Portable kidney machine*: If a person's kidneys fail, he must 'go on the machine' or die. 'The machine' is a fate so grim that the suicide rate is high. Miniaturization has made it possible to build portable kidney machines. This not only lets the patient lead a fairly normal life, travel and so forth, but also his blood is cleaned steadily as with a normal kidney; he is no longer cumulatively poisoned by his own toxins between his assigned days or nights 'on the machine.'

"This is new. A few have already made the switch but all kidney victims can expect it soon. The suicide rate has dropped markedly— life is again worth living; hope has been restored.

"*Computerized-Axial Tomography*, or CAT, or 'brain scan': They strap you to a table, fasten your skull firmly, duck behind a barrier, and punch a button—then an automatic x-ray machine takes endless pictures, a tiny slice at a time. A special computer synthesizes each series of slices into a picture; a couple of dozen such pictures show the brain in three-dimensional, fine detail, a layer at a time.

"*Doppler Ultrasound Stethoscope*: another microminiaturization spinoff. This instrument is to an ordinary stethoscope as a Rolls-Royce is to a Model-T Ford."

Witness stands up, turns from side to side. "Look at me, please! I'll never be Mr. America; I'll never take part in the Olympics. I've climbed my last mountain.

"But I'm here, I'm alive, I'm functioning.

"Fourteen months ago my brain was dull-normal and getting worse, slipping toward 'human vegetable.' I slept 16 hours a day and wasn't worth a hoot the other 8 hours.

"Were it not for the skill of Dr. Norman Chater, plus certain spinoffs from the space program, today I would either be a human vegetable or, if lucky, dead of cerebral stroke.

"My father was *not* lucky; from a similar disorder it took him years to die—*miserable* years. He died before the operation that saved me

215

had been invented, long before there was medical spinoff from space technology.

"Am I elderly? I'm 72. I suffered from a disorder typical of old age, almost never found in the young.

"Am I handicapped? Yes, but my handicaps do not interfere with my work—or my joy in life. Over forty years ago the Navy handed me a piece of paper that pronounced me totally and permanently disabled. I never believed it. That piece of paper wore out; I did not.

"Mrs. Heinlein and I spent 1976 and -77 on blood drives all over this nation. We crisscrossed the country so many times we lost track. It was worthwhile; we recruited several thousand new blood donors—but it was *very* strenuous. By the end of '77 we badly needed a rest, so we took a sea voyage. She and I were walking the beach on Moorea, Tahiti, when I turned my head to look at a mountain peak—and something happened.

"I balanced on my left leg and said, 'Darling, I'm terribly sorry but I think I've had a stroke. Something happened inside my head and now I'm seeing double and my right side feels paralyzed.'

"Mrs. Heinlein half carried me, half dragged me, back to the landing—got me back aboard.

"A shipmate friend, Dr. Armando Fortuna, diagnosed what had happened: a transient ischemic attack, not a stroke. When we reached California, this was confirmed by tests. However a TIA is frequently a prelude to a stroke.

"Remember that spinoff, computerized-axial tomography? That was done to me to rule out brain tumor. No tumor. The neurologist my physician had called in started me on medication to thin my blood as the clinical picture indicated constriction in blood flow to my brain. This treatment was to continue for six months.

"But in only two months I was failing so rapidly that I was shipped to the University of California Medical School at San Francisco for further diagnosis. Remember the *image enhancer* and that dog at the University of Arizona? I said that dog was *not* hurt. They did it to me, with *no* anesthesia; it did *not* hurt.

"The catheter goes in down here"—witness points at his right groin—"and goes all the way up and into the aortal arch above the heart. There three very large arteries lead up toward the brain; the catheter was used to shoot x-ray-opaque dye into each, in succession. The procedure took over two hours … but I was never bored because the image enhancer included closed-circuit television of the fluoroscopy with the screen right up here"—witness indicates a spot just above and to the left of his head—"above me, where the radiologist and his team, and the patient—I—could see it.

"How many people ever get a chance to watch their own hearts beat? Utterly fascinating! I could see my heart beating, see my diaphragm rise and fall, see my lungs expand and contract, see the dye go up into my brain … see the network of blood vessels in my brain suddenly spring into sharp relief. It was worth the trip!

"They spotted what was wrong; my left internal carotid was totally blocked. So the left half of my brain was starved for oxygen, as it was receiving only what leaked over from the right side or from the vertebrals where the network interconnected, principally at the Circle of Willis under the brain.

"But this is your speech center"—witness touches left side of skull above ear—"your word processor, the place where a writer does all his work. No wonder I was dopey—could not write, could not study, could not read anything difficult.

"My left internal carotid is still blocked; the stoppage is too high up for surgery. So they sent me to Dr. Chater at Franklin Hospital, who moved my left superficial temporal artery to feed the left side of my brain. This operation is pictured on pages 62 and 63 of the April 1978 *Scientific American*, so I will omit grisly details; if surgery interests you, you can look them up there.

"The procedure is this: Scalp the patient from the left eyebrow, going high and curving down to a spot behind the left ear back of the mastoid. Cut away from the scalp the temporal artery. Saw a circular hole in the skull above the ear. Go inside the brain into the Sylvian fissure, find its main artery, join the two arteries, end to side. The left anterior lobe of my brain is now served by the left *external* carotid via this roundabout bypass. Dr. Chater did the hookup under a microscope with sutures so fine the naked eye can't see them.

"Check by *Doppler ultrasound* to make sure the bypass works, then close the hole in the skull with a plate that has a groove in it for the moved artery. Sew back the scalp—go to lunch. The surgeon has been operating for four hours; he's hungry. (The patient is not.)

"They placed me in a cardiac intensive-care room. When I woke, I found in my room a big screen with dancing lights all over it. Those curves meant nothing to me but were clear as print to the I.C. nurses and to my doctors—such things as EKG, blood pressure, respiration, temperature, brain waves, I don't know what all. The thing was so sensitive that my slightest movement caused one of the curves to spike.

"I mention this gadget because I was *not* wired to it.

"Another space-technology spinoff: This is the way Dr. Berry monitored our astronauts whenever they were out in space.

"Colonel Berry had to have remote monitoring for his astronaut patients. For me it may not have been utterly necessary. But it did mean that I was not cluttered with dozens of wires like a fly caught in a web; the microminiaturized sensors were so small and unobtrusive that I never noticed them—yet the nurses had the full picture every minute, every second.

"Another advantage of telemetered remote monitoring is that more than one terminal can display the signals. My wife tells me that there was one at the nursing supervisor's station. Dr. Chater may have had a terminal in his offices—I don't know. But there can't be any difficulty in remoting a hundred yards or so when the technology was developed for remoting from Luna to Houston, almost a quarter of a million miles.

"*Space spinoff in postoperative care:* a *Doppler ultrasound* stethoscope is an impressive example of microminiaturization. It is enormously more sensitive than an acoustic stethoscope; the gain can be controlled, and, because of its Doppler nature, fluid flow volume and direction can be inferred by a skilled operator. Being ultrasound at extremely high frequency, it is highly directional; an acoustic stethoscope is not.

"It generates a tight beam of ultrasound beyond the range of the human ear. This beam strikes something and bounces back, causing interference beats in the audible range. It behaves much like Doppler radar save that the radiation is ultrasound rather than electromagnetic. Thus it is a *noninvasive* way to explore inside the body without the dangers of x-ray ... and is able to 'see' soft tissues that x-ray can't see.

"Both characteristics make it especially useful for protecting pregnant mothers and unborn babies. I am not departing from the call; babies unborn and newly born, and mothers at term *must* be classed as 'temporarily but severely handicapped.'

"*Doppler ultrasound* was used on me *before, during,* and *after* surgery.

"After my convalescence I was again examined by *computerized axial tomography.* No abnormalities—other than the new plate in my skull.

"This brain surgery is not itself a spinoff from space technology ... but note how repeatedly space spinoffs were used on me before, during, and after surgery. This operation is *very* touchy; in the whole world only a handful of surgical teams dare attempt it. Of the thousand-odd of these operations to date, worldwide, Dr. Chater has performed more than 300. His mortality rate is far lower than that of any other team, anywhere. This is a tribute to his skill but part of it comes from his attitude: he *always* uses the latest, most sophisticated tools available.

"I was far gone; I needed every edge possible. Several things that tipped the odds in my favor are spinoffs from space technology.

"Was it worthwhile? Yes, even if I had died at one of the four critical points—because sinking into senility while one is still bright enough to realize that one's mental powers are steadily failing is a miserable, no-good way to live. Early last year I was just smart enough to realize that I had *nothing* left to look forward to, nothing whatever. This caused me to be quite willing to 'Go-for-Broke'—get well or die.

"Did it work? I have been out of convalescence about one year, during which I've caught up on two years of technical journals, resumed studying—I have long been convinced that life-long learning helps to keep one young and happy. True or not, both my wife and I do this. At present I am reviewing symbolic logic, going on into more advanced n-dimensional, non-Euclidean geometries, plus another subject quite new to me: Chinese history.

"But I am working, too; I have completed writing a very long novel and am about halfway through another book.

"I feel that I have proved one of two things: either I have fully recovered ... or a hole in the head is no handicap to a science-fiction author.

"I must note one spinoff especially important to the aged and the handicapped: *spiritual* spinoff.

"'Man does not live by bread alone.' Any physician will tell you that the most important factor in getting well is the will to live—contrariwise, a terminal patient dies when he gives up the fight.

"I have been in death row three times. The unfailing support of my wife sustained my will to live … so here I am. In addition I have believed firmly in space flight for the past sixty-odd years; this has been a permanent incentive to *hang on, hang on!* My wife shares this; she decided years back to die on the Moon, not here in the smog and the crowds. Now that I am well again I intend to hang in there, lead a disciplined life, stay alive until we can *buy* commercial tickets to the Moon … and spend our last days in low-gravity comfort in the Luna Hilton, six levels down in Luna City.

"Foolishness? Everyone in this room is old enough to know by direct experience that today's foolishness is tomorrow's wisdom. I can remember when 'Get a horse!' was considered the height of wit. As may be, *anything* that gives one a strong incentive to live can't be *entirely* foolish.

"I get a flood of mail from my readers; a disproportionate part of it is from the very old and the handicapped. It is impossible to be a fan of my fiction and not be enthusiastic for space travel. Besides, they *tell* me so, explicitly, in writing.

"Examples:

"A college professor, blind from birth. He's never *seen* the stars; he's never *seen* the Moon. The books he reads and rereads—has read to him by his secretary—are about space travel. He went to a lot of trouble to look me up … to discuss our space program.

"A teenage boy, tied to a wheelchair, who wrote to ask me whether or not he could become an astronautical engineer—some 'friend' had told him that it was a silly ambition for a cripple. I assured him that an engineer did not need legs even on Earth's surface, advised him in what courses to take, and referred him to a story by Arthur C. Clarke in which a double amputee, both legs, commands a space station.

"A housewife with epilepsy, *grand mal*, who doesn't expect ever to be able to go out into space ... but finds her greatest interest in life, her major relief from the tedious routine she must follow, in our space program.

"A *very* large number of elderly people who wrote to me immediately after the first landing on the Moon, all saying, in effect, that they thanked the Lord that they had been spared long enough to see this great day.

"I could add examples endlessly. Just let me state flatly that my files hold proof that the aged retired, the shut-ins and the disabled of all ages get more spiritual lift out of space flight than does any other definable group of our citizens. For many of them the television screen is their only window on the world; something great and shining and wonderful went out of their lives when the Apollo Moon program ended.

"Even if a space program had no other spinoff, isn't *that* sort worth 5¢ a day?"

AFTERWORD

Later: No, to most citizens of the United States the entire space program plus all its spinoffs is not worth even 5¢ per day; the polls (and letters to Congress) plainly show it. And they won't believe that 5¢ figure even if you do the arithmetic right in front of their eyes. They will still think of it as "all that money" being "wasted" on "a few rocks."

It is easy to prove that the space program paid for itself several times over in terms of increased gross national product ... and in new technology ... and in saved lives. But they won't believe any of that, either.

NASA has two remarkable records: first, a space program far more successful than anyone had dared hope; and, second, the most incredibly bumbling, stupid, inept public relations of any government agency.

A Congressman's counsel pointed out to me that NASA and other government agencies were by law not permitted to advertise themselves. Oh, come off it!—it does not matter whether a man is called a "public information aide" or a flack; a press agent defines himself by what he does. The man who was NASA's boss flack all during the Moon program had the endearing manners of Dennis the Menace. He's gone now—but the damage he did lives on, while our space program is dying.

Still ... if you aren't willing to give up and start studying Mandarin or possibly Japanese, you can write to your congressman and to both your senators and tell them how you feel about it. If you do, send copies to Don Fuqua (Democrat, Lower House) and to Barry Goldwater, Sr. (Republican, Upper House). A strong space program has many friends in both parties and in both houses—but it is necessary to let them know that they have friends.

I shot an error into the air.
It's still going ... *everywhere*.

—L. Long

FOREWORD

One would think that a "prophet" unable to score higher than 66% after 30 years have elapsed on 50-year predictions would have the humility (or the caution) to refrain from repeating his folly. But I've never been very humble, and the motto of my prime vocation has always been: "L'audace! Toujours l'audace!"

So the culprit returns to his crime. Or see Proverbs XXVI, 11. And hang on to your hats!

—— THE HAPPY DAYS AHEAD ——

"It does not pay a prophet to be too specific."

—L. Sprague de Camp

"You never get rich peddling gloom."

—William Lindsay Gresham

The late Bill Gresham was, before consumption forced him into fiction writing, a carnie mentalist of great skill. He could give a cold reading that would scare the pants off a marble statue. In six words he summarized the secret of success as a fortuneteller. Always tell the mark what he wants to hear. He will love you for it, happily pay you, then forgive and forget when your cheerful prediction fails to come true—and always come back for more.

Stockbrokers stay in business this way; their tips are no better than guesses but they are *not* peddling dividends; they are peddling happiness. Millions of priests and preachers have used this formula, promising eternal bliss in exchange for following, or at least giving lip service to, some short and tolerable rules, plus a variable cash fee not too steep for the customer's purse ... and have continued to make this formula work *without ever in all the years producing even one client who had actually received the promised prize.*

Then how do churches stay in business? Because, in talking about "Pie in the Sky, By and By," they offer happiness and peace of mind *right here on Earth.* When Karl Marx said, "Religion is the opium of the people," he was not being cynical or sarcastic; he was being correctly descriptive. In the middle nineteenth century opium was the *only* relief from intolerable pain; Karl Marx was stating that faith in a happy religion made the lives of the people of the abyss tolerable.

Sprague de Camp is Grand Master of practically everything and probably the most learned of all living practitioners of science fiction and fantasy. I heard those words of wisdom from him before I wrote the 1950 version of "Pandora's Box." So why didn't I listen? Three reasons: 1) money; 2) money; and 3) I thought I could get away with it during my lifetime for predictions attributed to 2000 A.D. I never expected to live that long; I had strong reasons to expect to die young. But I seem to have more lives than a cat; it may be necessary to kill me by driving a steak through my heart (sirloin by choice), then bury me at a crossroads.

Still, I could have gotten away with it if I had stuck to predictions that could not mature before 2000 A.D. Take the two where I *really* flopped, #5 and #16. *In both cases I named a specific year short of 2000 A.D.* Had I not ignored Mr. de Camp's warning, I could look bland and murmur, "Wait and see. Don't be impatient," on all in which the prediction does not look as promising in 1980 as it did in 1950.

Had I heeded a wise man on 2 out of 19 I could today, by sheer brass, claim to be batting a thousand.

I have made some successful predictions. One is "The Crazy Years." (Take a look out your window. Or at your morning paper.) Another is the water bed. Some joker tried to patent the water bed to shut out competition, and discovered that he could not because it was in the public domain, having been described in detail in *Stranger in a Strange Land*. It had been mentioned in stories of mine as far back as 1941 and several times after that, but not until *Stranger* did the mechanics of a scene require describing how it worked.

It was *not* the first man to build water beds who tried to patent it. The first man in the field knew where it came from; he sent me one, free and freight prepaid, with a telegram naming his firm as the "Share-Water Bed Company." Q.E.D.

Our house has no place to set up a water bed. None. So that bed is still in storage a couple of hundred yards from our main house. I've owned a water bed from the time they first came on market—but have never slept in one.

I designed the water bed during years as a bed patient in the middle thirties: a pump to control water-level, side supports to permit one to float rather than simply lying on a not-very-soft water-filled mattress, thermostatic control of temperature, safety interfaces to avoid all possibility of electrical shock, waterproof box to make a leak no more important than a leaky hot water bottle rather than a domestic disaster, calculation of floor loads (important!), internal rubber mattress, and lighting, reading, and eating arrangements—an attempt to design the perfect hospital bed by one who had spent too *damned* much time in hospital beds.

Nothing about it was eligible for patent—nothing new—unless a sharp patent lawyer could persuade the examiners that a working assemblage enabling a person to sleep on water involved that—how does the law describe it?—"flash of inspiration" transcending former art. But I never thought of trying; I simply wanted to build one—but at that time I could not have afforded a custom-made soapbox.

But I know exactly where I got the idea. In 1931, a few days after the radio-compass incident described in the afterword to "Searchlight," I was ordered to Fort Clayton, Canal Zone, to fire in Fleet Rifle & Pistol Matches. During that vacation-with-pay I often returned from Panama City after taps, when all was quiet. There was a large swimming pool near the post gate used by the Navy and our camp was well separated from the Army regiment barracked there.

I would stop, strip naked, and have a swim—nonreg (no life guards) but no one around, and regulations are made to be broken.

Full moon occurred about the middle of Fleet Matches—and I am one of those oddies who cannot sink, even in fresh water (which this was). The water was blood warm, there was no noise louder than night jungle sounds, the Moon blazed overhead, and I would lie back with every muscle relaxed and stare at it—fall into it—wonder whether we would get there in my lifetime. Sometimes I dozed off.

Eventually I would climb out, wipe my feet dry with a hanky, pull on shoes, hang clothes over my arm, and walk to my tent in the dark. I don't recall ever meeting anyone but it couldn't matter—dark, all male, surrounded by armed sentries, and responsible myself only to a Marine Corps officer junior to me but my TDY boss as team captain—and he did not give a hoot what I did as long as I racked a high score on the range (and I did, largely because my coach was a small wiry Marine sergeant nicknamed "Deacon"—who reappears as survival teacher in *Tunnel in the Sky*).

Some years later, bothered by bed sores and with every joint aching no matter what position I twisted into, I thought often of the Sybaritic comfort of floating in blood-warm water at night in Panama—and wished that it could be done for bed patients … and eventually figured out how to do it, all details, long before I was well enough to make working drawings.

But 1) I never expected one to be built; 2) never thought of them (except for myself) other than as hospital beds; 3) never expected them to be widely used by a fair percentage of the public; 4) and never dreamed that they would someday be advertised by motels for romantic-exotic-erotic weekends along with X-rated films on closed-circuit TV.

By stacking the cards, I'm about to follow the advice of both Bill Gresham and Sprague de Camp. First, I will paint a gloomy picture of what our future may be. Second, I'll offer a cheerful scenario of how wonderful it *could* be. I can afford to be specific as each scenario will deny everything said in the other one (de Camp), and I can risk great gloom in the first because I'll play you out with music at the end (Gresham).

GLOOM, WOE, AND DISASTER—There are increasing pathological trends in our culture that show us headed down the chute to self-destruction. These trends do *not* require that we be conquered—wait a bit and we will fall into the lap of whichever power cares to occupy us. I'll list some of these trends and illustrate (rather than prove) what I mean. But it would be tediously depressing to pile up convincing proof—I'm not running for office. I *do have* proof, on file right in this room. I started clipping and filing by categories on trends as early as 1930 and my "youngest" file was started in 1945.

Span of time is important; the 3-legged stool of understanding is held up by **history, languages**, and **mathematics**. Equipped with these three you can learn anything you want to learn. But if you lack *any one* of them you are just another ignorant peasant with dung on your boots.

A few years ago I was visited by an astronomer, young and quite brilliant. He claimed to be a longtime reader of my fiction and his conversation proved it. I was telling him about a time I needed a synergistic orbit from Earth to a 24-hour station; I told him what story it was in, he was familiar with the scene, mentioned having read the book in grammar school.

This orbit is similar in appearance to cometary interplanet transfer but is in fact a series of compromises in order to arrive in step with the space station; elapsed time is an unsmooth integral not to be found in Hudson's Manual but it can be solved by the methods used on Siacci empiricals for atmosphere ballistics: numerical integration.

I'm married to a woman who knows more math, history, and languages than I do. This should teach me humility (and sometimes does, for a few minutes). Her brain is a great help to me professionally. I was telling this young scientist how we obtained yards of butcher paper, then each of us worked three days, independently, solved the problem and checked each other—then the answer disappeared into *one* line of *one* paragraph (*Space Cadet*) but the effort had been worthwhile as it controlled what I could do dramatically in that sequence.

Doctor Whoosis said, "But *why* didn't you just shove it through a computer?"

I blinked at him. Then said slowly, gently, "My dear boy—" (I don't usually call Ph.D.'s in hardcore sciences "My dear boy"—they impress me. But this was a special case.)

"My dear boy ... this was *1947*."

It took him some seconds to get it, then he blushed.

Age is not an accomplishment and youth is no sin. This young man was (is) brilliant, skilled in mathematics, had picked German and Russian for his doctorate. At the time I met him he seemed to lack feeling for historical span ... but, if true, I suspect that it began to itch him and he made up that lack either formally or by reading. Come to think of it, much of my own knowledge of history derives not from history courses but from history of astronomy, of war and military art, and of mathematics, as my formal history study stopped

229

with Alexander and resumed with Prince Henry the Navigator. But to understand the history of those three subjects, you *must* branch out into general history.

Span of Time—the Decline of Education

My father never went to college. He attended high school in a southern Missouri town of 3000+, then attended a private 2-year academy roughly analogous to junior college today, except that it was *very* small—had to be; a day school, and Missouri had no paved roads.

Here are some of the subjects he studied in back-country 19th century schools: Latin, Greek, physics (natural philosophy), French, geometry, algebra, 1st year calculus, bookkeeping, American history, World history, chemistry, geology.

Twenty-eight years later I attended a much larger city high school. I took Latin and French but Greek was not offered; I took physics and chemistry but geology was not offered. I took geometry and algebra but calculus was not offered. I took American history and ancient history but no comprehensive history course was offered. Anyone wishing comprehensive history could take (each a one-year 5-hrs/wk course) ancient history, medieval history, modem European history, and American history—and note that the available courses ignored all of Asia, all of South America, all of Africa except ancient Egypt, and touched Canada and Mexico solely with respect to our wars with each.

I've had to repair what I missed with a combination of travel and private study ... and must admit that I did not tackle Chinese history in depth until this year. My training in history was so spotty that it was not until I went to the Naval Academy and saw captured battle flags that I learned that we fought Korea some *eighty years* earlier than the mess we are still trying to clean up.

From my father's textbook I know that the world history course he studied was not detailed (how could it be?) but at least it treated the world as *round*; it did not ignore three fourths of our planet.

Now, let me report what I've seen, heard, looked up, clipped out of newspapers and elsewhere, and read in books such as *Why Johnny Can't Read*, *The Blackboard Jungle*, etc.

Colorado Springs, our home until 1965, in 1960 offered first-year Latin—but that was all. Caesar, Cicero, Virgil—Who dat?

Latin is not taught in the high schools of Santa Cruz County. From oral reports and clippings I note that it is not taught in most high schools across the country.

"Why this emphasis on Latin? It's a dead language!" Brother, as with jazz, in the words of a great artist, "If you have to ask, you ain't never goin' to find out." A person who knows *only* his own language does not even know his *own* language; epistemology necessitates knowing more than one human language. Besides that sharp edge, Latin is a giant help in *all* the sciences—and so is Greek, so I studied it on my own.

A friend of mine, now a dean in a state university, was a tenured professor of history—but got riffed when history was eliminated from the required subjects for a bachelor's degree. His courses (American history) are still offered but the one or two who sign up, he tutors; the overhead of a classroom cannot be justified.

A recent *Wall Street Journal* story described the bloodthirsty job hunting that goes on at the annual meeting of the Modern Languages Association; modern languages—even English—are being deemphasized right across the country; there are more professors in MLA than there are jobs.

I mentioned elsewhere the straight-A student on a scholarship who did not know the relations between weeks, months, and years. This is not uncommon; high school and college students in this country usually can't do simple arithmetic without using a pocket calculator. (I mean with pencil on paper; to ask one to do *mental* arithmetic causes jaws to drop—say 17 x 34, done mentally. How? Answer: Chuck away the 34 but remember it. $(10 + 7)^2$ is 289, obviously. Double it: $2(300 - 11)$, or 578.

But my father would have given the answer at once, as his country grammar school a century ago required *perfect* memorizing of multiplication tables *through 20 x 20 = 400* ... so his ciphering the above would have been merely the doubling of a number already known

(289)—or 578. He might have done it again by another route to check it: (68 + 510)—but his hesitation would not have been noticeable.

Was my father a mathematician? Not at all. Am I? Hell, no! This is the simplest sort of kitchen arithmetic, the sort *that high school students can no longer do*—at least in Santa Cruz.

If they don't study math and languages and history, what *do* they study? (**Nota Bene!** Any student can learn the truly tough subjects *on almost any campus if he/she wishes*—the professors and books and labs are there. But the student must *want* to.)

But if that student does not want to learn anything requiring brain sweat, most U.S. campuses will babysit him 4 years, then hand him a baccalaureate for not burning down the library. That girl in Colorado Springs who studied Latin—but no classic Latin—got a "general" bachelor's degree at the University of Colorado in 1964. I attended her graduation, asked what she had majored in. No major. What had she studied? Nothing, really, it turned out—and, sure enough, she's as ignorant today as she was in high school.

Santa Cruz has an enormous, lavish 2-year college and also a campus of the University of California, degree granting through Ph.D. level. But, since math and languages and history are not required, let's see how they fill the other classrooms.

The University of California (all campuses) is classed as a "tough school." It is paralleled by a State University system with lower entrance requirements, and this is paralleled by local junior colleges (*never* called "junior") that accept any warm body.

UCSC was planned as an elite school ("The Oxford of the West") but falling enrollment made it necessary to accept any applicant who can qualify for the University of California as a whole; therefore UCSC now typifies the "statewide campus." Entrance can be by examination (usually College Entrance Examination Boards) or by high school certificate. Either way, admission requires a certain spread—2 years of math, 2 of a modern language, 1 of a natural science, 1 of American history, 3 years of English—and a level of performance that translates as B+. There are two additional requirements: English composition, and American History and Institutions.

The second requirement acknowledges that some high schools do not require American history; UCSC permits an otherwise acceptable applicant to make up this deficiency (with credit) after admission.

The first additional requirement, English composition, can be met by written examination such as CEEB, or by transferring *college* credits considered equivalent, or, lacking either of these, by passing an examination given at UCSC at the start of each quarter.

The above looks middlin' good on the surface. College requirements from high school have been watered down somewhat (or more than somewhat) but that B+ average as a requirement looks good ... *if* high schools are teaching what they taught two and three generations ago. The rules limit admission to the upper 8% of California high school graduates (out-of-state applicants must meet slightly higher requirements).

8%—So 92% fall by the wayside. These 8% are the intellectual elite of young adults of the biggest, richest, and most lavishly educated state in the Union.

Those examinations for the English-composition requirement: How can anyone fail who has had 3 years of high school English and averages B+ across the board?

If he fails to qualify, he may enter but must take at once (no credit) "Subject A"—better known as "Bonehead English."

"Bonehead English" must be repeated, if necessary, until passed. To be forced to take this no-credit course does *not* mean that the victim splits an occasional infinitive, sometimes has a dangling modifier, or a failure in agreement or case—he can even get away with such atrocities, as "—like I say—."

It means that he has reached the Groves of Academe unable to express himself by writing in the English language.

It means that his command of his native language does not equal that of a 12-year-old country grammar school graduate of ninety years ago. It means that he verges on subliterate but that his record is such in other ways that the University will tutor him (no credit and for a fee) rather than turn him away.

But, since these students are the upper 8% and each has had not less than three years of high school English, it follows that only the exceptionally unfortunate student needs "Bonehead English." That's right, isn't it? Each one is eighteen years old, old enough to vote, old enough to contract or to marry without consulting parents, old enough to hang for murder, old enough to have children (and some do); all have had 12 years of schooling including 11 years of English, 3 of them in high school.

(Stipulated: California has special cases to whom English is not native language. But such a person who winds up in that upper 8% is usually—I'm tempted to say "always"—fully literate in English.)

So here we have the cream of California's young adults; each has learned to read and write and spell and has been taught the basics of English during eight years in grammar school, and has polished this by not less than three years of English in high school—and also has had at least two years of a second language, a drill that vastly illuminates the subject of grammar even though grasp of the second language may be imperfect.

It stands to reason that *very* few applicants need "Bonehead English." Yes?

No!

I have just checked. The new class at UCSC is "about 50%" in Bonehead English—and this is normal—normal right across California—and California is no worse than most of the states.

8% off the top—

Half of this elite 8% must take "Bonehead English."

The prosecution rests.

This scandal must be charged to grammar and high school teachers ... many of whom are not themselves literate (I know!)—but are not personally to blame, *as we are now in the second generation of illiteracy.* The blind lead the blind.

But what happens after this child (sorry—young adult citizen) enters UCSC?

I TELL YOU THREE TIMES I TELL YOU THREE TIMES I TELL YOU THREE TIMES: A student who *wants* an education can get one at UCSC in a number of very difficult subjects, plus a broad general education.

I ask you never to forget this while we see how one can slide through, never do any real work, never learn anything solid, and still receive a bachelor of arts degree from the prestigious University of California. Although I offer examples from the campus I know best, I assume conclusively that this can be done throughout the state, as it is one statewide university operating under one set of rules.

Some guidelines apply to any campus: Don't pick a medical school or an engineering school. Don't pick a natural science that requires difficult mathematics. (A subject called "science" that does *not* require difficult mathematics usually is "science" in the sense that "Christian Science" is science—in its widest sense "science" simply means "knowledge" and anyone may use the word for any subject ... but shun the subjects that can't be understood without mind-stretching math.)

Try to get a stupid but good-natured adviser. There are plenty around, especially in subjects in which to get a no-sweat degree; Sturgeon's Law applies to professors as well as to other categories.

For a bachelor's degree:

1) You must spend the equivalent of one academic year in acquiring "breadth"—but wait till you see the goodies!

2) You must take the equivalent of one full academic year in your major subject in upper division courses, plus prerequisite lower division courses. Your 4-year program you must rationalize to your adviser as making sense for your major ("Doctor, I picked *that* course because it *is* so far from my major—for perspective. I was getting too narrow." He'll beam approvingly ... or you had better look for a stupider adviser).

3) Quite a lot of time will be spent off campus but counted toward your degree. This should be fun, but it can range from hard labor at sea, to counting noses and asking snoopy questions of "ethnics" (excuse, please!), to time in Europe or Hong Kong, et al., where you are in danger of learning something new and useful even if you don't try.

4) You will be encouraged to take interdisciplinary majors and are invited (urged) to invent and justify unheard-of new lines of study. For this you need the talent of a used-car salesman as *any* aggregation of courses can be sold as a logical pattern if your "new" subject considers the many complex relationships between three or four or more old and orthodox fields. Careful here! If you are smart enough to put this

over, you may find yourself not only *earning* a baccalaureate but in fact, doing original work worthy of a Ph.D. (You won't get it.)

5) You must have at least one upper-division seminar. Pick one in which the staff leader likes your body odor and you like his. ("I do not like thee, Dr. Fell; the reason why I cannot tell—") But you've at least two years in which to learn which professors in your subject are simpatico, and which ones to avoid at any cost.

6) You must write a 10,000 word thesis on your chosen nonsubject and may have to defend it orally. If you can't write 10,000 words of bull on a bull subject, you've made a mistake—you may have to *work* for a living.

The rules above allow plenty of elbowroom; at least three out of four courses can be elective and the remainder elective in part, from a long menu. We are still talking *solely* about nonmathematical subjects. If you are after a Ph.D. in astronomy, UCSC is a wonderful place to get one ... but you will start by getting a degree in physics including the toughest of mathematics, and will study also chemistry, geology, technical photography, computer science—and will resent any time not leading toward the ultra-interdisciplinary subject lumped under the deceptively simple word "astronomy."

Breadth—the humanities, natural science, and social science—1/3 in each, total 3/3 or one academic year, but spread as suits you over the years. Classically "the humanities" are defined as literature, philosophy, and art—but history has been added since it stopped being required in college and became "social studies" in secondary schools. "Natural science" does not necessarily mean what it says—it can be a "nonalcoholic gin"; see below. "Social science" means that grab bag of studies in which answers are matters of opinion.

Courses satisfying "breadth" requirements
Humanities

Literature and Politics—political & moral choices in literature
Philosophy of the Self

Philosophy of History in the Prose and Poetry of W. B. Yeats
Art and the Perceptual Process
The Fortunes of Faust
Science and the American Culture (satisfies both the Humanities requirement and the American History and Institutions requirement *without* teaching *any* science or *any* basic American History. A companion course, *Science and Pressure Politics*, satisfies both the Social Sciences requirement and the American History and Institutions requirement while teaching still less; it concentrates on the post-World-War-II period and concerns scientists as lobbyists and their own interactions [rows] with Congress and the President. Highly recommended as a way to avoid learning American history or very much social "science.")

American Country Music—Whee! You don't play it, you listen.
Man and the Cosmos—philosophy, sorta. Not science.
Science Fiction (I refrain from comment.)
The Visual Arts—"What, if any, are the critical and artistic foundations for judgment in the visual arts?"—exact quotation from catalog.
Mysticism—that's what it says.
(The above list is incomplete.)

Natural Science requirement

General Astronomy—no mathematics required
Marine Biology—no mathematics required
Sound, Music, and Tonal Properties of Musical Instruments—neither math nor music required for this one!
Seminar: Darwin's Explanation
Mathematical Ideas—for nonmathematicians; requires only that high school math you must have to enter.
The Phenomenon of Man—"—examine the question of whether there remains any meaning to human values." (Oh, the pity of it all!)
Physical Geography: Climate

The Social "Sciences" requirement

Any course in Anthropology—many have no pre-req.

237

Introduction to Art Education—You don't have to *make* art; you study how to teach it.

Music and the Enlightenment—no technical knowledge of music required. This is a discussion of the effect of music on philosophical, religious, and social ideas, late 18th-early 19th centuries. That is what it says—and it counts as "social science."

The Novel of Adultery—and this, too, counts as "social science." I don't mind anyone studying this subject or teaching it—but I object to its being done on my (your, our) tax money. (P.S. The same bloke teaches science fiction. He doesn't *write* science fiction; I don't know what his qualifications are in this other field.)

Human Sexuality

Cultural Roots for Verbal and Visual Expression—a fancy name of still another "creative writing" class with frills—the students are taught how to draw out "other culture" pupils. So it says.

All the 30-odd *"Community Studies"* courses qualify as "social science," but I found myself awed by these two: *Politics and Violence,* which studies, among other things, "political assassination as sacrifice" and *Leisure and Recreation in the Urban Community* ("Bread and Circuses").

Again, listing must remain incomplete; I picked those below as intriguing:

Seminar: Evil and the Devil in the Hindu Tradition.

Science and Pressure Politics—already mentioned on page 237 (Volume II) as the course that qualifies both as social "science" and as American History and Institutions while teaching an utter minimum about each. The blind man now has hold of the elephant's tail.

The Political Socialization of La Raza—another double header, social "science" and American History and Institutions. It covers greater time span (from 1900 rather than from 1945) but it's like comparing cheese and chalk to guess which one is narrower in scope in either category.

The name of this game is to plan a course involving minimum effort and minimum learning while "earning" a degree under the rules of the nation's largest and most prestigious state university.

To take care of "breadth" and also the American history your high school did not require I recommend *Science and Pressure Politics*, *The Phenomenon of Man*, and *American Country Music*. These three get you home free without learning *any* math, history, or language that you did not already know ... and without sullying your mind with science.

You must pick a major ... but it must *not* involve mathematics, history, or actually being able to *read* a second language. This rules out *all* natural sciences (this campus's greatest strength).

Anthropology? You would learn something in spite of yourself; you'd get interested. Art? Better not major in it without major talent. Economics can be difficult, but also and worse, you may incline toward the Chicago or the Austrian school and not realize it until your (Keynesian or Marxist) instructor has failed you with a big black mark against your name. Philosophy? Easy and lots of fun and absolutely guaranteed not to teach you anything while loosening up your mind. In more than twenty-five centuries of effort *not one* basic problem of philosophy has *ever* been solved ... but the efforts to solve them are most amusing. The same goes for comparative religion as a major: You won't actually *learn* anything you can sink your teeth into ... but you'll be vastly entertained—if the Human Comedy entertains you. It does me.

Psychology, Sociology, Politics, and Community Studies involve not only risk of learning something—not much, but *something*—and each is likely to involve real work, tedious and lengthy.

To play this game and win, with the highest score, it's Hobson's choice: American literature. I assume that you did not have to take Bonehead English and that you can type. In a school that has no school of education (UCSC has none) majoring in English Literature is the obvious way to loaf through four years. It will be necessary to cater to the whims of professors who know no more than you do about anything that matters ... but catering to your mentors is necessary in any subject not ruled by mathematics.

Have you noticed that professors of English and/or American Literature are not expected to be proficient in the art they profess to teach? Medicine is taught by M.D.'s on living patients, civil engineering is taught by men who in fact have built bridges that did not fall;

law is taught by lawyers; music is taught by musicians; mathematics is taught by mathematicians—and so on.

But is—for example—the American Novel taught by American novelists?

Yes. Occasionally. But so seldom that the exceptions stand out. John Barth. John Erskine fifty years ago. Several science-fiction writers almost all of whom were selling writers long before they took the King's Shilling. A corporal's guard in our whole country out of battalions of English profs.

For a Ph.D. in American/English literature a candidate is not expected to *write* literature; he is expected to *criticize* it.

Can you imagine a man being awarded an M.D. for writing a *criticism* of some great physician without ever himself having learned to remove an appendix or to diagnose *Herpes zoster*? And for that dissertation then be hired to *teach* therapy to medical students?

There is, of course, a reason for this nonsense. The rewards to a competent novelist are so much greater than the salaries of professors of English at even our top schools that once he/she learns this racket, teaching holds no charms.

There are exceptions—successful storytellers who *like* to teach so well that they keep their jobs and write only during summers, vacations, evenings, weekends, sabbaticals. I know a few—emphasis on "few." But most selling wordsmiths are lazy, contrary, and so opposed to any fixed regime that they will do *anything*—even meet a deadline—rather than accept a job.

Most professors of English *can't* write publishable novels ... and many of them can't write nonfiction prose very well—certainly not with the style and distinction and grace—and content—of Professor of Biology Thomas H. Huxley. Or Professor of Astronomy Sir Fred Hoyle. Or Professor of Physics John R. Pierce. Most Professors of English get published, when they do, by university presses or in professional quarterlies. But fight it out for cash against *Playboy*, and Travis McGee? They can't and they don't!

But if you are careful not to rub their noses in this embarrassing fact and pay respectful attention to their opinions even about (ugh!) "creative writing," they will help you slide through to a painless baccalaureate.

You still have time for many electives and will need them for your required hours-units-courses; here are some fun-filled ones that will teach you almost nothing:

The Fortunes of Faust

Mysticism

The Search for a New Life Style

The American Dilemma—Are "all men equal"?

Enology—history, biology, and chemistry of wine-making and wine appreciation. This one will teach you something but it's too good to miss.

Western Occultism: Magic, Myth, and Heresy.

There is an entire college organized for fun and games ("aesthetic enrichment"). It offers courses for credit but you'll be able to afford noncredit activity as well in your lazyman's course—and *anything* can be turned into credit by some sincere selling to your adviser and/or Academic Committee. I have already listed nine of its courses but must add:

Popular Culture

—plus clubs or "guilds" for gardening, photography, filmmedia, printing, pottery, silkscreening, orchestra, jazz, etc.

Related are *Theater Arts.* These courses give credit, including:

Films of Fantasy and Imagination—fantasy, horror, SF, etc. (!)

Seminar on Films

Filmmaking

History and Aesthetics of Silent Cinema

History and Aesthetics of Cinema since Sound

Introduction to World Cinema

Sitting and looking at movies can surely be justified for an English major. Movies and television use writers—as little as possible, it's true. But somewhat; the linkage is there.

Enjoy yourself while it lasts. These dinosaurs are on their way to extinction.

The 2-year "warm body" campus is even more lavish than UCSC. It is a good trade school for some things—e.g., dental assistant. But it offers a smorgasbord of fun—Symbolism of the Tarot, Intermediate Contract Bridge, Folk Guitar, Quilting, Horseshoeing, Chinese Cooking, Hearst Castle Tours, Modern Jazz, Taoism, Hatha Yoga Asanas, Aikido, Polarity Therapy, Mime, Raku, Bicycling, Belly Dancing, Shiatsu Massage, Armenian Cuisine, Revelation and Prophecy, Cake Art, Life Insurance Sales Techniques, Sexuality and Spirituality, Home Bread Baking, Ecuadorian Backstrap Weaving, The Tao of Physics, and lots, lots more! One of the newest courses is "The Anthropology of Science Fiction" and I'm still trying to figure that out.

I have no objection to any of this ... but why should this kindergarten be paid for by *taxes*? "Bread and Circuses."

I first started noticing the decline of education through mail from readers. I have saved mail from readers for forty years. Shortly after World War Two I noticed that letters from the youngest were not written but hand-printed. By the middle fifties deterioration in handwriting and in spelling became very noticeable. By today a letter from a youngster in grammar school *or in high school* is usually difficult to read and sometimes illegible—penmanship atrocious (*pencil*manship—nine out of ten are in soft pencil, with well-smudged pages), spelling unique, grammar an arcane art.

Most youngsters have not been taught how to fold 8½" x 11" paper for the two standard sizes of envelopes intended for that standard sheet.

Then such defects began to show up among college students. Apparently "Bonehead English" (taught everywhere today so I hear) is not sufficient to repair the failure of grammar and high school teachers *who themselves in most cases were not adequately taught.*

I saw sharply this progressive deterioration because part of my mail comes from abroad, especially Canada, the United Kingdom, the Scandinavian countries, and Japan. A letter from any part of the Commonwealth is invariably neat, legible, grammatical, correct in spelling, and polite. The same applies to letters from Scandinavian countries. (Teenagers of Copenhagen usually speak and write English better than most teenagers of Santa Cruz.) Letters from Japan are invariably neat—but the syntax is sometimes odd. I have one young correspondent in Tokyo who has been writing steadily these past four years. The handwriting in the first letter was almost stylebook perfect but I could hardly understand the phrasing; now, four years later, the handwriting looks the same but command of grammar, syntax, and rhetoric is excellent, with only an occasional odd choice in wording giving an exotic flavor.

Our public schools no longer give good value. We remain strong in science and engineering but even students in those subjects are handicapped by failures of our primary and secondary schools and by cutback in funding of research both public and private. Our great decline in education is alone enough to destroy this country ... but I offer no solutions because the only solutions I think would work are so drastic as to be incredible.

Span of Time—Decline in Patriotism and in the Quality of Our Armed Forces

The high school I attended (1919-24) was an early experiment in the junior and senior high school method. The last year of grammar school was joined with the freshman class as "junior high" while the sophomores, juniors, and seniors were "senior high."

There was a company of junior ROTC in junior high and two companies in senior high. Military training gave no credit and was not compulsory; it was neither pushed nor discouraged. A boy took it or not, as suited him and his parents. Some of the subfreshmen (aet. ca. 13 an.) were barely big enough to tote a Springfield rifle.

Kansas City had a regiment of Federalized National Guard, with one authorized drill per week, 3 hours each Wednesday evening. For this a private was paid 69¢, a PFC got a dollar, and a corporal got big money—$1.18.

The required & paid weekly drill was not all, as about half of the regiment showed up on Sundays at the "Military Country Club"— acres of raw wood lot until the regiment turned it into rifle range, club house, stables, etc. No pay for Sundays. Two weeks encampment per year, with pay. For most of the regiment, this was their only vacation, two weeks then being standard.

That regiment ran about 96% authorized strength.

About 1921 Congress authorized the CMTC, Citizens Military Training Corps. It proved very popular. A month of summer training in camp at an Army post, continued through 4 years, could (if a candidate's grades were satisfactory) result in certification for commission in the reserve. Civilians submitted to military discipline in CMTC but were not subject to court martial. Offenders could be sent home or turned over to civilian police; depending on the offense. There were few offenses.

CMTC candidates got 3¢ per mile to and from their homes, no other money.

In 1925 I was appointed midshipman. There were 51 qualified applicants trying for that one appointment.

240 of my class graduated; 130 fell by the wayside. *One* of that 130 resigned voluntarily; all the others resigned involuntarily, most of them plebe year for failure in academics (usually mathematics), the others were requested to resign over the next three years for academic, physical, or other reasons. A few resigned graduation day through having failed the final physical examination for commissioning. Three more served about one year in the Fleet, then resigned—but these three volunteered after the attack on Pearl Harbor. 28 of the 129 who left the service involuntarily managed to get back on active duty in World War Two.

So with four exceptions all of my class stayed in the Navy *as long as the Navy would have them*. About 25% were killed in line of duty or died later of wounds. Neither at the Academy nor in the Fleet did I ever hear a midshipman or officer talk about resigning. While it is likely that some thought about it, all discussion tacitly carried the assumption that the Navy was our life, the Fleet our home, and that we would leave only feet first or when put out to pasture as too old.

Enlisted men: When I entered the Fleet, *before* the Crash of '29 and about a year before unemployment became a problem, Navy recruiting offices were turning down 19 out of 20 volunteers; the Army was turning down 5 out of 6. The reenlistment rate was high; the desertion rate almost too small to count.

Span of Time—Today in the Armed Forces

I have said repeatedly that I am opposed to conscription at any time, peace or war, for moral reasons beyond argument. For the rest of this I will try to keep my personal feelings out of the discussion—as I did in the rosy picture painted above. I reported *facts*, not my emotions.

I will not review details showing that the USSR is today militarily stronger than we are as the matter has been discussed endlessly in news media, in Congress, and in professional journals. The public discussion today concedes the military superiority of the USSR and centers on *how much* they are ahead of us, and what should be done about it. The details of this debate are of supreme importance as **the most expensive thing in the world is a second-best military establishment,** good but not good enough to win. At the moment the three-cornered standoff is saving us from that silly way to die ... but I cannot predict how long this stalemate will last as key factors are not under our control, and neither our government nor our citizens seem willing to accept guns instead of butter on the scale required to make us too strong for anyone to risk attacking us. Polls seem to show that a controlling number of voters think that we are already spending too much on our Armed Forces.

What I set forth below comes primarily from an article by Richard A. Gabriel, Associate Professor of Politics, St. Anselm's College, Manchester, New Hampshire, author of *Crisis in Command*. I lack personal experience with Army conditions today but what Dr. Gabriel says about them matches what I have heard from other sources and what I have read (I belong to all three associations—Army, Navy, Air Force—plus the Naval Institute and the Retired Officers Association; I get much data secondhand but no longer see it with my own eyes, hear it with my own ears).

Readers with personal experience in Korea, Viet Nam, and in the Services anywhere since the end of the Viet Nam debacle, I urge to write and tell me what you know that I don't, especially on points in which I am seriously mistaken.

Summarized from "The Slow Dying of the American Army," Dr. Richard A. Gabriel in *Gallery* magazine, June 1979, p. 41 et seq.:

Concerning the All Volunteer Force (AVF): Early this year the Pentagon admitted that all services had failed to meet quotas.

30% of all Army volunteers are discharged for offenses during first enlistment. Of the 70 per 100 left, 26 do not reenlist. The desertion rates are the highest in history ... and this fact is partly covered up by using administrative discharges (—i.e., "You're fired!") rather than courts martial and punishment—*if* the deserter turns up. But no effort is made to find him.

According to Dr. Gabriel, citing General George S. Blanchard and others, hard-drug use (heroin, cocaine, angel dust—not marijuana) is greater than ever, especially in Europe, with estimates from a low of 10% to a high of 64%. Marijuana is ignored—but let me add that a man stoned out of his mind on grass is not one I want on my flank in combat.

Category 3B and 4 (ranging down from dull to mentally retarded) make up 59% of Army volunteers ... in a day when privates handle very complex and sophisticated weapons and machinery. Add to this that the mix is changing so that a typical private might be Chicano or Puerto Rican, the typical sergeant a Black, the typical officer "Anglo." And that officers are transferred with great frequency and enlisted men with considerable frequency and you have a situation in which esprit de corps *cannot* be developed (an outfit without esprit de corps is not an army unit; it is an armed mob—R.A.H.).

Today we have more general officers than we did in World War Two. Our ratio of officers to enlisted men is more than twice as high as that of successful armies in the past. But an officer is not with his troops long enough to be "the Old Man"—he is a "manager," not a leader of men.

Dr. Gabriel concludes: "The most basic aspect is the need to reinstate the draft."

I disagree.

My disagreement is not on moral grounds. Forget that I ever voiced opposition to slave soldiers; think of me as Old Blood-and-Guts willing to use any means whatever to win.

Reinstating the draft would *not* get us out of trouble, even with the changes Dr. Gabriel suggests to make the draft "fair."

As everyone knows, we were in the frying pan; shifting to AVF, instead of producing an efficient professional army, put us into the fire. Dr. Gabriel urges that we climb back into the frying pan—but with improvements: a national lottery with no deferments whatever for any reason.

I can't disagree with the even-steven rule ... but my reason for thinking that Dr. Gabriel's solution will not work is this:

A lottery, even meticulously fair, *cannot* make a man willing to charge a machine-gun nest in the face of almost certain death. That sort of drive comes from emotional sources. Esprit de corps and patriotism *cannot* be drawn in a lottery.

Conscription works (among free men) only when it is not needed. I have seen two world wars; we used the draft in each ... but in each case it was a means of straightening out the manpower situation; it was *not* needed to make men fight. Both wars were popular.

Since then we have had two non-Wars—Korea and Nam—in "peacetime" and using conscript troops. **And each non-War was a scandalous disaster.**

I don't have a neat solution to offer. If the American people have lost their willingness to fight and die for their country, the defect cannot be cured by conscription. Unless this emotional condition changes (and I do not know how to change it), we are whipped no matter what weapons we build. It could be overnight, or it could continue to be a long slow slide downhill over many years—ten, twenty, thirty. But the outcome is the same. Unless *something* renews the spirit this country once had, we are in the terminal stages of decay; history is ending for us.

Our foreign masters might graciously let us keep our flag, even our national name. But "the Land of the Free and the Home of the Brave" will be dead.

Time Span—Inflation

The Winter of '23-'24 I paid a street vendor 5¢ for a five billion mark German note and I paid too much; 5,000,000,000 DM was worth a trifle over 1¢. A bit later it was worth nothing.

In 1955 at the foot of the Acropolis I bought a small marble replica of the Venus of Melos for 10,000 drachma. I wasn't cheated; that was 3.50 USA.

There are the British pound, the Turkish lira, the Italian lira, the Mexican peso, and several others; all mean one pound of silver. Look up "exchange" and "commodities" in your newspaper; grab your pocket calculator and see how much each is inflated.

When I was a child of four or five my brothers and I used great stacks of hundred-dollar bills as play money. Confederate—

After two centuries, "Not worth a continental," still means "worthless." Memory is long for the damage done by inflation.

Before paper "money" was invented, inflation was accomplished by adding base metal to silver and/or gold while retaining the name of the coin. By this means the Roman denarius was devalued to zero during the first three centuries A.D. But inflation did not start with Caesar Augustus. In the early days of the Republic before the Punic Wars the cash unit was the libra (libra = lb.—pound = 273 grams, or about 60% of our pound avoirdupois, 454 grams). That's too large a unit for daily retail use; it was divided into 12 unciae (ounces).

A "lb." of silver was called an "as." 1/12 of that, struck as coinage, made efficient currency. Now comes war and inflation—

Eventually the "as"—once a pound of silver—was so debased that it amounted to a penny, more or less. Augustus, by decree, went back on a silver/gold standard and created the denarius, 3.87 grams of fine silver. He made 25 denarii equal in value to one aureus (7.74 grams of gold), or a ratio of 12.5 to one. ("Free and unlimited coinage of silver at a ratio of sixteen to one!" The Great Commoner and the august Emperor had similar notions about hard currency.)

One Augustan denarius equalled in gold at today's London fix ($385/troy ounce) a nominal $3.83, or about 3/10 of a gram of gold. This tells us nothing about purchasing power; it simply says that the Augustan denarius was a solid silver coin almost the size and weight of the solid silver quarter we used to have before the government foisted on us those sandwich things. How much olive oil or meal that would buy in Rome around 1 A.D. can be estimated from surviving records—but all the gold in Rome could not buy an aspirin tablet or a paper of matches. No way to compare. And hard money was not supplemented by printed money, bank checks, and transactions that take place entirely inside computers—but I can't go into how those phenomena affect purchasing power without writing a book twice as long as this one on fiscal theory (which I am quite willing to do but nobody would buy it).

What Augustus did was to stabilize Rome's money by defining it in terms of two commodities, each intrinsically valuable, each stable in supply, each almost indestructible, and he defined also the legal ratio between the two coinages—an effort to circumvent Gresham's Law, unknown then but Augustus appears to have had a gut feeling for it. (Not Bill Gresham—the other one. Thomas Gresham.) But a bimetallic standard has its problems; the free economy ratio tends to drift away from the legal ratio, and Gresham's Law begins to work. But this happens very slowly with hard money and is not the disaster that printing-press inflation is, or the debasing of hard money.

Caesar Augustus died in 14 A.D.

His corpse was hardly cold before the vultures got to work. Tiberius, Caligula, Claudius, Nero—even Claudius did nothing to stop the robbery. Titus attempted an Augustan return to honest money in 80 A.D. but he died in September the following year; his successor was a disaster even as Caesars go.

"Put not your trust in Princes." Debasement of the currency continued under every Caesar for the next two centuries. Diocletian (reign: 294-305) inherited a worthless denarius; he returned Rome to the bimetallic standard at a level barely below that of Augustus. But he increased enormously the bureaucracy, instituted the harshest of taxation to pay for his "reforms," and decreed price-fixing—which worked just as it always does.

On his retirement (not assassination[!]) debasement was resumed while taxes stayed high, and Rome was on the skids. The decline and fall of the denarius and of Rome paralleled each other.

I'm tempted to discuss France's incredible inflation and collapse thereof during the French Revolution (and three more French inflations since then), and the inflations of several other countries in other centuries. But they are monotonously alike and differ from debasement primarily in the fact that the invention of paper "money" permits the corruption of legal tender to get utterly out of hand before the people notice it. In Germany in the early twenties people used to take wheelbarrows to the grocery store—not to fetch back groceries but to carry money to the grocer. But the early stages of disastrous inflation feel like "prosperity." Wages and profits go up, old debts are easier to pay off, business booms.

It is not until later that most people notice that prices and taxes have gone up faster than wages and profits, and that it is getting harder and harder to make ends meet.

There is a strong emotional feeling that "a dollar is a dollar." (Hitler called it, "Mark is Mark!") But you can reexamine it in terms of prices on bread, or how many minutes to earn a dollar. And don't forget taxes! If you aren't working at least the first three months of each year to pay taxes before you can keep one dollar for yourself, then you are on welfare, one way or another. You may not think you are taxed that much—paycheck deductions and hidden taxes are extracted under anesthesia. Try dividing the Federal Budget by the number of wage earners *not on the public payroll*, then take a stab at where you fit in. Don't forget the same process for state, county, and city. There are Makers, Takers, and Fakers, no fourth category, and today the Takers and the Fakers outnumber (and outvote) the Makers.

Today it takes more dollars each year to service the National Debt than the total budget for the last and most expensive year of the Korean War. I am not going to state here the amount of our National Debt. If you have not heard it recently, you wouldn't believe me. If you don't know, telephone your Congressman and ask; he has a local office near you. If the telephone information service can't (won't) tell you, the city room of *any* newspaper does know his number.

Our National Debt will *never* be paid. We are beyond the point of no return. Inflation will continue and get worse ... and the elderly on fixed incomes and the young adults trying to start families will continue to bear the brunt.

Every congressman, every senator, knows precisely what causes inflation ... but can't (won't) support the drastic reforms to stop it because it could (and probably would) cost him his job. I have no solution and only one piece of advice:

Buy a wheelbarrow.

The Age of Unreason

Having been reared in the most bigoted of Bible Belt fundamentalism in which every word of the King James version of the Bible is the literal word of God—then having broken loose at thirteen when I first laid hands on *The Origin of Species* and *The Descent of Man*—I should have been unsurprised by the anti-intellectual and anti-science ground swell in this country.

I knew that our American temperament, practical as sharp tools on one side, was never more than three quarters of an inch from mindless hysteria on the other side. I *knew* this—my first long story was "If This Goes On—", a yarn based on the assumption that my compatriots were capable of throwing away their dearly-bought liberties to submit to a crude and ridiculous religious dictatorship.

(In forty years of letters about that story no one has ever criticized this assumption; I infer that I am not alone in believing it.)

I had read much about the Ku Klux Klan during the Tragic Era, talked with many who had experienced it, then experienced its nationwide recrudescence in the early 1920's. I had seen damfoolishness from dance marathons to flagpole sitters, and had made considerable study of crowd behavior and mass delusions. I had noted, rather casually, the initial slow growth of anti-science-&-intellect-ism.

Yet the durned thing shocked me.

Let me list some signs:

a) I CHING;

b) Back-to-nature cults;

c) The collapse of basic education;

d) The current respectability of natal horological astrology among "intelligentsia"—e.g. professors, N.Y. lit'rary people, etc.;

e) "Experts" on nuclear power and nuclear weapons who know nothing whatever of mathematical physics and are smug in admitting it;

f) "Experts" on the ecology of northern Alaska who have never been there and are not mathematically equipped to analyse a problem in ecology;

g) People who watch television several hours a day and derive all their opinions therefrom—and expound them;

h) People who watch television several hours a day;

i) The return of creationism—"Equal time for Yahweh";

j) The return of witchcraft.

The mindless yahoos, people who think linearly like a savage instead of inductively or deductively, and people who used to be respectful to learned opinion or at least kept quiet, now are aggressively on the attack. Facts and logic don't count; their intuition is the source of "truth."

If any item on the above list strikes you as rational, I won't debate it with you; you are part of the problem.

But I will illustrate what I mean in categories where I think I might be misunderstood.

a) **I CHING**—easier than "reading the augurs" but with nothing else to recommend it. Chinese fortune cookies are just as accurate—and you get to eat the cookie. Nevertheless this bit of oriental nonsense is treated with solemn seriousness by many "educated" people. It is popular enough to make profitable the sale of books, equipment, magazine articles, and personal instruction. Paralleling I CHING is the widespread use of Tarot cards. Fortunetelling by cards used to be a playful parlor game, a mating rite—a nubile girl limited by the vocabulary and public manners of the Mauve Decade could convey to a rutty young male almost any message by how she chose to "read his fortune"—with no impropriety. But neither he nor she took the cards seriously.

Tarot cards formerly were used only by Gypsy or fake-Gypsy fortunetellers; they were not an article of commerce, were not easy to find. Today they are as easy to buy as liquor during prohibition, and also books on their "interpretation." Reading the Tarot is taken with deep seriousness by a dismaying number of people—having the Hanging Man turn up can cause great anguish.

b) **Back-to-nature cults**: I do *not* mean nudist resorts or "liberated" beaches. The growing realization that human bodies are not obscene is a sane, healthy counter trend in our crazy culture. By back-to-nature cults I mean people who band together to "return to the land" to grow their own food without pesticides, without artificial fertilizers, without power machinery, self-reliant in all ways ... but with no comprehension that a spading fork implies coal mines, iron ore, blast furnaces, steel mills, factories, etc., that any building more complex than a log cabin or a sod house implies a building-materials industry, etc.

If all of us tried to go back-to-nature, most of us would starve rather quickly. These back-to-nature freaks can't do arithmetic.

c) **The collapse of basic education**—no need to repeat.

d) **Natal horological astrology**—Baseline: fifty-odd years ago astrology was commonly regarded as a ridiculous superstition, one all but a tiny minority had outgrown. It is now the orthodoxy of many, possibly a majority. This pathological change parallels the decay of public education.

Stipulated: Ancient astrologers were scientists in being able to predict certain aspects of descriptive astronomy such as eclipses, positions of the sun, moon, and naked-eye planets, etc. Whether or not they believed the fortunetelling they supplied to their kings, patrons, or clients is irrelevant. The test of a science is its ability to predict; in the cited phenomena the Chaldean priests (for example) performed remarkable feats of prediction with handcrafted naked-eye instruments.

It has long been known that Sol is the heat engine that controls our weather. Recently, with the discovery of solar wind, the Van Allen belts, etc., we have become aware of previously unsuspected variables affecting us and our weather, and successful predictions are being made empirically—no satisfactory theory.

"What sign were you born under?"—I don't recall having heard that question until sometime after World War Two. Today it is almost impossible to attend a social gathering (including parties made up almost solely of university staff and spouses) without being asked that question or hearing it asked of someone else.

Today natal horological astrology is so widely accepted that those who believe in it take it for granted that anyone they meet believes in it, too—if you don't, you're some sort of a nut. I don't know what percentage of the population believe in natal horological astrology (sorry about that clumsy expression but I wish to limit this precisely to the notion that the exact time, date, latitude, and longitude of your birth and the pattern of the Sun, Moon, and planets with respect to the Zodiac at that exact time all constitute a factor affecting your life comparable in importance to your genetic inheritance and your rearing and education)—I don't know the percentage of True Believers but it is high enough that newspaper editors will omit any feature or secondary news rather than leave out the daily horoscope.

Or possibly *more* important than heredity and environment in the minds of True Believers since it is seriously alleged that this natal heavenly pattern *affects every day of your life*—good days for new business ventures—a bad day to start a trip—and so forth, endlessly.

The test of a science is its capacity to make correct predictions. Possibly the most respected astrologer in America is a lady who not only has her daily column in most of the largest newspapers but also annually publishes predictions for the coming year.

For ten years I clipped her annual predictions, filed them. She is highly recommended and I think she is sincere; I intended to give her every possible benefit of doubt.

I hold in my hand her predictions for 1974 dated Sunday January 13, 1974:

Here are some highlights: "... Nixon ... will ride out the Watergate storm ... will survive both the impeachment ordeal and the pressures to resign—will go down in history as a great president ... will fix the responsibility for Pearl Harbor" (vindicating Kimmel and Short) ... "in ... 1978 ... the cure for cancer will be acknowledged by the medical world ... end the long search." (1974) "The dollar will be enormously strengthened as the balance of payments reflects the self-sufficiency in oil production." "The trouble in Ireland will continue to be a tragic situation *until 1978*." (Italics added—R.A.H.) "Willy Brandt" (will be reelected) "and be in office for quite some time to come. He will go on to fantastic recognition about the middle of 1978." (On 6 May 1974 Brandt resigned during a spy scandal.) She makes many other predictions either too far in the future to check or too vaguely worded. I have omitted her many predictions about Gerald Ford because they all depend on his serving out the term as vice president.

You can check the above in the files of most large newspapers.

e) & f)—no comment needed.

g) & h) need no comment except to note that they are over-lapping but not identical categories—and I should add "People who allow their children to watch television several hours a day." (Television, like the automobile, is a development widely predicted ... but its major consequences *never* predicted.).

i) **The return of creationism**—If it suits you to believe that Yahweh created the universe in the fashion related in Genesis, I won't argue it. But I don't have to respect your belief and I do not think that legislation requiring that the Biblical version be included in public school textbooks is either constitutional or fair. How about Ormuzd? Ouranos? Odin? There is an unnumbered throng of religions, each with its creation myth—all different. Shall one of them be taught as having the status of a scientific hypothesis merely because the members of the religion subscribing to it can drum up a majority at the polls, or organize a pressure group at a state capital? This is tyranny by the mob inflicted on minorities in defiance of the Bill of Rights.

Revelation has no place in a science textbook; it belongs under religious studies. Cosmogony is the most difficult and least satisfactory branch of astronomy; cosmologists would be the first to agree. But, damn it; they're *trying*!—on the evidence as it becomes available, by logical methodology, and their hypotheses are constantly subjected to pitiless criticism by their informed equals.

They should not have to surrender time on their platform; space in their textbooks, to purveyors of ancient myths supported only by a claim of "divine revelation."

If almost everyone believed in Yahweh and Genesis, and less than one in a million U.S. citizens believe in Brahma the Creator, it would not change the constitutional aspect. *Neither* belongs in a science textbook in a tax-supported school. But if Yahweh is there, Brahma should be. And how about that Eskimo Creator with the unusually unsavory methods? We have a large number of Eskimo citizens.

j) **The return of witchcraft**—It used to be assumed that Southern California had almost a monopoly on cults. No longer. (Cult vs. religion—I am indebted to L. Sprague de Camp for this definition of the difference. A "religion" is a faith one is born into; a "cult" is a faith an adult joins voluntarily. "Cult" is often used as a slur by a member of an older faith to disparage a newer faith. But this quickly leads to

255

contradictions. In the 1st century A.D. the Christians were an upstart cult both to the Sanhedrin and to the Roman priests. "Cult" is also used as a slur on a faith with "weird ideas" and "weird practices." But this can cause you to bite your tail even more quickly than the other. "Weird" by whose standards?

(Mr. de Camp's distinction implies something about a mature and presumably sane adult becoming a proselyte in a major and long-established faith, such as Islam or Shintoism or the Church of England ... but the important thing it implies is that a person born into, let us say, the Presbyterian Church is not being odd or unreasonable if he remains in it all his life despite having lost all faith; he's merely being pragmatic. His wife and kids are there; he feels that church is a good influence on the kids, many of his friends are there. It's a comfortable habit, one carrying with it a degree of prestige in the community.

(But if he changes into a saffron robe and shaves his pate, then goes dancing down the street, shouting, "Hare Krishna!" he won't keep his Chevrolet dealership very long. Theology has nothing to do with it.)

One of the symptoms of this Age of Unreason, anti-science and anti-intellect, in the United States is the very prominent increase in new cults. We've never been without them. 19th Century New England used to breed them like flies. Then it was Southern California's turn. Now they seem to spring up anywhere and also are readily imported from abroad. Zen Buddhism has been here so long that it is usually treated with respect ... but still so short a time (1950) that few American adults not of Japanese ancestry can claim to have been born into it. Ancient in Japan, it is still a cult *here*—e.g., Alan Watts (1915-1973), who moved from Roman Catholic priest to Episcopal priest to Zen priest. I doubt that there is any count on American Zen Buddhists but it is significant that both "satori" and "koan" were assimilated words in all four standard U.S. dictionaries only 16 years after Zen Buddhism penetrated the non-Japanese population.

And there are the Moonies and the Church of Scientology and that strange group that went to South America and committed suicide en masse and the followers of that fat boy from India, and—look around you. Check your telephone book. *I express no opinion on the tenets of any of these*; I simply note that, since World War Two, Americans have been leaving their "orthodox" churches in droves and joining churches new in this country.

Witchcraft is not new and never quite died out. But it is effectively new to most of its adherents here today because of the enormous increase in numbers of witches. ("Warlock" is insulting, "Wizard" barely acceptable and considered gauche, "Witch" is the correct term both male and female. The religion is usually called either "the Old Religion" or "the Craft" rather than witchcraft.)

The Craft is by its nature underground; witches cannot forget the hangings in Salem, the burnings in Germany, the fact that the injunction, "Thou shalt not suffer a witch to live" (Exodus XXII, 18) has usually been carried out whenever the Old Religion surfaced. Even during this resurgence only four covens have come to my attention and, not being a witch myself, I have never attended an esbat (easier to enter a tyled lodge!).

The Craft is *not* Devil worship and it is *not* Black Mass but both of the latter have enjoyed some increase in recent years.

If witchcraft has not come to your attention, search any large book store; note how very many new titles concern witchcraft. Most of these books are phony, not written by witches, mere exploitation books—but their very existence shows the change. Continue to show interest and a witch just might halfway reveal himself by saying, "Don't bother with that one. Try this one." Treat him with warm politeness and you may learn much more.

To my great surprise when I learned of it, there are over a dozen (how much over a dozen I have no way to guess) periodicals in this country devoted solely to the Old Religion.

Time Span—The Cancerous Explosion of Government

Will Rogers told us that we were lucky in that we didn't get as much government as we pay for. He was (and is) emphatically right ... but he died 15 August 1935. The Federal government spent $6,400,000,000 in the last 12 months of his tragically short life. The year he was born (1879) the Federal government spent $274,000,000—

an expensive year, as we resumed paying specie for the Greenback Inflation, $346,700,000 of fiat money.

What would Will Rogers think of a budget of $300 billion and up?

(Figures quoted from THE STATISTICAL HISTORY OF THE UNITED STATES, Prepared by the U.S. Bureau of the Census)

Census Year	Population	Fed. Employees State & Local Total Pub. Emp.	Fed Receipts Fed. Expenditures Surplus/Deficit	Fed. Public Debt
1910	91,972,266	388,798 ?	$675,512,000 693,617,000 (-)$18,105,000	$1,146,940,000
1920	105,710,620	655,265 ?	$6,648,898,000 6,357,677,000 $291,221,000	$24,299,321,000
1930	122,755,046	601,319 2,622,000 3,223,319	$4,057,884,000 3,320,211,000 $737,673,000	$16,186,310,000
1940	131,669,275	1,042,420 3,206,000 4,248,420	$6,900,000,000 9,600,000,000 (-)$2,700,000,000	$50,700,000,000
1950	150,697,361	1,960,708 4,098,000 6,058,708	$40,900,000,000 43,100,000,000 (-)$2,200,000,000	$256,900,000,000
1960	178,464,236	2,398,704 6,083,000 8,481,704	$92,500,000,000 92,200,000,000 $300,000,000	$290,900,000,000
1970	203,235,298	2,981,574 9,830,000 12,811,574	$193,700,000,000 196,600,000,000 (-)$2,900,000,000	$382,600,000,000
19809	-222,000,000	(3,600,000) (14,500,000) (18,100,000)	($300,000,000,000) ($310,000,000,000) (-)($10,000,,000000)	($525,000,000,000)

(1980 figures are extrapolations = wild guesses) (Too timid?) *Much* too timid!—as you knew when you read them, as I knew when I prepared them. I plotted all of the above figures on graph paper, faired the curves, *suppressed what I knew by memory* (even refrained from consulting World Almanacs to bridge the 9 years since the close of compilation of *The Statistical History*) and extrapolated to 1980 by the curves—*not* tangent, but on the indicated curve.

By the best figures I can get from Washington today (20 Nov 1979) the budget is $547,600,000,000; the expected deficit is $29,800,000,000; and our current Federal Public Debt is estimated at $886,480,000,000. (!!!)

The end of the Federal fiscal year, September 30, is still over ten months away. In ten months a lot of things can happen. Unexpected events always cause unexpected expense ... but with great good luck the deficit will not increase much and the National Public Debt will stay under $900,000,000,000.

In case of war, all bets are off.

What is happening is what always happens in fiat-currency inflation: After a certain point, unpredictable as to date because of uncountable human variables, it becomes uncontrollable and the currency becomes worthless. Dictatorship usually follows. From there on anything can happen—all bad.

The Greenback Inflation did *not* result in collapse of the dollar and of constitutional government because gold backing was not disavowed, simply postponed for a relatively short time. The Greenback Party wanted to go on printing paper money, never resume specie payment—but eventually we toughed it out and paid hard money for the Greenbacks that had financed the Union side of the war. From 1862 to 1879 gold and silver were not used internally. Our unfavorable balance of trade for 1861-65, which *had* to be met in gold, was $296,000,000. Hard times and high taxes—but we made it.

The French Revolution inflation was unsecured. Between April 1790 and February 1796, 40 billion livres or francs were issued. New paper money (Mandats) replaced them that year; the following year both sorts were declared no longer legal tender (waste paper!)—and 2 years later Napoleon took over "to save the Republic." (!)

We could still keep from going utterly bankrupt by going back on some hard standard (gold, silver, uranium, mercury, bushels of wheat—*something*). But it would not be easy, it would not be popular; it would mean hard times for everyone while we recovered from an almighty hangover. Do you think a Congress and a President can be elected on any such platform?

One chink in the armor of any democracy is that, when the Plebs discover that they can vote themselves Bread & Circuses, they usually do ... right up to the day there is neither bread nor circuses. At that point they often start lynching the senators, congressmen, bankers, tax collectors, Jews, grocers, foreigners, any minority—take your choice. For they know that *they* didn't do it. The citizen is sovereign until it comes to accepting blame for his sovereign acts—then he demands a scapegoat.

I used official figures without comment to show where we have been the past 70 years ... and how we got into the mess we are in. But, while I think our government is more nearly honest than some others (see "Inside Intourist" Afterword, page 158 (VolumeII) there is a lot of hanky-panky in those official figures. Example: Social Security taxes go into the general fund and are spent. If Social Security were *in fact* insurance (the basis on which the gimmick was sold to us by FDR's "New Deal"), the receipts would be segregated and invested and not shown as income ... *OR* a competent insurance actuary with staff would calculate the commitment and it would show in the National Public Debt.

(The fact that a debt is amortized over the years doesn't stop it from being a debt. It was an amortized mortgage that got me into this racket. The prospect of years and years of future monthly payments spoiled my sleep.)

The only way the Government can go on paying Social "Security" to my generation is by taxing you young people more and more heavily ... and each year there are more and more old people and fewer and fewer young people. It won't help to run the printing presses faster; that causes food to rise in price, rents to go up, etc.—and people over 65 start putting pressure on Congress ... and there's an election coming up. (There's *always* an election coming up.)

One thing I learned as a wardheeler was that (with scarce exceptions) people in my age group want one of two things: 1) They want to keep on clipping those coupons and collecting those rents and they don't give a damn what it does to the country, or 2) they want that raise in Social Security (Townsend Plan) ("Ham & Eggs") (you name one) and they don't give a damn what it does to the country.

(I don't claim to be altruistic. Just this pragmatic difference: I am sharply aware that, if the United States goes down the chute, *I* go down with it.)

I use the term *"Federal* Public Debt" because what is usually termed the "Public Debt" is by no means our total public debt. There are also state, county, city, and special-district debts. It is difficult to get accurate figures on these public debts but the total appears to be larger than the Federal Public Debt. I can't make even a wild guess at the Social Security commitment ... but our *total* public promises-to-pay have to exceed two trillion dollars. How much is a trillion? Well, it means that a baby born today owes at least $4,347.83 to the Federal Government alone before his eyes open. (No wonder he yells.) It means that the Zero Population Growth family (who was going to save us all—remember?) of father, mother, and 2.1 children owes $17,826 in addition to private debts (mortgage, automobile, college for 2.1 children).

Of course papa won't pay it off; that debt will grow larger. But it will cost him $2000 a year (and rising) just to "service" his pro-rata; any taxes for which he gets *anything at all*—even more laws—is on top of that.

A trillion seconds is 31,688 years, 9 months, 5 days, 8 hours, 6 minutes, and 42 seconds—long enough for the precession of the equinoxes to make Vega the Pole Star, swing back again to Polaris, and go on past to Alpha Cephei. Or counting the other way it would take us to 29,708 B.C.... or more than 25 thousand years before Creation by Bishop Usher's chronology for creationism.

I don't understand a trillion dollars any better than I do a trillion seconds. I simply know that we had better stop spending money we don't have if we want to avoid that Man on Horseback.

But I don't think we will stop "deficit financing," the euphemism that sounds so much better than "kiting checks."

You may have noticed that 1970 figure for public employees (not my extrapolation for 1980, but the official 1970 figures straight from the United States Bureau of the Census).

That figure does not include the Armed Forces. It does not include some special categories. It is easier to learn the number of slaves imported in 1769 (6,736) than it is to find out exactly how many people are on public payrolls in this country. And it is not simply difficult but *impossible* to determine how many people receive Federal checks for which they perform no services. (Or food stamps. Are food stamps money?) But one thing is certain: the number of people eligible to vote who *do* receive money from some unit of government (aid to dependent children, Supreme Court justices, not growing wheat, removing garbage, governors of states, whoever) exceeds the number eligible to vote but receiving no pay or subsidy of any sort from any unit of government.

Have you read the Federal Register lately? Have you *ever* read the Federal Register? Under powers delegated by Congress certain *appointed* officials can publish a new regulation in the Federal Register and, if Congress does not stop it, after a prescribed waiting time, that regulation has the force of law—it *is* law, to you and to me, although a lawyer sees nuances. I have vastly oversimplified this description, but my only purpose is to point out that "administrative law" reaches into every corner of our lives, and is the major factor in the enormous and strangling invasion of the Federal Government into our private affairs.

I can't see anything in the Constitution that permits the Congress to delegate its power to pass laws ... but the Supreme Court says it's okay and that makes my opinion worthless.

I'm stopping. There are endless other gloomy things to discuss—the oil shortage, the power shortage (not the same thing), pollution, population pressure, a projected change in climate that can and probably will turn the problems of population and food into sudden and extreme crisis, crime in the streets and bankrupt cities, our incredible plunge from the most respected nation on Earth to the most despised (but we are nonetheless expected to pick up the tab). Bill Gresham was right but he told only half of it: you not only don't get rich peddling gloom; it isn't any fun.

So now come with me—

"OVER THE RAINBOW—"

The new President had not been in office ten days before it became clear to his own party as well as to the "loyal opposition" that he was even more of a disaster than the defeated candidate had predicted. Nevertheless the country was shocked when he served even fewer days than the ninth President—killed in a crash, his private plane, himself at the controls; dying with him his three top aides: White House chief of staff, press secretary, appointments secretary.

No U.S. or Canadian news medium said a word about alcohol or incidents in the dead President's past; they treated it as a tragic accident. Papers and TV reporters elsewhere were not as reticent.

The Speaker of the new House saw the ex-Vice President first (even before the oath of office) as the Speaker's seniority in line of succession enabled him to do. He came right to the point. "I am ready to take this load off your shoulders. We both know that you were picked simply to support the ticket; no one ever expected to load you down with *this*. Here's how we'll do it: You resign at once, then we'll meet the press together—after I'm sworn in. I'll do most of the talking. I promise you, it won't be a strain on you."

"I'm sure that it won't be. You're excused."

"*Huh!*"

"You may leave. In fact I am telling you to leave. I thought you had come to stand beside me as I take the oath ... but you have something entirely different in mind. You would not enjoy staying; I would not enjoy having you stay."

"You'll regret this! You're making a mistake!"

"If a mistake was made, it was made at the Convention. By you and five others, I believe; I was not present. Yes, I may regret it but this is what I undertook to do when I accepted the nomination for the Vice-Presidency. Now get out. *Pronto!*"

The new President sent for the Director of the Budget forty minutes after the swearing in. "Explain this to me."

The Director hemmed and hawed and tried to say that the budget was too technical for anyone not in public life before—

—and was answered, "I'm accepting your resignation. Send in your deputy."

It was almost a week before this call was made: "Admiral? This is the President. If I come to your home, do you feel well enough to see me?"

There was a tussle of wills that the Admiral won only through pointing out that it was never proper to subject the President of the United States to unnecessary risk of assassination ... and that with his new car, fitted for his wheelchair, he still went to the Pentagon twice a week. "I'm old, I admit; I was born in 1900. But I'm not dead and I'm quite able to report to my Commander in Chief. And we both know that threats have been made."

The President won the next argument. On being wheeled in the Admiral started to get out of his chair. "Do please sit down!"

The old man continued to try to rise, leaning on the arm of his nurse. The President said quickly, "That was expressed as a request but was an order. Sit down."

The Admiral promptly sat back down, caught his breath and said formally, "Ma'am, I report—with great pleasure!—to the President of the United States."

"Thank you for coming, sir. In view of our respective ages ... and your health, I felt that it was a time to dispense with protocol. But you are right; there are indeed a flood of threats, many more than get into the news. I don't intend to be a target ... at least until we have a new Vice President sworn in."

"*Never* be a target, Madam. You would be mourned by everyone, both parties. Uh, if I may say so, you are even more beautiful in person than you are on the screen."

"Not mourned by everyone, I'm certain, or I would not have to be cautious about assassination. As for that other, I'm not beautiful and you know it. I know what I have. I project. But it's not physical beauty. It's something that a pro—a professionally competent actress—does with her whole being. Her voice, her expression, her hands, her *body*. A gestalt, with regular features the least important factor. Or not present, as with me."

The President smiled, got up and went around the big desk, leaned over the Admiral, kissed his forehead. "But you are an old dear to have said it."

He cleared his throat, noisily. "Ma'am, what is your opinion in the matter against that of millions of men?"

"We've dropped that subject. Now to work! Admiral, why is it that there has been so much difficulty with nuclear power plants ashore but never any trouble with your nuclear submarines?"

The President slapped her desk, glared at the leader of the delegation. "Stop that! Han'kerchief head, you've come to the wrong church. In this office there are *no* Blacks—or Blues, Whites, Greens, or Yellows—just Americans. Besides that, you claim to be a Black representing Blacks. Hmmph! That's a phony claim if I ever—"

"I resent that, Mrs. Ni—"

"*Pipe down!* 'Madam President,' if you please. And one does *not* interrupt the President. I said your claim was phony. It is. I'm at least three shades darker than you are ... yet I'm smooth brown, not black." She looked around. "I don't see a real sooty black in your whole delegation. Mmm, I see just one darker than I am. Mr. Green, isn't it? That is your name?"

"Yes, Madam President. From Brooklyn."

"Any white blood, Mr. Green? Perhaps I should say 'Any Caucasian ancestry?'"

"Possibly. But none that I know of, Ma'am."

"We're all in that boat ... including all whites. A person who claims to be absolutely certain of his ancestry more than three generations back is accepting the short end of a bet. But since you are from Brooklyn, you can help me pass a word. An important word, one that I'll be emphasizing on the networks tonight but I'll need help from a lot of people to let *all* the people know that I mean it. A Black who gets elected from Brooklyn has lots of Jewish friends, people who trust him."

"That's right, Madam President."

"Listen to my talk tonight, then pass it on in your own words. This nation has split itself into at least a hundred splinter groups, pressure groups, each trying for a bigger bite of the pie. That's got to *stop!*—before it kills us. No more Black Americans. No more Japanese Americans. Israel is not our country and neither is Ireland. A group calling

265

itself La Raza had better mean the human race—the *whole* human race—or they'll get the same treatment from me as the Ku Klux Klan. Amerindians looking for special favors will have just two choices: Either come out and *be* Americans and accept the responsibilities of citizenship ... or go back to the reservation and shut up. Some of their ancestors got a rough deal. But so did yours and so did mine. There are no Anglos left alive who were at Wounded Knee or Little Big Horn, so it's time to shut up about it.

"But race and skin color and national ancestry isn't all that I mean. I intend to refuse to see *any* splinter group claiming to deserve special treatment not accorded other citizens and I will veto any legislation perverted to that end. Wheat farmers. Bankrupt corporations. Bankrupt cities. Labor leaders claiming to represent 'the workers' ... when most of the people they claim to represent repudiate any such leadership. Business leaders just as phony. *Any*one who wants the deck stacked in his favor because, somehow, he's 'special.'"

The President took a deep breath, went on: "Any such group gets thrown out. But two groups will get thrown out so hard they'll bounce! I'm a woman and I'm Negro. We've wiped the Jim-Crow laws off the books; I'll veto any Crow-Jim bill that reaches this office. Discrimination? Certainly there is still discrimination—but you can't kill prejudice by passing a law. We'll make it by how we behave and what we produce—not by trick laws.

"I feel even more strongly about women. We women are a majority, by so many millions that in an election it would be called a landslide. And *will* be a landslide, on *anything*, any time women really want it to be. So women don't need favors; they just need to make up their minds what they want—then take it." The President stood up again. "That's all. I'm going to devote this term to those 'unalienable rights'— for *everybody*. No splinter groups. Go tell people so. Now git ... and don't come back! Not as a splinter group. Come back as *Americans*."

They moved toward the door. Their erstwhile leader muttered something. The President demanded, "Mr. Chairman, what did you say?"

"I said," he answered loudly, "you aren't going to have a second term."

She laughed at him. "I thought that's what I heard. Burr head, I'm not worrying about being reelected; I worry only about how much I can do in four years."

(Editorial in the Springfield *Eagle*)
LIFE INSURANCE?

The President's surprise nomination of the House Minority Leader for the vacant vice-presidency has produced some snide theories, one of the nastiest being the idea that she fears a plot on her life by the wheeler-dealers who put the late President into office, so she is spiking their guns (literally!) by rigging things to turn the presidency over to the opposition party should anything happen to her....

... prefer to take her at her word, that her objective is to get the country unified again, and that a woman and a man, a Republican and a Democrat, a White and a Black, could be the team to do it.

The Speaker of the House has still not commented, but his floor leader and the nominated minority leader appeared with the President when she announced her choice. The Senate President Pro Tempore said, "I see no reason why confirmation should not go through quickly. I've known Don for thirty years; I trust that I am not so narrow-minded that I can't recognize presidential caliber in a man of another party...."

... customary to be of the same party, there is a custom just as long standing (and more important) that a President have a Vice President he (she) trusts to carry out his (her) policies.

Let's back them to the limit! Let's all be *Americans* again!

"Thanks for coming."

"Madam President, any time you send a car for me, then scoot me across the country in a hypersonic military jet, thanks should be the other way. My first experience above the speed of sound—and my first time in the Oval Office. I never expected to be in it."

She chuckled. "Nor did I. Especially on this side of this desk. Let's get to work." She held up a book. "Recognize this?"

"Eh?" He looked startled. "Yes, Ma'am, I do. I should."

"You should, yes." She opened to a marked page, read aloud: "'—I have learned this about engineers. When something *must* be done, engineers can find a way that is economically feasible.' Is that true?"

"*I* think so, Ma'am."

"You're an engineer."

"I am an *obsolete* engineer, Ma'am."

"I don't expect you to do the job yourself. You know what I did about fusion power plants."

"You sent for the one man with a perfect record. I've seen the power ship moored off Point Sur. Brilliant. Solved an engineering and a public relations problem simultaneously."

"Not quite what I mean. I consulted the Admiral, yes. But the job was done by his first deputy, the officer he has groomed to replace him. And by some other Navy people. Now we're working on ways to make the key fission-power people—safety control especially—all former Navy nuclear submariners. But we have to do it without stripping the Navy of their Blue and Gold crews. On things I know nothing about—most things, for this job! I consult someone who *does*—and that leads me to the person who can do it. Since I know very little about how to be President, I look for advice on almost everything."

"Ma'am, it seems to me—and a lot of other people—that you were born for the job."

"Hardly. Oh, politics isn't strange to me; my father held office when I was still a girl at home. But I did my first television commercial at fourteen and I was hooked. If I hadn't been 'resting' between contracts, I would not have accepted the Governor's appointment—I was just his 'exhibit coon' but the Commission's work did interest me. Then I was still an 'exhibit coon' when he saw to it that I was on his favorite-son slate. Then, when the three leading candidates deadlocked, my late predecessor broke the deadlock in his favor by naming me as the other half of his ticket. I went along with it with a wry grin inside, figuring, first, that the ploy wouldn't work, and second, that, if he *did* get nominated, he would find some way to wiggle out—ask me to withdraw in favor of his leading rival or some such."

She shrugged. "But he didn't—or couldn't. I don't know which; he rarely talked to me. Real talk, I mean. Not just, 'Good morning,' and, 'Did you have a comfortable flight' and not wait for an answer.

"I didn't care. I relished every minute of the campaign. An actress sometimes plays a queen ... but for four months I got to *be* one. Never dreaming that our ticket would win. I knew what a—No; *de mortuis nil nisi bonum*, and we must get back to work. What would you do about pollution of streams?"

"Eh? But that one has already been solved. By one of the Scandinavian countries, I believe. You simply require every user to place his intake immediately downstream from his discharge of effluent into the stream. In self-protection the user cleans up his discharge. It's self-enforcing. No need to test the water until someone downstream complains. Seldom. Because it has negative feedback. Ma'am, complying with a law should be more rewarding than breaking it—or you get positive feedback."

She made a note. "We could clean up the Mississippi that way. But I'm fretted about streams inside states, too. For example, the Missouri, where it is largest, is entirely inside the State of Missouri."

"Ma'am, I think you'll find that you have jurisdiction over *all* navigable streams."

"I do?"

"Ma'am, you have powers you may never have dreamed existed. A 'navigable stream' is one only three feet deep, I think. You may right now have the power to order this under law already on the books. If there is a paragraph or even a clause on placement of inlets and outlets, you almost certainly can issue an executive order right away. Today. The boss of the U.S. Engineers would know. General Somebody. A French name."

She touched a switch. "Get me the head of the U.S. Engineers. How would you dispose of nuclear power plant wastes? Rocket them onto the Moon as someone urged last week? Why wouldn't the Sun be better? We may want to go back to the Moon someday."

"Oh, my, no! Neither one, Ma'am."

"Why not? Some of those byproducts are poisonous for hundreds of years, so I've heard. No?"

"You heard correctly. But the really rough ones have short half-lives. The ones with long half-lives—hundreds, even thousands of years, or longer—are simple to handle. But don't throw away *any* of it, Ma'am. Not where you can't recover it easily."

"Why not? We're speaking of *wastes*. I assume that we have extracted anything we can use."

"Yes, Ma'am, anything *we* can use. But our great grandchildren are going to hate you. Do you know the only use the ancient Romans had for petroleum? Medicine, that's all. I don't know how those isotopic wastes will be used next century ... any more than those old Romans could guess how *very* important oil would become. But I certainly wouldn't throw those so-called wastes into the Sun! Besides, rockets do fail ... and who wants to scatter radioactives over a couple of states? And there's the matter of the fuel and steel and a dozen other expensive things for the rockets. You could easily wind up spending more money to get rid of the ashes than you ever got from selling the power."

"Then what *do* you do? They say we mustn't sink it into the ocean. Or put it on the Antarctic ice cap. Salt mines?"

"Madam President, honest so help me, this is one of those non-problems that the antitechnology nuts delight in. Radioactive wastes aren't any harder to handle than garbage. Or hot ashes. Or anything else you don't want to pick up in your bare hands. The quantity isn't much, not at all like garbage, or coal ashes. There are at least a half dozen easy ways. One of the easiest is to mix them with sand and gravel and cement into concrete bricks, then stack them in any unused piece of desert.

"Or glass bricks. Or let the stuff dry and store it in steel barrels such as oil drums and use those old salt mines you mentioned—the bricks you could leave in the open. All by remote manipulation, of course; that's the way a radioactives engineer does everything. Waldoes. That's old stuff. No trouble."

"I thought you said you were obsolete."

He grinned sheepishly. "Ma'am, it's easy to talk. As long as I know that young fellows will have to do the tedious drudgery that goes into making anything new work. But the solutions I've offered *are* practical. No new discoveries needed."

"How about air pollution?"

"What sorts, Ma'am? The two main sources are internal combustion engines—trucks and autos—and industrial smokes. Quite different problems."

"Pick one."

"Transportation pollution is going to solve itself soon—either the hard way or the easy way. Oil, whether it's our own or from the OPEC, is too valuable to be burned in cars and trucks; it's the backbone of the chemical engineering industry—fertilizers, plastics, pesticides, lubricants, and so forth. So, quite aside from the energy problem, we need to stop burning it. We can either wait until it's forced on us catastrophically ... or we can turn to other transportation power voluntarily, and thereby become self-sufficient in oil for peace or for war. Either way, transportation pollution is ended."

"But *what* other transportation power, Doctor?"

"Oh. Half a dozen ways, at least. Get rid of the I.C. engine completely, both Otto cycle and Diesel cycle, and go back to the external combustion engine and steam. The I.C. engine never did make sense; starting and stopping combustion every split second is a guarantee of incomplete combustion, wasted fuel, and smog. Air pollution. External combustion has no such built-in stupidity; no matter what fuel, it burns continuously and can be adjusted for complete combustion. The Stanley Steamer used kerosene. But that's petroleum again. I would use wood alcohol as a starter—it hurts me every time I pass a sawmill and see them burning chips and slash.

"But wood alcohol has its drawbacks. We may burn hydrogen someday. Or learn to store electricity in less weight and less space. Or store energy in a flywheel. But all of those, even hydrogen, are simply ways to store energy. It still leaves an energy problem."

"Hydrogen, too? But you said we would burn it. No?"

"We'll burn it for some purposes; in some ways it's the ideal fuel; its only ash is water vapor. But, Ma'am, we don't *have* hydrogen; we have *water*—and even with perfect efficiency—never achieved—the

EXPANDED UNIVERSE: VOLUME TWO

energy you get out of hydrogen by burning it cannot exceed the energy you must use in getting that hydrogen by electrolysis of water. So you must generate electricity first."

"I see. No free lunch."

"Never a free lunch. But the energy problem can be solved several ways ... through renewable resources. We've been using nonrenewable resources—coal and oil and cutting trees faster than they grow."

"Renewable resources—windmills and water power and sun power?"

"Wind and water power are fine but limited. I mean effectively unlimited power. Such as this new wrinkle of thermoelectric power from the temperature difference of deep ocean and surface ocean. But there aren't too many really convenient places to do that. You named the one energy that is unlimited and convenient anywhere. Sun power."

"So? What desert is convenient to the Gary steel mills?"

"Not desert, Ma'am; the Sierra Club wouldn't like it."

"I plan to tell the Sierra Club that they are *not* the government of the United States. But in stronger language."

"I look forward to hearing you, Madam President. The Sierra Club loves deserts and hates people. But our deserts aren't sufficient. Sun power, yes—but *unlimited* sun power. In orbit."

South Africa Enraged

United States Surprise Return
to Gold Standard at $350 per
Troy Ounce of Fine Gold Has
Bourses in Turmoil

"New Policy Obvious Concomitant of
Return to Balanced Budget," Says
Treasury Secretary Spokesman

"The Way to Resume is to Resume."

By ADAM SMITH
Finance Editor

WASHINGTON—The Treasury Secretary, after reading aloud to the Press the President's brief announcement of resumption of specie payments immediately at $350/oz., emphasized that this was not a tactical maneuver to "strengthen the dollar," not an auction of bullion such as those in the past, but a permanent policy consistent with the administration's total policy. "A return to our traditional policy, I must add. A century ago, for 15 years, war caused us to suspend specie payments—but never with any intent to accept the vice of fiat money. Since 1971, as sequelae to 3 wars, we have had a similar problem. By letting the dollar float until the world price of gold in terms of dollars settled down, we have determined what could be called the natural price. So we have resumed specie payment at a firm gold standard. God willing, we will never leave it."

This was in answer to the London *Times* correspondent's frosty inquiry as to whether or not the Secretary thought anyone would want our gold at that price. The Treasury Secretary told him that we were not "selling gold" but promising to redeem our paper money at a gold-standard price. The *Times'* question was inspired by the fact that at the close of market Friday the London fix was $423.195 per troy ounce, with the Zurich fix, the Winnipeg fix, and the Hong Kong fix (the last only hours before the Washington announcement) all within a dollar of the London fix.

PRAVDA: "—capitalistic trickery—"

Moscow has not had a free market in gold since pre-1914 but, as a gold-producing country, its response to our resumption policy has been even more acid than the shrill complaints from Johannesburg. The Zurich gold market did not open today. London opened on time but the price dropped at once, with the first purchase at $397.127, which slowed but did not stop the decline. Winnipeg opened an hour late; the reason became clear when the Prime Minister announced the tying of the Canadian dollar to the U.S. dollar at one-to-one—a *fait accompli* as the two currencies have hunted up and down, never more than 1% apart, for the past several months.

The timing of the announcement gave the world a weekend in which to think things over, the purpose being presumably to reduce oscillations. The New York Stock Market responded with an upward surge. The Dow-Jones Industrials closed at ....

"Mr. Chairman, are these unofficial figures I have in front of me—that each of you has in front of you—correct? Or have my informants been leading me down the garden path? The figures on the use of hard drugs, for example?"

"Madam President, I don't know quite how to answer that."

"You don't, eh? You're Chairman of the Joint Chiefs and for four years before that chief of staff of your service. If these figures are not right, how far are they off and which way?"

"Ma'am, that is a question that should be put to each of the Services, not to me."

"So? General, you are relieved of active duty. A request for retirement will be acted on favorably, later today. You are excused. General Smith, take the chair."

The President waited until the door closed behind the ex-Chairman. Then she said soberly, "Gentlemen, it gives me no pleasure to put an end to the career of a man with a long and brilliant record. But I cannot keep in a top spot in my official family a military officer who can't or won't answer questions that, in my opinion, must be answered if I am to carry out my duties as Commander in Chief. If he had answered, 'I don't know now but I'll start digging at once and won't stop until'—but he said nothing of the sort. I gave him two chances; he brushed me off." She sighed. "I suppose he dislikes taking orders from one with no military experience; I do not assume that my sex and skin color had anything to do with it. General Smith, you are in the chair by default; I can't ask you about the other Services. How about your own? Hard drugs."

"I suspect that this figure is conservative, Ma'am. I've been trying to get hard data on hard drugs since I was appointed to this job a year ago. In most cases we need evidence from medical officers to make it stick ... and all our doctors are overworked; we don't have nearly enough of them. Worse yet, some of the doctors are pushers themselves; two were caught."

"What happened to them? Making little ones out of big ones?"

"No, Ma'am. Discharged. In civilian practice, I suppose."

"For God's sake, *why?* Has the Army forgotten how to hold a court martial? Two drug pushers, simply sent home and still licensed to practice medicine—and to prescribe drugs. General, I'm shocked."

"Ma'am, may I say something in my own defense? Then you can have my request for retirement, if you wish it."

"Please. Go ahead."

"These cases occurred before I became Chief of Staff. At the time these two were caught, I was Superintendent of the War College; drugs are not a problem there. When last I had troop duty, I *did* have a policy of treating use of hard drugs as a criminal offense, as permitted and required by regulations. But the very most I ever managed was to get some sent to the V.A. for hospital cure and rehabilitation. Under the present rules, if a man has a good lawyer—and they do, usually—he can get away from courts martial and appeal to a civilian judge. That usually ends it."

"Madam President, may I add something?"

"Certainly, Admiral."

"Have you heard of the mutiny in the *Somers* about a century and a half back?"

"I—Yes, I think I have! A novel. *Voyage to the—Voyage to the First of December*. Right?"

"There was a novel some years back; I think that was the book's title. I haven't read it. Then you are aware that it was a tragic scandal, with mutineers hanged at the yardarms. What I wanted to say was this: I think the figures on drugs in the Navy are about right—lower than in the Army, of course; the circumstances are different. But what is killing the Navy—aside from a shortage of career officer material—is that both mutiny and sabotage are out of hand ... because offenses that used to rate hanging from the yardarm are now treated as 'Boys will be boys.' A great deal of it does derive from a change in the legal structure, as the General said. I would rather have five ships properly maintained, properly manned, shipshape and Bristol style, than ten ships undermanned and shot through with men who should never have been accepted in the first place. A stupid and sullen seaman is worse than no one at all."

The President said, "Judges, chapter seven."

The Admiral looked puzzled. The Marine Commandant suddenly said, "Gideon's Band!"

"Exactly. I suspect that we have been trying to meet quotas—numbers of men—rather than placing quality first. I'm sure it's not as simple as that, but that does seem to be part of it. General, does the Air Force have any different slant on this?"

"No, Ma'am, I think the Navy and the Corps both speak for me. And the Army ... although Smitty's problems are different from ours. Our worst problem is hanging on to trained men ... because what we teach them, flying and electronics especially, are very salable on the outside. I want to add something, though. Marijuana is not on the list of drugs. It may very well be true that grass is no worse than liquor. But neither one mixes with driving a flying machine. Or anything in an airplane. But grass is harder to cope with. A stash is easier to hide than a bottle, and it is harder to tell when a man is stoned than when he is drunk. And much harder to prove. I welcome suggestions."

"I think we all do. Although I think we've pinpointed one essential. Quality before quantity. Gentlemen, we'll let this marinate about ten days while all of us try to spot all of the basic things that are wrong ... then meet again and exchange ideas. In writing. Call the shots as you see them, don't be afraid of hurting feelings, pay no attention to sacred cows. Admiral, you found things wrong with the military legal system; please analyse the matter, with specific recommendations. If you truly feel that we need to go back to keelhauling and hanging at the yardarm, say so."

"I do not, Ma'am. But I do think the present rules are more suited to a Scout camp than to a fighting force. Punishment should be swift and certain; mutineers should not be coddled. We need a new code."

"Work on it. I assume that you have legal aides. Mr. Secretary of Defense, I have not intended to monopolize the floor. Before we adjourn, I want you to give us your opinions on problems of discipline. I would like to hear comment on those figures I supplied, all categories. But you aren't limited to that. Feel free to bring up anything. I think that discipline in the Armed Forces is as serious a problem as I face ... and the most difficult."

"Discipline is not one of the duties of the Secretary of Defense."

"So? What are your duties?"

To manage my department. Discipline belongs to these gentlemen. Not to me. And certainly not to *you*. You are way out of line."

"You forgot something, sir. The President is in the direct line of command, at the top, and cannot avoid responsibility for any aspect of her command. The Secretary of Defense is *not* in the line of command; he is an executive secretary for the President. However, since you see your job as merely managerial, and not concerned with morale and discipline, I won't press you about it. I have your signed resignation in my desk, inherited from my predecessor. I'm accepting it. At once."

The ex-Secretary leaned back and laughed. "How just like a woman! Ruffle her feathers and she flies off the handle. But it's okay, Shortie; I didn't intend to stay this long. After the Chief died I was ready to quit. But Charlie asked me to stick around a little longer, keep an eye on you. I know what you did to him the day of the tragedy, standing in his way when he was entitled to the job. You never were anything but an election poster. Didn't anybody ever tell you that?"

"You may leave now. You're excused."

"Oh, I'm leaving; I've got a press conference in ten minutes. Just one thing: You said Joe probably disliked taking orders from you because you've had no military experience. Nonsense. Any top brass expects to take orders from a civilian. But no real man will take orders from a nigger, much less a nigger wench."

The Marine was out of his chair so fast that it overturned, snatched the ex-Secretary out of his chair and got a hammerlock on him—but beat the others to it only by being closest.

"Down on your knees and apologize, you jerk! That's the *President of the United States* you're talking to!" The Marine General's Deep South accent, ordinarily carefully corrected, came out in full force, thick as gumbo.

"Make him take his hands off me!"

"Keep him secure, General. And thank you, sir. But don't rough him up more than necessary. Admiral, if you will be so kind as to check, I think you will find two Marines and two Secret Service men just outside that door. Please ask one of them to telephone for two White House Police. I want this person removed from the building and not allowed back in. Nor back into the Pentagon, ever. Most especially not into his former office."

"A pleasure, Ma'am!"

"Thank you, sir. I hope to see you all here at the same time a week from Thursday. General Smith, I ask you to remain chairman pro tem, in addition to your regular duties. Adjourn when it suits you. I'm withdrawing now; I want to lie down. I find that I am a bit shaky...."

```
CND 406CRH
CHEYENNE-LEGISLATURE BOTH HOUSES PASSED OVER-
WHELMINGLY FIRST AND SECOND READING EMERGENCY
MEASURE RESTORING PAUPERS OATH FOR RECIPIENTS
OF ANY PUBLIC ASSISTANCE OF ANY SORT REPEAT
ANY SORT IN RESPONSE TO GOVERNOR'S IMPASSIONED
CLAIM THAT THERE WOULD BE NO MONEY FOR THE
BLIND AND THE TOTALLY HELPLESS UNLESS STATE
RETURNED TO NINETEENTH CENTURY TEST OF ELIGI-
BILITY MORE MORE
CND 409CRH
CHEYENNE-AMERICAN CIVIL LIBERTIES UNION WILL
FILE CLASS ACTION IN FEDERAL COURT TO STOP RES-
TORATION OF PAUPERS OATH AS PREREQUISITE FOR
PUBLIC ASSISTANCE.
```

"Come in, Senator! Thank you for doing me this favor!"

"Madam President, it would be a pleasure to call on you at any time even if you were not President. Perhaps more."

"Uncle Sam, I don't know what that means but I like it. Now to work! Would it suit you to work for me?"

"You know it would, my dear—but I have a constituency."

"I don't mean resign and take a job here. But can't you pair votes, or something? I need a lot of help from you right now and more later."

"Anything the President wants, the President gets. Yes, I can always arrange a pair … even when I'm only nominally out of the District." He looked down at her. "Trouble?"

"Work I don't know how to handle. I've got to appoint twenty-three judges and I can't put it off much longer. And I don't know how to tell a knucklehead from an Oliver Wendell Holmes. See that tall stack? And that one? Those are the written opinions—or other legal writings if they are not already judges—from the candidates for judgeships. No names on them, and other identifications blacked out. Just identification numbers. I thought I could read this mess and tell which ones had their heads screwed on tight. I can't. I don't understand legalese, I'm not a lawyer."

"I'm not a lawyer either, bright eyes."

"No, but you're the world's leading semanticist. I figured that, if you couldn't understand something, then it was really nonsense."

"It's a good approach. If a person of normal intelligence, and a reasonably full education, cannot understand a piece of prose, then it *is* gibberish. But you shouldn't be doing it; you have a country to worry about. I don't have time, either, but I'll take time; my staff are quite competent to wipe the noses and hold the hands of my constituents for a while. I'll arrange it."

"Then you'll do it! Uncle Sam, you're a dear!"

"But I want a bribe."

"You do? I thought *I* was supposed to be offered bribes, not have to pay them."

"I'm eccentric. I take bribes only from pretty little girls I've known a long time."

"You're eccentric, all right. What is that thing you wear on your head? A cow pat?"

"My dear, you're colorblind. Madam President, I have a proposed amendment to the Constitution I want you to sponsor … and by great good luck I just happen to have a copy of it on me."

"I'll bet you sleep with a copy of it on you. No, just put it on the desk. Now tell me what it is supposed to accomplish."

"It permits a citizen to challenge the Constitutionality of any law or regulation, Federal or any lesser authority, on the grounds that it is ambivalent, equivocal, or cannot be understood by a person of average intelligence. Paragraph two defines 'average intelligence.' Paragraph three defines and limits the tests that may be used to test the challenged law. The fourth paragraph excludes law students, law school graduates, lawyers, judges, and uncertified j.p.'s from being test subjects. I call it 'the Semantic Amendment.'"

"No, you don't; you call it 'the Plain English Amendment.' Show biz, Uncle Sam. Senator, under this amendment could a person challenge the income tax law on the grounds that he has to hire an expert to make out his form 1040?"

"He certainly could. And he would win, too, as no three I.R.S. men can get the same answers out of identical data if the picture is at all complex."

"Hmm—What if he's bright enough but can't read?"

"Paragraph three."

"How about the Federal Budget? It isn't law in the usual meaning but Congress votes on it and it has the force of law, where it applies."

"First paragraph. It quacks like a duck, waddles like a duck—it's a duck."

"I'll try to study this before I fall asleep tonight. Senator, this one we're going to put over!"

"Don't be too certain, Madam President. Lawyers are going to hate this ... and the Congress and all the State legislatures have a majority of lawyers."

"And every one of them not anxious to lose his job. That's their weakness ... because it's awfully easy to work up hate against lawyers. Senator, this bill will be introduced by lawyers. Both Houses. Both parties. Not by you, you're not a lawyer. Uncle Sam, I'm an amateur president but I'm a pro in show biz. It'll play in Paducah."

The two Presidents were seated alone at the front of the crowded grandstand. Two kilometers in front of them a spaceship, small compared with the Shuttle assemblage, but close to the size of the Shuttle alone, stood upright in the bright Mexican mountain sunshine. A voice from everywhere was counting:

"—sixty-one seconds.... one minute .... fifty-nine .... fifty-eight—"

She said, "How are you coming with Spanglish, Señor el Presidente?"

He shrugged and smiled, "As before, Doña la Presidenta. I know it is simple; I hear your people and ours talking in it ... and I understand them. But I don't have time to study. When I leave office—" He spread his hands.

"I know. Perhaps two years from now—I can't believe I've been in office only six years. It feels like sixty."

"You've accomplished sixty years of statecraft; the whole world is awestruck."

"—forty-one ... forty ... thirty-nine—"

"There never was anything really seriously wrong with my country, Mr. President. We made some silly mistakes, then compounded them by being stubborn. The Fence, for example. What's the point in a Fence that doesn't work? So I had it torn down."

"Madam, your most creative act of statesmanship! Without that act of faith, you and I could never have put over our Treaty of Mutual Assistance. And the dozen major advances we have started under it. This. You and I would not be sitting here."

"Yes. No more wetbacks and *this*. Mr. President, I *still* don't understand how a beam of light can put a spaceship into orbit."

"Neither do I, Madam President, neither do I. But I believe your engineers."

"So do I but it frightens me."

"—fifteen ... The Binational Solar Power Zone is now on standby power ... nine ... eight—"

"*Oh!* Will you hold my hand? *Please!*"

"—four! ... three! ... two! ... one! ... *LIGHT!*"

A single inhalation by thousands, then came the everywhere voice in soft, reverent tones: "Look at that bastard *go!*"

"—direct from O'Neill Village, Ell-Five. It's a beautiful day here, it's *always* a beautiful day here. But today is our happiest fiesta ever; little Ariel Henson Jones, first baby born in space, is one year old today. All four of her grandparents are here, her father's parents having traveled all the way from Over-the-Rainbow, Ell-Four, via Luna City Complex, just to be here on this great day. Don't repeat this but a little bird, a parrot, told me that one of Ariel's grandmothers is pregnant again. I won't say which one but it's *personal* good news for *all* of us here in the sky because, if true and I can assure you it is, it is one more and very important datum in the rapidly growing list to show that youthfulness in all ways is markedly extended simply by living in free-fall. Correction: the mild acceleration we experience at the skin of our Village ... but which we can leave behind completely at any time for free-fall sports at the axis.

"*And you* can enjoy them, too. This newscast comes to you sponsored by O'Neill Village Chamber of Commerce. Visitors welcome.

You haven't *lived* until you ride the Light Beam, the cheapest way to travel per thousand kilometers ever invented by a factor of at least one hundred ... and not uncomfortable even the first few seconds since the installation of the new total-support hydraulic couches. Also you haven't lived until you've seen our free-fall ballet! You think Las Vegas has shows? Wait till you see a Coriolis torch dance. Or what free-fall does for a hundred-centimeter bust. Oh, boy! Or if you like to gamble we'll take your money with brand-new games as happily as Monte Carlo or Atlantic City. See your travel agent for a variety of package vacations.

"Or more than a vacation. Buying a share in the Village is cheaper than buying a house in most cities down heavyside. But if you are young and healthy and possess certain needed skills your migration into the sky can be subsidized. Phone the placement office here for details, same rates as from San Francisco to New York. Wups! Almost forgot to tell you: knowledge of industrial Spanglish required, plus some Brownie points for any other language you know...."

It *could* be that way, over the Rainbow. As Madam President said, there never has been anything incurably wrong with our country and our world—just a horrid accumulation of silly mistakes that could be corrected with horse sense and the will to do it.

We have a lot of healthy, intelligent people with a wide spread of useful skills, trades, and professions. We have a wonderful big country not yet too crowded and still wealthy in real wealth—oh, bankrupt on paper but that can always be corrected with real wealth, will, and work. Actually it's easier to be happy and get rich than it is to go down the chute. This country has so much going for it that it takes a lot of work combined with wrong-headed stubbornness to ruin this country. It's not easy.

In the meantime don't go away. There are still a lot of sacred cows I haven't kicked but plan to … someday. So, unless I'm hit by a taxicab while swiveling on my cane to ogle pretty girls, I'll be back.

THE END

Made in the USA
Columbia, SC
17 August 2021